C L

Janice Galloway's books include the novels *The Trick is to Keep Breathing*, which won the 1990 MIND/Allen Lane Book of the Year Award, and *Foreign Parts*, which won the 1994 McVitie's Prize. In 1994 she also won the E.M. Forster Award, presented by the American Academy of Arts and Letters. *Clara* won the Saltire Scottish Book of the Year Award. She lives in Glasgow.

Janice Galloway

CLARA

V

VINTAGE

To the memory of Ken Hetherington,
the best of teachers

Published by Vintage 2003

10

Copyright © Janice Galloway 2002

First published in Great Britain in 2002 by
Jonathan Cape

Vintage
Random House, 20 Vauxhall Bridge Road,
London SW1V 2SA

Random House Australia (Pty) Limited
20 Alfred Street, Milsons Point, Sydney
New South Wales 2061, Australia

Random House New Zealand Limited
18 Poland Road, Glenfield,
Auckland 10, New Zealand

Random House (Pty) Limited
Endulini, 5A Jubilee Road, Parktown 2193,
South Africa

The Random House Group Limited Reg. No. 954009
www.randomhouse.co.uk

A CIP catalogue record for this book
is available from the British Library

ISBN 978 0 099 75051 2

The Random House Group Limited supports The Forest Stewardship
Council (FSC®), the leading international forest certification organisation.
Our books carrying the FSC label are printed on FSC® certified paper.
FSC is the only forest certification scheme endorsed by the leading
environmental organisations, including Greenpeace. Our
paper procurement policy can be found at
www.randomhouse.co.uk/environment

MIX
Paper from
responsible sources
FSC® C016897

Designed by Janice Galloway and Peter Ward

Printed and bound in Great Britain by Clays Ltd, St Ives PLC

Durch alle Töne tönet
Im bunten Erdentraum
Ein leiser Ton gezogen
Für den, der heimlich lauschet.

Through all the bluster and clamour
of this rainbow-illusion called Earthly Life,
one note, soft and still, sounds
for the secret listener.

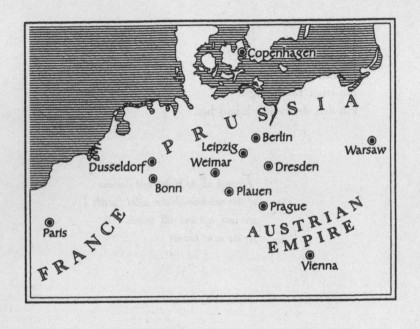

Clara

Frauen Liebe und -Leben Op. 42

Woman's Life and Love

a revised edition of eight songs with piano accompaniment,
with passages from

Carnaval Op. 9, Fantasia in C Op. 63 , Kinderszenen Op. 80,
Kreisleriana Op. 16,
Album für die Jugend Op. 68 ,
Gesänge der Frühe Op. 133,
Trio for Violin, Violoncello and Piano Op. 17

———•———

Additional material including
nocturnes, ballades, marches, variations, overtures
and works by new composers.

———•———

Finale

Concerto for lone piano
Work in progress

$\mathcal{T}$he sea in a blue bowl, a face staring up from its surface.

Touch and it breaks. For all that, it's not fragile. Watch and what scatters on the water's surface comes whole again, the same as before. These eyes are wide, their images so clear each lash is visible to the root. Her lids are sugar-pink, the skin of her temples creaseless. The downward tilt would suggest sadness if it were not their natural set: they have looked this way all along. Look hard as you like, they don't change. The depth of these eye sockets, the slab of her brow is how she is arranged, that's all. The nose is not pinched, the full lower lip devoid of sensuality. So far as can be managed, this face is blank. Inscrutable. As it should be. A pianist must develop more than technique, more than musicianship, more, even, than luck. She needs the capacity to deny fear. Passion one might take for granted: its control is the medium through which all else flows. That every emotion evoked by music is created through containment is a commonplace. For all the shimmering detail of this reflection, then, the depth of her training is the only thing that shows. It's something she is proud of, something for which she is thankful every day. Facing an audience gets no easier. She's faced thousands before now, learned comfort in logistics. More means further away. Thousands she can take in her stride; to them, she is no more than a projection. Today, however, there will be only a handful: there will be no stage. Close enough to see stitching on her sleeves, to smell her if they choose, to test her solidity and this she has accommodated as best she can. What's not new is mended, what's mended is pressed: whatever else, she will not be shabby. With one hand, she reaches and unties her hair from its night-knot, slackens the ribbons at the top of her gown, checks her face a last time. It stares right back. *You'll do*, she thinks, trusts it to be true. She'll do.

Water, soap, one linen towel. Clothes, heaven help her, this black, sober assembly. She laid them out herself, every piece.

Chemise. Long, cloth. No trimmings.

Corset. Light-boned, of white silk elastic, its back ready-laced, the front to be fastened by straps, buckles, ribbon ties.

A short camisole, summer-weight.

One flannel vest.

One horsehair and linen crinoline, stiff as book board.

Two skirts of percale, plain.

Two skirts of plain muslin, starched, unflounced, tied at the waist.

Two starched cambric skirts with broderie anglaise trim.

One petticoat of thick silk, pleated beneath, black.

Plain stockings, black lisle.

No hoops, no watch-sprung cages to fasten, nothing requiring more than one pair of hands. The dress, when it comes, has flat pleated folds from the shoulder to centre front, the sleeves and undersleeves both tight. It doesn't fit as well as it might, but should last a long time, as bombazine does. Bombazine, her father always said, is durable cloth. It does not reflect the light. It takes some time fastening buttons, catching eyelets and hooks, even seeing them against the muffle of the material, but time is in plentiful supply. Setting the piping straight on her sleeves, she scans the room for her jacket, the borrowed bonnet, the boots recobbled and buffed to a sheen, and wishes for clouds. Let it not swelter. She closes her eyes and a picture of earth baked dry by the sun appears, ground bleached to solid chalk. Rain, if it came, would bring mud, viscous slicks of it, roads running to vapour. Let it not rain either; the clouds alone will do. On the far side of the room is her unmade bed, its spill of pillows; the window, the single chair. She crosses the room in this dress heavy as slate, its drag at her legs unsteadying. She sits by the window till the cloth stops whispering, then sits some more. No one else in the house is awake, but the sun is rising, altering the sky. Soon, the others will be stirring in their separate beds, remembering what's been learned by heart. Choristers, a violinist, the conductor, the composer. They'll bring flowers, and she'll make a point of thanking them. It matters to remember simple kindness. Then Hannes will offer his arm. Thin as a wishbone. It will feel surprisingly strong, steady. He will open the door, pause on the threshold, then lead her outside.

Behind her forehead the sensation of pressing is getting worse. To help it clear, she looks out of the window again, watches colour seeping through the grass like fog. She watches it come. A long time ago, on a morning like this, she watched a man walk on to a stage. One of a crowd, she stared up at his unkempt hair, the loose fit of his neckless shirt. And the man stared back. The only child in the world, it seemed: he looked directly at her. The fist on her lap clenches, releases, spreads its fingers into a starfish. Hands have a memory of their own; they will know what to do. For now, she must only wait, rehearse the habit of mental discipline, prepare.

She hears birdsong. Getting louder.

For now, at least, she has nothing to do but wait.

ONE

Seit ich ihn gesehen

Since first I saw him

*H*alf-light and rain.

The path of the street shines along the rim of guttering. Look up.

Behind the glass, a girl, a little girl, a young woman, maybe, is looking back. She can't see you, she won't object. You can look as long as you like. The light is bad but she's distinct enough, hair pulled back and her eyes full almond shapes, the size of bay leaves. Wide. She has a generous lower lip, a gypsy mouth; skin pale as cheese. You see braids and ribbon, the sheen of dark hair slatted with something that might be pearls, can almost smell the lavender, pomade. Nine, perhaps? This dark, at this distance, it's impossible to be sure. She shifts, half in shadow. Whatever else, she's certainly a child. No one is with her. Nothing moves and rain glints on the paving. Once in a while, she presses a hand against the glass, blurring an outline on the pane. Her mouth opens a little as though she might speak. But nothing comes. There is only stillness, the silent house. This curiously undiverting, undiverted child, watching. Waiting.

Hand.
This is a hand. My hand.

There are web partitions between the fingers. The function of the skin is to protect and cover. The function of the joint is to flex; of the muscles to clench and release. The nerves and circulatory channels cannot be seen. Their function is sensory evaluation, animation. Life. Long tendons reach the fingertips, slip through a bracelet of bone in the wrist.

Everything comes from the shoulder.

She looks at her hand, these fourteen crooks, the chicken-leg muscle under the thumb, its tight parcel of buried bones. So many bones.

Her hand.

His.

Listen! You can hear it plain.

Someone is playing exercises.

His hand, the solid pressure he exerts upon the keys. Not Czerny, not Hummel – he plays his own. Simple but effective, the same half-melodies over and over, designed for discipline, the honing of muscle. Aesthetics be damned: training is what comes first. His fourth finger sticks and it starts again, staccato next time, contrary motion, sliding between major and minor, just to keep his fingers trim. No pauses; no sooner does one finish, than it turns on its heel and starts again. This is the start of everything: stubborn pursuit of self-defined perfection through tedious hours of the same, the same. Practice, patience, whatever you like to call it. He has his own name. *He* calls it endurance and it abideth for ever. The little G minor triplets passage runs into the distance, vanishes like a mouse. Then he catches it by the tail and drags it back, backwards. Clever, a mental arithmetic that falls into place quite naturally after a while, happens almost without thought. And while it's happening, something else slips in alongside. Listen again: something married to, but not one with, the keys. Something human for a start. Take a moment, allow yourself: it's there, quite clear. A woman, singing. Her voice is high, expressionless, saving itself for more. A voice that puts itself through its paces: a ladder of five ascending notes, tonic to dominant, back again. That done, it cranks up a semitone, does it fresh: a five-note bloom and fade again, another semitone, again. Soon it's as high as you think it can go and – it does it one more time. It's not Johanna, silent Johanna. Johanna wouldn't have sung if her life depended on it. It's not a student because a student would have been with Papa, working in tandem, not elsewhere, trying to swim against the piano that ignored everything but itself. Whose, then? The same answer comes back

12

every time. Mother. Her mother's voice. There's no one else's it could have been. Does knowing make the voice more beautiful, more keenly felt? Perhaps. Another, surely there will be one last flourish, and the woman will appear entire around it, if only in your imagination; the voice will come into itself. So you wait. Your ears strain, waiting. Only the piano keeps going, churning the same cycles, oblivious. For whatever reason, the voice has gone. You can't even remember it. The texture of the sounds, the edge of it against the ear. Gone.

Sound.

That memory is made of sound before it's made of anything else, she has no doubt. That it is not as ephemeral as it appears she has no doubt either. After the kiss, the glass of lemon water, the scent of orchids is gone, it's gone. But a fragment of music somehow remains. And she knows that when she is alone in bed, in the early hours before dawn, music comes whether she likes it or not: a sliver of Chopin, one stubborn phrase of Beethoven, the edges and elbows of countless songs. And these. Her earliest memories, maybe, but something etched inside the skull, heard again and again till they stuck for ever and one in the same. Father raising his inventions to the sky. Mother, in another place entirely, singing.

Sing. One word. Sing!

She doesn't speak, has never spoken. Four years old and not a word. Some people say she's deaf or simple; others that she's both. *Poor Herr Wieck!* She hears them herself. Leering down with faces like owls, mouths open wide so the rotted places in their teeth show. *Hello!* they roar. *Hello, little lady!* in warm clouds, heavy with pig fat, garlic, tobacco. She peers out at them, protecting her nose behind the grey mask of someone's skirts, unblinking. Unfocused. After that, they give up. They turn to father, the baby with a face like a bloater, knock horseshit from their shoes – anything but persist with this awkward child. Never speaks. Never smiles. Thin as a stick with monstrous eyes; they can't even say she's pretty. Never mind. They give her sweets anyway, let her father take them away, wag his finger in mock-warning, let the talk turn to other things. Weather, they say. Who's married, who's sick, who's died. Business ah! Business. The fascinating Subject of Business and How it Thrives. And even at four, she knows what business means. Business means pianos. It also means Mother and all those notes, tickets, money and students, but mostly pianos. This talking, mouths chewing verbal cud, always runs for some time. After that, there is remarking about the state of the roads, who has dropped in or out of the subscription series, concerts and optional cooing at Gustav – this last always brief. Gustav is only a baby and, by definition, not interesting. He doesn't cry, yet. He squeaks like a stood-on puppy; only the housemaid listens. She picks him up and claps his hands together till she has something better to do, then she puts him down again. He can't even sit upright. So much for Gustav.

Then what? They scan with their eyes, working out the farewell strategy and she's still there, oblivious to the blatancy of it, staring. Every time they turn round, eyes. The child's entire repertoire. Last is an exchange about Frau Wieck's father in Plauen and that's the sign. When the talk turns to Grandpa, it's almost over. Absent people are the ends of conversations. Sometimes sick people, sometimes dead, but the merely absent will do. Alwin is an exception. Alwin is not here but no one will ask after Alwin. Asking after a child is not much done and this particular child less than most. Too small to walk, too big to carry, Alwin says goodbye in the hall and stays there. His white pudding face watches over Johanna's shoulder till Papa shuts the door and the face slides away and you hear him cry. Alwin cries all the time. No matter. That the girl-child says nothing has its good side. And when he looks down, to include her in his deliberations, to indicate more fully for their amusement whom he means, there she is, looking back. She watches them put their hats on and when Papa puts his on too, it's sure: the talking is done. That's what hats-on means. *Done.* To prove it there are farewells, the looking-over of shoulders, waves. Then there is walking. Where you walk is away. The sound of walking is footfalls to the Eilenburg Road, brass keys clanking in Father's pocket. Nothing but footfalls for miles.

Höhe Lilie. ❦ Mountain Lily.

Their letters come addressed to a flower.

Grey walls rising three floors. *Mountain Lily.* More the latter than the former, thinks Friedrich, when he thinks of his house name at all, which is seldom. What people think of his house is not his concern. It's a plain house, neither elegant nor grand. Sufficient is the word that springs to mind: this house is pleasingly adequate. There is a door and matching shutters in dutiful loden; ten solid apartments and loft space, all necessary. There are music rooms, workshops, the warehouse; a spread of bedrooms, a sitting room, parlour, kitchen. One servant's room, one servant, three big windows, eleven pianos. That's what bulks up the space. Pianos. They're not slight beasts, not dainty. Varnished edges sharp enough to cut, snap-shut lids, shin-battering pedals, stops, stands. Watch boys lifting them for transport and you'd see – pianos, even small ones with painted lids and silver candle sconces, all nymphs and weeping trees, are brutes. Unwieldy lumps. Stand between them and they crack, moan, breathe out wood; a little girl could get lost among their brown bull legs. That she never does is just as well, for the pianos keep coming. He trades one, puts one out for hire, two more appear. Teaching, trade, sale and barter; livelihood, aspiration; this house is made of pianos. That's what people come here for. The hall is full of silhouettes; cheaper than miniatures. One bears a passing resemblance to Schubert, another Beethoven. Everyone has these. As for the rest, Lord knows who. But trying to concentrate, to *think* in this place, is impossible. This house has no peace. It rings and resonates, echoes from all its corners. Pianos. Voices. *Sound.*

Sing!

Someone does. She has never heard anyone refuse. The very idea. *Sing!*

Girls come with their hair curled tight, sheet copy under their arms; young men with more hope than talent and what they come for is *him.* For Father to tell them what to do and he does, he certainly does. *Sing!* It's the same for everyone, even the pianists, especially the pianists. *Sing!*

They make scales and arpeggios, domino shapes of sound to make their throats and fingers supple, their pitch true. *The voice is your beginning!* he shouts. It's how every lesson starts. They sing till the whole street can hear them, it carries through walls. Later there are only pianos: the same pieces faltering, recurring, snipped into bits. Bad days, there are crashes and howls, even curses. Father is a passionate man. He kicks things, usually instruments. The old ones. *Better that than Other Things*, he says and you know he is offering a joke. It's also not a joke because he's right. Father is always right. This is how it is: a reliable constant. He takes full responsibility, he says, for being in the right. If he is not, they may apply for refund of fee and no one ever does. Proof.

During the day, all day, the music rises. Standing over the practice room ceiling, upon the floorboards of elsewhere, she can feel it buzz beneath the soles of her canvas shoes. Music makes sensation, it vibrates along the bones. There are hearts on the toes of her slippers; the clean, delicate stitching that is her mother's own. The laces are white and loose but nobody minds. Or is preoccupied. Johanna is always there, but rocking a crib, building a pyre of sticks for a fire, grating something green. There is a chair to play with, shutters to hide behind. There is a kit violin, pegs, balls of crushed paper, a frazzle of old strings. Ivory inlays, fresh covers for naked keys, scatter the table like dead giant's teeth. They can be looked at, even touched, these things: tuning pegs, metal prongs, studs and buttons, shreds of red velvet in wooden boxes fixed with brass. These things are particular; the very look of them fills her with warmth. *Treasure.* Not that she knows the word herself. She calls nothing anything, gives no clue she would like to. Princess, hero, fairy tale – the same. Why should she know? No one reads to her. Johanna has never learned and in any case uses speech like pepper: sparing, seldom, sometimes not at all.

Wieck reads, he reads a great deal but only to himself and things so tedious he sometimes throws them at the wall and goes out walking to escape. Letters too! They can make him spit. That words can stir such violence; mere black marks on a page! A remarkable thing, but that passing observation is enough. A teacher, a dealer of pianos, a musician, a composer in his own way – father has too much to do already without pointless observation of the commonplace, thank you. He's important. Once he lived on bread and water, hid his shirt cuffs in public lest the fraying show, but he built his Life with Unswerving Dedication and Selfless Effort and now – well, look at him. He signifies. Music changed his life for ever and he'll tell the story to anyone. He's not proud. Six free lessons from Milchmeyer, and his destiny, he says, was altered. Milchmeyer was a cripple in a metal crate but a Great Man nonetheless, a Great Pedagogue such as one meets once in a lifetime and to whom Great Gratitude is owed. Spohr too – Spohr is a Great Man and Weber. He knows because they answered his letters, they *took the time*. Great Men all. Great Men have shaped Our Lives. He's in a good mood when he tells her these things: his face looks less solid. He doesn't read to her, perhaps, but he tells her tales about his life, Great Men and Jesus. If she can't hear or comprehend, what's the loss? He can speak enough for a household, the voice of one trained to know and disseminate the will of God, so who need add or interrupt? He speaks because he speaks. He does it well. He'd tell an empty room, maybe, and the child is at least more than that.

Mother does not read because she is a singer. She has the house to run, Hanna to tell what to do, all this singing and playing that father directs her in, night and day. There is a lot to direct, she can see that, and Vigilance is Eternal. Between come concerts but mostly Mother's work is Vigilance: the training of the voice, practice, digital dexterity, programming, the concert to come. And her name is pretty as a petal. Marianne. That's everything there is to know. Everyone. Friedrich and Marianne. Mama and Papa. Alwin and Gustav are only little boys who make too much noise and need things all the time, and nobody mentions Adelheid. Adelheid had no birthdays – what is there to say? The Lord giveth etc and acceptance is a lesson that none may avoid.

After that, there is only one left to name: Johanna. *Hanna*, the boys say; *Hanna*, easy for baby mouths. Mama and Papa are easy words too but it's Hanna they say first. Johanna smells of fat and ashes. Her breasts are a mattress of flesh. When she reaches behind for the buttons at the back of your dress at night, one arm on each side, you can hardly breathe. She's warm and she's *there*. At bedtime, when the people are coming, she takes them upstairs. They have nothing to contribute to these *soirées* but absence and they know it very well. Gusts of cold air come upstairs from the front door while they undress; through the skylight, the sound of hooves. Trilling and tail ends of practice come through the floor, the sound of adult men roaring greetings. Nonetheless, she must sleep. And Johanna nips out the candles with her fingers, not afraid of the flames, to make the dark.

In the frazzled stink of tallow is another country and the child lies in it, given up to thinking, listening – the things they suspect she does not do. Listening involves not moving. Not moving to a Very High Degree. Some children can lie so still you'd think they'd stopped breathing, and this one's better than most. She lies in the dark like a dead thing till the dark sucks her in and she supposes that is sleep. It never seems like sleep. It seems like waiting. Words come, sometimes, as she lies there and she hears them clear: *Insolent. Deceitful. Proud as sin.* The wash of Father's voice made eerie in the darkness from his bedroom down the hall. *Silence*, muffled only slightly through three walls' thickness. *Indolence itself!* And she wonders why he is up so late, what kind of lesson it can possibly be. There is no music now, just loud words, a sound that could be crying. A kind of lesson the child does not yet understand. Her breathing hurts when it happens, like something struggling to climb out of her from the inside; she clutches her nightdress over her chest till it passes. She sweats and her eyes leak till the quiet comes back, and her own silence is part of it. That way the peace will come back quicker. She doesn't know where this certainty comes from; it's true, that's all. Some old knowledge held in the lungs, the ribcage tells her. So she waits, still and silent, till the last shout fades, till the quiet tells her only she is awake, and she can lie down again, rest a while, wait some more. The boys snore like piglets, turning the air hot with their breath, and there is the scent of milk and bile, wet wool. The more she stares at the dark, the darker it gets and she sleeps, despite herself, she sleeps, her little hand over her mouth, not knowing whether her eyes are open or shut.

Then morning comes, all blue with pale stripes, the rag rug under-foot, fallen quilts, the boys grizzling. There is light like a happy thing through the window where the shutters don't meet and Johanna with a facecloth, a dowsing in a jug, as though the night never was. Johanna picks up fallen clothes, checks them for loose ends, signs of unravelling. Johanna cooks and mends. She washes, irons and starches. She clears the grate and leads it, builds fires, polishes brass, wood and iron surfaces, washes glass with vinegar. She orders kitchen supplies, deals with tradesmen, draws up household inventories, minds children, arranges hair when necessary, makes shirts, aprons, caps, slippers and bibs. Johanna sews. She pulls you away from the fire and the window if you wait there too long. She cleans their teeth at night, the length of her pinpricked fingers slathered in salt. Huge, bloody as sausage, the nails bitten past the quicks to half-moon slivers, red-rimmed. Johanna's hands. After years, decades, the child they ministered to will be able to conjure them at will. She will be able to recall the smoothness of her face, the smell of her, heady as last week's soup, that her eyes were grey. But no voice. No matter how hard she tries: nothing. Johanna didn't speak enough to leave a trace. She's been told again and again: *Didn't speak so you'd notice*, the approval with which it was said. Then again, she must have said something, at least now and then; she must have uttered their names. Her name. How do you discipline a child without speaking her name?

Clara.

It means limpid. Light.
  Her father chose it.

Clara. Say it. Clara. He holds a watch in front of her face. It swings to and fro on a chain. Gold or brass, perhaps, beautifully polished. The child's eyes make half her face dark. They tilt at the corners like a Slav's.
  Clara. You may hold Papa's watch if you say it.
  The reflection in her pupils shows the face of a man, doubled; twin timepieces, swinging.

⤛═◉═⤜

No one at home thinks she's deaf.

Not in their heart of hearts. The child takes instructions, clears her plate, comes when she is called. Eventually. She doesn't laugh much and, thank God, seldom runs. She is not as clumsy as most of her age, can walk good distances unassisted and has no perceptible need of toys. As for her silence (here the man of the house raises himself to his full height), some would say that is an admirable trait in a woman. Then he looks at his wife. He looks hard. Family, he says, that's what matters; people in town may say what they like. People are always saying something. It's beneath his dignity to say anything back. Time will tell, he says. *We'll see.* What he sees before long are the lines between her brows. He notices more than once, little furrows. It seems they only appear when he does. He tries experiments, watches her with Johanna, Alwin, and it's true. With them, there's nothing. Her forehead's flat as a field. When he comes back — so do the lines. He does it several times for sheer curiosity, to see this semblance of adult concern on a little girl, and it makes him smile. They make her look like a spaniel, he says, a pup. The lines are consistent, however: as though she is trying to make sense of the unfathomable. She knows I take her intelligence for granted, he says, not like some. Here, he says, gives her a penny. The frown stays put. It has to be admitted: something about the observation is infinitely pleasing.

Not long after this, he decides to act. This plan has been waiting its moment and the frown lines are it. He will use the concentration he inspires and, to begin that use, he reaches for the dead centre of the keyboard. One note, clear and resonant. C. He looks her in the eye. He plays it again, sings it.

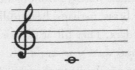

He plays it again, waits. Waits. Then her face lights like the sun from behind a cloud and her mouth opens. She sings. C, she sings. C for Clara! Again. Again. He does this for three minutes, choosing five different notes. He times it, never strays more than a sixth, returns to where he began. Then he smiles. What's more, she smiles back. A very small smile, true, but discernible. Her brow, he notices without even trying, is completely smooth. *We'll see*, he says. *We'll see.*

What everyone sees already is the child takes after him. There is no mistaking her paternity. She has her mother's nose, which for ever means her mother's profile, but the rest of her face is all Friedrich, God help her. That apart, she doesn't give much away, which is, after all, as it should be; he would give nothing away if he could help it either. That's something else people say, and Friedrich knows. He doesn't care. People say a great deal more than their prayers, he says, and that's the end of it. Especially if one has a presence. He says this last part as though it might be contempt but it's relish too – you can hear it. He is a Figure in his Community and his community is not inconsiderable: Leipzig.

It's not Dresden and God knows it's not beautiful, but Leipzig has its points. Hard work and trust in God can get a man far in this place: the Gewandhaus, the orchestra, the university where Goethe was a young man, the scrawl of book and music publishers, the handspan of newspapers and textile merchant money backing it up – the place has enough. And, let us always remember and be grateful, it's not Pretzsch. God forbid he should ever have to return to Pretzsch. True, the average Leipziger has a taste for gossip but people gossip everywhere; it is not to be avoided. In any case, gossip matters little or nothing. Diligence, Patience and Craft, he says, these are what matter; not what idle people say. They have a counted-stitch motto of these very words beside the mantel, low on the wall so the child can see. A pattern of browns and blues, nothing she can read. But the words are shapes she knows already. She can touch the threads with her fingertip. Meanwhile, her father says – he looks at his watch – work on the concerto, the second movement in particular. Attend to your poor arpeggios. Sewing can wait. Directives before he leaves. It's a habit. Frau Wieck has a concert in two weeks; but then she always has a concert in two weeks and the rest of the time there is plenty else to do. She puts the dress down, the panel she is stitching unfinished. Her needle glints in its dark-blue folds.

Herr Wieck looks at his daughter, addresses her alone. Apply the highest principles and expect favours from no one, child. No one.

No one. A vast word for a small head.

He looks at her watching him, her hair parted like a split damson. Whether she hears him or not, she understands. He is sure she understands.

No one save Papa, he says. He smiles, broad, wide. His eyes glitter. Save me.

⊹═◦═⊹

When he calls her he calls her by name.

Clärchen, Little Clara. My Clara.

First-borns, they say, make solid citizens: prepared for, fussed over; complicity with the adult world is assured. Second-borns are rebels, dissenters. The near miss, it seems, grates. Thirds and fourths fare more according to personal whim, strength or weakness; and the youngest, wherever they occur, can twist the world round their effortless, pretty fingers. Monday's child, of course, is fair, Tuesday's is graceful and no one wants to give birth on a Wednesday if they can help it. Predictions and games, where's the harm? They shield folk, however temporarily, from implacable statistics. Which everyone knows not from learning but what they see, and what they see is that children die. One in four. Stillbirths to accidents, complications and disease, hands fresh from the cavities of cadavers to those of labouring women, wiped once or twice on still-bloody aprons. One in four won't make the age of five. Visit the graveyard and the evidence is everywhere, every coffin maker has stock in varying degrees of tiny size. Women die too, especially in hospitals – dear God, none but the desperate, the destitute or the dead enter *hospitals* – the whole business of medicine and its institutions is fraught. Rumour has it they guess half the time and so they do, but people fall sick, people feel pain and one must do something. Patients, however, are wary. Unless death is likely in any case, the processes of birth must do as they will and that means one in four. Town and country, rich and poor, in no

22

order one could reasonably foresee, avoid, account for; without resort to numbers, everyone knows the odds.

Friedrich lusted for Clara irrespective of her sex.

Before he knew what she was, who she was, he knew what she would be: the greatest pianist he could fashion, his brightness, a star. He never allowed himself to think she would not survive. He had worried for Adelheid and what had it meant? The crunch of his miniscule fists, the blue cast of his lips. Adelheid died before there was much to see, but what there was, Friedrich remembered. He remembered very clearly. White-blond, unlike either parent. Some children are like that; they lack a stamp of physical belonging. As though they were built in error. His first-born, then, was a failure.

Clara arrived on the first day of the working week, full head of dark hair first, eyes open if the midwife was to be believed. The weight of her in his arms, when he held her, was solid. His true first-born, he thought. He felt her struggle against the shawl. And there and then a tightness in his chest welled up, so sudden, so powerful, he was forced to sit lest he fall. It was a sensation he had never experienced before and it frightened him more than a little. He sat with his eyes closed, listening to his own breathing as it shuddered under control, steadied itself. The smell of her, like warm fruit, soothed him. But soothing was softness, and softness counted for nothing in this life. His eyes still closed, the moment suggesting itself, Friedrich prayed. He absorbed the subtle scent of her and prayed for iron. She would see strength, this child. She would acquire it, too. This time, it would be different. Done, he looked down at her wide-open eyes, her jet-black head, saw her looking back. It was not foolish to think so. This child was here for the duration.

What her mother thought he never asked. The Lord gave and the Lord took away, and why was not a question. Marianne, he felt sure, was grateful for Blessings Bestowed. Marianne's life was full of Blessings – he reminded her often – including a body that healed quickly, a mind that soaked up notes like a blotter and the capacity to perform *well*. These were not to be buried beneath maternal obligations. The housemaid was a suitable nurse, dumb as a sheep, perhaps, but capable. He was sure

Johanna was capable. After three months of screaming colics and night feeds, Marianne was sure too. She bound her breasts and handed the child over. Johanna it was, then, who saw to feeds and chewing rusks, the awkwardnesses of mittens, bibs and bonnets. She boiled wetting cloths and nightdresses, tiny pinafores and gruel. She worked the baby's legs and arms, kept an eye on the stair edge, placed ornaments on higher shelves, cleared up vomit, spills, shit and fingerprints; saw off wind and night terrors with equal efficiency if she heard them. By the time of Alwin's arrival she was practised; by the time of Gustav's, mechanical. When Marianne took to sleeping in the afternoons, Friedrich found the little girl trailing him. Stopping when he stopped, waiting. What's more, he let her. He had plans for the child and they could begin now, more unconventionally than he had imagined, but certainly now. He showed her the workrooms, let her sit in on lessons, encouraged her to listen if she could not articulate. He swung his watch like Mesmer, repeated her name.

Father.

Father taught. Father talked a lot in a noticeable voice. He instructed. He had a straight back, a scratchy face. His boots were shinier than any other boots she had ever seen or could imagine; they made music on the cobbles from their leather soles. Father walked. He certainly walked. He walked off tempers and to increase his joy of living. He walked to cafés and meeting houses, to avoid excessive coach fares and to enjoy the Rosenthal. And after all that, there was more. Walks were not just walks, dear me, no. They were meetings and connections, parades and snubs. They were A FUNCTION OF SOCIAL ORDER. EXERCISE IN FRESH AIR. Strengthening the body in general and the lungs in particular, walks made PROTECTION AGAINST DISEASE AND CONTAGION. They MAIN-TAINED PRESENT HEALTH AND PERSPECTIVE, CONTROLLED YOUTHFUL EXCESSES AND ENCOURAGED CRITICAL REFLECTION. Walks were lessons and discipline, sound preparation for a sound and godly life. And walks were silent. Along the river, through moors and woodland, over pebbles, tracks, fields, bells and walking sticks were all one heard and rightly so, rightly so. On their walks, the Wiecks walked.

Start at the green door. When it closes, follow the heels in front (black, regular, heavy of tread) right through the Neumarkt, past the hawkers and water boys, the porters and haulers. Buy nothing. Keep walking. Past the gutterless streets, the two crossed hunting horns on the house that marks the end of University Square, past the newspaper offices, the broken wall scrawled with foreign words, the names of homesick soldiers, to the city gates, then on again till the road turns brown, becomes indistinguishable from dirt. This is one way to the edge of Leipzig, before the road to somewhere else. It's nowhere. Other people stop here, make circuits round the town like dancing bears. Not you. You keep walking. Soon, there is no road at all, only footpaths, hedgerows, puddles. Stand still and the toes of your boots disappear, sink whole into mud that sucks when you try to reclaim them, draws down. Keep walking.

The memory is clear to the end of her life and why is no mystery. They did this every day. Father and daughter, she from the age of four with her white baby bonnet and loosened strings. When it rained his coat (mud green, the colour of a river in spate) smelled like wet chickens. His skin stank of leather and the stick he carried in his hands. Her memories carry blisters, the sensation of skin loosening, tearing away from the tissue beneath at every step, the tang of wet woodland filling her nose. Her feet were damp: the price of owning only one pair of stout boots, of not drying them as fully as she might. But wet boots were her affair, no one else's. She would not complain. She bit her lip as she saw her mother often do, did it without thinking, and kept going, the hem of her pinafore turning darker with every step, the trackless mud paths splashing. Up and overhead, however, was a lattice of leaves with light razing between, a watery sun promising more. Up there was the whole sky, and Father himself, lofty as a monument, his hat brim an eclipse. Grey hair flared at his temples, the studs on his heels clapped like hooves and he was handsome, she thought; a man not to be trifled with.

Once he caught her looking at him, not watching her feet at all but him, and whether he was pleased or not was hard to say. His face changed not at all, but he stared down the length of his considerable nose and spoke: The sky is growling, listen! *The sky is growling.* These words, their strangeness. That the sky might *growl*, might be a threatening thing despite the fact that God lived there, was impossible to believe. For a moment, and only a moment, doubt made a trapdoor in her stomach. What, she wondered, split-second dazzled and terrified, what if God did not help them when the growling came? And then, as she thought it, it did. Thunder. The sky rolled darker and the low rolling noise of a coming storm made her turn her head, and single spits of rain smacked close to her eyes. Seconds later, the sky opened like a tear in a shop awning and she heard his footfalls behind her, picking up speed as he moved away. Afraid of being left here, she turned on her heel, saw him ahead of her and started running. Perhaps her foot caught on her skirt hem, perhaps she slipped on rotted leaves; perhaps she had no excuse at all. But she remembers falling, tumbling headlong, the trees flipping over her head and a cracking of twigs loud in her ears. There was pain, but nothing pressing; a peppering of dirt on her hands.

And when she raised her eyes, sure that now he had marched away without her, there he was, raised to his full height, looking back. He glanced at her hands and eased back his shoulders. *Up,* he said. *Up.* And Clara stood. She refused to cry out despite the stinging, refused to allow any halt in her stride. She hitched her dress to her ankles and merely walked. In the time it took to reach him, something was decided. *You'll do,* he said gently as she reached his side. *You'll do.* Whatever it meant, it pleased him. Only then did he reach out to her. He dusted her hands, smoothed her coat over her flat child-hips ignoring the downpour as though it was not there. When they set off once more, he walked closer to shield her and she was quite sure. Father was not afraid of anything. Everything came right. Lest he feel forced to slow down, be disappointed that he had misjudged her, she widened her step. He looked down, then, watched her doing it. She was quite sure he was smiling.

And Mother? Ah. Mother.

Mother sang. Mother rocked her sometimes, rocked without her sometimes. Mother stayed at home with Mozart, swollen as a sow. Mother played. Mother played.

Clara would never remember her mother taking the stage pushing her belly in front of her, but she would recollect the fullness of her dress and the body beneath, a handing over of flowers, a suggestion of embrace. That they had gripped her mother's body while someone was living inside it always came as a shock; a queer, unseemly thing to be able to recall. It spoke of something intimate, a closeness at one time unremarkable. One embraced Mother, she was the shape she was. It may have happened only once, but it happened. She recalls a baby, a red face and wizened hands, upturned saucer eyelids purple and twitching. Which brother is uncertain. She remembers a picnic in a muddy field, the sleeve of a gauze dress caught on a thorn bush, a torn fingertip leading to outraged misery, Father shouting. A hand clutching her own, tight enough to hurt. She recalls her mother standing next to her, far back from the platform, the crowding close of people. When Clara thought of her mother, she thought of singing, the anchors she once thought written notes made on the page, cloth. She thought of terrible fear and pity mixed. She thought of Woyzeck.

Whose idea it had been she could not say. But she had been there. She forgot it for years but it came back, piecemeal, slow, from the bottom of mud. And what came was this. A man between soldiers, their blue jackets shutters on either side of his white face; stand-on-end hair, a dust-pale shirt, black-red lips. He talked to himself, or at least his mouth moved. His teeth were brown. In prison, they said, he had bitten iron bars. The imprisonment was uncontested nonetheless. Woyzeck had killed a woman because she would not walk in public with him, and because she would not love him as he wished. He had taken her to the riverside – she went, it seemed, without suspicion – and there, at the water's edge, stabbed her till the tide turned purple. Afterwards he ran away. He hid the knife in his shirt. But they found him talking out loud about what he had done and they took him to the Rathaus to decide what to do. Voices did it, he said. They had incited him; angels and devils beneath the ground. He was misunderstood, the world despised him, and the voices had told him the source of his misery and how to put it right. They locked him up immediately, watched him pace his cell. He tore at his hair till it stood on end. He talked incessantly to what was not there. His warders said Woyzeck was mad, from lack of love, from motherlessness, from bad luck, maybe, but mad all the same. Dr Carus, however, did not. Dr Carus – Clara knows Dr Carus, likes the chime of his name against hers, that he comes to their house and sings, plays the piano prettily – said his voices were nothing particular: loneliness was all that crazed him and since Dr Carus was a doctor and his opinion counted, Woyzeck was found sane enough to be publicly killed.

All this she did not know as she stood there, at least not in detail. Of course not. She saw only what she saw, heard only the voices on all sides. The afternoon Clara recalls is mostly a man, a platform, a terrible sword. And she knew that words had been the cause. Something had spoken in his ear and he had listened. Woyzeck, the whispered-to, the murderer, standing on a purpose-built raft in the middle of Leipzig, a show for the public gaze and she, somehow, had seen. She recalls him kneeling down, his shock of hair red as brushfire, his shut eyes and these whispering, silent, red-black lips. The rest is only telling. He refused a blindfold so the sword was to be drawn behind him. It was thought kinder. He had written a prayer and spoke it aloud. After that, perhaps sensing the movement of the swordsman, he had shouted aloud. *Think of me on your wedding day.* What did it mean? A foreigner in a foreign land, hearing things, talking nonsense in his final moments. That they cut off his head in one slice, that her mother had held her hand, that her father had been there – all this was theory. A four-year-old with a nun's expression, one of the citizens of Leipzig come to see justice dispensed, there to learn, she seemed singularly to have failed.

Her father had not been irritated by the crowds or the watching, the holding high of children that they might see; he found the whole thing merely vulgar. Even if they had not held up the head afterwards like the bloody French, the crowding and selling of souvenirs was difficult to thole. Woyzeck's last words, however, amused him and he repeated them often. Love may well be a path to ruin, he said crisply. Undisciplined passion most certainly is. He looked down his long nose at Marianne, the bride of his heart, pulling on his gloves. Beware, he said, smiling after a fashion, the primrose path of wedding days.

⊷⊶⊷

Not long after this, then. Not long.

There was a journey to see Grandma in Plauen, her mother all in grey. She recalls the colour, the scrub of the cloth against her face, the cold crush of its linen folds. It must have been summer because of the flowers, something fresh and yellow in a vase, Easter long gone. Of the events prior to this journey, the decisions that led to it, she knows nothing even now. That something serious had happened, something to split a life in two, did not show. Plauen was only Plauen; they had been to see Grandma before. Viktor in the crook of Mother's arm, still feeding from her body when he got the chance, Grandmother throwing a ball. Alwin and Gustav had not come too but this was nothing new. The baby was new, he required to be shown; his brothers were not an issue. Mother smelled of blood and the dog followed her. The dog would not sit still if she came near. People visited as ever but their talk was lower, more hushed and someone, someone unplaceable, took her on their knee and rocked her. It made her uncomfortable, a stranger swaying her back and forth.

Over days, the whole visit became cloying. It was too long, too purposeless. Too clearly not home. The birdsong was too loud and the air was always sticky, pending thunder. After a while it dawned. There was no music. Home was stuffed with it: the same phrases of the same concerto for days on end, ringing on in echoes in spaces in your own head. Here in Plauen the piano lid stayed shut. Mother didn't touch the keys at all. A book appeared in Clara's mind, red morocco covers with embossed lettering, W-E-B-E-R, each figure raised and dusted with gold. The pages inside were thick, their edges curled and dark with use. Perhaps she missed the book, the music it held inside. Sometimes she was almost moved to speak, but didn't. Not more than a baby herself, but she knew already. This terrible hiatus. There was only so much longer it could go on.

Saxon Law, Napoleonic Law. It's all the same.

Children are property; men are property owners.

It was certainly the law.

Soon Clara, newly five, sits next to strangers near open window spaces of a post-chaise. She wears the new boots that were the present from her grandfather, her best pinafore, the apron Grandmother stitched with her own hands. It's not cold but Mother's face looks bitten and her hands shiver. All Grandmother does is sniff. Someone opposite wears a coat like a ploughed field, doesn't speak for the whole journey. He spits on the floor and Mother moves her feet. Blots of phlegm shine like eggs, sliding as the chaise rocks. He says nothing, this man, only coughs and spits, and does not admit anyone else is there. Mother, however, talks a lot — *Look, Clara, the trees! The rabbits! Soon you'll see Alwin again; won't it be good to see Alwin?* — talking far too much, truth be told, wrapping Viktor tighter in his cowl. *How Gustav will have missed you!* For a moment when she says this Grandmother seems to laugh but it isn't that. Nothing feels like a joke. The man with the coat has a yellow face and when his eyes meet hers, an accident, she looks away. When the man coughs again, she fetches a scarf up to Clara's nose, holds it there, tight. Grandmother takes the baby and Mother fusses in the bag beneath her feet. The bag has stockings and dresses, pattens, a winter cape. She saw them packed. Why, she has no idea. The winter cape stays in Plauen, too awkward to ferry back and forth, but not this time. This time everything, everything of Clara's at least, is coming too. Where Mother's bags might be never occurs. They will be somewhere. They're not a child's concern. Through the open window space a distant steeple hoves into view, back out again. The trees turn russet, horses run in the fields. The coat-man coughs. His whole body rattles. There is nothing to play with, nothing to see.

Then comes Altenberg; Altenberg with fresh horses and pie sellers, pumps for water, an inn. This time, there is also Hanna in her old cap and dun skirts, with a bag on her arm, her knitting, and the sight is so pleasing the child breaks rules and runs. Johanna stands there, laughing to see her do it — as if she would forget her Johanna even after these months! As if! And Johanna strokes her cheek as though they had arranged to meet here, as though nothing was unusual in this place, this happenstance, at all. She has bread and apples in her bag, a pastry twist. Clara may choose. Since no one says they are not, she assumes them birthday presents, maybe from Papa too, and thinking it fills her up so she wishes only to own them, not eat. In any case, there's the rest of the journey to go and the carriage jolts. It would not do to be sick, the same length of journey to go. For that's what's coming. It's clear now. What else can they be doing in this place? Altenberg, a crossroads, the way to somewhere else. All five together; they are met up as they should be and they're going home. No one else seems to know, however.

Mother and Johanna stand apart; don't greet each other. Even when Clara holds up the pastry to Viktor's lips, knowing he is asleep and can't eat pastry in any case, no one smiles. When the porter shouts for passengers and it's time, Clara turns to wait for their first move. She watches their faces. The horse brasses clank. Mother and Grandmother do not move. Something calls in the wood, one bird to another, and everyone stands as still as a picture. The driver tests his whip.

Just as Clara begins to be uncertain they are leaving at all, Johanna's hand slips into her own, tugging. Tugging the wrong way. Clara watches her mother and grandmother stay put, feels herself inched forward, away from them without her co-operation. Johanna keeps pulling, more definitely now, and Grandmother, still within touching distance, calls as if from far away. *You'll see Mama soon*, she says, *very, very soon*. Viktor is held out, a package being shown off, and Clara can't understand. Why should she look at Viktor now? And despite her rheumatism, her weakness in the joints, Grandmother kneels. Clara has never seen her grandmother kneel and is faintly appalled. What is she doing? *Viktor is staying with Mama*, Mother says. *Goodbye, Clara*. Johanna's hands are clinging like mud, sucking her away. *We will see you soon. Very soon*. Without being able to account for the footsteps that take her there, Clara's boots find the first of the coach steps and begin to stumble upwards out of habit. Grandmother is struggling to her feet again and Viktor is waking up. Clara can see a hand emerge from the layers, its scorched redness against the white. He cries and no one comforts him, no one says anything at all. The horses move from hoof to hoof and, from inside the carriage, someone's hands are reaching down. They bracelet her arms and Clara pushes up on her toes to help. It is what a good girl does. She helps. As she rises, lifting out of sight, the child checks over her shoulder one last time. There is a glimpse of Grandma folding like paper, hands lifting to cover her mouth, Mother's face the colour of milk, then nothing but arms, black woollen sleeves against them, the scent of leather. Something is wrong. Johanna pushes, someone in the carriage hauls. Something is terribly wrong.

After that? The sound of rain.

The cold seeping through the woollen blanket over her knees.

Johanna, silent as stone. That's all.

That's all.

Presumably he collected her. Presumably someone held her, even if in passing, as they helped her down. If only for that short period of time, it's something. If she had not been so sure on her feet they might have carried her, which affords embrace by default, but she seems to have had no aptitude for that kind of artifice, no way to ask. Her father's daughter, she returned to the house at Leipzig on her own two feet, blisters starting on her heels. A new house with no flowers in its name. This house had no name at all. Papa was up and waiting, of course. He did not ask where her mother was. Maybe he knew. Maybe everyone knew but her. Her brothers were already asleep, he said, leading her up stairs she only half remembered. He would take her to her room. *Brother. Her room.* She had been in Plauen too long, could picture only Viktor, her grandmother's bed, yet that was not his meaning. For here she was, going up different stairs entirely, to a room that smelled like staleness and crumbs, not babies; a room that was nonetheless hers. *Hers.* You are home now, he said. With Papa. Home with Papa where you have always been. And he drew the shutters. And always will be. She heard them thud shut. A jug of cold water sat near the bed, a blue flannel. One candle. Johanna prised what was left of the pastry from Clara's hand, pushed gently till the rim of the mattress was near enough to lift her towards it in one swoop. Her feet did not reach the floor. Slowly, one eyelet at a time, Hanna worked on the laces of her boots.

Next day she ate no breakfast. Her father noticed but did not force. A man who was once a domestic tutor, who understood children, he knew best when to leave alone. The violent shaking of the coach, airless interiors and poor roads — the after-effects of travel on a child's system were only to be expected. Besides, fasting had its limitations; he saw no need to insist when nature would do it without his intrusion. In time, he told Johanna, in time. She'll eat when she's hungry. Soon after, he found her standing at the window, her chin barely reaching over the inside sill. What held her attention? Outside, he saw only a man grooming a dray, carters unloading wood. No carriages. No one coming. She kept looking out nonetheless. He fetched his hat, then issued Johanna with the day's directions. The housekeeper now, the only woman of the house, she needed little telling, but checking was never wasted, in his opinion.

On his way out he saw a bundle of what appeared to be rags in the parlour. Not rags. His daughter, flat on her stomach. It took a moment to realise she was peering under the couch. A mouse, silverfish, something must have caught her eye. Something small. Who can tell what happens in the mind of a child? He had left full orders for the day, set to begin at eight. Let her lie watching silverfish till then, he thought, suddenly indulgent. Johanna would set her right only minutes from now. To be perfectly sure, he warned the new housemaid to check for vermin, reminded Johanna to set Clara to polishing the forks, then left with his house and spirits to rights. The sky was clear, cloudless. Herr Wieck would not show it was anything else. He walked to the Coffeebaum, ticking lists in his head, making plans, many plans. First, exercise: the best medicine for a troubled digestion. It was clear the child's digestion was at fault. After lunch, whether she had eaten or not, he would take her out. He would take her out for four miles. After that, sleep. After that? He made many plans.

Six days after her fifth birthday, then, near four o'clock in the evening, her father led Clara to the piano. He pulled his daughter, his brightness, next to him, tilted her chin, raised her right hand close to her face and looked at her. Hard. Five, he said. Five. Look.

He raised his hand to the window that she might see the spread of his fingers, the bright translucent blood colour in the spaces between.

The thumb is One. This here is Two. This, Three. He counted out loud till each was called something. Five, he said. One. Two. Three. Four. Five. Then he raised her left hand and did the same again.

Clara, *Clärchen*, this child chosen for greatness, waited till he was done, then she looked at him, her face steady, her mouth a tight line. *I know this*, her eyes said. *I know this already.*

To his credit, Friedrich laughed.

+→○←+

Clefs are the keys to the kingdom.

Not quite a joke, but close. *Kingdom.* When he said it she fancied vast stretches of territory, huge brass locks tooled with iron studs, tumblers the size of fists sludding into place. The gates to other, more magical, worlds. *Clefs are the keys.* Her head filled with pictures, ideas: what these keys might open if they became wholly her own. That they would she had no doubt. No one did. The thing was never in question. It was only a matter of acquisition.

First, I stress the necessity for the Young of frequent open-air Exercise. Second, I am opposed to forcing or delaying the Work of Active Education. If a Child is attracted to something, and can understand it tolerably well, teach! Do not worry unduly about his Age! Remember it does no good to allow a Child entirely his own way, but neither is it good merely to drill him. One must take pleasure in one's Calling, and interest the Pupil in the Work before him. Find his Natural Enthusiasm! As for Moral Education, the most important – I stress that to teach the Child to be a Good Man is the Highest Goal of Humanity. The power of the Christian faith to this end will be denied only by those with no Religion at all, so teach that too. There are those, of course, who say Children should be taught no Religion before the age of ten because Children lack the necessary understanding. To them I say: Religion, and especially with Children, should be a matter not only of Understanding but also of the Heart. God, Religion and Virtue vibrate together in response to the slightest touch when one is young. Spare no reasonable rod. To do so is to give in to easy sentimentalism that will later give cause for regret. A Child remembers little of Childhood, of how things begin, of the Necessary Coercive Discipline of the new: they retain only the Good Effects which result. The Mind and the Tree bend best when young. And Children forget. They forget. That may be borne in Mind.

In whose mind, though? Whose?

This sickly boy, the runt of five brothers. Nobody else in the family played or even liked music much; no one in the whole town, when he came to think of it. Pretzsch. Between Wittenberg and Torgau on the Elbe. Nowhere. From his bedroom window he watched coopers spring-load barrels into shape, his neighbours cobbling shoes, metalworkers and hedge-cutters, sawers and bangers, people who butchered meat. Almost everyone in town had brown nails and the tanner's were black. Friedrich's were white. The sight of them flicking the pages of books, pale as the paper itself, gave his mother pleasure. Quiet pleasure, but pleasure nonetheless. Sometimes he read aloud from these books while she worked in the kitchen, mixing blood into pudding meal, boiling dough; by and large, though she never said, they bored her. Some of them bored Friedrich too, but that was beside the point. When he looked out of the window, saw what surrounded him, he knew one thing. Books were his future. Nobody laughed at the short-sightedness, the occasional sickness of an *academic*, it was taken for granted – that's how Bookish Sorts were. His hands were hopeless, his father said, not much troubled; *he'd better be good with his head* and where head workers went was college. What for? Not music. He liked music – who didn't – but music wasn't *work*. Music, like doctoring and jurisprudence, was a pastime for rich boys, a marriage market enhancement for girls. Someone needed to teach such but it wouldn't be Friedrich. Friedrich had never had a lesson in his life. He could self-teach all he liked, but without lessons, *real* lessons, who in their right mind would call him *professor?*

Religion, on the other hand, *that* was a living. Religion was what every clever boy from a nothing background studied: it made him into a something. Snotty clerks from Paris had pared down the opportunities, it was true, posts and promotions in that direction were not what they were, but what else was there? Besides, he looked the part. The skin of his face broke out, it peeled and worried at him, his hair was always needing cut: the church was clearly his natural home.

Fifteen, then, with one jacket, the legs of his trousers a comedy, he left home for Torgau and learned. He learned to walk everywhere, talk loudly to cover the noises from his growling gut, hide his threadbare shirt cuffs under the shiny rims of his jacket sleeves. He learned how stupid and lacking in anything of foresight, vigour or intellect those who surrounded him were. He learned not to point it out. He learned the value of geniality and found he was good at it: for all he hardly drank and gambled less, he was popular. People who could tell a joke, he found, were. He practised anecdotes, caricatures and casual asides in his shaving glass, keeping his chin keen. He played the school's clavier and let drunkards sing to his accompaniment, as though he didn't mind at all: for an hour's playing, teaching himself before the others were even awake, it was fair trade. And playing the clavier mattered. Not just because it did, but because it was the thing.

Once a week, a local carter brought him bread, his mother's hand-prints baked on the crust. Before long, he found something to go with it. His landlord's little daughter needed a tutor, a cheap tutor; the landlord's wife made good soup. Soup wasn't money but it was soup, and exchange wasn't robbery. Soup for reading would do. It came as a surprise how well teaching suited, however. The way the child looked at him when she grasped a new idea was gratifying; this growing clarity between her brows came from him. He was forming something, he felt, as he watched her struggle over her diphthongs, spit out sense: forming *her*. Soon, a boy from a richer family earned him mutton on Sundays, a place at the table to eat it. And places at tables meant introductions, something he'd never have achieved by birth. He met minor officials, prissy administrators and lesser dignitaries, all with children and tables of their own. A student at Wittenberg, a proper university boy now, it was no more than he deserved. He was, he fancied, a real pedagogical catch, and those who paid him found few reasons to argue. He drilled the children well, threw religious teaching in for nothing and, apart from a tendency to mount a high horse now and then, had no real vices. He learned the value of good notepaper, a legible hand, how to spell *soirée*.

He saw the rage for pianos – every girl in Vienna played, they said, every house held a Pleyel or a Graf, a Broadwood, a Stein – was no passing fad. Burning now, he begged six lessons from Milchmeyer; Milchmeyer, with his callipers, the rims of grease round his stockings; who thought he knew how much it meant to the poor boy to give him something for nothing; who told him there was nothing in this life to fear; Milchmeyer who would never know exactly what he started, but who did it anyway. He wrote to Spohr, Weber, Meyerbeer, yearning to hear something of fellow feeling. He learned a little of composition, a lot of musical theory and he spoke to Bargiel, the house piano teacher. He spoke a great deal to Bargiel. Mozart earned his bread this way, made rank count for nothing against talent. If the French had assisted nothing else with their butchering each other, their revolting and tearings apart, they had at least achieved this: ownership of land and title, possession of wigs and swords no longer governed everything. Despite what his parents believed, futures these days were no longer fixed. You could earn them. And music, the teaching of notes and fingers, was a highly desirable commodity.

By the time his religious studies were done, young Friedrich knew something. He knew something spiritual and something material, one and the same, and he knew it better than he knew anything else. God no longer wanted Friedrich for a priest, if he ever had. Lord no! God wanted Friedrich for the piano. What else explained his fascination, his feeling of kinship for the instrument? Something about its hamstrung innards, its rickle of ivory slats, kept drawing him almost against his will.

Dependent and tyrannical, willing and resistant, the piano soothed and irritated in equal measure. You could spend your life trying to tame the brute, coaxing it, pursuing its relentless demand for mastery. What music it could make: an orchestra in a box! It was peerless. Yet it was nothing, no more than a stranded whale, without a human operative. Without *him*.

Further, though he would never have said it out loud, there was something about the piano Friedrich *admired*. It wasn't too strong a word. There was something unyielding, something stoic in the demeanour of the pianoforte he admired very much. Yell at it in frustration, kick it now and then; weep, beg the beast to yield something beautiful this time – the piano went on being exactly what it was. No pity, no giving save what was deserved and not always that much. Exactly like God, he thought once, once only, then banished the thought as blasphemous. It needed no philosophy, this feeling. And what he felt was this: singing was a Profound Thing, a Passionate Thing, the body itself as music; but the piano, this stiff black box in the corner of the drawing room, since first he touched his fingers to the keys, watched the hammers flail like anemone fronds, was Meant for Him. Realising its earning potential was merely the final push in a jump he'd have taken anyway, sooner or later. As things stood, sooner made sense from every angle. It took some time for him to write to his father, crafting the right line. He hit it eventually and, when he wrote the words, he wrote them with satisfaction. *I will, it seems, make of my hands a hopeful thing after all.*

Meanwhile, Friedrich taught. From one minor member of the nobility to another, a *Hauslehrer* chafing only slightly at his livery, he listed rules and plotted his next life, as teachers do. While war altered the landscape, the rules around him, while teachers were ten a penny and roaming the streets like tinkers, he taught as though his life depended on it. Afterwards, while Germany went about the business of making itself afresh, he found his business partner; within months, a wife. He'd travelled to the eye infirmary in Leipzig for treatment and when they cleared the pus out of his eyes he saw her. Marianne. A French name. Something, call it romance for the sake of argument, seemed a viable option. She played, she sang, she looked decorative, she was eighteen. Eighteen. Eleven years younger than himself, a little headstrong, but (here he preened himself when he told the tale so folk would appreciate the humour) possessed of excellent taste. She laughed at his jokes. And she was well connected, well trained. Her grandfather was a flautist, a composer: the name Tromlitz was *known*.

With no further need for its medical services, his eyes keen as blades, he came back to Leipzig again, again. There were food shortages, threats of more; walls needing to be rebuilt. But the town was tough, its people were tough. They were survivors. They'd nurtured Bach and books, had no nobility to speak of; its censors and town clerks did not swagger as much as in other places he could name. There was a university. A great battle had been fought and won here, Leipzig writing itself further into the roots of the future. There were many families, many daughters. Many, many claviers. On the fourth trip, old Tromlitz introduced Friedrich to half the Gewandhaus orchestra and Marianne wore a muslin sheath, a French collar round her slender neck. He had no doubts left. Leipzig would suit him very well indeed.

Herr Wieck has a fine house, a busy house. It sits on the slope of a hill, is solid and dry. Anyone can show you where it is, over the warehouse. He makes his living from Steins, Broadwoods and dummy keyboards, buy, sale or rent. Finger stretchers, strings and tuning forks, old bits of baby grand, physiharmonicas, second-hand violins, whole actions, manuscript loans, books, a lending library of sheet music straight from Vienna – he does it all. He holds *soirées* where all sorts turn up – publishers, composers, the opera director, editors of music rags, students, doctors with refined tastes, their hangers-on and, if they can sing, their wives and daughters. They play till the small hours so the whole street hears. He wrote a letter to Paganini once; got within touching distance of Beethoven. His wife ran away, it's true (they recall that third appearance at the Gewandhaus, the concerto when she sat before the keys *at some distance* – mere days before their third was born) but they'll say this: she left with good reviews. Excellent reviews. He's the best teacher in Leipzig – in Saxony! Anyone will tell you. Little places, big ears. Folk know each other by repute or gossip or self-advertisement. *Everyone* knows Herr Wieck.

Leipzig, he thinks, looks well. Every night he stands at his window looking out and over the rise and fall of this city, and that it looks any other way does not enter his head. These twisty lanes leading off behind Grimaisse Strasse are unthreatening; no city walls shut at night, no curfew, no palatial residence or *in situ* royalty to raise taxes for no good reason at all. There's paving underfoot and the streets are lit. Even when the moon passes behind a cloud, one may see. Every evening he checks it's still the case, and it is. Which means peaceful. Now, and at last, Leipzig is a stable place in which plans can flourish away from sudden catastrophe, riots, looting and revolution and amen to that. They conscript like everywhere else, but that's no concern to Friedrich now. He slipped through his twenties, his thirties, intact; they'll not pursue him now. Leipzig is safe as houses haha. So. Two sets of shutters, a glass of Rhenish, the inordinate satisfaction of the solitary evening to come. Tonight he'll spend it with Rousseau.

Only Berliners call Rousseau seditious these days; that's Berlin for you. That's why he wouldn't live there. It's too fancy and it's full of bureaucrats. It's too full of Berliners. Whatever they say, he knows the truth: Rousseau is the best of pedagogy and this is the best translation. He knows because Bargiel told him and he has no reason to mistrust Bargiel. Leather-bound, well-thumbed; some places fall open without forcing. He stands at the fire to let it do that, choose for itself what he should read. After a while he moves to the settle. Never lie when you can sit, sit when you can stand, stand when you can walk – he knows that, but it's been a long day. He sits. Before long, he puts his book spine up beside him, scrambles a pen into ink and writes something down. He scans his own notes from years before, jottings he made last month, earlier this week, today. He makes notes on these notes, stands again, tracks a pile of manuscripts on the table. One he checks again, memorises a sequence, making sure. Certitude takes effort, always worthwhile, but effort nonetheless.

After that, he trims the candles. They're cheap and smoke but they're what there is and he has more to do: lists of pupil progress, letters of account, schemes for the lessons ahead. Later, he'll filter pieces in order of technical difficulty, select exercises, build his repertoire of options. He does this every week, often more than once. Dussek. Clementi. Czerny. Eberl. Gelinek. Woelfl. Müller. These are his work, Great Teachers are his work. They run in his head till the ink is dry in the pot, till his eyes turn pink. Duty is duty, after all! Berger. Ries. Cramer. Hummel – well. Hummel goes without saying. Hummel is the greatest teacher of all time. That one day he will join him goes without saying too. He waits up in the night, imagining fresh lettering on the spine of a hand-tooled book while Hummel's words to the already wise dance before his eyes.

Notes on Fingering

1 Simple finger-order in successions of figures
2 Passing the Thumb under other fingers or other fingers over the Thumb (ie. vice versa)
3 Omission of fingers in acquisition of technique
4 Changing a finger with another on the Same Key
5 The passing of a shorter finger under a longer or a longer over a short (ie. vice versa)
6 Change of fingers on a key with note repeated, more-over the frequent repeated use of the same finger on several keys
7 Alternation of hands; interposition of the hands; fluidity of the hands
8 All of the above with concentration on fourth finger
9 The fourth finger
10 The fourth

He falls asleep making imaginary corrections, improving on the best. Future generations are whispering in his head. Herr Wieck, they say, they say it admiringly and without doubt, Herr Wieck is the greatest authority. It goes without saying.

Except for Sunday, which is the Lord's day, mornings are lessons. Every day the same. Lessons are in the room downstairs, where other girls take theirs. The *other* girls, that is, the ones who pay. She waits for him like anyone else in the corner of the stairhead room, a pupil waiting for her teacher. Which she is. He is. Now. There must have been a time when music, staved and stuck to the page, was something unfamiliar. It stands to reason. No one begins with the page. Yet these seed-pod heads, their sticks and legs, attenuated hairpins and crack-backed rests have always been there, strewn on tables and piled in corners, scattered on the music stand where mother, oozing when her babies cried in other rooms, gave in and fed them where she sat at the keys. Falling ringlets of stave brackets, the arcs and bows of phrasings, time signatures, random confettis of sharps, flats and naturals seemed always to have been comprehensible; stair runs of semiquavers, no matter how dense, more loaded with meaning than any alphabet. It's how things are, have always been.

So is the room in which one waits: familiar, unchanging, known down to the chips in the painted window ledge. An empty vase, two candlesticks, a wooden box stuck over with shells, an ornamental porcelain in the shape of a dancing shoe are the only other things to see: the same five things on the mantelshelf. And every week, it seems, she wonders the same five things about them: who it was that paid money for the useless shoe; why no one misses the vase for flowers; where the shells have come from, what they are when they're not stuck to a box, if it's true they're skeletons that once held their animals inside. Just as she reflects there is nothing interesting whatsoever about candlesticks, there he is. Punctual. Watching his watch to prove it. The Mind and the Tree, Clara, he says, opening the door for her to come in. What do they have in common? She doesn't know. *They bend*, he whispers. *They bend*. She looks intently when he tells her here is a new language to learn. French as well as mother tongue, Italian too — she will not believe how much Italian. And, of course, singing. Clara, the child who almost never speaks, tries to think about language, singing. Mother. Tongue. The two words come easily together for her. She sees how they fit. Her eyes meet his and lock there, saying it. She understands.

So. Lessons. Practice. Handwriting and study of theory.

Sometimes in the evenings there are house concerts.

She may listen, she may watch, she may sit. Sometimes she may just sit, restraining her extremities as a matter of course. A musician must learn to sit still and expressionless, waiting his or her turn. Grimaces are the province of hopeless amateurs. This is a lesson too. Everything, it seems is lessons. Aphorisms. Notes. Sit still and watch. These are the materials of all learning.

Duty is the Highest Happiness.
Little and Often is the Surest Way.
Play always as if you played for a Master.
Trust God and your Teacher.
The Mind and the Tree etc.

Sometimes lessons were immediately recognisable and open; other times it came about by a kind of stealth. Things that did not seem to be lessons at all at first, would turn out to have a Moral, a Serious Test of Diligence concealed within – a sudden fall or a carriage ride, the apparently unearned offer of a sweet – but Papa was always watching, assessing, noting whether Clara behaved as he would wish. As her Best Self would wish. The mark of the Finest Teacher, he said, is that he Keenly Observes, and he does it a lot. Somewhere in the middle of these early lessons, then, when the talent to observe had become something named and something deliberately to refine, it happened. Something in detail and through the fingers first. An icy bloom under her palm never fails to bring it back, entire: the sensation of looking down from somewhere dizzy. The feeling that at any moment, without warning, she might fall.

The street was two floors down, only a sliver of it visible. The glass creaked in its frame when pressed, a rusty sound like ice, not enough to pull away. Up, the sky was bright blue, buzzing, full of beasts; hairy black blots that rose on warm currents from the nostrils of coach horses, flies the size of thumbs. They zoom into your mouth if you hold it open, Papa told her, but they can't come through brick, through glass, so in here is safe. Two floors up, a vantage point on the whole world. Down there on the paving, someone invisible was whistling. Behind her, without turning, she could hear Johanna wheezing, Gustav baby-snoring, Alwin scraping on a slate. Audible warmth. Thick, slow, torpid, a heat-dazed fly hovered just outside, eye to eye with her on the other side of the glass. Then the door opened. And everything, everything changed.

Papa was filling the room, enormous somehow, waving his arms and mouthing and for a moment, one horrible, stomach-clamping moment, she thought he was weeping. Then she realised he was laughing and felt so blessed with relief that she laughed too. Alwin looked at them and smiled, sharing something he suspected might be a good thing though he didn't know what. She didn't know either, but a joke was better than . . . better than whatever the alternative had threatened to be. But there was something not right hanging in the air, a disturbance the laughter didn't shift. Despite the laughing, maybe because of it, Father didn't look like himself. His cheeks were too red, everything about him was too loud. Then she heard the words. Your mother, boys! he shouted. The pianist, Fräulein Tromlitz of Plauen!

Alwin's eyes were round as plums.

We shall have to become accustomed to her new name! He arched an eyebrow, catching his breath and in the moment's silence, Clara felt her smile having nothing to do with her, unfixing from her face.

Madame Bargiel! he roared, his face like an actor in a play. Madame Bargiel!

Startled by the noise, the suddenness, Gustav woke. He started crying.

Your mother, Clärchen! he shouted, not even looking like her father any more, laughing all over again, Madame Bargiel! This time so loud that Alwin joined in, squealing like a kitten, almost dancing with delight while Clara struggled to understand exactly what it was she had been told. For one inspired moment she looked down at her dress, hoping the answer was there, but there was nothing but blue cotton. Then Gustav started wailing, the same terrified monotone he made in the middle of the night, and Johanna lifted him up one-handed. Though Alwin was in no distress, her free hand seized him too and, before either of them had any idea they were going, she careened both children out of the room. Clara glimpsed the tail ends of Johanna's skirts, Gustav's legs dangling, before the door closed and there were only her and Papa. The laughter, inside and out, stopped dead. Clara heard Johanna's heavy footfalls fading on the stairs, Alwin beginning to scream. She did not look up. When the screams faded too, the only sound was her father's breathing, so close she felt it gusting on her arm. After a while it levelled out. When he no longer sounded like a horse, he walked to the window, stood as though looking into the distance. Perhaps, the child thought, looking at her father's back, perhaps Johanna would come back to fetch her. She kept her breathing shallow, noiseless, and waited. From outside, beyond glass, came the thrumming of monstrous flies. Soon, she thought, if she kept very still indeed, someone would fetch her. If she waited like a good girl, someone would come, very, very soon.

⊷══◉══⊷

Pot-bellied Herr Bargiel.

Mother and Herr Bargiel. *Frau Bargiel.*

Words were full of questions. Mother had a different name. Not Clara's, not Papa's. She was someone else. She wondered about Viktor, Viktor who stayed, whether his name would be different too. *Viktor Bargiel*, a stranger. A Berliner. Berliners had different manners (none, Papa said), different faces – everyone knew that. It was living in Berlin that did it. Just from being there, Viktor would be unrecognisable. So, she realised suddenly, would her mother. Mothers are always mothers, she felt sure this couldn't be undone. Brothers were a less certain quantity. Alwin and Gustav belonged to Papa just as she belonged to Papa. They always would; he had told them so. Viktor, however. Who did Viktor belong to? Maybe Viktor belonged to nobody. Mother and Herr Bargiel and a baby they don't own. What if – she thought with a shock – what if they sent him back? If they sent him back and *Papa didn't want him?*

She remembered her mother's face at the Altenberg crossroads, Grandmother's hands. She remembered a baby's face quite clearly, tiny hands reaching beyond the edge of his blanket. Suddenly, it seemed, she remembered all sorts of things. *Dear Jesus*, she prayed, under her breath in case anyone heard. *Be kind to Viktor*.

Their ground-floor window throws a gangly shadow. Students out staggering home late see it pacing, not at peace. They point it out to each other, snort like pigs with cider apples. Wieck is burning candles! Whatever's on his mind, it's serious – he's spending money to see it by. Law students: that's the kind of thing they find amusing. One of them is dressed as a woman. He throws up against a wall before they move on, singing sentimental songs. Singing them badly. They hope he hears. *Sing!* one shrieks, and they laugh again. But two of their number have a lesson with him tomorrow. No matter how hung-over, they'll be there, practised and polite. You might laugh, taking the gamble he doesn't recognise your voice disguised and in the dark, but you don't get on his wrong side.

Inside his house, though, the teacher hears every word. What's more, he can identify the timbre of voices through walls with near medical accuracy, and that without even trying; he knows who they are all right. Boys who can't even spell *thrift*, let alone practise it. Law students, he mutters. He says it under his breath like it's a nasty disease. Tonight, though, he doesn't really care. He has more to think about. He has *Logier. His Method*. Friedrich likes this word, *Method*. He likes *System* too, but *Method* is better. And who these days thinks of Logier without thinking of his *Chiroplast?* The whiff of science in the very name excites. A length of wood with little straps of canvas and leather; buckles, tiers and hollows: it's simple enough. From what he has read, he has grasped the idea very well. The board attaches to the piano and the child attaches to the board, each finger caught like a ferret in a trap, then the restraining band is clamped in place over the knuckles. Result? The hand held *just so* every time – without the pupil being able to disrupt the fact. Now! If the importance of hand position cannot be overestimated – and it can't – this peculiar little pillory has its attractions. To hell with finger stretchers, thumb belts and Lordknew what else – *this* is the Coming Thing. In Vienna, people were queuing to have their children strapped to it, paying excellent money. If he introduced it here, persuaded Logier himself to give a lecture or two, it might work untold good for the hands of the town, especially for little hands, little, malleable hands.

He thinks of Clara's fingers, her wrists that need all the help they can get. Then his eyes water. The candles are sending out distress signals, smoking their last. Rather than light more, he should make up his mind and get to bed, just choose. Kalkbrenner had already endorsed the thing. The French liked it, the Italians; even the Austrians, who preferred dancing to hard work, who abhorred anything remotely newfangled unless it was a recipe, had taken the Chiroplast to their hearts. Only the English had reservations and what did they know about music? Besides, applied properly and with the right addition to fees, the thing would pay for itself in a matter of months. Enough thinking. He snuffs the last limp wick, sniffs with satisfaction. Law students! Ha! He wouldn't light the fire with a law student. Let none say Herr Wieck is not a man of action, a man to be reckoned with! Herr Wieck, the innovator, is buying.

Clara has a class. Not just lessons any more, a class. Three together, they will learn from each other and reduce Wieck's new pupils list. These days, everything is advantage. The other girls have beautiful hair. It's pleated and coiled like earmuffs. They have pale skin the colour of ham rinds and their eyes are pink as potatoes. Side by side with Clara, they play scales in triplicate, petticoats rustling as they stretch for the pedals, miss. Girls in lace-for-lessons frocks, smelling of outside and hairdressing. Rich girls. They speak even when they are told not to and on occasion, rare occasion, when Papa is out of the room, Clara speaks back. Mostly, however, they play, which is to say they work, and straight ahead of them sits the same book. LOGIER it says, white on black cover: THE METHOD. It sits on the stand, so much a part of the hours at the keys they can see its chapter headings, its smooth list of contents, even when they close their eyes.

Ease and Grace

Of Notes and the Stave

The Clefs

Of Different Sorts of Notes

Of Sound

Of Rests

Duration of Sound

Thumb of R.H.

Thumb of L.H.

Of Time

Of Comparative Note Values

Of Sharps, Flats and Naturals

Double Bars

Of the DOT

Reckoning a Crotchet Rest

Of KEYS

Of Scales

The CHORDS, sprinkled

Marks of Abbreviation

The PAUSE: duration at Pleasure

Her first book. All her life Clara would be able to conjure this list, the frontispiece with attendant angels; the warm and gingery smell of its paper pages. These words would rise before her eyes when she could not sleep, recall the feel of the leather straps against her knuckles, reining her in. She would run them in her head till her eyes grew heavy again, fade away with her father's voice repeating them in her ears.

Reckoning a Crotchet Rest

The PAUSE

Duration of Silence

Silence

Yes, but what else? These lessons were for all comers – what did he add *in particular*? The hours he spent, every day over years, to make the genius she was to become, what did he actually, minutely, repeatedly *do*? All her life people ask this question. It's natural; people want to know all sorts of things, it's what people are like. All her life she has no real answer. The Chiroplast, the fingerstalls pushing wood against her fat knuckles, their straps and frippery, made no lasting impression. He got rid of it, taught pupils to strengthen their fingers on the back of a chair, developed an antipathy to mechanical devices. He played first and she played back is the essence of what he did. The diaries are there, she smiles; his books may be read. But they tell nothing beyond general principles, they argue; nothing that marks him off from the common herd of teachers, nothing *felt*, and she fails repeatedly to give them more. What is she to say? Even for her, reading his words brings only the memory of his writing, the meticulous nips and tucks of the quill in his hands, not the *feel* of lessons. That's not transferable in words; at least, none she knows, none she will ever record. Words are weak things, attempts to grasp what's abstract, what's sensory, what's spiritual. What's gone.

Exercises, she says. She has to offer something. There were exercises. She lists pieces, the order in which they were learned. If pressed, she can dictate his most-used phrases, his preoccupations. He placed much stress on Evenness, she says. On Touch and Dynamics. On Strengthening of the Fingers, on Cautious use of the Pedal and Good Legato Style. She talks Hand Position, Stretching, Octaves in Both Hands, Attack from the Arm. She repeats herself, reprises; affirms these things had their place. Yes, there were two half-hour keyboard and two fifteen-minute singing lessons as he says in his textbook; they are not wrong to trust this as truthful: two hours' practice every day, a daily walk to accommodate and preserve her Joyousness of Youth and offer her limbs and mind to the keen fresh air – all, moreover, without tiring, without tedium, without complaint. Neither her education nor his care of her childhood years, she insists, were restricted, indeed, she saw more, attained more, met more than most: harmony with Herr Weinlig, voice with Herr Miksch; Dorn, Dehn, Reissiger, Prinz (composition, counterpoint, orchestration and violin respectively) – what more could he have given?

She makes the same explanations a dozen times, a hundred times in the course of her life, somewhere between pity and despair at ever making her meaning clear, knowing they imagine this compacted into the same year or two, the same day; knowing this explaining will never be done. *Of course* there were times when study was not uppermost; he took her to the opera time without number, she played at all his *soirées*. No, she will say, her childhood was quite unforced, quite normal. She says nothing of willingness, engagement; it wouldn't occur. She had a gift; willingness didn't come into it. There was Duty and there was Art. For the sake of both, there were lessons, that's all. Lessons. Like blood, like breath. Like bone.

An envelope arrives from Plauen. Inside, white ribbons. He tears the letter up, instructs Johanna to add the ribbons to the child's stock of clothing, not to mention the sender. He can think of no immediate reason why the child may not have ribbons. Later, he returns with a sack. Kittens. Little boys, he says; they'll need smacking. He sets them down and they huddle, shivering. She must flick their noses when they are naughty, he says. Feeding will be her responsibility; Johanna and Lise have enough to do. He lifts them by the scruff to show how it's done. Handfuls. She is astonished by the blue of their eyes, the slightness of their bones, like twigs inside a fur purse. They squeal. Of course, he says. He's surprised by the question. Of course they are hers. No one else wants them. Their legs flail in mid-air, trying to reach solid ground.

He comes into the kitchen unexpectedly and his children are eating soup. Well, he thinks, and the sight of it pleases him. Nourishing, plain, cheap – soup is an inspiration and inspiration is what he needs. While they concentrate on the optimal manipulation of their spoons, he will write something. Today is the first day of his own method – *method à la Wieck*. Not too proud to start here, in a servant's room on a chair with a broken wicker seat, he cracks the spine of the new notebook and begins. *Three planes*, he writes, while his children ignore him, *physical, intellectual, moral.* The placing of things in threes has sound precedent. His training in religion makes him appreciate this more than most. He takes a deep breath and goes on. *Three ideals: musicianship, discipline, singing tone.* To help him choose what to write next, he observes the children. Then he sits back and watches some more. The absorption at the table, the repeated application of little fingers to their task, draws him. Filling the spoons is easy work; fetching them to the mouth without undue spillage is the test. Before long, the boys give up and mop with their bread but Clara keeps going. Her mouthfuls are small and she chews thoroughly.

After church this Sunday, he had thought he might permit Alwin to join their daily walk for the first time. He had imagined them walking under the lindens, his own dark, square-shouldered shape, the sudden drop to the outlines of his children walking beside him, his own voice saying something of the debt of gratitude owing to God for the sacrifice of His Son. Easter was a good time to approach an explanation of the meaning of self-sacrifice, something unequivocal, fit for small heads. This bread-slopping, however, this splashing of beans and vegetables, brings second thoughts. The boys can stay at home with Johanna; he'll keep the sermon idea and walk with Clara alone. The last sentence is his prize. He gives it a line to itself, his best cursive.

Bend. Guide. Above all, teach.

He watches the words drying on the page, enjoys the uniformity of his own script. *Teach.* Not too soon, though, only when the moment is ripe. That's good too – he'll add it later. Alwin is finished. He sits waiting in the wreckage of his bib for Johanna to come and mend him. Gustav fishes for carrots with his hand. No more than babies yet, button-faced and blond, they look like his own father. Clueless. Only Clara is dark; only she eats with any degree of precision. Her eyes are too big, any prettiness undercut by the down-tilt of her eyes, but that matters little. Her playing is already sound, her progress solid. Something can be made of this child, something strong, and he, Friedrich Wieck of Leipzig, teacher and dealer in pianos, is sure enough to say it out loud. His throat constricts even when he thinks it. *Virtuosa.* A glittering word. *Virtuosa.* Clara, her soup bowl still more than half full, has no idea. A single drip, like a blood spot, splashes from the spoon end on to her pinafore, but she doesn't see. Lack of vanity, he thinks. An artist must cultivate a certain vanity and he can help with that too. *Posterity will record it began here,* he thinks. When he closes his book, the children stand, scrape their chairs back, look up expectantly. Johanna! he roars. Change Clara's pinafore! Send her clean to the piano room in half an hour! Brush her hair! Johanna sees lightness, a spring in his step as he leaves. Almost out of earshot, she hears him bellow over his shoulder, a parting shot, I have been cooking something in our kitchen! She hears him laugh out loud.

She will make a visit across town. Herr Bargiel and his wife, he says, request it. At the end of the week, he says. She counts. Her counting is strong. Four days. Over those days she practises legato technique. She learns to gloss and refine so no taint of nervousness is audible, to play with a fluency and smoothness that do not betray her age. When the day comes, she stands waiting at the door for his blessing in a new pinafore and he doesn't notice. He holds out a letter for her to take. *Madam!* it starts. He's written it so dark it shows right through, even when the letter itself is folded. *Madam!* Impossible not to see. Frau Bargiel's instructions, he says. I shall expect to hear they have been carried out. She takes the letter and for some reason curtsies. He makes no remark. He doesn't even say goodbye.

Not sure what it means, what any of it means, Clara walks with Hanna to an unknown district of Leipzig, she hoping only one thing: that she should not disappoint. Walking back, she hopes exactly the same, only with less of a clue how this hope is to be realised. Papa will want to know things – he said it himself. What things? That she handed over his letter and played well he would take for granted. What else should she say? That the woman in the grey dress had looked different, smelled different? That it had taken some time not to call her Frau

Bargiel but Mother? That her eyes and nose had run when Clara asked if she might sit at this different piano, see what music belonged to this unfamiliar house? She can't find good words for these kinds of things. Should she say there had been pears, plums and apples, two kinds of bread, four cheeses, as many meats, beans, butter and cake – all on the table *at once?* That Viktor took his food from his mother's fingers, easily, as if he did it all the time? That Herr Bargiel gave her a clasp for her hair and said it matched her eyes? She had no interesting words for these things either. She would have nothing to say. Walking beside her, taking her home, Herr Bargiel was no help. Crossing the square, he reached to take her hand, but she pulled away and he affected not to notice. Counting their footsteps to cover the silence, each closer to Papa, she imagined the kittens, waiting at home to be fed, lengthened her stride without thinking. She slipped a glance at Herr Bargiel, keeping pace beside her, hoping he would not suffer on her account but she would have to tell: he encouraged her to eat cake. Confession was good for the soul, Papa said and it always cheered him to hear her do it. Two pieces of cake. She would certainly tell.

Take the clasps out of your hair, he says. That dark amber shade is not your colour. You look ridiculous, he says, you look matronly. Then he gives her a sugarplum. The clasp goes into a box in his own room; later it will go for sale. One day, Clara returns from the Bargiels' with something else, a soft little body made of stuffed cloth with real hair and staring eyes. It has an odd set to its face that reminds her of someone she knows but can't quite place, and she is afraid of it. All the way back from the Bargiels' it sits in her pocket, Clara's hands avoiding contact with its smooth cup-and-saucer skin. She avoids speaking of it too, and Father asks only what she played. There is no deception in not saying, she tells herself. He didn't ask. Next morning when she comes for her first lesson, however, he is holding it out in his hand. She tells where it came from, that they told her to take care of it. Yes, they called it *her*, as though it were a real girl; tried to help her choose a name.

Wieck lifts the flaccid little body up to the light, peers at it. What name? he asks.

None. Clara could think of nothing to call it.

And do you like – her? he asks. He is smiling as he asks, his face gentle. He keeps it gentle.

She knows the answer, speaks plainly. No, she doesn't like the doll one bit. It looks like Minna, the maid next door.

He laughs at the time. Later, however, the doll face comes unbidden into his head, its lidless gaze clouding his thinking. He buys Friar's Balsam for inhalation, wonders if he is coming down with a chill. The veins in his temples throb and Clara's lesson makes them worse. Sloppy phrasing, poor trills and turns, the same slip in the same place more than once were not what he expected. He lets her do it till his collar feels too tight, then grabs the music from the stand, looks at it hard. No, he says, it's not upside down. He puts it back on the stand, moves closer to her shoulder. The mistake comes back, sawing at his nerves, making them so much dead wood. You! he snaps. You sound like a machine! Like a monkey on a barrel organ! Is this how you repay me? This? He opens out another page and an exercise his wife used to play tumbles from between the leaves quite by accident. She picks it up quickly and plays four bars before he stops her completely. You would kill me with stupidity! he spits, so loud she jumps. Is this what your mother teaches you? This ingratitude? He dabs his forehead with the back of his hand and pronounces sentence. Trilling exercises. Three days of trilling exercises, nothing more. When she's fit for music again, then she may play. He goes out walking in the fresh air, but feels no better.

For three days, Clara plays nothing but trilling exercises, one hand, both hands, inverted and in contrary motion, tuneless and sniffing like a tap. *It will teach her the error of her ways*, he thinks, trying to attach a point to both their misery. *It will teach her better trills.* Even when he forgives her, he's aware dimly that he's not at peace. Neither is she. He takes her in a new dress to hear a symphony by a deaf man, a Great Man, but the pleasure feels stolen, on shifting ground. At night, guilt clogs her throat like porridge and she nips Gustav's arm for the relief of hearing him cry. She lied. She knows what this punishment is for. The doll doesn't look like Minna at all. The eyes and the shape of the mouth. It looks like Mother. It looks like her.

But the consequences of lying are not over for her yet. Something terrible happens and she is sure it is punishment of some kind, a warning never to keep silent in the face of her father's questioning again. Hanna leaves. It must be so for who would dismiss her, the more constant female presence in Clara's young life. She almost cries but Father sees the sheen start on her eyes and draws her up just in time. Servants don't stay for ever, he says and it's true. There is nothing to argue against. But standing at the door while Johanna comes out with her bag, a limp bunch of evergreens that were picked for her that morning, is hard. She smells of muslin and curds so there will be cheese in the kitchen later. Cheese but not Johanna. Papa will pay for the ride only so far, then she will take a wagon into the countryside outside Leipzig and for miles after that. Hohenzollern. What kind of name is that? Hanna is going to a place that doesn't sound like anything at all. The child may only imagine wilderness, empty countryside, Johanna on a wagon with potato sacks around her, disappearing round a dark bend of the road into nothing. She might as well be falling off the edge of the world. Hanna goes all the same. Clara's last sight of her shows a strand of blonde hair, blonde, not grey after all, falling from her cap as she withdraws into the van and the rain starts.

The rain certainly starts. Before it stops, the boys begin violin lessons, Father's shouting gets louder and the Bargiels move to Berlin. *Berlin.* It means the same as vanished. Mother, Viktor, the piano, everything, gone. Wieck, however, seems more cheerful than he has been for some time. His headaches, his strange fits of moodiness, lift and so does his business. Before long, he's in Vienna with Graf and Stein, a consequence of thriving, so Lise tells them the news instead. She picks Sunday morning because that's the day she takes them to church. Viktor is dead, she says. The house keys rattle on her hips. He's buried, so there's an end of it. She tells them cleanly, without expectation and they walk back home as though nothing were any different.

Inside, Clara goes to the sitting room and just sits. The curtains are drawn to keep the upholstery from fading. She plays with the cats till they run elsewhere, then lifts down Papa's biggest book from its stand in the corner. Black dashes and hoops. Hünten. Haslinger. Döhler. Spohr.

Moscheles. Mozart. Field. Schubert. Weber. Beethoven. Hummel, of course. Clementi. Czerny. Lots of Czerny. Nothing is an exercise, she remembers. Play everything as music. On an instrument that works only by hitting, striking, the strenuous belting of its innards, she wills herself to replicate the human voice. *Sing, Clara, sing.* The book open before her, she imagines playing, playing without hesitation or fear, exactly as he would wish her to play. She imagines his big hand resting on her shoulder at the closing bars, just one; the warmth of it a blanket from collar to sleeve seam, the faint smell of coins and leather. That's what she imagines. His hand.

The night of his return, the self-same night, he takes her to the opera and the theatre is vast. It has stars on the ceiling. When she was small, she might have thought it was the sky itself, but now she knows that's not true. Now she's rising seven and she knows many things. She knows Czerny's Toccata and she knows the sky is very big indeed. People can disappear into it. Men come and shake her father's hand, hold it tight, and even with no one's skirts to hide behind she is not afraid. She can stand her ground. The opera is full of people hiding, being lost and frightened. There's a Bad Queen who sings high enough to shatter plate china. Her Husband hates her because he hates all wickedness. The Daughter gets lost but is found again, this time – hurrah! – by the father who will surely teach her to be Good. A man with feathers and a lock on his mouth can't speak but he can sing and he does it very well. She likes this opera but is afraid of the Queen, of what might have happened to make her so terribly wicked, and is really quite pleased when it's over. They go home in silence, just the two of them, as they always do after an evening out. After music, her father says, is no time to talk.

Next day she plays the Toccata and he says nothing, but he smiles. He calls her *Clärchen* for the rest of the day. *My Clara.* After lessons, she pushes the hated doll between the floorboards and skirting where they part company, watches for a while to be sure it doesn't try to come back out. What's buried is gone, Lise said, and it's true. She waits a full five minutes to be on the safe side, then goes back to the music stand, the thing she is beginning to call *work.*

Sing, Clara, sing!

Simplicity. Modesty.
A quiet movement of the Fingers without
Undue Jerking of the Arm.

By degrees, she sings.

TWO

Der Herrlichste von Allen

The Best of All

$\mathcal{M}$y diary begun by my father, the 7th June 1827
and continued by Clara Josephine Wieck

Now the decisions have been made that this life will be remarkable,
someone must record it. It stands to reason. And who better than her
father/her teacher/her guiding light. Who should teach her to catalogue
time, to name the dates and how to spend them, that her time is not now,
not ever, her own? Who should teach her that impressions are not
enough, but names, places, facts must be detailed enough to look back
upon, reuse when needed for verification, classification, durable proof?
Whom does she belong to, after all? Whom?

My diary. His own hand. *Mine.*

The rules emerge and stick. His daughter is *I*, he is *father*; he sees and
knows everything. Since this is a history, he begins with dates: the where-
fores and whens of birth, what house, which town – pack drill. Soon, the
feel of a pen in his hand makes him bold. *Today my father divorced my mother,*
he writes, but it's no more than fact. Not much further down the line, he
imagines he has a talent for the descriptive. *This is how I walked on stage, why
I chose this dress,* as though he would know. *I did not play any wrong notes and
got much applause.* After a while he can't stop. *Father deserves my greatest devotion
and gratitude for his ceaseless efforts on my behalf,* he writes – no sense of irony
at all. She doesn't feel what he can't conceive of; his priorities, her hopes
and fears are all the same thing. Whatever he writes, he has no doubt
she'll take on trust, and why should he? After he's gone – by which he
means dead – people will cite him as her voice, read this telling as
though it's her own and she will not correct them because there will be
no need. *Who's the monkey? Who's the organ grinder?* He never needs to ask.

What he doesn't write himself he dictates, amends, expands; he marks it up with editorial glyphs. Scribblings, jottings, notes and letters to inconsequential friends – these she may scratch out on her own; the diary, however, the *Diaries* are *Posterity's*, which is to say an Authorised Version, and his, without saying, is the authority that applies. The child, the adolescent, the young woman whose life these books purport to record may have sat at desks or tables, checked her spelling on the blotter, smeared the nib *just so*; maybe a window behind her filled with watery spring or full summer skies. But he is always at her elbow, watching. Between the ages of seven and thirteen, the ages beloved of Jesuits, he's there in the flesh; thereafter she knows the ropes. There's no danger. Between breaks from copying expenses, copying letters to promoters, copying letters to hire pianos for tours, copying letters demanding fees, letters raging at cities for being cities, provincial backwaters for being provincial backwaters, at audiences whatever their stripe, at bad critics, faint-praise critics and hacks in general, she may write unsupervised. She may write to his heart's content.

Dear Mother
You have as yet heard Nothing from me but now I
can write a little a little it is modest to say a little **I will**
send you Herr Bargiel is it impolite not to mention Herr **a**
Letter which will please you will be proud of my spelling
I am trying my handwriting you will not recognise my handwriting on the envelope will have to break the seal to see who
I had Presents on my eighth Birthday remember my
birthday there was cake and singing and I wished **from dear**
Bertha and from my dear Father from dear Father I
got a beautiful Dress you should see it all in white he says
I will look like a snowflake in it and play like a storm **and**
from Bertha I had Aschküchen and Plumcake and a
fine Knitting-Bag I can't sew or mend well Papa says
And I played Mozart's E♭ Concerto that you used to
play with an Orchestral Accompaniment it was our
house with flowers the same Mozart the same pedalling did he

make you use the sustaining **and Herr Matthäi, Lange, Belke and a lot of Others** they always come do you know who they **played with me It went very well and I never stuck at all only my Cadenza did not go easily where I had to play a Chromatic Scale three Times** the same scales a ruler under my wrist passing the thumb beneath **I was not at all frightened but the Clapping troubled me** my bow is not good I am ungainly and embarrassed to bow so close in our own parlour **Emilie Reichold and M Kupfer played too** Emilie looks like an angel she is blonde where I am **The day before my Birthday I went to Malger with father** father is reading this **Please give my Love to Grandmama and my Brothers** little brothers **who send their love** love **to you Now you will write to me** hear me **won't you –**

Your obedient Daughter
Clara Wieck Leipzig September 14 1827

ps Dear Mother I will come to see you soon and then I will play a great many Pieces with four Hands with you And I have sung and played through so many Operas already such as Oberon, Die Schweizer-familie, Der Schlosser, Die Zauberflöte which I have seen in the Theatre too My dear Father has ordered me a beautiful Piano from Herr Stein in Vienna because I have been industrious and can play and sing at the same time all Spohr's Songs and the Concerto went without a Mistake Goodbye C

Well, then. Herr Probst. Herr Hofmeister. Herren Fink, Marschner and Matthäi, Herr Stein Banck and Lyser. Sofie. Emilie. Francilla with her own copy of the Schubert, the phrasings mercilessly pencilled in. Doctor Carus, Frau Carus and their young guest from Zwickau. Fans and summer evenings. The men lit cigars and the music and flies escaped together through the windows into the street. In winter, the windows steamed, music stiffened on the stands.

If happiness matters, these were significant days. She knew at the time. They were hers for the taking and she took. Already the boys, her brothers, were secondary. She certainly took.

Dressing in front of the half-mirror the day of his wedding, Wieck liked what he saw: his stock fresh-starched and the shirt collar so high it hid his cheeks. Nothing else was new but the shirt cost plenty, and he had paid on time. He took a pride in that. Fräulein Fechner wore what she called silver, though it wasn't. It was yellowy grey, like phlegm. When Papa said it matched her eyes and gazed down at her, Alwin had to hide his face. They all knew Fräulein Fechner from before. She met them in the street and asked after the house and its doings. *Their* house and its doings. Now they would see much more of her and it would be her house too. She knows when to be quiet and thank the Lord she had no musical opinions, Wieck said, raising a glass and everyone knew it was meant to be amusing. It wasn't. It was just true, but they raised their glasses, they drank. *The Bride and Groom. Health and Happiness. Long Life and Little Trouble* haha. Reverend Fechner, who looked like a pig, was their grandfather now, someone said, and Gustav, newly five, burst into tears. In the fuffle that followed, the spill of wine and water mixed, Clara heard her father call the former Fräulein *Dearest*. Reverend Fechner was smiling, his daughter hanging on his arm. While she did it, Friedrich stood on a chair to make a speech. Forty-three years, he began, is a certain age; an age at which one can be trusted to know one's mind. Some people cheered. For all that, he went on, I have been some time deliberating this choice. Today, however, I need only look at my children, he said – and he did, he looked at Alwin with buttons squint, Gustav choking, Clara doing nothing save staring back – to know my hope has not been misplaced. I salute, he raised a glass, their New Mother! Clara, in a white dress, white lace drawers and slippers, nothing new at all, played Cramer and Clementi, routine crowd pleasers. Later there was singing and money for the boys, a bower made of sheets to play with.

For three days afterwards, Clara watched this woman move through her new rooms, perfectly at home. The scent of toilet water coiled from Father's bedroom, the mantelpiece sprouted pansies. They'll fade behind our backs, Papa said, they'll only wilt. He said it packing. He packed dresses, sashes, shawls and shoes, clasps, ribbons and jewellery for his daughter while Clementine packed her own. Honeymoon or no, Clara was coming too. Dresden, he said, was a beautiful city, full of important people; people who would know an artist when they heard one. A first recital outside home deserved something special and Dresden was it. It wouldn't do so badly for himself or Frau Wieck – *Mother*, she was *Mother* now – either. He smiled when he said it, aiming to charm. *Mother*. She supervised the leaving arrangements for the boys herself – *little meat and no pastry* – to prove it. They must learn to call this nineteen-year-old with no bosom *Mother*. Before long, however, Clementine sat alone in the back row of the Blind Institute, Beethoven flying past her ears, while her new husband sat near the piano, in case. The girl's shadow, cast from afternoon sunlight, threw double on the facing wall, its twin arms, its twenty fingers, moving. *My daughter*, she thought, feeling for pride, not able to see for the forest of heads in front, the sightless crowd. *My own husband's daughter.* She stood at the end when everyone else did, though it took her by surprise, and became part of the general throng. Clara, from the front of the stage, saw her: a pink blob among the dark ranks of institute uniforms, her face round as a pie. And at that moment, as her father took her arm to raise it in triumph and the applause rose further,

Clara realised what she liked best about her stepmother. Clementine couldn't play if her life depended on it. She couldn't play a note.

⊶≡◎⊜⊶

Lambs and cherries, cake-shaped domes under a clear sky.

Memories of first things are strong with some. That first week in Dresden, for example: Clara recalls it with tangible clarity her life long, enough to teach her a lesson she never forgets, viz looks aren't everything; they're seldom anything at all. The people as beautifully turned out as the place — so much silk! Old-fashioned tricorn hats! — and so stubbornly antique in their tastes they made her uncomfortable. Dresden made her feel lost. Leipzig might be ungainly, it was rainy and pinched and dour to the bone, but it never made her feel ill at ease. It was home. For those who travel, a feeling of *home* is what matters.

On her travels in years to come, far from anything remotely like home, Mme Schumann would be approached time and again by complete strangers who felt they knew her because of her fame. Sometimes they would want to talk about themselves — their set-aside hopes, lost ambitions, their belief they'd have turned out as she had if only they'd had the luck. Other times, whether the inclination served her or not, they'd prefer her to be revealing — for newspapers, history books, a *bon mot* to offer up to their friends. They'll ask about her memories, what she recollects of all the places she has seen, the people she has met, her life, her life. If pressed, she'll say she can describe only fragments. She'll say pieces of her past filter to the surface when she smells a certain type of cigar smoke, for instance, when a certain kind of light strikes a certain kind of tree a certain way. But, she'll insist, that is common to each of us; it's not worth the mention. Most memory is friable as dust and no one can be expected to remember everything. Dresden, however. She may admit recalling a first visit to Dresden; a first impression of Berlin, its streets wide as shipping canals; a first sight of Zwickau through the trees, all slants and heavy thatch, cows wandering through back lanes; the bruises occasioned by the journey to Schneeberg or Magdeburg in winter in an unsprung carriage. She may mention Copenhagen (dainty), St Petersburg (vast), or London (charcoal-grey) and they'll marvel at her ability to recollect itineraries. That the approach to Altenberg, its crossing point crazy with horses, seized her with panic all her life; that the view of the Hartz mountains at dusk could make her weep; that Hamburg filled her with rage while Vienna felt of possibility; that many things come to her vivid as last week or worse, much worse, she'll keep out of words, keep out of knowing if she can.

Then, though, nine years old, only what was recorded seemed true. Especially in his handwriting. Facts concealing truth − her family were practised in it. That her head, not words, always captured too much of what happened around her was something of which she was not especially aware but it happened all the same. Eyes like inky sponges, fingers nervy as spider limbs, hair swept up over neatly pierced full-lobed ears, Clara Wieck recalled everything without trying.

The night of her first concert in Leipzig, she waited alone at home, watching her own hand melt a pattern of mist on the cold window. The sheen on the guttering, his words in her ears: *Glass coach, it will be a glass coach.* And already late. He had gone ahead to prepare, trusted her to be there, and all she could do was wait. It will come, she promised herself. What else could she do? He had said so: it would come. She imagined a carved gemstone drawn by white horses, its interior exposed through the transparent sides like a lantern, only velvet and she inside. Snug. By the time something arrived she didn't question; anything would do. A plain brown affair with a dray and a loud man roaring her name barely waited for her to get inside. There was no glass, only other girls in cheap dresses, but they had been waiting for her. They said so. Before long, the houses outside looked not only unfamiliar but alien. She tried to memorise the slant of these roofs, wondering if it was some kind of test. *I am Clara Wieck and I have a concert at the Gewandhaus.* She couldn't even say her name. *I am to play the piano with Demoiselle Reichold. People are coming.* Not a word. She imagined her father at the hall, staring at his two watch faces, screwing his eyes up to see the nothing that was arriving on the Gewandhaus Road, and that finished her. She had no choice.

I am an artist.

Six faces turned to look at her.

And I have a concert at the Gewandhaus.

And the frowning child with the awful eyes burst into shivering, face-drenching, silent tears.

It was simply enough resolved. The wrong coach had the wrong Clara — mistaken identities, that was all. The Gewandhaus coach handed over a footman's daughter when pursued and, laughing at the luck of it, carried the grey-faced little piano player to her concert only sixteen minutes late. She was here, at least, the coachman said, she was here. She had to be lifted down, not able to take her hands away from her face, her new fan dangling from her wrist by a cord. *Clara. Clara.* The voice he used in public, winkling her out like a whelk. *Clärchen.* Softer still. People are always taken to the wrong house the first time they play in public. She looked through the lattice of her fingers to see if anyone was looking at the baby who needed to be humoured in this way. *It's the law!* he whispered. His smile in the dark made his teeth long and yellow, and he held out a sugarplum. Too sticky, even with gloves; she knew the rules. So she opened her mouth like a bird, let him feed her instead. Chewing, she let her hands fall, smoothed them on her new white dress. He dusted sugar from her lips, straightened, lifted his head up, up, and she did the same. She recalls clearly his blue velvet collar back, his profile as he turned, waited in the wings, the drop in his smile as he glanced beyond. Mlle Perthaler was finishing her third solo. Mlle Perthaler plays like a child, he said and, easing off her gloves, dusted chalk on her palms. Like a monkey in a dress. He moved aside and there was the stage. The piano. Mlle Perthaler leaving as the clapping rose, huge in the room like random gunfire. He took her by the elbow. They walked together towards the light.

All that recorded it was his handwriting, his mild summary. *It went very well and I did not play any wrong notes but got much applause.* One did not want her to appear vain after a *shared* concert, after all. From time to time, though, and for years afterwards, Clara thought of Emilie Perthaler whose share was the beginnings of another career, who remained in her mind as a name. Whether she married, had money, a living husband who

68

knew her name. When she stopped having a career. Every so often, though never said to a soul, Clara wondered what became of Emilie.

⋯⋙◉⋘⋯

Six-octave Stein, three pedals. Kalkbrenner (Moses Vars). NB Less movement of the body and neater bow – receive applause with MORE GRACE (bend from waist). Mozart/Beethoven. Continue Kalk., add Field, Moscheles, Ries, Hünten (Op. 26?). Hummel and Czerny as before.

Students come and go. They come thicker, faster, some of them grown men. She hears their lessons from other rooms and knows something. She plays better. Father spends time with some of them, though; goes out to student lodgings to hear their music, music they write themselves. They all compose, some better than others, and she must too. It's expected these days; it's part of the training. New work, he says. Lifeblood. In the coldest part of the year she learns there will be no more lifeblood from Schubert, not this season, not any season. Some of Papa's students turn up weeping on the doorstep; another doesn't come for lessons at all, just stays in his room, howling like a dog. If genius were proof against dying it would not have happened, he says, but it's not. Demonstrably, it's not. Schubert is as suddenly dead and buried as Viktor and that's an end of it. When Alwin plays badly, Wieck cuts his lesson time and gives the extra to her. All Schubert. Work is the cure for grief, he says. Most of these young pups wouldn't know grief from a hangover: everything is an excuse for laziness. Most of them don't know they're born. Alwin, nursing a bruise, his mouth tight shut.

⋯⋙◉⋘⋯

The night he took her to see Paganini she wore blue. He remarked on it, dropping the second watch in his waistcoat. *You will remind him of Italian skies*. He strode up and down the same bit of rug, ranted about the Miracle of the Age, the privilege of being alive In This Hour. Some people, he said straightening his waistcoat front, dusting off invisible crumbs, *some people* said he hadn't many concerts left in him. He was sick, they said, dying! HA! The boys' eyes grew round as eggs, watching him. He sawed with two knitting needles, pretending a bow and a fiddle. His hair stood on end. They had never seen him so jovial. The devil! Lightning! he said. People say anything – most of it stupid. Then he demanded the boys get ready for bed. If they weren't so stupid themselves, they might be coming too. Paganini was a virtuoso to redefine virtuosity, he said, adjusting his best cravat, yet even Paganini began with scales. He grabbed his hat, fought his gloves, took Clara by the arm so suddenly it hurt. Your sister will hear something tonight, not because she is lucky, but because she is industrious! he roared, then rushed them both downstairs. Halfway down the street he stopped, spoke back for his sons, for Clementine, the cats – whatever was sure to be hanging on his every word, to hear. And another thing – prayers. Ask God for an end to idleness. Make them say long prayers. Tripping over her own feet, blue suiting her better than it ever had before, Clara followed him. Eh, Clara? he wheezed, somewhere between a laugh and a cough. Long prayers!

Of the concert, however, all she recollects is enormity, astonishment, an overpowering welter of sound: nothing that broke into distinct elements to tick off a list. How did he look? A chalky face and black eyes. A spider. How did he play? Like three men at once. What did he play? Things she had never heard the like of before, impossible to describe. And his nose! The most Jewish-looking man you will ever see, they said, and she supposed they were right. Jewish or not, the applause was endless. Outside in the low fog of late hours, her hands still burned. They went backstage and a skinny four-year-old with his father's pallor, though not his nasal dimensions, welcomed them in. She gave him two bunches of grapes, one white, one black, and the Great Man squeezed her hand, his tendons tight as punches, his skin damp as dough. His face was hollowed with missing teeth, his hair lank, his shirt soaked through. The child held on to his leg and Paganini kissed him, exhibiting his foreignness for all to see. Nonetheless, her father was happy; he was demented with happiness. Invitations to the rest of the concerts, invitations to sit on stage, invitations to play, invitations to receive letters of introduction through which would come more invitations – he and Paganini might be lost brothers. From nothing, he said, from less than nothing, M. Paganini has made himself a life. He has earned for himself, Clara. Only those of us not born into money know what that means. He has a talent and by God he earns with it, he makes an independence and forces their respect! Remember, Clara, what you earn by yourself is yours. You need depend on nothing, no one else. You have a means to prosper and, he sniffed, to save your family should the need arise. This is what Great Men teach us. Spite them! Prosper! And look what you may become!

Clara listened and said nothing, which was what she was meant to do. He was not talking to her now, in any case, but to himself. Or a Clara some years later, someone who would know what he meant one day. And perhaps she would. For now, all she needed to do was preserve the silence while he spoke his secular sermons; understanding any of it was extra. Both knew without saying, both were content. The best always knew their own, he said, as they strolled along gutters towards their house, their home, he knows we are his kind.

Clara thought about the Great Man's terrible thinness, the smelling salts and brown lotions in his dressing rooms, the bandages and sleeping masks. His kind looked sick. She thought of those cold hands touching hers, the kisses of a skull face. Dying? Father said, swinging his cane as he walked. *People will say anything!*

As they did. They do.

Before long, they say them about Clara too.

Next time in Dresden their letters open doors. If the girl played for Paganini, she could play for Dresdeners too. Dresdeners, like everyone else in this respect at least, are not averse to Paganini. And when she plays, she does it so well they are suspicious. They say things the like of which she has never heard before. She's really a dwarf in her mid-twenties; a midget in a childish dress, a shooting star that will fade. They say she is forced to practise till she drops, can't read, can't write; is the tool of a tyrant out to make his own name and a fortune. Even if she's none of these, the sophisticates observe, she's not very pretty and will probably (here they snap their fans) *never marry*. Wieck hears the stories; he saves them up. What a joke! He'll dine out on these. She chases butterflies in the park, his little girl, and no one notices her; sit her at the ivories and they notice so hard it hurts. The difference makes him laugh till he cries. He tells lies about her age, you know, someone whispers in a salon bulging with stuffed beasts, glass-eyed birds, that's him over there. Really? says Friedrich, screwing an eyeglass in place to look at a man he's never seen before, that no one's seen before. Ugly fellow! Lisped at by aristocrats who say *Pretzsch?* astonished, *Pretzsch?* as though it were, or should be, unimaginable. *We don't know anyone from Pretzsch, do we?* Friedrich roughens his speech on purpose, rubs his hands in sheer delight. It's a game and he's winning; they can say what they like. He's confounded the lot of them. Counts tell stories about her, titled women and their daughters give her earrings, stroke her hair.

She's invited to the palace by Princess Louise. Twice. Princess Louise looks like a frog, Friedrich thinks; who is she to wear a coronet? What talent do these people possess? There is no stopping his revolutionary zeal, his desire to show them their heredity is nothing at all next to ability. *This is the coming world!* he says, he writes it home. But he wears the prescribed clothing when he takes her through the palace gates, bows when he must. It pleases him to toss his hat at flunkeys who may not complain, who must call him *sir*. What do they look like in their ill-cut livery, their awful wigs? Ha! Not like him, that's for sure. Next time, while he looks on dressed to the nines, the sensation proceeds entirely to his liking. During her improvisation – the *Wundermädchen* also improvises! She composes! – someone swoons. It could be the unusually warm spring weather, the claustrophobia of the small room, it could be the new vogue for tighter stays, but Friedrich doesn't think so. He knows what he thinks. If they're reeling now, what will they make of her next time? The time after that? *The teacher must be a lion, a genius!* they say, and he is forced to agree, but he's in no hurry. Only fools rush and Wieck is no fool. Not yet. To date this is his finest hour and the best thing about it is his certitude. He knows without doubt. He's just begun.

Beginnings, he thinks.

His eyes are on the yarn, the loose ball winding under his wife's hands. The rest he holds four-square, at arm's length.

By definition, he knows, beginnings are transient. They pass into *what comes next.*

Clementine pulls a knot free, snips the cord running between them and starts a fresh ball.

One thing, he says, we'll not go to Dresden. He'd been offered bribes of Pleyels and Lordknew what else to take her there, but *no*. When the Beethoven was more grounded, the attack for the Mozart more muscled, then he might consider it. Meantime, he says, sniffing, not able to wipe his own nose, there's some hard work to attend to. A little more composition, a full six months on Czerny, the basics of French and some violin – all the fiddle teacher wants is a mandolin! But he's in no hurry. All she needs is a little more – what was the word?

Hands, Clementine says. She means his.

His preoccupation having made the loop slack, he corrects his forearms and clears his throat. Time, he says. He nods in a decided manner. Everything comes to him who waits.

Yes, says Clementine. The wool pulls gently from her side. And *her* who waits. *Her* too.

Friedrich lifts his gaze, focuses on his wife. For the first time that evening he notices she is wearing a particularly fetching cap. Her hand that holds the ball is all but buried under strings. His half of the process, he decides, tightening the yarn, is easier. This is an occupation he does not mind. It's their wedding anniversary, after all, and the winding helps him relax. The letter waiting on his desk wasn't going anywhere and anyway, he needed this time to think how best to answer it. Frau Schumann of Zwickau was all please and thank you on the surface: everything between the lines was solid demand. *I beg you, I beseech you, as a husband, father and friend to my son EVERYTHING DEPENDS ON YOUR ANSWER* – he could see through it all right. Some mothers did that: they bullied and whined for guarantees. This one, however, did it more thoroughly than most.

Last year she had nipped at him for lessons – teach her boy or she would run mad with worry etc. The boy himself was studying law in

Leipzig, already had lodgings and money enough, it wasn't hard to say yes. Five months in, however, the boy changed his mind and buggered off to Heidelberg with barely a leave-taking and Friedrich assumed their contract done. Now, here he was again, getting his mother to do the asking, all stitched round with yards of self-pity about her fragile nerves, her vapours, her sickness to the soul, her husband's *untimely and tragic demise*. Frau Schumann was a Greek tragedy all on her own. *Can my youngest make a living of ART? My three other sons are VERY ANGRY,* she wrote. As well they might be. *They* hadn't spent three years barking up wrong trees, spending the family's money with nothing to show for it. *He has all but used up his modest fortune.* Ha! Theirs too, given half the chance! Now it seemed the boy wished to give up law for good and be a musician. Not a teacher, mark, nothing that earned a sure wage but a *virtuoso, the equal of Moscheles.* He had said that last time too, Friedrich recalled, yet had argued, absconded, and on one occasion disappeared for three whole days and nobody knew where he'd gone. Tracking him down had unearthed a great deal, mostly dives, drinking dens and unpaid tailors, not to mention Flechsig, Götte, Renz, and the other *poseurs* the boy was pleased to call his friends. Now, out of the blue, this letter from his formidable mama, begging and beseeching and arm-twisting to wangle him back to his old Leipzig teacher again.

Well, then, what was he to say? On the surface it was easy enough. Talent is talent; if the boy had it, Friedrich could train it and the Schumann lad certainly had it. He practised all the hours God sent and his playing was always full of — what? Colour? Imagination? Oddity? Full of *something*, at any rate, and Lord but he had big ideas! Art, Life, Meaning — he always had something to say, and a boy who called his teacher Maestro, who stood when that teacher entered the room, who wrote so earnestly, so loyally, so intensely, surely had *something*. And how he loved Beethoven! A reverence that bordered on the religious! On the other hand he was also naive, nervy and fond of histrionic books. He spent too much. Dress boots! Two frock-coats! Cigars and champagne! A little arrogance did the musical soul no harm, but arrogance allied to lack of insight — ah! That was a more tricky proposition. Technically, he was no match for Emilie Reichold, let alone Moscheles, and Clara, rising ten, had more discipline. What's more, his *attitude* was suspect. Friedrich had seen him lapping up applause, sighing and making cow-eyes at Agnes Carus within spitting distance of her husband, which did not suggest discretion or even common sense. He lacked concentration, he exaggerated, he flirted with married women and he drank like a drain. Then again, so did every other law student. If he lacked a fitting degree of manliness, he was also his mother's youngest by a long chalk. In his favour he had a clear if largely untutored gift for music and — what else? Something one could only call *himself*. That wide-eyed look about him, the open face. Simply, the boy was likeable. So esteemed a personage as Thibaut liked him, and Carus's good opinion was not to be sneezed at. Then Clara, Emilie, Matthäi, Glock. Even Glock's dog liked him. And Friedrich liked him too, so far as he could recall. Talk of livings, however, *whole happinesses*, futures — what is he to say?

Something touches his elbow then, brushes past. His hands, when he looks, are suspended in mid-air, holding nothing. What's more, the fire is low and a glass, one of the thick crystals that came as a gift with Clementine, sits waiting on the side table, half filled with something invitingly dark. Only the echo of his wife's skirts is left to show who put it there. He's done, then. For the time being. He lifts the glass, studies the deep red inside, then shuts his eyes and knocks it back, like medicine. This way, it takes a moment for the alcohol to hit, but when it does it has an effect. The effect comes, forces him back in his chair and slows his breathing, letting him ease into a discovery of something obvious, as he hoped it would. And the obvious is this: whatever Frau Schumann thinks, this boy isn't *his* problem. He's a businessman, not a fortune teller, and futures can't be cut and dried. It's not the boy's problem either — his desires in the matter are unmixed. As the wine floods out in his chest cavities, it's suddenly clear that no one's in a froth here but the widow, the mother, his Humble Servant Frau C. Schumann née Schnabel *ergo*, the problem, like her son, is all *hers*.

He knows what to do about it, too — he'll write and tell her. He'll tell her Friedrich Wieck is a Busy Man, a Man of Importance, a Man who can effect Great Things. He'll put the fear of God into the woman. He'll make a long list of the lad's shortcomings, hammer home the enormity of this thing she asks. Then he'll say – *yes. Yes.* THE PROMISE TO CHANGE is all he asks. And fees, of course, the requisite fees. In return, he'll offer to deliver ONE OF THE FINEST VIRTUOSI IN EUROPE. Ha! He can write capital letters too if he feels like it and right now he does. What's more, he can do it. Isn't Clara living proof? It strikes him, then, the picture of his daughter forming before him, that he should teach them together, that learning beside someone half his age could be the makings of the boy. He could lodge here too, absorb music at the master's elbow, and Clara's example, her constancy and dedication, might shame the man into moulding himself on the maid. That sounds pretty, now he thinks of it – he must remember to write it down.

As the last of his claret works its visionary effect, Friedrich sees his plan reach, extend beyond the present tense, become something of substance. He can fix Clara's concert for September, accept Robert on six months' probation the same month, show what *both* are made of. It's all very pleasing, very pleasing indeed. Clementine clears the empty glass unnoticed, goes to bed with only her Bible – something she's used to by now. Her husband has work to do. He stays up doing it, changing his life and everything in it in his most emphatic hand. In future years he will look back, wonder at how little a glimpse of anything the present tense affords; he will cut his heart to ribbons wondering it. For now, though, he thinks he is setting the world to rights. Near midnight, he signs his name and views his finished pages. Glowing, righteous, resolved.

Dresden, theory and distant guns fill the summer. There's fighting in Warsaw, Alwin says, a post-boy told him. He has no idea where or what Warsaw is, but ignorance in these matters is no drawback. Fighting, he says, and his whole face shines. Before he's tired of soldiers, there's news from Paris too. Revolutions. The French are making the very word their own. *Gun manufacturers and undertakers*, her father says, *they're making a killing*.

There's a ruined house by the Hallischen Tor. Go past the cabbage fields on the Rosenthal side and you can't miss it. Up close, it has pits in its walls, big enough for fingertips to fit inside, half its face eaten away. Other buildings in town have these pockmarks too, some healed over with fresh plaster, but this is the worst. Built near a crossroads. Prussians, Austrians, the French: they all came running this way. People died here. The Fleischerplatz lolled with corpses. After the battle they put them into piles, they stacked the pieces. Frau Nussbaum that lives in the Neumarkt found an arm on her windowsill, its hand sliced through like a crown joint. To this day she puts her apron over her head and cries for no reason. Clara has seen Frau Nussbaum, boys chasing her in the street, and knows it's true. She's heard other stories too. Father tells her not to listen. War drives weak people into madness, he says. Or gossip. Either will do. He says people who gossip over the vagaries of violence have as little brain as the mad ones and the mad ones, Frau Nussbaum included, should be put away. Yes, the night sky lit like a bonfire, the sound of guns and groaning was heard for miles; yes, he remembers too, but artists are above such things. War, he says, is not our concern. Clara hopes the soldiers, if they come back, when they come back, know. Meanwhile, people close their shutters, build stronger doors. Some leave altogether and the question of who will play at the next subscription concert at the Gewandhaus — *her first paying concert and all her own* — occupies no one. No one but Friedrich. Art stops for nothing, he growls, it never concedes. This is her entry into professionalism after all; he refuses to be deflected by the thoughtlessness of a few generals.

When the music press closes down, all advertisement with it, his rage is thick. It fills up rooms like sourdough and everyone gets a taste. One morning, when Clara stumbles on a simple triplet passage, he snatches the sheets from the stand and tears them to snowflakes before her eyes. The rest of the day she must spend writing a list of adjectives that best describe Bad Girls which, by coincidence, describe Bad Mothers too. All night, and for several nights after, the sound of ripping sheets makes her thrash in her sleep.

Alwin has no trouble sleeping; his playing, however, is helpless. One day, it's bad; even for Alwin, it's bad and he confesses he didn't practise. When the swelling won't go down, the doctor comes to look at Alwin's eye. It will get better, he says; no more stumbling on the stairs, eh? He chucks Alwin's chin, gives him an apple. And no peering at notes till it passes! Everyone smiles till the doctor is out of sight. Doctors know nothing about music, says Friedrich, and anyhow, there's nothing wrong with the boy's fingers. Alwin keeps the apple and plays with his eyes bound, resting. His scales, however, get no better. Alwin is as musical as a pig, Father says and Gustav laughs. Briefly. Sit up! he roars out of the blue at Clara one afternoon. Straighten your face! And Clara sits. She straightens perfectly.

One week later, after a week of solid fighting that can be heard as near as the outskirts of town, the Gewandhaus closes until further notice. Friedrich understands – a concert hall can't live without an audience, when tickets won't sell; all the same his face is set like a bear's and his knuckles are white.

Alwin's next mistake is pure folly. The same phrase fails him but he keeps restarting, tucking the violin back under his chin. He hasn't the sense to stop, so his father does it for him. He reaches, takes the violin, turns his son slowly. He looks directly into the boy's eyes. And Alwin, stupidly, asks to try again. Everyone in the room knows before it happens that something will. Even then, when Alwin's head tilts suddenly to one side and his legs crumple beneath him, it takes her by surprise. He looks like a calf in an abattoir, she thinks, something taken by a vast, unpleasant surprise. She almost laughs, then wonders if he's fainting, but that's not it. It's his hair. Staring makes it no different, simply more the case. Her father is pulling her brother's hair. The nine-year-old is almost kneeling now, tangled round the man's fingers as he's pulled lower still. With his remaining free hand, Wieck removes the violin to keep it safe and hands it to Gustav, who simply takes it. When Alwin yells, stumbling lower, his father tugs harder, and the boy begins sliding on the loose rugs, his feet churning in little circles. Even when he's prone it doesn't stop. It changes. Hauled by the hair, like a dog on a lead, the boy begins sliding across the polished floor. Clara can see the skin of his neck stretching as the hair begins to snap, her father's hand clutching tighter as he drags. I want to play, the child shouts, his voice splitting, I want to try! and they all know it won't work. Even Alwin knows it won't work, but he begs despite himself. Well-trained, Clara and Gustav do not look at each other, do not react at all. Anything at all might make it worse. There is nothing to do now but wait.

While her father begins in earnest, pacing the room with his burden whimpering behind him, Clara picks up the music on the stand. *Weber*, it says. *Sonata*. She reads the words over and over, rocking slightly on the stool, trying to keep her face expressionless. Weber. Other people, she thinks, ignoring the thuds behind her, the whimpers and shouting, other people are coming tonight. There will be fairy tales and laughing, food and wine. Tonight, she thinks, she'll play. Close to, something crashes. Even when the piano lid rocks and threatens to fall on her still fingers she doesn't flinch. Is this the way you repay a father? he roars. This ingratitude? You children will be the death of me! Gustav bites his lip. *Tonight*, she thinks. She keeps her eyes on the pages, the word *Sonata*, the serried ranks of notes. She'll play flawlessly, with all the meaning in the world. She concentrates, fighting her own eyes. She waits.

The concert comes, eventually. They remember her. The little girl with the doppelgänger — even the driver jokes. This time there's no mistake, no other little girl with the same name. All the way without mishap, without diversion; the night is all her own. The pianos are tuned, the programmes in plentiful supply, the orchestra sitting silent for a nod from her head. She concentrates, certainly. Clara Wieck does not play, has never played, without focus. All the same, she is aware of the black suits that surround her, the kindnesses of so many men. The only dress during the four-piano finale is hers. The Herz is faultless, they tell her; her Variations clever, for a girl. Did she write them all by herself? they ask, looking at her father in a knowing way. Nonetheless, Dorn calls her a *True Servant of Music* and kisses her hand. When they take their bow together at the close, she is aware hers is awkward, not assured, but they don't mind. Her father remarks on it, of course, but he's pleased. He even says so. *Work on your composition, Clärchen, the public want more!* She doesn't mind if they do.

Her own concert in front of so many is a different affair, more different than she had expected. That it would give her this feeling of alertness, this fizz in the head, was something she could not have anticipated. It's a difference she likes and it keeps her awake. She waits up, making conscious acts of memory: that her sash was grey, that the satin of her dress glowed almost yellow under the stage lamps, that she felt no tiredness at all. Tomorrow it will turn to dictation. *Tickets at 60 groschen*, he'll say, *outlay and return* and she'll write it down. Outside, the bells of the Nicholas Church chime midnight. It's moonless, the sky too cloudy for stars, but the lodger's lights are still on. Herr Schumann staying up late, again. She sits at the window in her nightdress, hanging on to what she can. Already it's tomorrow. Applause ebbs in her ears. His window flickers.

◦═◦═◦

Clementine's belly turns into Klemens just before Christmas. For two weeks the new baby, all boiled face and prawn hands, hardly moves. Watching him, Clara finds a picture of Viktor in her head and its vividness frightens her. Now Viktor was under the ground in Prussia somewhere and this one is here instead. Viktor had looked like Papa. This one – she wants to be charitable but one must tell the truth – this one looks like Reverend Fechner. Before long it has colic, gripes, wind, is swaddled so tight its face turns purple, which makes it look even more like Fechner. The nights are full of howling. Soon, she and Papa are going out together more often. *The Vampyre* is causing a sensation in Vienna, Papa tells her. Clara has seen every opera that's come to Leipzig, all that despair and suicide without turning a hair, but this *Vampyre* puts her out of sorts. It could be the baby's fault, it could be the dark nights, it could be all that swooning and lack of blood, but Clementine blames the lodger. He puts sheets over his head and looms at her from behind the sofa. He laughs when she shrieks and tells her ghost stories. He pulls sweets from behind her ears and lets her eat them without permission from her father. Only Clementine minds. Wieck's mind is on higher things. Distant things. He tells Clara before his wife: it's no slight. Women with babies can't travel. They have other things

80

with which to concern themselves. Clara Wieck and her father are going on tour.

Jouer. Jouer is to play. *Honoraires.* Fees are *honoraires.*
Papillons means butterflies.

Look at the map, he says. The black lines are rivers. Whole rivers. These stretches with no names are sea. One is fatter than the land mass, all water. It looks terrifying. She can't imagine so much water and says so. Water is irrelevant, he says. He brought the map to show her something else. There are new partitionings, new provinces. The map is old but it'll do for now, he says and he spreads it out on the floor. LEIPZIG is overwritten with SAXONY, splitting the word in two; DRESDEN, which takes such a long time to reach, is inches away, off to the right. She recognises CHEMNITZ and PLAUEN, BERLIN a spidery mass to the north. Past Westphalia, further than Frankfurt, on another page entirely, sits PARIS. The centre of the civilised world, Friedrich says, pleasure in his voice. Young Liszt who puts himself about so much; Herz, Pixis, Kalkbrenner, all live there. Heine too and who can blame him? The French were arrogant but they had cause, and Paris was it. Paris. A shattered egg at the top of pastry-shaped France. They speak another language. Clementine's brother, the painter fellow, speaks it like a native because he is. They have a relative *in situ* who can find them lodgings, help with translation, set up introductions. Friedrich is well aware of his luck. And now the so-called *unplayable* Variations are ready, so is Clara. Chopin. How on earth was one to pronounce it? At any rate, this *Chopin*, who plays, they say, *like no one else*, was on his way to Paris too and Clementine's brother knew someone who knew him! They'd meet, perhaps, get more introductions still. They might even — here he winks heavily — *storm the gates.* Haha. An excellent joke — *storm the gates.* No one understands it save the lodger. He doesn't laugh, but he lifts his eyes from his book at least. He looks up.

You think they have a sense of humour in Paris? Wieck asks.

The young man says nothing.

It's somewhere you've been? One of your student haunts?

No, the boy says. He's pink. Not Paris. Paris isn't — then he stops in mid-sentence, done.

Not what? Wieck asks.

Not. Switzerland.

Switzerland, Wieck says. Paris isn't Switzerland?

No, I didn't travel to Paris. I travelled to Switzerland. He coughs. Italy. Parts of Italy.

Ha! Wieck's eye fixes on the boy's face. He's in the mood for a joke. You avoided Paris on purpose! Every musician in the world holds the opinion Paris is what matters, what counts. But not you. Perhaps you think the Swiss more refined? That cow population is a greater indicator of a country's worth?

No, the boy says. Not at all. But in his opinion — in the opinion of some of his more travelled friends too — Paris was — overrated.

His neck colours darker in the silence.

What I mean, he says, stammering, is that a German way of thinking musically, independent of Paris, is something to consider. Dresden is as beautiful as Paris, Hummel says, and Weimar is just as —

Hummel? Wieck says. Hummel? His eyebrows go up an octave.

The young man stops.

The Hummel whose pupils retreat to this house in search of a teacher who has some understanding of method? Who hasn't produced a pupil who's stuck in the public imagination longer than one season? That Hummel? Wieck persists. Is that the Hummel you mean?

The boy shouldn't have mentioned another teacher. He knows that. Before it gets worse, he tries for lightness, mock-flattery. He fishes instinctively with charm. I must try to make you change your mind about leaving somehow. He smiles. Why — he casts around, nods at Clara — whom may I rely upon when you are gone?

He is appealing when he smiles, has a vague awareness of the fact. Wieck, no fool, draws him a look the length of his nose. Why, he says, folding the map as he speaks, Dorn will take care of your fingers upon request. It's already arranged. If you don't like it, Herr Schumann, I suggest you try the as yet undreamed-of prospect of relying on yourself.

The map, now folded into manageable size, slots neatly into his pocket.

If you are trying to say you will miss us, Robert, I have no doubt you are right. From the capital of the musical world, however, a place you have never been, you will not miss reports of our success. Take comfort in that.

The girl follows him out as he leaves, hair swinging behind her, pinafore squint, not even looking back. The three boys with whom he has been left wait, watching to see what he will do next, so he turns back to his book and pretends to focus on it. His chest is tight but he picks up a pen, tries to look idle, unaffected, while his head races to piece together Wieck's full meaning. Dear God, new rooms. He can't stay here with an absent man's wife, her apron barely concealing a fresh pregnancy. He'll have to find new rooms, hire an instrument all over again. He'll have to beg more money from his mother. SELFISH, he writes. His ears buzz. SELFISH his pen digging scores in the paper. POMPOUS, BOASTFUL, TEDIOUS not caring who sees. A BOOR, A MONSTER, AS RUDE AS A BEAR.

His writing is illegible in any case. HIS NATURE IS JEWISH AND HIS CAUSE IS MONEY. And damn him, he thinks, his eyes hot, wondering how soon he can stand up, find a drink, a smoke, the quickest means to a reassuring stupor, *damn him*. He's right. Not about Paris, not at all, but about his pupil's own weaknesses; about those he could not be righter. Herr Schumann would indeed miss the house, the company, the piano, the laid-on cooking, even the babysitting duties he had willingly taken up. He liked children. He liked telling stories. He liked the little girl out there cutting a career. A little girl, moreover, who had drunk in music with her mother's milk, and had not had to plead her case, to beg and cajole, not had to study the damnable, boring detail of law till, out of charity as much as anything else, someone had taken her on as someone fit to study music. And too late. Was it possible he was already too late? Clara was not thirteen, pigtails still trailing down her back. Her confidence surely came from ignorance, from lack of awareness of what in life can go terribly, irrevocably astray. Ignorance of sickness, mortality, loss. Herr Schumann feels suddenly older than his years, lonelier and unpleasantly wiser. He feels, maybe more than anyone may ever understand, that he will miss them very much indeed.

⊹≕◍═⊹

False starts and ill-mannered weather. Sickness, roadblocks and border guards twitchy as mice. No sooner had Wieck set up the Paris dates than everything was out of sorts. Everything conspired against him and even Schumann, no great observer of the practical world in anyone's book, noticed. Between politics and nature, he said, cheerful to the point of drunk, they'd need to stay put a little longer.

Heat and instability, the invariable combination, would eat the whole of June and July. He also told them, standing on a chair to do it, he was not one man now but two, a poet and a hero, each with a different name and a different temperament, though they liked each other well enough and, finally, Wieck laughed. Herr Schumann was a box of tricks, he said and ordered champagne. Two bottles. Straight on the slate. In August she was full of measles and Berlin was full of cholera, and that was the heat's fault too. Still blotchy on her September birthday, she walked with Schumann to Connewitz, leaving her father to his cursing and refixing of dates.

Herr Schumann was not like her father. Herr Schumann was frothy and talkative. He was writing a novel, an opera, a play, he said, then he was always writing something. He carried fat volumes of Jean-Paul Richter full of indecipherable jokes, Menzel and Schlegel, books of poems and pamphlets and handfuls of notes. Did she know Jean-Paul? he asked. Everyone should know Jean-Paul! He read her single lines, licking the words on his lips like salt. *Gottwald was blue-eyed and soft; Vult was a black-haired, black-eyed villain.* He lowered his voice. *Sunburned maidens with white teeth shaded their eyes with sickles that they might look undazzled upon the flute-playing student.* This, a favourite, he assumed to have more than a little to do with himself. *The flowers and the dead lie buried together,* he intoned, and he narrowed his eyes to see her shiver. *I have a secret,* he whispered, leaning so close her ear burned. *I am so sensitive that sometimes even music disgusts me.* And Clara, fresh as a peeled green onion, was shocked and thrilled to her roots. Then Clara believed every word the lodger said.

Her father, on the other hand, believed nothing: all those hints of despair, those melodramatic threats, the hypochondria — who could take that sort of stuff seriously? It was just Schumann, how he behaved. Keeping a clear eye on the future, forcing one's plans upon it — that was serious and Schumann hadn't enough manliness for that, not yet. Neither had he patience, and patience in the end was what won through. To prove it, after months of delay, he told her everything was ready. The world awaited Clara Wieck. In a matter of days, so did the coach tickets. Schumann turned morose and withdrawn. She wondered if he was sick.

On his last day at Grimaisse Strasse, though she would not know until she was a woman with children of her own, Schumann sneaked into Clara's already abandoned room and flicked through her drawers and papers. Her handkerchiefs smelled of starch, her old diaries splayed beneath like linen. He read more than he should, but she was a child. She had not the same need of privacy as an adult. It wasn't spying. And besides, he needed to know. She really was twelve years old. Really and truly. Quite so.

Clementine, pregnant again, saw them off as far as Bitterfeld, with the children. Schumann stood beside her, waiting.

She recalls his face, or thinks she does, growing smaller, whiter; the interior of the coach a black frame round his shrinking form. After that she thought of him hardly at all. If he got drunk for three days solid, wrote letters to himself, passed out, played Bach till he was dizzy, wept and laughed alone in his terrifying new rooms, she knew nothing of it. Not then. A poet and a hero. Christ. *Christ.*

Gone these six months, what did she do?

Weimar	Erfurt	Gotha
Eisenach	Arnstadt	Cassel
Frankfurt	Darmstadt	Mainz
Paris	Metz	Saarbrücken
Frankfurt	Hanau	Fulda

She learned faces, times of day, the different smell of another country's streets, the mean dispositions of foreign hotels. She travelled with her father. She played the piano.

What did *he* do? Ha!

He moved rooms twice, played, wrote, rejoiced, despaired and masturbated till his wrist cramped. He read. He read a great deal. He read about cholera and jaundice, typhus and flu. He studied Beethoven and cures for chronic skin complaints. He read Goethe, Bach, Herder and Wenzel, and enough Shakespeare to cause indigestion. He scanned texts on nervous debility. He devoured Hoffmann and Heine, Schubert and Chopin, essays on syphilis, sight problems and gout. He read letters from his mother, full of blame made to sound like love, bad love letters full of exquisite, racking pain. He felt guilt, fear, shame and loneliness. He worried. He didn't sleep enough. He read even more of Jean-Paul to while his sleepless hours — Lord! Here were men come back from the dead, looking into their own graves! Branches tapping the windows! — and slept even less. He was raddled with sensibility. He drank too much, hated himself, drank more, lit cigars, sang till the small hours and woke among sheets spattered with burn holes, butt-ends, trails of wine. He resolved to change. To *change*. To drink less, smoke less, spend less, to leave his cock alone. And so he did. Till next time, when it started all over again, again, again. Many times he wished for a soulmate, a dear friend, a brother in thought and spirit: someone as unlike his real brothers as possible. Some men were married and settled by his age, they were famous. Mendelssohn, the darling of London; Chopin with two concertos under his belt. Mozart — Christ! Mozart didn't bear thinking about. Some were in the army. Just thinking about the army brought him out in a rash. He dreamed they came to get him, all uniforms and bad boots and bayonets; that he told them his eyesight was poor and they drafted him anyway, woke sweating, sick, white. For comfort he read his journals and no comfort came. It was just as he thought. He'd become nervous.

A year ago – there it was in black and white! – he'd felt fit to trust his luck. He had given up his law books, landed the teacher of his choice, set his heart on music at last, at last. He had his portrait painted. He had chanced upon Variations by a young Polish composer in an out-of-town music shop and couldn't believe his ears; he had gorged on Jean-Paul, the only writer who *understood*. He had memorised great chunks of it, a repository for courage now and then, and muttered it under his breath when things seemed out of hand. *Niagara scattered in a thousand tiny rain-showers.* Thus fortified, he had played for the charity student at Wieck's, a mezzo with a dark voice who had followed him back to his rooms, who came inside without waiting to be asked, who slid her finger in his mouth to stop him suggesting she sing. Christel, sweet Jesus, a mouth round a thumb. He had Jean-Paul, he had this brilliant new Chopin, he had a woman. Something wholly unsuspected – a *woman*. For the first time he was a man, he thought. He was not alone. He was – what? The more he thought about it, the more the same answer came back. He was – two. Like Vult and Walt, Abelard and Héloïse, Hamlet. Everything meaningful sprang from duality; why not himself? Life darkened by great suffering led to sunrise: youth led to age. *Gottwald drank at the left breast, Vult at the right.* If Jean-Paul was right, and he was always right, the human being had a great double role in life that required only to be recognised. And he, the young Schumann, as the young god Schubert before him, would recognise and play it to the full.

Some days his head raced with new knowledge and he felt invincible, stuffed with *being*; other days he felt melancholy, even withdrawn – a splitting that had become more marked these past two years. Now, he understood this was not an inconsistency. It was a *ripening*. He was coming into his own as, patently, *two people*. In the same instant he knew this, he knew the first one's name: *Florestan*. Beethoven's hero, a man at the heart of a great operatic destiny. What more explanation was required? He was Florestan without a doubt. The other side named itself later, tumbling from the pages of a dropped book; a Saints' Day Almanac too near the edge of the table, brushed to the floor by the skirts of an angel, falling open at *Eusebius*. Saint Eusebius, martyred for his nobility of thought. And his name day was two after Clara's on the calendar. A sign. Robert picked up the book, trembling; on his fevered days, everything was a sign, and this might as well have come with thunderbolts, choruses, shafts of light. *Florestan* and *Eusebius*, he had it now! Both beyond question and both himself.

It certainly explained things. Those days when he felt his head was at war with itself, shifting his mood from laughing to crying irrespective of his own wishes – now it was obvious why. Perhaps they fought with each other, his two halves; perhaps they switched in rapid rotation. Whichever, he knew both were in his seeing, his hearing, his whole existence, which is to say this twinned state was his *normal state*, not madness, as once he had horribly feared. He had heard it said often enough that madness was akin to genius, indeed, some people *expected* the appearance of madness from their creative sorts. He had even seen some affect variations on lunacy the better to be thought *artistic* by potential patrons who hadn't a clue. What he had suffered had seemed wholly different. What he had suffered did not go away when the audience did; it had worsened into terrors and visions that scared away all joy of living and replaced it with mechanical writing, hideous drawings, things fit only to hide away and be afraid of. Now, however, now he grasped it. These were *birth pains*: the twins pulling in their separate, rightful directions. He was, now it had finished, simply *how he was*. How he *both* was, haha! A jest was the core of all meaning, after all. Not only that, but Gottwald was blue-eyed and soft, and Vult was a black-haired, black-eyed villain, and he, Robert Schumann of Zwickau, knew what this felt like *from the inside*.

He could remember his childhood and the proofs were there too, he could remember his *conception* and two selves had been present then too! Moreover, this maturing or whatever it was, was not finished yet. One day these two would merge to make one more, as he and Clara did when they played Schubert four-handed, the two of them side by side on the piano stool. This perfected self would be RARO — ClaRA RObert, a fusion yet to come. Florestan, Eusebius, RARO. These three explained everything: all his striving and present being, his promised future. They held the private code book for how he might plot the novel of his life. For the first time, *the first time*, he saw it all and with dazzling precision. He could stand at his window, open the shutters wide and see all the way to Alsace if he tried; all the way to America, the moon, the stars. He was at ease with himself — to be at ease with oneself, what a feeling that was! His first piece newly published, his sheets stiff with sex, his head full of champagne, Herr Schumann felt stout as Napoleon. How long had it lasted? Two weeks? Three? Then his cock started bleeding again, the novel, the opera, the poems dried up, and he turned twenty-one. He put Narcissus water and arsenic on his foreskin and stopped answering the door. He wept. Twenty-one! Draft age! A marker on a road that led only forward, the path behind him melting into oblivion. On bad days he suspected his youth was finished, his chances gone, his conscription to some lunatic skirmish on the Prussian border a foregone conclusion; on bad nights, he knew it for sure. Twenty-one. He drank himself senseless, burned candles, developed stomach cramps and a cough. He had syphilis, he knew it. Every twitch was a spiroid infection, worming deeper into his nervous system, his brain and bones. When his mother wrote that Julius, the brother who looked most like father, was coughing too, moreover coughing *blood*, Robert recalled a portrait he'd had painted when the world was at his feet and took to his bed, terrified. A likeness of himself, a doppelgänger, did nothing but tempt fate. *The storm comes*, he repeated it over and over, *the storm comes and the water is rising*. People were falling like skittles in Berlin — cholera, typhus, Lordknew what else. Cholera was the worst. Cramps and dysentery first, then stools like rice water flaked with bits of intestine. He knew this and more because Wieck told him.

Wieck told him other things, too, hurtful things about the slap-dashness of his playing that threatened to drive him mad, personal things about his *lack of manliness*, but those were the kinds of things Wieck said. To his sons he said worse, and they were children. The Old Man

89

had to be endured. He had to be endured because there was no arguing with him. Because he was the best teacher in Saxony. Because Robert could never find the words when he needed them. Most of all just because. Because he was *there*. No matter how confusing the rest of life became, you had something solid if you had Wieck. He was a rock and Robert was grateful for it. When he heard the rock was packing its bags for Paris, the shock to his system and all parts attached was frightful. *In six years I will make you a virtuoso to equal Moscheles*, he had said. Had he meant it? At all? Or did he mean that prize only for his daughter, a girl of barely twelve? He felt ashamed and pitiable suddenly, unable to speak. The girl, he remembered, noticed. I will miss you, Herr Schumann, she had said as they left. I will buy you something pretty in Paris.

And he had watched them go, the Chopin pieces he had discovered along with them, and gone back to his new digs alone. A long walk. He would reinvent, he thought, leaves blowing up at his face like slaps. He would change his whole direction. Spiteful, he chose a new role model. Belleville, Clara's nearest rival – moreover, a rival with breasts – struck him as a fine idea. He bought a new hat, a coat with longer frocking, a finger stretcher. Four hours a day he practised with his wrists high, looking somewhat effete but not caring. In addition, he weighted his fourth finger to make it strong. For a time it worked. Then it didn't. He added more weights. By the time Clara's accolades were arriving by post, his digit was curling in on itself, numb as a carrot. The more he read her reviews, the more glowing those reviews became, the worse his indisposition got. Holding the pen as best he could, he wrote to his coughing brother, his mother, his sisters-in-law, pouring out his fears. What if it never got better, if he could no longer play? What would happen then? His mother sent money as he hoped she would and Rosalie, sweet Rosalie, Rosalie who married his sniffy brother Carl, came all the way from Schneeberg with a cake. It didn't help. Dr Reuter and Dr Carus and Lordknew who came as well, but still his finger sickened. It drew towards the centre of his palm, like a spent penis. What, he thought, suddenly horrified, if it's punishment? *Only guilt brings nemesis.* What if everyone else could see this awful evidence of carnality too?

That evening, when Christel arrived with flowers and beer, he wouldn't even open the door. Safer, he decided, to keep himself and his extremities out of her way. He had wasted time, injured himself. He would waste no more. Eusebius would think only lofty thoughts; Florestan would be resolute. There would be no more brooding or late, lost nights, no more wrist-flexing under the sheets. No more dwelling on the debts, the awful letters from Mother with the catalogues of disease, blame and fear, no more empty bottles outside the door or fretting about his bastard fingers. The cure for despondency was discipline. Wieck told him that too. Wieck's advice was tough as hide but always sound. And since his hand stopped him speaking at the keys, he turned to the pen. The divine Schubert had done this; had turned to paper with a quill in his hand, had paced his room wringing his hands to find the phrase that would capture the graceful, the mad, the simply true. He would be like Schubert, then. He'd write. Not a novel, not an opera, not reviews, but *music itself*. He'd done it before, now he'd do it again, but in earnest.

Mere months later, when the blossom was back on the cherry trees and the nights no longer began at four o'clock, when Alwin arrived, running — *Herr Schumann, they're coming! They're home* — he was ready. He straightened his necktie, adjusted his cuffs. Past the Thomas Church, through the town square, along Grimaisse Strasse, his new sideburns brushed, his new pieces, the *Papillons*, pinned to perfection under a cover of cherubs, ivy, trailing vines. The hole in his boots, like Paris, was irrelevant. Jean-Paul himself had said it: *the butterfly is as powerful as the bear in the right hands*. His hands were the right hands and they carried the proof. He had something else to show for himself — for both himselves — and to the people who mattered. Wieck was home, Clara was home. He couldn't wait.

The new sister, four months old, was big as a cannonball. Klemens didn't know who she was and Gustav refused to take her hand. Cousin Pfund and Alwin, Emilie Reichold and mother, Schumann with his head tilted to one side waiting to hear what she had to say, knew who she was all right. They'd come to hear her show it off. Let Clara tell it, her father said.

Don't forget she came too.

Let Clara tell the story exactly as she recalls.

Well then.

Weimar	Erfurt	Gotha
Eisenach	Arnstadt	Cassel
Frankfurt	Darmstadt	Mainz
Paris	Metz	Saarbrücken
Frankfurt	Hanau	Fulda

Cold, unsprung coaches and no sleep, the acrid stink of piss-hardened whips and ancient horses, dragging another mile, another mile. Arriving late in the evenings with the towns shut and nothing to see, nothing to eat, almost never a welcome or a porter to carry bags; new rooms with old sheets and the noise of Papa snoring in the bed beside hers till morning filled up the window, if there was a window, to see what lay ahead; breakfasts of bread and afternoons of hiring and haggling, demanding and blustering, of contracts, bookings, accounts. She had studied, sung, composed. She had stood by while Papa made himself known to music society presidents, administrators, critics, tuners, dealers, bodice fitters, clerks, censors, town officials who took three days to process a request, then asked for another signature, another fee. And every day, after her three-mile exercise, she had made trips to hotel ante-rooms, the back rooms of dealers' warehouses, schoolrooms, parlours in rich people's houses to beg an instrument to play till the time came to view the brute they'd provided for the concert. Sometimes she wished she played the violin, the flute, something portable; most times she didn't. Pianists played pianos; this was how it was with her kind. Out-of-tune dust boxes to shipped-in Pleyels, they took what was afforded; they played. Pianists gave concerts, that was the correct word, they *gave*, and she had given a great many; in halls little more than barns with not enough light to see by, others in palaces, with royal families in matching sets waiting round a piano so patterned with inlays and painted land-scapes it seemed an affront to touch it at all.

She had played for Goethe with all his hair after eighty-one years, who fetched her cushions and sweets; for Spohr who held her hands and told her they were *treasures from God*; for Mendelssohn and Chopin who looked like princes till she saw them bear-fighting, giggling like boys in a salon ante-room. Yet how beautiful – she could think of no other word for it – Herr Chopin was when he listened! How fragile yet determined his face! And she had played for Kalkbrenner and for Herr Hiller and for Paganini, who remembered her and showed her his three more missing teeth; for officials and generals and countless teacup-rattling philistines, supporters and sniffers, for boors, bores and the merely curious. She had seldom been asked for an opinion. She had been given jewellery, medals, accolades, keepsakes, locks of hair from lovesick girls; gold clasps, emerald combs and money. Most of the jewellery was money now, too. But this was nothing to say. It wasn't a *story*. She had travelled with her father, she had played the piano – that was the long and short of it. She said so – and they laughed. Father too. Relief lightened the air in the room like orange zest.

The things you say. Her father smiled. He shook his head in a manner indicative of incredulity. *Ce n'est pas dire!*

And he told it himself, as he knew he would all along.

Weimar was full of snobs. Gotha housed only ignoramuses and farmers. Eisenach and Frankfurt were miserable. They could tear down Frankfurt and he'd not weep. There of all places, she played like an angel till Darmstadt, where perfectly tolerable people were served cold playing, this time *not the piano's fault*. Never mind! Performances aren't rewards. Not for anyone. And Paris? Where to begin? Paris stank. One tiny jug of water for washing in the morning and no more all day! Clementine's brother, however, couldn't be faulted, had even drawn an official portrait – Clara with no waist at all and her neck bare – that earned a few thaler *thank the Lord*. A new dress for *each appearance* and everything white, flat-soled shoes, only fresh flowers or seedpearls for her hair which should *always* be up. For himself, three pairs of yellow kid gloves, as many white stocks and half a dozen shirts *in one week alone*! Add laundry bills, hair-dressing, wraps and shawls, and one wondered why people put their daughters to touring at all. Salons reeked of smoke, stale Cologne, and

Frenchmen. Programmes didn't start till after ten at night, then everything was lumped together like stew — Spaniards lying full-length on the table with flowers between their teeth, chicken-faced sopranos with their dresses cut so low their nipples showed, divorcées reeking of cigars — he'd seen it all. And the crush! Four hundred in Kalkbrenner's tiny front rooms to hear Chopin play for fifteen minutes! And that hellish piano! What was it like, *Clärchen*? Eh? Kalkbrenner's instrument? A bag of bones, that's what, a disgrace. Yet Chopin thinks Kalkbrenner a magnificent fellow, so what is to be made of that?

Now, listen to what an honest German had to say, and in his own home, not to impress multitudes. In Weimar, Goethe himself said our Clara had the strength of six boys. *Six boys.* And she needed it in Paris! You don't play these French uprights, you fight them! You fight to win! And the true connoisseurs, of course, knew it. They knew the difficulties. Spohr, Pixis and Mendelssohn, Paganini — all Great Men, Good Men. Heine, however, was arrogant and Kalkbrenner was worse. Kalkbrenner was a precious, self-adoring sort, a prig without the talent to back it up. *In Paris we love Beethoven*, he said. *Programme her without Beethoven and only the claptrap you push upon her presently and you will reap little here.* Ha! Do you know what I said? He looked around the room fiercely. I said this! She plays Beethoven as she plays Schubert — at home and not for the mass until I say so, sir. He sighed. Until I say so.

For the first time since he'd begun, he leaned back in his chair.

Of course it was a regret not to have spoken to Chopin. You should see the way he looks them in the eye. As though he doesn't need their money and never will! They say he does not care if he only ever plays for a handful of people in his life, he will not be liveried entertainment. *Ha!* He repeated it, savouring the idea or ridiculing it, it was hard to know which. *He will not be entertainment.* Well, then. He slackened his collar. Well. A pity. People of spirit should stick together. But the young man is naturally reticent.

Clara watched him sink back further, drop the tension in his shoulders.

He is reticent. That's all.

Ferocity seemed to have been all that was holding him together.

Now he had allowed himself to spit it all out, he looked smaller. He looked thin and old and tired. The way, in fact, he had looked for weeks. She had recognised his story as she always recognised his stories. He had told what he saw. But she had seen other things, things around the edges of his vision; mere detail, of course, nothing so important as what his own eye had lit upon. But certainly other things. Many of them about Father himself. She had noticed his incredulity at the Paris protocols, his spluttering humiliation at being unable to afford the rate for the hotel found by Fechner, his face reddening in the accumulated heat as the evenings went on and on; the hateful French salons full of stuffed leopards and embroideries and paintings and peacock feathers and whispers that he never seemed to notice. She heard the content of the whispers too, sometimes wondered if she was meant to. But that wasn't it. That would have been to give her too much credence. They talked out loud like that because they thought her more or less insensible, because they assumed she had not a word of French to her name. And what they said! The father's infelicitous turns of speech, the passé colour of his coat, the not-quite fit of his yellow kid gloves. Lord, my dears, do you not pity her! Chopin thought him stupid, they said; Kalkbrenner thought him a buffoon and everyone in the world, it seemed, made fun.

Oblivious, his French not up to French as spoken by French persons, he led her to pianos, his velvet-covered arm under hers solid as truth. And inside the cocoon of whispering snobbery, his voice had sounded good like the voice of God. *Artists are your own; be in awe of none. As for the rest? Remember that none of these sorts, no matter how much they think of themselves, not one of them can do what we can do.* Then he left her to what she had come for, left her alone at one keyboard after another. And she had played. She had played very well. For all that, they seemed to see her as an amusement, someone so young playing so maturely, a girl playing with such *masculine strength*. That they thought her *pretty* seemed to matter more than any of it. She met Heine, who, for his politics and other things besides, had packed himself out of Saxony before Metternich had done it for him. He and his companion, knowing nothing of the applause she had received in Weimar and Cassel, thinking nothing but the applause of the city in which they stood counted, appraised her like a vase while she stood there in front of them: *Poor child! It seems as though she could tell a long story woven out of joy and pain, yet what does she know? Music.* Her face burned recalling it, even now.

And this was not the worst, not by any means. Audiences of aristocrats — well. It seemed they couldn't help themselves. Anyone who was paid for a living they regarded as no more than a servant. They talked through the music, petted dogs, ordered tea and yawned. If French, they smirked at her speaking in her own language because it was not theirs and asked how on earth she had learned so much *so far away.* How Chopin endured it she had no idea. She certainly understood why he hated to play. But Clara and Father endured it all for four concerts in small rooms, the sense of being tolerably amusing. This, then, was the Capital of the Musical World.

When word of cholera made him pack their bags she was almost glad. Through Metz and Saarbrücken, swathed in flannel, a heaviness grew in her stomach, her head. In Frankfurt, another name for hell, she woke with night sweats and her bones ached: no more than a passing chill but her father prayed and his face was grey. Shortly after, she bled. There was no hiding it. Her father said nothing but he ordered her bed stripped and demanded fresh sheets, let her patch herself with rags as best she could. This was something that happened, she knew, it was not cholera. Not, despite its awfulness, an illness at all. Sharing the room together, however, was becoming unbearable. As soon as she could dress herself, a cheap overnight coach and four had rattled them home. None of this had much to do with what people wanted to hear either, but it was what made the deepest ridges in her memory. Applause and performance she took for granted, yet they were triumph, success, the real story. She must learn to refocus her priorities, then she'd have something to say.

Thinking it through made her feel restless. She made her excuses, left the company in the sitting room, put on her oldest pinafore and headed for the kitchen. Lise gave her salts and vinegars, soda and lemon juice, a recipe for metal paste. That made, she worked. Hair scraped back, a necklace worth two years of Lise's wages round her neck, she set herself to polishing knives. Next time, she thought, scouring, when Papa said, *Tell Dr Carus how Paganini played, Clärchen; what Goethe said; what that rather stuck-up fellow Heine looks like; what refinement Mendelssohn, the son of a Jewish banker, can display*, she would say something dazzling. The reflection of her face appeared in the blades as she worked, her lips parted as though ready to speak. She was Clara Wieck. These hands had been kissed by adult men. *Parisians.* The great, the good and the very rich indeed had looked her in the eye, and she had looked straight back, knowing she had something to give. More to the point, that she worked and she *earned;* and that mattered, dear goodness, that mattered. One day, she thought, buffing till she broke sweat, she'd say something dazzling. *Ce n'est pas dire.* One day, she'd say something to surprise them all.

In the room above her head only Schumann remained. He had said all he had to say: his struggles with Dorn, his medical advice, his plans for a newspaper full of fresh ideas and critical insight, the pressing need for written musical activism. When even Wieck had had enough, the young man was still there, bright-eyed and unable, it seemed, to leave. No one moved him on. He had lived here once, was as good as the Old Man's son – one he treated rather better than his own, it might be said. Music was playing somewhere on the other side of the street and the candles were down. *Music, a recollection of the beautiful, of what lived and died upon the earth.* With no one expecting him, Jean-Paul foremost in his thoughts and nothing immediately pressing to do, Robert settled back into the chaise and lit a cigar. Being a virtuoso was a thankless, hellish life. For what joy it brought, little Clara was welcome to it. He blew smoke into the darkness, watched it drift. The edge of a book jutted at his hip from his hip pocket and he lifted it to the light to see. *Fruit Flower and Thorn Pieces: or The Married Life, Death and Wedding of the Advocate of the Poor, Firmian Stanislaus Sabienkäs.* A sign. He'd sit here a while, think. Read and learn, remember that Sabienkäs was restored to life. Tomorrow, and the day after that? He'd take up the cello; conduct, perhaps. To hell with performing. Even thinking it made his fingers stretch, all pain melting out. He'd write. The tip of his cigar a beacon. He'd compose.

THREE

Ich kann's nicht fassen, nicht glauben

I cannot, dare not, believe it

*H*e said she watched him.

That she sat at the keyboard thinking herself inconspicuous, unobserved, and simply watched. He saw her first at the Carus house, he said, remembered every detail: that he had worn a yellow jacket; that they had had him recite Schiller; that the quartet had been excellent; and that after, he had kept Flechsig awake all night ranting. Most of all he remembered that when he heard her play for the first time − when he heard her for the first time he had thought − he had thought her nose was too big. Ha! He could tease all he liked, she could do no more than tell the truth. She had no memory of their first meeting at all. Later he would claim she had more memories of his life than he had himself and she wouldn't argue. How and when it started, this reversal of retention, could not be pinned down and trying would have been a waste of time. What signified was that this had happened. She had become the guardian of his memory, not he of hers. Robert and Clara. What signified was that any of it happened at all.

Fräulein Wieck is not the only one who has seen far-off lands and people!

He pulled a bag from behind his back, tipped sand from its corners. He had been to Araby collecting stories! He made them stand on one leg, race, took them to the zoo and when the boys were sent to bed, stayed on with Clara reading some more; stories of fairies and donkey-headed men hiding in the grass, of Danish princes and women dressed as boys. He told her about a girl called Emilie whose brother played the piano while she danced, then she went under the sea and everyone cried, a story that always made him shudder. Later came the story about Estrella, a princess with yellow hair and an appetite for *ASCH*cakes who was loved by a poet and a hero, and Clara knew things she should not.

Before then, however, there was only Clara and Schumann and the woods at Connewitz, the playing of duets. They shared five-note themes on scraps of paper, made ciphers, fragments, musical jokes. He read her his poems and she watched his footing when they walked by the river, careful he should not fall. Byron and Schiller, the purple prose of Jean-Paul, his own purpler poems, mad kings and misunderstood daughters. She listened. She watched. She played.

⊷═◉═⊶

His hand was stiff/numb/worthless/temporarily indisposed.

It would take two days' rest/six months of medical attention/was incurable.

Whichever doctor was telling the truth, this was certain.

He couldn't play. The première of his own Opus. 2 was in other hands.

Twelve-year-old hands.

Hers.

⊷═◉═⊶

These pieces, he said, the *Papillons*, they are not really butterflies. Not at all. They are a masque, a ball, he said, but programme was not his intention. Continuity of musical thought, a solid aesthetic, that was first. Programme was more or less nothing at all. That understood, she might think of handsome people dancing if she chose, but to produce the *feeling* of a ball, nothing literal. The right-hand octaves in the third fragment should *glide*. A giant boot, he said, she might think of the octaves in exactly that way – a giant boot *gliding* in F♯ minor. She asked if she should fade the dominant seventh chord at the close, let it melt to nothing. He only smiled. She asked again. His work was difficult for some, he said, but not her. She would know what to do when the time came. She was his right hand where his own failed. His champion, the bearer of a torch. And she would play well. He had no doubts at all.

102

Afterwards, Rosalie came up to speak. Her husband's cough was worse, she said, but it would pain Robert to hear of it. He need not be concerned, that was a wife's duty. She would not have her sweet Robert pained if she could help it. Robert, knowing nothing of Paris pianos or his brother's respiration, was pained anyway. *She plays better than this*, he whispered. The butterflies were lumpy, the *Caprices* capricious as constipation. What's more, Clara's accent was affectedly Frenchified and she looked like a frog. Paris had done her no good. Six weeks later, on the evening of his twenty-second birthday and the better of four glasses of champagne, he changed his mind. She had played his Paganini studies exactly as he'd imagined them. In her white muslin she looked like a fairy, he thought. Was her dress filling out? He sank another glass, looked again. Playing this way, her skin sheeny as satin under muslin sleeves, her eyes focused entirely on the keys, Clara looked something more than pretty, something more, even than an artist. She looked, he thought, like a lamb returned to the honest, modest, German fold.

He stank of week-old mutton.

When he told her he spent his time in the slaughterhouse with his fist deep in the still-warm guts of sheep, she didn't believe him. He joked, after all, he teased. When the stink didn't fade and he told her again (the skin still attached, he said, they open them and leave their bellies gaping like mouths), she knew it was true. Old-fashioned or not, he'd try any cure. He wanted back the use of his hand. How he must suffer, she thought (the smell of fat and tissue clinging to him, dogs lifting their noses as he passed); how wretched he must feel. That November, he sat in the back row of a concert in Zwickau, his home turf, and watched 500 people crush towards the stage, but not for him. They knocked over music stands, pushed each other aside, begged for a touch from the artist's hand, an artist who had offered them Herz and flashy trill variations alongside that other stuff. Who cared who the composers were? She was what counted. Robert's mother watched it all, his brother Julius out of a sickbed and Rosalie, coughing now herself. She wore black net for her little boy that died, thick gloves to hide the tremor in her hands, and smiled for her brother-in-law. Your beautiful piece is too difficult, she said. But they will catch up some day, some day. Frau Schumann wept and smelled of damp; she clung to Clara's hand as though she'd known her all her life. That one is overfamiliar, Wieck said. She presumes.

Next day, when Wieck's back was turned, Frau Schumann invited Clara to her house to talk. They sat at an upstairs window and Rosalie brought cups. The sky was pending snow and black birds circled in the sticks of woodland just visible beyond the nearside roofs. Frau Schumann sipped and talked about the weather, music, the state of the roads. Clara looked strong, she said. Healthy, too, she'd be bound? Clara was doubtless someone who worked hard for her success and could confidently await the prospect of more – was she right? Clara smiled. Reply did not seem to be called for. *I see*, said Frau Schumann, delighted, *we will be great friends.* Robert travelled, she said. He had been as far as Italy. She wished he wouldn't. He caught colds so easily – and this business with his hand! It gave her headaches, sciatica, insomnia and chills just to think of it, but that, she supposed, was the price of being a mother. She sighed and patted Clara's arm. She took great comfort that Robert was settled in Leipzig, however. And with such nice people! Leipzig was not, after all, so very far. And yet. She inched closer and the hairs on the back of Clara's neck began to prickle. And yet! What fears she had for his future! Robert was – particular. Robert was – an *artist*. The other boys were like their father, she said, clutching and unclutching a badly embroidered handkerchief; they were sickly but untroubled by artistic yearnings. They worked with books. But Robert, she said, now beginning to sniff, Robert was *different*. Should she tell a story? Clara willed her silently not to. On it came, regardless, as somehow Clara had known it would. When he was just tiny, his mother — that is to say herself, Frau Schumann — had been ill; terribly, terribly ill. What could one do? Robert had been nervous from the start, easily given to fright and disappointment. And so sensitive! Like his sister, like Emilie, who — Frau Schumann's eyes brimmed suddenly, her sentence faltered. The story stopped. What came instead were statements.

I am almost seventy years old, Fräulein Wieck. Seventy. A widow. Her breathing sounded wheezy. All my other sons are settled, but still I have no peace. I worry. We are not rich.

Clara, helpless, looked out of the window hoping for a distraction, a clue what to say. Instead she saw Robert, fallen branches gathered beneath his arm, his collar turned up against the chill. She stared at him hard, hoping he'd turn, come inside. Hoping he'd at least see.

He has great gifts, Frau Schumann said. Great drive and obstinacy. He is not, you will agree, unattractive. This close she smelled of dried roses, dust. I sense you have a stout heart, she said. Courage and insight are not strangers to you. She placed her own fat hand over the girl's, covered it completely. *Anyone who hears you knows that.*

Clara wondered if she ought to find Rosalie, someone else, anyone else. The wheeze in Frau Schumann's chest was more pronounced now, her face florid. What if she was unwell? More to the point, something about the woman frightened her, her livid colouring, the way her eyes were never focused for long, restless, as though they were looking for something mislaid.

Suddenly the old woman caught Clara's wrist, gripped it hard enough to hurt. Some day, Frau Schumann said, she whispered, her eyes fixed, some day you will marry my Robert.

Clara bit her lip and looked, shaking, out of the window. At that same moment Robert looked up. He saw Clara gazing down at him, her sober, innocent little face. He blew a white plume of breath towards the window, wrapped his arms tighter round the bundle of kindling. He smiled.

⊷══◉══⊶

Klemens died.

Rosalie, raddled with a fever of her own, sent condolences. Schumann, still in Zwickau, did not. Clementine, spiteful with grief, made Clara a roster of household tasks. The girl was growing up, after all, nearly fourteen. Some girls in Torgau were married by that age. *This isn't Torgau*, Friedrich said, and tore up the roster in front of her face. Sewing, however, he encouraged. It saved a fortune in concert frocks. Every woman should sew. In the thick evening silences, Clara licked thread ends and pricked her thumbs, building a concerto in her head as her stitching got neater. Every achievement should lead to another, her father had said. It was called progress. Before long, she was three drafts into her first serious orchestral piece and two aprons to the good, an overture and nightgown to follow. On better days she and Emilie, another child too old for her face, dared the Connewitz road and went walking for hours. Her Great Friend, Herr Schumann, went walking there, Clara said. He stumbled on stones if she didn't watch out for him; his mind was on Higher Things.

When the Great Friend came back to Leipzig that summer raving with swamp fever, Emilie had no doubt it was all true. Confined to bed, he sent delirious notes and composed like a dervish. At night, when the heat died back, Clara wrote back, little themes to cheer him, five notes falling like rain. She thought of him in his flat in Reidel's Garten, at the other side of town, among his papers and quinine, lonely with infection. At least he had Gunther. It said something for Schumann that he was able to find such a friend. Clever, loyal, soft as a girl, Gunther had not moved out of their shared accommodation; that he was prepared to take his chances to nurse Schumann touched Clara very much. She hoped one day, if it came to it, she would find such a friend.

⊷══◉══⊶

Dr Kuhl, Dr Otto, Dr Portius, Dr Reuter, Dr Hartmann.

Physicians came and went, changed like handkerchiefs. If one did not like what they said, one could find a new one — it was easy enough. Changes of rooms, too, were beneficial, and new rounds of Titans, demigods, angels and devils, commonly called *friends*. One ran out of money, more came; it was a rule of nature, or so he said. Should she have seen anything untoward in this? Should anyone? Surely no one could blame them if they did not. He was suffering from malarial illness, after all; an identifiable cause will do for any number of symptoms. He was covered in bandages, a mummy; he scrawled in tiny, crunched letters from his sickbed, all but dead, but he had raised himself from winding sheets to write to her, only her.

> Tomorrow on the stroke of 11 I shall play the adagio
> from Chopin's variations and at the same time I shall
> think of you very hard, exclusively of you. Now I ask
> that you do the same so that we may see and meet
> each other, in spirit. Our doppelgänger will probably
> meet over the little Thomas Gate . . .

Whether traces of fever could thrive and carry on ink or paper she didn't know; that he would think of her *exclusively* and not his fingering she doubted, but she did as he asked. On the stroke of eleven and without music on the stand. If their spirits met, he never said. He was on to something else, head racing, blood pressure pushing him on. He smoked, drank, composed. He walked to Connewitz. He expounded theories, stayed up late, wrote poems compulsively and spoke in rhyme. What he did not do was rest. What he did not do was go to Zwickau as his mother asked, he did not even send flowers. Someone else took his corner for Julius's coffin, someone else again for Rosalie's. Turned under the soil without him, they complained in dreams. His solution? To refuse sleep. He burned hundreds of candles and didn't eat. He switched doctors again, developed an occasional tic in one eye and forbade his mother to write anything but good news — his nerves couldn't take it, he said, and no one argued. At least, so Clara heard. Touring again, she hardly saw him. Soon, almost no one did. A rumour that he had tried to jump out of the fifth-floor windows of his new rooms, scattering broken glass and poems the length of Burgstrasse, circulated while she was playing in Plauen, but had run its course by her return. She would have declared it a lie in any case. Schumann was gentle and learned, a man of sensibilities; only a lunatic would do such a dreadful thing. Lunatics were not gentle and refined, ergo Herr Schumann was not a lunatic and people who implied *anything to the contrary* were creatures below shame. She would have fought like a tigress. If she had heard the further story that his friend Lühe slept with him to stop him jumping again — ah, but she didn't. Neither did she see him. After Gunther and Lühe called in Dr Reuter, no one saw Herr Schumann for some considerable time.

✦═◎═✦

Beethoven, Mendelssohn, Bach.
Schubert. Beethoven.
Beethoven.

Her repertoire was changing. That was growing up, her father said; not household rosters, *that*. On the day of her confirmation, in the first month of 1834, he handed her a letter in his best handwriting, clear as an edict. On the verge of womanhood, it advised, she should strive to be independent. Independent, virtuous, dutiful, noble and pious. She should also, it went on, rest safe in the knowledge that her truest adviser and helpmate was her father/her teacher/her friend/himself. He had dedicated ten years of his life to her training and hoped she would not forget. He neglected to mention the custom she had brought, the pupils and dealers, the money she had earned for the household, or that her success had made his name. Of course not: that would have been beside the point. For the purposes of filial education, his beautiful letter served just the way it was. She understood. Of course she did. That, after all, was growing up too.

There was more. Nanny took her to be fitted for a corset. It hurt. A quarter of an hour to lace it, the silk and whalebone, spiral brass wire and eyelet holes pressing against her back and ribs. That afternoon she couldn't sing. She cried instead, had pains all over. Growing pains, Clementine said; one grew, it was painful. Three pairs of corsets were a minimal requirement for young ladies in Paris! Some girls wore them in bed! Clementine was pregnant again, sick as a poisoned stray. One corset, she said, and that just for special – *one* corset. Be thankful for the father who lets you get away with it, she said, digestive acids tainting her breath sour. Be thankful you're a musician. Freedom of movement, my eye. Musicians get away with murder.

⊷══◎══⊶

From January to April Schumann barely put his nose beyond the Coffeebaum. It was warm there, full of good beer and coffee: a place a man might hatch ideas. He's busy, her father said. He's with Knorr and Hartmann and Schunke finally starting this newspaper he had talked about so much. Schumann wants to be a critic and write deathlessly on the state of music – Well! There were worse things to do. Lordknew what happened to Gunther and Lühe, those baby-faced men who ran about with him, laughing at his jokes and begging him to play the piano that they might swoon during the holidays. Now this Schunke fetches and carries, looks out for him, checks he eats. These days, he said, Schunke gets to be the demigod and Schumann doesn't break wind without telling Schunke first. Anyhow, he can't visit. He's at the Coffeebaum up to his eyes in his newspaper stuff. Then he left for the Coffeebaum too. She heard a little, now and then. They were a band, a league of warriors with Schumann at its head; Florestan and Eusebius (both of them Schumann) were *David* now too; *the Philistines who opposed True Art* were the enemy against whom the warriors would fight – to the metaphoric death if need be. The Davidsbund believed in Freedom, but who did not? Freedom, then, as represented by an idea of political liberalism, the individual and his philosophical extemporisations upon life, would be the only legitimate basis for culture and Art! Or *her* extemporisations – yes, quite.

The Davidsbund, then, opposed bad music, showy music, music that was not music, competitions of virtuosity (Thalberg and Liszt's gladiatorial bout of pianism before a mob in Paris being a case in point and arguably not a case in point), and all else that was mere entertainment, tinsel, glitter, show. They battled for a public liberated from meretriciousness; their politics would be composed entirely of aesthetics. Goethe, they whispered, was *Antique*; Wenzel was the shape of the New. And they would fight! Not with swords but with reviews and articles, and win the soul of Real Music with words. Well, she thought, it sounded fine enough. Some of it she almost understood. That there was enough to attack was unarguable; she played some of it herself. And if someone had to take up arms against it to champion *True Art* it excited her to think it was Schumann. It took up his time, however. It took up lots of his time. By Easter he still hadn't visited but her father brought a note back that told her she'd been chosen – in her absence, of course – as a warrior too. A *Davidsbündlerin*, it said; one without a place at their table, it's true, but a member of the sacred band nonetheless. *Chiarina*, he called her, his handwriting an amiable scrawl. *Chiarina*. She set it open on the table, next to her Beethoven Sonatas, her notes for composition, her pen and her French grammar. It showed her name, his regards. His fondest regards.

Chiarina, Zilia, Chiara.
   Jeanquirit, Serpentius, Fritz Friedrich. Charitas. Estrella.
   Felix Meritis, the most good-hearted of men.
   Jonathan, *God have pity on his miserable soul*, Jonathan.

Schunke was there when they unveiled the first edition of the *Neue Zeitschrift für Musik*, Schumann at his side. A prosaic enough title for such a radical music paper, as he said, but rather the content than the title should make waves. Clara listened to the speeches, watched. Having seen neither man for some time, she watched more. She stared. Schunke was gaunt as a grasshopper, almost the same colour. Schumann, on the other hand, the formerly sickly Schumann, resembled a broker with his smart new suit, his fattening, contented chin. They called each other by their warrior names, this being the inaugural occasion of their fighting talk-sheet, *Jonathan*'s smile as watery as *David*'s was hale. *David*, she thought, watching Schumann shake hands with Knorr and some greasy town official, *David* the anointed of Samuel who killed Goliath the Philistine. Schunke, the most trusted of David's freshly appointed band, coughed and held a pasty-white hand to his mouth. *Jonathan*, she thought. The beloved. Jonathan died. She fetched the young man a chair, watched him sit. The lips that mumbled their thanks into a handkerchief were pale-blue. She sat beside him anyway, and together, in companionable silence, they watched Schumann, his chestnut hair curling over his collar, the sheen of excitement on his healthy, helpless face.

The last stage in his recuperation was Dr Reuter's idea. Schumann had taken to Dr Reuter. The man was more a friend than a physician these days and besides, Robert had no need of medicine. He was sure of that. He took Reuter for a drink at the Coffeebaum and explained it all, and Reuter didn't even blink.

Very well, he said, genial as ever. You don't need medicine. Perhaps what you need — he laughed to seal their closeness — is a wife. Wives, I am told, cure all sorts of things.

His exact words — *what you need is a wife*. Well, then! Robert thought and thought, and saw no reason why this shouldn't be true. Full of it, he went to his old friend Wieck and told him too. Wieck's reaction was immediate. He sent his daughter to Dresden. Urgent study, he said, packing her bags himself for quickness, her harmony teacher insists. Ernestine, the boarder not long arrived from Asch, was sad to see Clara go, and so quickly. Only a few days before she had pinned feathers in the younger girl's hair, dabbed her neck and non-existent bosom with rose-water. In return, Clara had muttered confidences. *I like Schumann best of all our acquaintances*, her eyes earnest as a nun's. No one else in Leipzig made Ernestine feel more trusted, more worldly wise than Clara. For Ernestine, a girl separated from her family for the first time, alone in this town, this had been a treasurable thing. Now, seeing her little friend away on a coach journey that would last Lordknew how long, Ernestine's composure broke. She wept. She wept right down to the bile. Fortunately, Schumann had a handkerchief. A plain one, but the baron's daughter was grateful nonetheless. When the coachman snapped his reins, Robert blew Clara a kiss. Wieck drew himself to his full height. Years after, unimaginable stretches of time gone past, Clara would still recall the drench of loss that filled her. Ernestine, seventeen, big-breasted, pitifully naive, promised to write.

※

It was fostered, of course.

The Voigts, the Caruses, Lordknew who else, tinkering lightly in other people's lives. When Clara returned, briefly, for the christening of her new sister, the changes were plain enough: Schumann sporting a rake's moustache, refusing to find it even mildly amusing, Ernestine was cool as a herring. They played duets now, her father told her, spent whole evenings together practising. Behind her father's back, she saw Schumann fetch her former friend a glass, their fingers touching on its crystal stem. Estrella, he called her. *Estrella*. Everyone had seen it coming. Even Schunke, dying on a couch in the Voigts' back room, his vision restricted to four walls and a diet of minced liver, saw it coming. Everyone save Clara. By the time Baron von Fricken arrived asking after his daughter – rumours had reached him as far as Asch – she was undeniably part of a pair. Shock made Clara stupid. How did one treat the *betrothed*? Was that what they were? What had she said that was foolish, not knowing? Pains in her stomach kept her awake.

Back in Dresden, holed up with the Serres in their rambling house in Maxen, a place that might as well have been the end of the earth, she tore through her lessons like a fire in a rush field. She walked. She planned choruses, *études*, a whole concerto in her head. She sight-read Bach till there was none left to sight-read, razed Beethoven to the bone. When Ernestine and the Baron left Leipzig, *Herr Enthusiast* with them, she wasn't sorry. The time for stories, chases and childish pursuits was past, would not come back. One grew, it hurt; this was how things were.

112

Herr Banck, the singing teacher, turned up repeatedly at the door and her father did not send him away. She had better, she thought, get used to it. In Magdeburg she bought a brooch and a new pair of shiny earrings; in Halberstadt she opened a ball in a bare-shouldered gown; in Brunswick each Müller in the Müller quartet thought her a charmer and by Hannover the most handsome of the four declared himself in love. Quartets were too much trouble, grumbled Wieck; they could manage the other concerts alone. Through Bremen, through Hamburg, he could not get her out of bed till after daybreak, found her tastes in hairdressing tending towards the coquettish. She asked for new dress trimmings, better pianos, her laces to be done tight. Very tight. She spoke back. *No. He heard her himself. I have played already today. I am indisposed. No.*

His hair greyer, his strength unequal to his indignation, Wieck took stock. So far, this tour had yielded stuck pedals, stupid audiences, stupider critics, the recalcitrance of his own flesh and blood and less cash than it should have. And Berlin was still to come. Enough, dear God, enough. He couldn't face Berlin. With the exception of his first wife, who could? Spring was coming. He wanted Easter cakes and linden blossom, a walk through the Rosenthal. He cancelled Berlin and dragged his daughter to the coach station knowing exactly what he wanted: Berlin to go to hell, tickets for Leipzig, his own life back. He wanted home.

Back at their own front door, the first thing they found was Schumann, pacing back and forth on the top doorstep, as though he'd been waiting there all along. Without his ridiculous moustache and without Ernestine, he looked much more like himself. These new pieces were finished, he said, bright as a flower. Also he had bought up all the shares in the newspaper so it would be run *properly*, ie by himself. He was – he said it with some satisfaction, keeping his eye on Wieck as he did it – the sole editor and publisher of the *Neue Zeitschrift für Musik*. A businessman, Wieck said, prepared to be mildly impressed, and the boy agreed. He had even been on business trips, to talk *money*, with his brothers in Zwickau, on which subject his mama sent greetings to the esteemed Herr Wieck and hoped to be remembered. Everyone sent greetings, everyone – not already here. He didn't mention Ernestine by name. He didn't allude to her or give any indication she had ever existed. Asch,

Clementine whispered between clenched teeth. After their – disagreement she went back to Asch. Whatever the story, it would have to wait. Schumann left no gaps in his conversation for it to be otherwise.

Listening, lifted by the tide of his enthusiasm, it took some time for Clara to realise there was no mention of Schunke either. Schunke, his Jonathan, his *dearest brother*. Don't ask, Clementine whispered, telling it anyway: a death rattle you could hear two streets away – she heard it herself. No wonder Schumann, his nerves the way they were, had stayed away. He stayed away *months*; Schunke's going was uncommonly – Frau Wieck chewed the word like a dough ball – slow. In the sitting room a vase of lilies dripped pollen on the window seat; the air was choking with the scent. Schumann, too brittle by half, talked only to Wieck who in turn talked only of his trials, his tribulations, how spoiled his daughter had become. When the Reverend Fechner, come for an unimaginable month, started on the subject of his gall bladder, Clara couldn't help herself. She wept. Great tears rolled down her face and she did not know why. Tiredness, said Clementine, ushering the girl to one side, patting her shoulder. Excitement after the tour, her awkward age. A good night's sleep would mend it. She turned to her husband, her face soft. It would pass, she said. Everything did. It would certainly pass.

❧═◦═❧

Carnaval.

Like the Papillons, but not. A higher kind of Papillons.
Jests on four notes. Look.

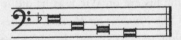

SCHA. All the playable letters of his name.

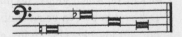

ASCH. Ahem. A town on the Bohemian border.

From these figures, everything else followed. Finally the Sphinxes

these not to be played but meditated upon. Seen and not heard. Silent music? Silent music, just so.

Here is Florestan,

and here is Eusebius.

Chopin. As though he is speaking to us. Make him limpid, the core of a shell. Chiarina — well! Chiarina is a force to be reckoned with. The rest she will see for herself. He will not say too much.

Did she see? She saw.

Préambule. Pierrot. Arlequin. Valse Noble.

Eusebius. Florestan. Coquette.

Réplique. Papillons.

ASCH – SCHA (Dancing Letters).

Chiarina. Chopin. Estrella.

Reconnaissance.

Pantalon et Colombine.

Valse Allemande/Paganini.

Aveu. Promenade.

Pause.

Marche des Davidsbündler contre les Philistins.

Chiarina came before Estrella, separated by a very slender Chopin. She certainly saw. All the same, nothing prepared her for their openness: these little pieces torn out of sheer joy, their trickery on the fingers, the grand, lumpen joy of the Grandfather's Dance that emerged from hiding inside the other folds. First things first, her father said. Fingering, dynamics, exact use of the pedal, then poetry. Herr Schumann has ideas but they — scatter. This is not so easy for the public to understand. They need grounding, solid earth under their feet. Provide it, Clara. Make these pieces into something whole and you will carry them anywhere, pieces for only you. Be the hands he no longer may rely upon and he will be grateful. He may come closer to us, offer something more. Wieck had his mind on more exclusive pieces, that little something extra with which to carve their names. He should have remembered his daughter was a more literal being altogether. Clara, he said, make something of him. Everything rests on you.

Mendelssohn arrived on the last day of August, caught Leipzig in full sun. Chopin, impeccably thin, a visitor to none if he could avoid it, paid a house call in October rains. Hiller played her waltzes for his own delight. Clara Wieck was a name. On her sixteenth birthday, a blue dress among black suits, she played, she sang, she even, one might say, sparkled. The Variations, a chorus and her first concerto composed and complete, why should she not sparkle, at least a little? Mendelssohn himself, the new Mozart, the new conductor at the Gewandhaus, cherished her like an old friend. When Hiller and Schumann sang to her, and in Mendelssohn's presence, she thought she would faint from sheer pride. Schumann, not caring who heard, called her his right hand, and so she was. He could not do without her. She was his friend, his confidante, his truest musical adviser. *Sometimes*, he said, and he meant it, she felt sure he meant it, *I forget where my thoughts end and yours begin.* And he danced with her, his footing somewhat awkward but willing, entirely willing. Two months later, on a smoke-skied November evening, in the dark glow of the lamp as she lit his way downstairs, he told her she resembled an angel: she was a gilded star among purple clouds, the most noble thing he knew.

She laughed, fleetingly, watching his face. It was, she realised, no joke. There he was in the door frame, black ghosts of trees and the stars as bright as pins behind his back. For a moment, with nothing to say or remark upon, neither of them moved. Shivering with cold, with something, he looked into her eyes. She noticed his height next to hers, the breadth of his shoulders, the man-smell of tobacco from his coat. His staring made her uneasy and oddly hot, almost dizzy. As he drew closer, closer still, her eyelids fluttered shut by instinct. *Fait accompli.* One week later, after a concert where her applause, her encores, did not stop for an hour, while her father fetched smelling salts for his mother, he kissed her again. This time she closed her eyes knowing why. His mouth was soft, like something melting over her; his jacket buttons rubbed against her breasts. Holding her upright, clinging, he told her he had never cared for any but his Clara; she was his equal in every way. And Ernestine? Ah! Ernestine was betrothed to another and had never really been his choice. This wasn't strictly true, but no matter. For now, there was only the moment, this secret, this. This.

That her mouth did not bruise, that this thrilling thing she had found did not show, amazed her. That people could look but not see. For two weeks this luscious, intimate trickery was almost a game. Now and again, Frau Wieck wondered aloud why Herr Schumann always stayed so late, why duets in the study so often turned silent. Frau Wieck was no fool. She said nothing till Schumann's special gift, a rope of pearls on crushed red velvet, arrived on Christmas Eve. Pearls, she said, catching her husband's eye, how extravagant! Some called them bridal beads, but this was voguish. Pearls – did they not? – meant tears. The young man was not to know, perhaps. But his gift meant tears. Wieck lifted them out of the case, held them up to the tree candles. Pearls, he said. He looked at Clara. She saw the Reissigers, the Kaskels, the Kragens, people with nice big houses somewhere else, register in his eyes; she heard the wheels in his head calculating baggage. Pearls meant Dresden. She could see it coming. Major Serre and Mrs Serre. The Maxen suburbs and Dresden, all over again.

Look. He loved her. He wanted the best for her.

She was sixteen, a child. Not allowed to choose her own dresses, never mind – this. She was an artist, a virtuosa, the realisation of the years of work, planning, spending and only now beginning to come into her own. To assist her to understand what this meant, Herr Schumann was forbidden access to the house and the intimacy of the house – was this clear? Clara watched the handful of letters she had dutifully given up consigned to the Serres' marble fireplace, Schumann's name silvering in the flame, his carefully chosen paper twisting and blackening to ash. It was very clear indeed. After a fortnight, Nanny brought news from Leipzig – Herr Schumann missed her; his doctor went round to do his washing or he'd not be clean; he got drunk and he pined – but news was not enough. After five weeks, Clara astonished herself. She sent him a note. Mark and do not forget – the note was her idea. Her father was leaving for three days. Come, she scribbled, ink blotting on the repeated entreaty, come. This arrived in his hand the same day as another, from Zwickau. His mother was dead, his brothers distraught. Come, they wrote, come. For once, he felt no indecision. His priorities were horribly clear. The funeral and the remnants of his sorrowing family were south. He took the first coach he could and headed into the sun. He headed east. For Dresden. Clara. Her.

Look. Given a choice between sure pain and possible comfort, which would you choose? Between duty and seizing the day? For years Clara's thoughts would return to it, be unable to understand his decision. His mother's funeral, dear Lord, yet he came to her. For years the guilt did not go away. Whatever drove him was bigger than himself, bigger even than duty. Then, he called it Destiny. He called it Fate. Fate's handmaidens, maids, friends and accomplices, slipped notes and coins; they dealt with the practicalities. Holed up with the Reissigers for guards, there was little Clara could do and Schumann was not a practical soul even at the best of times. Chaperoned by an accomplice, she went walking to the woods outside Maxen the same day her father left on his three-day mission and there he was, a mourning band on his arm, a razor burn on his cheek, turning purple in the cold and with someone Clara didn't know. Two third parties — it had its conveniences. They walked back together as four, but only two went up to Clara's rooms. Alone in this strange place, he took off his travelling coat but did not kiss her. Not immediately. He touched her face. His hands were frozen, she noticed, stiff and scarlet. He had brought her a gift — the poems of Burns bound in red morocco, some Schiller. Books, he said. Books, beer and a woman singing — that's what he would wish for the place he called home, and he had brought her the first part. He almost smiled. They sat on the sofa, close but without touching. Someone paced on the gravel outside, back and forth. When it died away he began to talk. He had a story to tell.

When he was small, he said, he imagined everything else was too. Nothing could be bigger than Zwickau, he thought. Then the soldiers came. He had no recollection of Napoleon, the Empress on a horse. But he remembered the soldiers, whole batallions of them, crowding the streets. He recalled blue jackets, yellow jackets, the crush of hats and boots, his whole hand enveloped in his mother's as she dragged him through the mass. Then someone pushed between them, he stumbled perhaps — and she was no longer there. His whole arm felt light with absence, his chest seized with fear. The legs of soldiers made a forest on every side and, when he looked up, all he saw was a crack of sky, as one might see from the bottom of a well. Three years old, motherless, what did he do? He ran. Maybe he thought to catch up with her or maybe he panicked — who can say? At any rate, that's what he did. He ran — straight into a mountain of stinking wool. Before his eyes the wool became a jacket, the jacket a man, the man a cripple. One sleeve was folded right up to the shoulder, slack from the nothingness inside. And above that, what was left of a face. Held together by a bandage the colour of cheese, there was half a jaw, half a nose, a gaping socket where an eye had been, puckered as a clam. If the other remained, he did not remember. Probably he ran again — he couldn't say for sure. Neither could he recall how mother and son were reunited; that they were was certain and that was what mattered, after all.

But for days after, he said, stumbling slightly on the words, even knowing he was in his own bed, he would wake from sleep with his heart pounding, see this face all over again. He would weep with pity, sweat with terror, wish he had held tighter to his mother's hand. Before long, however, his mother took ill. Distraction, she called it, morbidity. He was sent to Frau Ruppius till she was better. Frau Ruppius was kind enough, he said quickly. There was plenty to eat. But now when he woke in the night and found himself alone, he would climb up on the windowsill and look out. He had waited in his nightshift, looking out over the vista of Zwickau, and tried to make his mother come back by sheer dint of wanting it. Frau Ruppius, he said and she heard a smile in his voice, Frau Ruppius would find him in the mornings, damp to the collar. Maybe I cried a lot, he said. Children do.

Clara said nothing. There were things if only she could think of them, things someone wise might say. She could tell him about her own wakings as a child, the nameless terror that showed itself the same way. But it wasn't the time. She stroked his hair awkwardly instead. He didn't draw away. He leaned towards her, put his head in her lap. He seemed almost drowsy.

A house full of books, he said, you should have seen the books! Hamann. Herder and Voltaire. *Critique of Pure Reason* with a golden urn pressed into its leather spine. Shakespeare in English, German, French. Goethe and Jean-Paul. Lord, Clara, that you never had books!

He reached for her hand, kissed it again, again. He would give her books. He would give her everything of value he owned. He paused. He had other things to tell her too, things that . . . happened before. But they would come. They would tell each other their whole lives one day, take a whole life to do it. The only thing he could not give was a mother.

He was tilted, his face towards the fire then, and she felt a wetness on her fingers, however, as he kissed her palm. He was crying, but silently, almost imperceptibly. It tore at her heart to know it. His grief made no sound at all.

The loss of a parent is a terrible thing, he said eventually. But I lost my mother before. I lost her twice before. Now, somehow, she has come back. She has always come back.

Clara's neck prickled. She had never heard him speak like this before. She had never heard anyone speak like this before.

Something would come of all this, he said. Of herself, himself. They were particular people and their meeting was not chance. She would see.

Her father had not taken to things kindly, but he'd calm down. He'd remember their friendship, tighten up whatever screws had come loose and come round. He'd do right by them both, she'd see. And though his mother was gone, she — Chiarina — *she* was here.

The wool of his jacket pleated as he turned, the fibres twisting. His shoulder dug a hollow between her legs as he raised himself a little, looked up. He didn't smile, just looked, his jawline firm in the orange half-dark. She offered a wineglass with unsteady fingers, pressed it to his lips. She watched him swallow, the plumb line in his neck rise and fall before his cheek rested back on her lap. Could he feel the heat of her, her heartbeat pulsing?

I have a picture in my mind, Clara.

She said nothing, only closed her eyes, waiting. For some time there was only the sound of ashes sifting, embers cracking in the grate.

When he spoke again his voice was very soft. *I picture another Frau Schumann.*

His lips brushed the silk of her dress, burning a kiss through to her thigh. *Clärchen*, he said. Are you true?

If the Reissigers had returned there and then, if Napoleon himself had come back with an army, she would not have noticed. Nothing was bigger than this house, this room, their place within it. *Yes,* she whispered, the echo of it in her head sounding cavernous, immense. *Yes. Yes.*

Wieck found out, of course. He raged, of course. He raged for the next six years and one day at a time.

The first day, he raged like this:

Sophie Kaskel was an accomplice! The Reissigers were incompetent buffoons! Hanna, who had left in a wagon headed west ten years ago, was a slattern and the absent Marianne, Frau Bargiel, former-pianist-turned-wife of a sickly ivory tinkler in Prussia, was the source of all deceit and treachery! He raged at his sons, who for all their ingratitude had never done this. He raged at the deceased Frau Schumann, the deceased Herr Schumann; at his current wife in Leipzig for not anticipating; at the whole of Leipzig for aiding and abetting. Sophie Kaskel would go to the bad, the Reissigers could go to hell and the boy? Boy? A man of twenty-six! Rage was too good for him. He had a pistol, a *pistol* – his voice cracked on an accelerating crescendo – and he'd shoot him like a dog if he came near their house again! Did she understand? He'd shoot!

The second day, another tack. He was sore and his heart grieved, he said. He looked at the mantel. He had the justified anger and bewilderment of one who had always done his best and been betrayed. He was shaken to his soul. And what had done this? A daughter. He sighed. But then a daughter without duty was no daughter at all. Ponder this: a father who was ashamed to call his daughter his own. A daughter for whom he had provided everything, for whom he had given up ten years of his own life, yet a daughter who rose against him and against all his clearly expressed wishes when his back was turned. What would Clara Wieck make of such a daughter? What words would Clara Wieck use to describe her? Who had given Clara Wieck the education that enabled her to describe anything at all? *Ad infinitum* in the same vein.

The third day he said nothing much, merely radiated coldness like a black sun. Walking everywhere with her, even to the privy and back again; silent in spite of her best playing; insisting on childish exercises; cutting all Schumann from her repertoire; reading homilies from the Bible, from Rousseau, from Shakespeare, especially Shakespeare, on the subject of ingrate daughters, he implied the error of her ways.

The fourth day he demanded all the letters in her immediate possession. There would be no more, he promised. *No more.* The one she had carefully hidden, the best one, he ran to ground inside her sleeve. He read it. He read it out loud.

Zwickau Post Office, after 10 at night
I'm nearly asleep. I've been waiting for the express
mail coach for two hours. The roads are in such bad
shape I might not leave till 2 o'clock, they tell me. But
you stand before me, my beloved Clara, Oh! so close
I could touch you! I used to be able to describe my
deepest feelings for them with a bit of style, but I can't

any more. If you didn't know already how I feel, I wouldn't be able to tell you. Just love me a lot, you hear! I ask a lot because that's what I give – a lot. Today was very busy – my mother's will, accounts of how she died, all unbearable. Your radiant image shines through all this darkness though, and helps me see it through. I can also tell you my future is looking more secure. I won't be wasting any time – I've a lot to achieve before I'll be able to see what you can see every day just looking in the mirror. Meanwhile you'll want to keep on being an artist – I mean you will carry your own weight, work with me as well as share my griefs and joys. Write to me about that.

Anyway, I've decided on a plan. The first thing I have to do when I get back to Leipzig is to knock my practical affairs into shape (I've already sorted out the emotional affairs, I think – your father can hardly refuse when I ask his blessing) then tackle my career, whatever that's set to be.

Meanwhile I'm trusting in our guardian angel, for we have one. We surely do! Fate means us for each other – I've known that a long time now, but wasn't sure you'd laugh if I'd said so. Enough to say everything that's so broken into little pieces today will come clearer later. You probably can't even read this – the main thing is MY LOVE FOR YOU IS BEYOND WORDS. It's getting dark in here, passengers are sleeping right next to me. Outside, it's snowing, it's howling a gale. But I'll bed down in the corner, sink my head in a pillow and think – only of you. Farewell my Clara!

Your Robert

He read out every word, articulating each as though it belonged to a foreign language, then kept the lot. She had imagined him making another ritual pyre; that he didn't was his masterstroke. Now she would think of him scrutinising them at his leisure, picking over every tenderness, every imagined intimacy again, again. It was, she thought foolishly, the worst day of her life. Alone in her room, for no reason she could think of, Clara tried to picture her mother. Not Clementine, her mother. Mother was a woman with brown hair. Reddish perhaps. Light ash. She had blue eyes or hazel, possibly grey. They had a violet cast. She had high colour, sallow skin, was as pale as a candle and her ears were pierced. Or not. It seemed suddenly important, wholly impossible. She couldn't remember her mother's face.

The fifth day? He took it from the top.

Day One. *Da capo*. All over again.

✦

Dresden	No letters
Gorlitz	No notes
Breslau	She carved, pencilled, inked his name on thin air

What did she do? She composed to keep her head from hurting, pieces not like Schumann's, not like Chopin's, like — like no one else's. For company she took extra singing lessons, exercises in orchestration. She put her faith in the biding of time. God loved patience. She knew it for a fact. She played. She played.

What did he do? Ah! At first he refused to believe it. He got drunk, he languished, he clung to his landlady who gave him a rent cut and a beer. He clung to the prose of Jean-Paul and the poetry of Schiller. He clung to Christel who clung back till both had mild abrasions. Then he found the ink. He wrote. He sent no letters but he wrote a great deal. A sonata, *To Clara from Florestan and Eusebius*, was delivered to the Wiecks' front door in May. A sonata made of five notes falling. C-L-A-R-A. Forwards and backwards and buckled into distant shapes, turned on its head and still plain as day. C-L-A-R-A. Let the pages fall at random, glance even for a moment and there it was — C-L-A-R-A — pulsing through the music like vesicles through meat.

Wieck took one look and fetched the letters he'd been hoarding since Dresden. He asked his daughter to hold them and went to her room. He emptied a little carved box with a painted pastoral scene, another stuck with Rhine pebbles. He emptied the middle drawer of her desk. He riffled the pages of her manuscript books and shook her clothes. For good measure, he raked through her linen and under the soap. He had no need to do these things, only to ask, but he did them all the same. Over two hours he rounded up every scrap of paper over which Schumann's fingers had traced, every fragment that ever called her *Dear*, every letter and seal, and sent them back, on the spot and without explanation. Schumann, he felt, would catch his drift. If he thought it his daughter's drift too, so much the better.

Schumann received them later the same afternoon. He had expected acknowledgement of some kind, but the return of his own handwriting took him by surprise. He tipped the porter, since Wieck had not, put the letters where he wouldn't see them and went out. Banck was welcome at her house. He taught her singing, it seemed. *Singing.* He stayed out till he found Christel. He asked her to sing Schubert, then he wept into her hair and fucked her till he passed out. Days running, he woke to the same headache, the same reek of spilled beer, sex and nicotine, the same sense of déjà vu. Only one thing could be worse than this, he thought, reaching for something to retch into, and that was knowing it would happen again tomorrow. His head felt sliced. He stood, stumbled, caught hold of the edge of his chair. Papers fell on the floor. This time, he picked them up. His fingers shook. He watched them till they stopped, then made coffee, very black, drank two sobering cups. Then he went back to his piano. He recharged his pen. C-L-A-R-A he wrote.

C-L-A-R-A He had work to do. C-L-A-R-A Another piece to write. C-L-A-R-A Another, another. C-L-A-R-A Pieces stuffed with her C-L-A-R-A alive with her C-L-A-R-A roaring her na

me

The snow came early. Her father bought her a muffler and a wool-lined bonnet, silk underthings. They'd pack easily and the north, he believed, was always cooler. In Naumburg the roads were sheet ice. She almost slid under a set of moving coach wheels and took the stage an hour later, healthy as a cabbage. In Jena she premièred her new concerto, the ink barely dry on its finale. She had, Wieck boasted, no fear. What's more, the public liked her. Herr Banck liked her too. Carl, her father called him. *My boy.* By Weimar, Banck liked her too much and was sent packing. He turned up again in the new year, sprouting sideburns, flashy cuff studs. Mendelssohn turned up too, a fiancée who looked like a baby in tow, and all five went walking in the Rosenthal. Banck walked too near, her father some few feet ahead with the couple, laughing a good deal. After half an hour, Clara stopped at the side of the road to stamp snow from her boots, waiting till they went on without her. She watched him go, counting seconds, clattering her heels like a Spaniard. The snow would not budge. It swallowed the soles and tips of her boots and, despite her new gloves, she stooped instinctively to dig it off. Ice flaked on to her green velvet fingers, burrowed into the pile like rock salt. The elegant seams down the sides of her hands begin to seep. She stopped, then, looked out over the place that should be the Rosenthal and was now only whiteness. Bleached blankets for miles and still falling. If she kneeled here, waited long enough, the snow would cover her along with everything else. She had heard of it happening, beggars fallen in gutters by night who died and were buried by winter, not found till spring, their faces dark as pig's liver. These drifts at the side of the path, crusted with blue ice, ice that would crack at the lightest touch, could do it already. She reached out one hand, felt the carapace brittling under her fingers. She pressed again, through to the hidden cache of powder. Again, till her hand was sunk in snow up to the wrist. She held it there, letting the cold burn and her whole skin surface shiver. Instinctively, her fist closed, tightened on numbness. It soothed her, this grip; it gritted her jaw. Only when the cold was unbearable did she withdraw, the rim of her sleeve spangled white as christening cake. The glove was ruined, of course; her father's

Christmas gift, his money, so much stiff, spoiled cloth. What if – she felt her face flush – what if she threw them away? For one glorious moment she imagined them, hurling off like so much boiled kale, the graceless arc they would make over the solid lake. One moment. And when the moment was done, she felt the dead ache in her hands. Her knuckles were lilac, beginning to swell. She was to play this afternoon. For this, at least, she might be missed. On the path behind her the light was dimming, the dark shapes of her companions already disappearing behind the trees. Before anyone turned back, saw her idling here, thinking nothing and thinking it too much, she gathered her skirts in her soaking hands and shifted one foot at a time out of the snow. She gathered herself together and ran.

In the event, they were not far ahead and no one had missed her at all. Mendelssohn and her father were discussing concert programmes, while Banck talked to himself in the direction of the affianced Mlle Jeanrenaud. Mlle Jeanrenaud was not a musician. This much Clara knew already. Mlle Jenrenaud was not anything but a Protestant and pretty. And fifteen. Clara had worked out the numbers and knew it for a fact. Mlle Jenrenaud was fifteen.

The *Appassionata*, Mendelssohn said. Clara has played enough box office. Let the Berliners hear Beethoven; some Bach, Chopin, Henselt. The *Songs without Words*; I will give her a personal copy if she will promise to make me sound grand and she will. I am told she plays them better than me.

Mlle Jeanrenaud laughed. A pretty laugh. It plumed in the cold air like thistledown. Lord, Felix! she said. Such a serious programme – and for a young woman! So much competence will only frighten young men away! She turned to look at Clara, freshly arrived from Lordknew where. What do you say, Fräulein Wieck? With this pretty face, surely you don't want to frighten the young men away?

Clara felt hot and cold at once, wishing the ice beneath her feet would part and drown her, take her away from this terrible embarrassment. But Clara, thank the Lord, didn't need to open her mouth. Wieck stretched some three inches taller and did it for her.

Mademoiselle, he said, he said it as though the word were the name of a hideous disease; you forget whom you address. This is Clara Wieck. His eyes narrowed. This young woman can carry a load that would fell a carthorse and needs no consideration to the contrary. My daughter is an artist, Mademoiselle, not a woman of any sort. I tell you that you may remember. Pray that you do.

The two-mile trek home was all crunching snow, the sound of breath through woollen mufflers. Wieck, Clara, Banck and, some way behind, Mendelssohn and his bride-to-be, muttering, almost amused, to each other. But then, silent walking for Clara was nothing new. All the way, keeping her wet gloves out of sight, Clara picked over Mlle Jeanrenaud's words, wondered at their meaning. Why should good music frighten young men away? Banck sniffing like a tap, her hands singing with pain to the bone, a question that would not, would never, let her be.

⋘◉⋙

Berlin – ha! Berlin was a sink!

Its people were arrogant, insolent and snobbish; its officials were crooks; its reviewers jealous and its hall fees scandalous. And they thought themselves famous for wit! Berlin had wit as human beings had infections, without redeeming effect. Further, its hotels were overpriced and its food not worth the effort of mastication. He wheeled her before its public nonetheless and watched them cheer. For *Glorious Clara* they'd queue two days for tickets, clap till their hands were sore. Everyone loved her, except idiots who thought Beethoven was boring, and Bettina von Arnim. *How pretentiously she seats herself at the piano, showing off without the music on the stand!* Von Arnim said, her head sprouting ostrich feathers. *Her forehead will distend, puffed up from inside with notes. Döhler would never be so vulgar.* Then Döhler was a man and no threat. The most famous woman in Europe, her father crowed, the great Bettina von Arnim, whose talent for poetry was finished, who no longer bedded famous men, who had no musical sense and a face like an arsehole, was jealous – that was the simple truth. His daughter was a *triumph. He* was a triumph. Their enemies were smashed, Berlin was a gold mine, and Bettina von Arnim –

he laughed — *the most famous woman in Europe* — was afraid of little Clara Wieck.

The first free day he took her walking. Wear your best, he said, the expensive stuff, then he walked her for miles. The place was full of book-shops, even more than in Leipzig and Leipzig was stuffed. Everything else was street sellers, markets and hawkers, beggars and hurdy-gurdy men with dogs on ropes, starving farmworkers wondering why they came to the city at all. People; the place was choking with people. Even walking down the river's-breadth avenue of the Kurfürstendamm, there was no room for everyone. People pushed. They shoved and elbowed total strangers. They hooted with laughter at nothing. These are Prussians, her father said. Only observe. Observing as best she might, she trailed his steps to piano workshops and sheet-music suppliers till her feet were tired, then walked some more, past a lane of pretty lime trees, into a more cluttered series of backstreets and twisting alleyways. Beyond this, another great thoroughfare hove into view and Friedrich sighed. He took both of them to a house directly on the main street with horses reeking outside, children running, a garden box in the window with skinny shoots struggling through the dirt. She stood at the stepless front door, dressed like a prize pig, till he beat it with his stick — twice — and it opened.

Frau Bargiel's hair was auburn. Streaked with grey, but auburn.

Of course it was.

Her eyes were dark and deep-set and, Clara realised with a shock, level with her own. They were the same height. She and this woman who was her mother — the same height. Herr Bargiel, too — a tree of a man in her mind — was no taller than Papa. And how thin! The half-brothers she had never seen shook her hand. No one cried when she played, which was a blessing, but when she left Frau Bargiel — her mother, it took active remembering, her *mother* — clasped her hands. Clara saw the same patterns of muscle, the same risen veins from scales and studies, encasing her own. We are alike, she thought, exactly alike. A taste like flowers filled her mouth as they stood there, waiting at the door, a taste Clara could not identify till her mother kissed her cheek. Elderflower. Her mother's kiss tasted of elderflower. If Wieck shared this recollection with his daughter he didn't say. That woman's voice, he said as they walked back, is becoming shrill. That is what querulousness does: it toughens the female vocal chords. He checked the top button of his daughter's coat to keep her warm, reminded her cancellations were costly. This might be a short trip but they were here to earn, after all.

In Hamburg she earned a good deal but ate plain. Rich food fudged the mind, he said; a touch of hunger kept one sharp. By Hannover she lost her appetite completely. In Brawnschweig, after less applause than usual, she developed restless sleep and took to lying in. The Picture of Indolence, he called her, waking her well after seven. You can't get out of bed without me. Reviews were glowing but not reprinted back in Leipzig and it dampened his spirit. He wanted them to know. If Schumann couldn't oblige, what use was his wonderful *Neue Zeitschrift*? His sole editorship? What use at all?

As the carriage rocked from ditch to ditch on the way home he found the answer. Two consecutive editions, not one, carried mentions of Clara Wieck, Schumann's prose style all over them if not his name. The first was a review. Her concerto, it said – it said it in clipped typeface, neatly set – could certainly be mentioned but could hardly be the subject of serious criticism. It was, after all, the work of a lady, *ahem*. The other paper held worse: a caricature, a lady pianist accompanied by a side-whiskered singing-teacher in fancy cuff studs. The man was clearly a fool and the lady pianist sweated like a stallion, read the caption; moreover, she was a clear harpy of ambition and pride, all of which led one to the conclusion that at best this lady was sexless, but more probably she was, in fact, *a man*. She read it twice, wondering what had possessed him. This so-called review was spite and deliberate cruelty and – it had to be a mistake. She was beginning over again when her father directed her attention to look outside. A couple, a woman and a man, were waiting ahead on the grass verge. Clementine and a young man in a yellow coat. She peered at them with her heart choking till she saw the sideburns, the dark hair. It was Banck, Banck and her stepmother come to welcome them home. *My dear Clara*, he said, helping her down. *How welcome you are in Leipzig! The whole town has been reading about your triumph!*

When he grasped her waist firmly and smiled, a generous, wholehearted smile, the pressure in her chest would contain itself no longer. She fell on his breast, his saffron velvet lapels, and wept. And wept. And wept.

Whatever they say in books, love needs allies. Two against the world – even when the two are mother and child – is of short-lived allure. Love needs nurture as a plant does or it stunts, it goes off the path, is prone to chance and accident, malevolent intent. It needs family, sworn-to-silence maidservants, confidantes and sympathisers. It needs signals and codes, snatched glimpses and hopeful journeys, courage, tears and terrible tests. It needs reflection. Action. Contact. The slightest sober reflection will tell you, and Clara, it should be said, had a talent for sobriety. Schumann, however, had not. Headstrong, keen to learn the hard way, he had read *Romeo and Juliet* and understood Juliet not at all. She had not enough fire, he was fond of saying, too little of impulse. Romeo's impulsiveness killed them both, quite, quite, but that Romeo was a poet and a hero to the last absolved all. Nonsense, of course, but people drew to him in any case, offered to feed him up and smooth his lovelorn brow. He had the charm of the dazed, the bewildered, the withdrawn, and when he didn't have that he had the charm of talent, intensity, daring. He had people on his side. He had his sister-in-law, Thérèse; his female enthusiasts, who variously thought him a Dreamer, a Dark Horse, a Sweet and Studious Sort who needed Understanding or Mothering, depending on their age. He had Berger and Lipinski, and a string of other come-and-go friends thought him a Fine Fellow and Becker, the magistrate, who thought him a Genius and Noble Heart. He had his reviewers, his publisher and a good barman, and nobody cared what they thought but they were there. He had Mendelssohn, *Felix Meritis*, the most genial of men; a talent so luminous he betrayed no flaws, whose orchestra worshipped him in common with every concert goer who saw him, heard him, watched him conduct, and a man like *that* for his friend, that alone said something.

Mendelssohn, however, could walk about the city with the woman of his choice on his arm. Chopin was prone to influenza and his lungs were frail, but he could play his own work with his own hands. And either, not needing her, not wishing to do more than exchange pleasantries, could visit Clara Wieck. Everyone but him, specifically not him, could hear her play, let their eyes linger on her neck, her fingers, hear her sing. His chest constricted when he thought about it, Banck, her so-called singing teacher, touching her, urging her to flow from the diaphragm, asking her to pucker her mouth into an O. One night he tried to write her a letter, filled with beautiful thoughts, but the words began melting, letters first, then whole lines, sliding off the page, seeping into the dust, not dust but earth under his feet. Graveyard, he thought, I am in a graveyard yet it was full of people, and most of them he knew. When his mother walked towards him from behind the curtain he woke, bolt upright and freezing, his room ringing with absence. For a long moment he knew only that he was afraid.

Then he stood up. Asleep at his desk, he had cramped his limbs, his back hurt when he walked. For fresh air, to revive himself, for something to do, he opened his shutters, crunched his eyes against the early light. The clouds were pregnant with coming snow, the trees scrawny, the street a long way down. No people. He might, he thought, be anywhere at all. He opened the glass panelling then, let the cold soothe his eyes. Horses in the far field snorted dragon breath, pawing at the frozen ground. A first flake of snow fell against his cheek and he did not brush it away. If he stood there long enough, he thought, peering into the grainy distance, he might see her house. If he tried harder, he'd see as far as Connewitz where they had gone walking. As far as Zwickau, where he had been a child, Zwickau and its terrible river, where last he had seen his sister clothed in little more than water. He had not thought of his sister for years. At that moment, he not only thought of her, he saw her. Long-dead Emilie Schumann, the set of whose features he had all but forgotten, was looking up at him from the gutter under his window, her face full and white as the moon. When he looked again, though, it was only himself. Himself, a reflection in the still puddles, the granite-crushing street below. I will not be mad, he said. He said it aloud. Not mad.

Reuter arrived some time after ten. He had been doing Schumann's laundry. Someone had to. He came upstairs with his arms full and the door was not locked. The bed was dishevelled, books strewn on the floor, Schumann himself inside his window arch, rigid as a splint, staring up at the falling snow. The doctor placed the folded cloth on the nearest chair, gently, soundlessly. And waited. After a moment the figure at the window spoke. *I have made up my mind*, he said. His voice was soft but calm, quite calm. When he turned, his waistcoat covered with melting spangles, whole beads of melted ice; his face was grey. *I will cut her out like a sore. A sore.* He closed the window himself. When given, he folded his frozen fingers round a cup of warmed wine and sugar. He drank. Reuter did nothing but sit with him, not talking. The stillness, it seemed, was significant. At noon, Reuter went out and returned with rolls, coffee, fresh meat. Only he ate. Robert sat where he sat for the rest of the day.

Was it logical? Think it through. Weather clears, colds mend. Sit some things out and they pass. But others sit like a stone in the heart and do not move. Either you learn to put up with a stone in the heart, or – and this was not easy – or you plucked it out. Putting up was not in his nature. Upsetting facts, situations, people – how could one put this? – upset him. He'd lasted and his lasting had yielded no reward. Now, for his own sanity, this infatuation for Clara, for *Mademoiselle Wieck*, was over, finished, behind him and if manufacturing a spite against her helped him do it, that's what he'd do. She was heartless and had done terrible things, even if he couldn't say offhand what they were. Even if they changed every time he told the tale. Herr Banck could have her, he said, and he meant it. He meant every word for exactly as long as it took to say them. Then, three days later, Banck left Leipzig: Wieck had ordered him off his premises, they said, told him never to come back and he had offered no resistance. Typical of him, Schumann thought; true or not, it was typical of that worm Banck to leave without a fight. He walked for miles thinking it, then went back to his rooms and slept like a beast, his head and heart completely untroubled.

After three days he woke, refreshed. His head was ringing with sound. He washed, combed his hair, dressed in his fanciest things and lit a cheroot. He went to his piano. Florestan and Eusebius, he thought. He took a deep drag, examined his cigar end. Fire and Light! He picked up a quill. C-L-A-R-A, he wrote. No blots. C-L-A-R-A. Whatever was dawning on the page, it was beautiful. All he had to do was let it come. That afternoon, Becker interrupted to give him news. Clara would play Schumann at her next concert! Programmed it herself and the Old Man hadn't thrown it out. She had *insisted*. What's more, she wanted her letters back. Becker had come from her directly to get them: every sheet her father seized and returned to sender – did he understand? She wanted them back!

Robert put down his pen. He looked at Becker and lit another cigar. He blew a smoke-ring, then gave his answer.

No, he said. Tell her – tell her one may not have what one has already given up. But tell her – tell her she may have new ones. I will write to her afresh. There and then, he sent Becker for flowers and checked his calendar. Aurora's Day. Aurora's Day – a new dawn. God was sending messages and he heard every word! He'd write, and right now. After all this time, he felt justified. In seventeen months she had given him not one word – now that was what he asked. *Send one word, just one*, he wrote, *and that will be your confirmation. If you give it* – what? He paused long enough to refill his pen. If she gave it, he'd send a formal proposal of marriage with full assurances, financial statements, etc by return, straight to her father. Becker would help with the wording – Becker was good at wording. All he needed was this thing she had denied him for so long – one word. To hell with waiting. *One word*. He could hardly sit still. Her answer came next morning. Eusebius Day. He snapped the seal and there it was. Yes, in bold handwriting. He couldn't miss it. Yes. *Yes*. This time, he knew it, he felt it in his blood. This time the Old Man would not say no!

⊷⊶

He said no.

Not immediately. But thoroughly. So there would be no misunderstanding. Clara was already spoken for, he said. Art had spoken for her. Schumann would only make her unhappy, not intentionally, but completely nonetheless. Schumann had too little money, too much taste for champagne and cigars. Was it not a father's duty to protect his daughter from penury and unhappiness? Besides, her talent, her public. He had not raised a daughter to this pitch for her to play like a clock-work doll only for cliques of her husband's friends, for the applause of a few. On top of which, no real artist — Schumann considered himself an *artist*, did he not? — would wish upon the object of his love the obscurity which would undoubtedly follow their marriage. Schumann should not forget the extent of her fame, her solid, hard-won reputation; the standard of living she was entitled to expect, and as he had no fortune — well! It would be whispered Schumann had married Clara Wieck only for her money, which would place an intolerable strain on both parties. Further, Mendelssohn thought this union inadvisable. *Mendelssohn*, did Herr Schumann see? Further, Frau Wieck thought Herr Schumann shallow, labile and deceptive — and surely everyone knew that Clara secretly admired Herr Banck? Finally, she was too young. What did she know of love? Housewifery? The thousand upon thousand sacrifices that domesticity and motherhood entailed? No, this Schumann should find someone else, someone with less at stake, for his attentions, then Schumann would retain Wieck's respect. That should suffice. He was a man, was he not? He would take this to heart, this fatherly advice. Yes, Clara was in her room. She was composing. With a Russian pianist, a charming fellow. No Schumann might not leave a birthday gift. Schumann might not see her. Schumann might write, provided he understood that his letters would be read openly to the household. He might see her, of course — Wieck had no desire to hide his daughter in an ivory castle! — but he might see her in public places, for example, from the paying seats in the back row of a concert hall. Otherwise, Herr Schumann should keep his distance. The days of Herr Schumann's lodging here, of Clara's childhood, were over, was this plain? Herr Schumann's presence *upset* the household. His daughter needed all her concentration for her forthcoming tour, a *very serious tour* with implications for his daughter's career. Since Herr Schumann had never made a serious tour and his insight into these matters was limited, Wieck would be plain. Herr Schumann should Stay Away. He should Cultivate Absence. And he should begin now. Wieck wished him good luck and good day, and did not call for Lise to show him out. When the young man did not move, Wieck looked him straight in the eye, a dead shot, a duellist. *Goodnight, Herr Schumann,* he said quietly. *Goodnight.*

⋆⇒◎⇐⋆

What did she do?

She wrung her hands, talked of love to the Old Man, begged to be understood. Pah! Had she no fire? No fight? He wanted a girl in armour, someone to *defend him.* Instead she fretted, conversed with brick walls, told him to wait. Ten years her senior, a man with shoulders as square as an accordion, he did not know what to do. He lasted a month, meeting her in anguished, heart-thumping secret, then his patience snapped. Furious, he turned up under Wieck's nose at the Gewandhaus. He wore a red coat, a signal from the back of any hall, a bright, stuck smile. Her last concert in Leipzig before Wieck dragged her off again, and how long would he have to wait this time? Six months? A year? They had exchanged secret rings, he was her betrothed — he had a right to see her! That night, everyone did — everyone who bought a ticket, at least. The hall was stuffed. And when she appeared, smothered in white silk, some fancy new dress he had never seen before, he loosened his collar to try to keep his face composed. Like dying, he thought, like drowning and trying not to let it show. This woman he had held in his arms yesterday for five minutes, maybe ten, Nanny patrolling the end of the street in case anyone came, this *vision* stood before him as she stood before everyone else. She was herself and not herself, near and far, for him and not him, and the faces around him seemed to know. *Let them see,* he thought, rising to his full height, *let them.* But he blushed for some nameless shame despite himself, and looked up again only when the hush fell, the two great ranks of the Gewandhaus quieting down to a ripple of fans, a solitary cough.

And she played, Lord how she played! Love agreed with her. It filled out her playing, opened it into something wide, ripe, warm. Had he not been such a musician, he might have thought she played only to him. But

he knew too much. That's the trick of Art, he thought – to offer intimacies to a roomful of strangers. Play well, play like *this*, and every clot in
the audience thinks it speaks only to them. He could see them thinking
it. Po-faced Leipzigers, people who would not turn a hair for Chopin,
who called that magnificent pianism *somewhat thin*, clapped and bayed like
moonstruck mutts; they stood. He watched her eyes scan the crowd, pick
him out, move on. She wore pearls in her ears, white combs. Afterwards
she wrote in her secret diary. *I felt nothing*, her own words, *I felt dead inside*
– and he believed her. Yet he recalled her face that night, its momentary
pause just for him. Then its turning again to the crowd, acknowledging
the applause, and the shine in her eyes. She was two people his Chiara,
Chiarina. Maybe more than two. It occurred to him, then, occurred as
no more than a passing observation, that he hardly knew her. She had
become a woman, someone who was learning to experience pain and not
show it. A woman with sweat on her breastbone, who performed physical work before the public gaze. A woman – he heard them saying it as
they left the hall – *a woman with a soul as great as a man's.*

He walked home alone, locked the door, lit a lamp and turned the
flame low. His head was ringing. He opened his writing desk and picked
up a handful of letters, some spattered with seal. *What good would riches be
to me with a broken heart* flipped open as it fluttered to the floor, its single
page wide. *Forgive him for my sake . . .* he read as it fell. *This pain has attacked
the foundations of* – next, folding under itself.

> *May God Almighty whisper to you what I feel so ardently but –*
> *Nanny will bring it –*
> *For God's sake be careful! I am*
> *nothing but a poor, weak girl but steadfast*
> *until*
> *how greatly I love you!*
> *death*

         – one after another,
like petals between his fingers, his rug thickening with words. Prague and
Vienna, he thought. Six months. At least six months, this empty space

he felt when he thought of it, growing all the time. One last letter, flat as a coin, had dropped on to the desktop. He picked it up, balanced it in his hand, then opened it one fold at a time, like a medicine paper. *I've promised my father to be cheerful and devote a few more years to music and the World. Could your love ever falter? If so, you would have broken a heart that loves only once.* One day, he thought, one day sheer rage would break him clean in two.

FOUR

Der Ring

The Ring

$\mathcal{T}$his journey between Leipzig and Dresden, the autumn light on the Elbe.

Every tour begins here.

She knows the ruts and bends in the road, every sign and stile. He will not say how long they are going for, how many concerts he expects her to play, but he has told her to be cheerful. You are eighteen, he says. Eighteen. What do you know? The carriage rocks under the shade of red trees, out again. Since Bitterfeld the carriage has been theirs alone. Nanny, sitting silent with the travel keyboard on her lap, father with a trunk under his seat. What is your one skill, one talent? And who gave you that, child? Her carpet bag is full of programmes, a draft list of fees, city plans. Are you to bury your art now? he says. You would only weep, he says. Think of your gifts. Put them first. Be cheerful. And she tries. She does. What she feels, however, clattering over stones and dust tracks that become more Bohemian by the mile, is not cheer. Not sorrow or even irritation. What she feels is nothing at all.

Nothing? Come now. In Prague?

There are domes in that city to rival the sky. October chill hugs the river and the lamps on its bridges look like stars trapped in wedding veils, ghost shapes in glass. She has never seen so many marionettes, so many houses painted green, blue, sugar-pink. She has never heard such Mozart or eaten such dumplings. She has never, never taken so many curtain calls. *More than Paganini,* her father crows, counting every one, *more than any man in this city!* No feeling at all? It seems improbable, certainly, but then again what *is* probable about performers, their preoccupation, this thing they do?

Cellists raddled with rheumatoid, gastric, or mental fever may still render melodies with the sweetest, most joyful expression. Tenors have haemorrhaged to death behind handkerchiefs rather than quit the stage, sopranos executed flawless *bel canto* at the funerals of their children. *Let the orchestra stay together, let the piece sound rehearsed enough, let my tuning hold, my nerve not fail, my wig stay put. Let me not think too much. Let me render this music as I hear it — have always heard it — in the dark secret space of my own head, beautiful and without taint and above all, dear God, Let Me Not Fail.* In the last-moment prayers of performers, *feelings* only interfere. Hours into years of practice, solitude and repetition, war with tedium and physical limitation made to look like grace, elegance, ease — what use is feeling to that? What are they after, these performers and liveried few? This relentless determination to sublimate a life — what drives it? Music? Yes, music of course, *music*, but more than the comfort or communion that is music as most understand it, more than music in its ingenuous, embraceable form. Beyond the domestic, beyond the possible, almost, *this* music, the language of the concert hall and its terrifying show, demands all. Is it a desire to conquer or the desire to serve? A requirement to display or hide? Is its impulse born of sensitivity or instability? Is it merely an outlet for the incurably vain and overreaching? Is it some form of love? Is it driven by the imperative of making a living or supreme disregard for same? Is it simple lack of talent in any other direction? Does it matter?

Not to Clara. Before now, it never occurred to her to wonder *why* one played, one simply did. One still does, of course, but now she learns something new. It lends power, this thing she can do. People *admire* it. And through the notes, on something else's behalf, she may feel anything she likes. She may feel rage and wonder and soul-grinding sorrow; pleasure and peace, and it's all much the same, for this thing she can do turns feeling into something else. Fuel, perhaps, the drive to play to a pitch of perfection and keep going. Her stride grows more purposeful. Her back is straighter, her mouth firmer, her gaze more fixed. Sitting at the keys in a swath of white silk she looks as incorruptible as steel.

Wieck sees it, too, the square set of her jaw, and because he is not as far-seeing as he fancies, he rejoices. The advance of the Swedish army on to the platform wouldn't break that concentration, he thinks, just listen! They called her *poetic* once, *Poetry Itself. A Story woven out of Joy and Pain*, whatever that meant. They remarked on her strength — *six boys' worth*

– and in that they did not lie. Now she is all that and something else too, something so rapt, so tenacious, that even the back row of the stalls feel it bristling their necks. *Passionate*, they say. *Passionate. Full of striving and moment and nobility of soul.* Wieck hears them and likes the *moment* part. He likes *striving* and *nobility* too. As for the other thing, that is because she plays Tomaschek. Bohemians, he thinks, they find Tomaschek *passionate* no matter who plays it. But the saying goes on and her playing is roomy as the sea. Men follow her, sniff around their hotel rooms even when her father is in. They send gifts and carriages, sweets. And for all they find her smaller, almost childlike in the flesh, they will not leave her alone.

Her father lets them lounge in the hired parlour, even dine with her, and when they are gone he dictates accounts. He warns her against spendthrifts, indecisive sorts and hypochondriacs; that a woman with a growing reputation must beware of men without much notion of – he pauses, flicks dandruff from his lapel – *honour*. Men, he continues (leafing her notebooks for hidden letters, something in code) men who pursue barons' daughters till they find they may not inherit then – *pfft!* (he shrugs like an actor playing Shylock and raises his brows) turn their attentions elsewhere. Consider carefully, Clara, he whispers, his stubble grating her cheek. Disinheritance is something which disinclines Herr Schumann. His voice is smoke. *I will disincline Herr Schumann how I must.* When she leaves the room he follows, snapping at her heels. He will bury your playing! he roars as she closes her bedroom door. Even without conscious effort! He will burden you with financial cares and ruin all my hopes! He rattles the handle, furious at the sound of her turning a lock. He will foist children upon you! Make you nothing more than a breeding cow! And what then, lady? Without a penny from me, what then?

She has no peace. When she is asleep, his voice cuts through, picking at what wounds it can find; if she wakes, it's there still, rising up through the invariably thin boards. *I know when she is writing*, she hears, lying in her nightdress, trembling. *Deliver letters after the manner of an Italian play, Nanny, letters I have not read with my own eyes and I will know.* She has no doubt he's telling the truth. He intimidates the maid. He intimidates her friends, her acquaintances. When there's no one else he intimidates thin air. So she waits. She gets very good indeed at waiting. And when she is sure he is out of the hotel for longer than half an hour, when she is sure he is sleeping or impressing someone in the hotel parlour without her, she writes it to her Robert, every word. *We'll need enough money, and money of our own. We can do nothing without enough money.* Her eyes fill so the words quake. *A ring is an object, no more. Make your promise and mean it, that's all.* That's all.

By Vienna, she's a powerhouse. Blue shocks crackle from her fingertips and watch hands spin at her touch. While her father sleeps in the afternoon, even his energy exhausted by relentless travel, not unpacked, not fed, she checks the road from her window, waiting for Nanny to bring her the post, coded, double-sealed, secret post, bound in blue ribbon, and this brings little relief either. *Now I find out you think so little of rings, I must say I don't care for yours any more. I stopped wearing it from yesterday. I dreamed I was strolling past some deep water and — and I threw the ring in. I almost threw myself in after it. Not that you would care. Anyway, let's talk money since money is something you wish to discuss. I have enough, don't worry. Less than your father demands but his demands are ridiculous and the only person who can't see it is you.* What has she said to make him say these things, she wonders over and again; what can she say to take them away? *I'd like to tell you some day about a dark secret, a serious psychological affliction I fell prey to some time ago, but the telling will take a while. You'll hear it all some day, then you will have the key to my curious personality.* This is not Florestan, not Eusebius. The man who writes here is someone else. *I am not at all satisfied with my life these past few weeks; the separation from you and the pain of the insults I've suffered depresses me so I can't do anything — then I mope for hours. I look at your picture there in front of me and wonder how this will all end.* Someone different altogether. *I was at Miss Novello's recently. We spoke French together. She's become very popular here — a good-looking girl, a face as <u>magnificent</u> as her voice. Are you playing your concerto of your own accord? There are beautiful ideas in the first movement but it didn't make a strong impression on me, I'm afraid.* Is it feasible he would toy with her? *The lovely and <u>very talented</u> Miss Laidlaw wrote to me — she has a fancy for me I think. She gave me a lock of her hair before she left, I just thought you should know.* That he would enjoy toying with her? Is this mere teasing or deliberate spite, a form of love-lettering that more sophisticated persons enjoy? Is this the Creative Mind at work? Sadness? Or – what is it – this noting of afflictions, locks of hair, dreams of leaping into lakes? She grasps phrases, glimpses, appeals and blame, and it almost makes her afraid. Full of remorse, pity, something more bearable than confusion, she thinks herself insensitive for mentioning money and resolves to do better. Parts of his letter are delightful, after all – his signature, his name in his own hand, the words *dear* and *dearest* – and delight must be grasped where it is found. She grasps it tight. For two hours in a hired room she practises, this paper his hands have caressed tucked neatly beneath her corset bones, then hides it under the bolster of her hotel bed. Sleepless, hearing the paper crackle as she turns, she thinks of him in Leipzig, but it doesn't help. The bed rocks, all seasick horsehair as Nanny gets in beside her and curls away. Before long, Nanny's snores make fog in the half-dark. It's winter in Vienna. Tomorrow she will walk in the Prater, gawp like the other tourists at the Imperial Palace. The rest of the day will fill with visits and hiring, practice rooms and dealers, contracts, form-filling; the days after will be the same. *I dreamed I was strolling past some deep water.* This foreign hotel room is dark as a pit. Words flip in its depths like fish.

A professor calls. He comes right to their hotel with letters of introduction, gifts of ham, pickled cabbage and flowers. Vienna welcomes you! he booms, confident for a whole city. The Viennese give presents, he says. We are fond of giving. The Leipzigers have nothing to give back and he knows. Fischhof, he spells his name so they won't forget. F-I-S-C-H-H-O-F, professor at the conservatoire. He takes them for coffee, walks with them to try out a Broadwood, a Stein. He offers opinions unasked and smiles a great deal. He will not be shaken off. He lounges on the sofa all afternoon telling anecdotes. Wieck despises anecdotes but he endures. The day Beethoven kicked the piano tuner, the day Schubert lost his favourite collar-studs, what Wölfl's tailor thought, and an interminable list of his students who turned pages once for Thalberg, Paganini, Clementi. He endures it all but it doesn't end. After cakes, in deference to Mademoiselle Wieck, Fischhof gives his opinions on Women of the Keyboard. The Mlles Blahetka, Belleville, Laidlaw and

Pixis are young things, he says, passing novelties. Great Austrian ladies of the past could put them to shame. Marie Bigot de Morogues who first played the *Appassionata* to the great master himself, Dorothea von Ertmann to whom Beethoven dictated corrections – though both were well-married and played (here Fischhof coughs) only for a select few. Then again there was Josepha Aurnhammer. Hahaha. Josepha Aurnhammer. Not that he'd met her but his father had, and she was indeed remarkable. Fat as a cow and ugly as an udder. Haha. Pockmarked. For all that, Mozart himself was her encourager – and what ambition the woman had! Already unattractive, what did she care it put men off? They still used her compositions at the conservatoire, and excellent compositions they were – for a woman. Worked all the hours God sent and no compunction about fending for herself. And thank goodness for that, eh? He leans forward, and all his chins quiver. For who would have had her, haha? Hahahahahaha! Who in Christ's name would have had her?

A further week and it's certain. The city of Beethoven, the city of Schubert it may be, but Vienna is also stupid. It's fat and complacent and hogtied with red tape. They are Saxon, they are Lutheran, they are foreign; no hire is simple for they are not Viennese. These people have their heads pinched in, Wieck thinks; they are insular and *amateur*. The professor of their famous conservatoire wouldn't pass water, never mind muster, in Leipzig. The Viennese have no rigour. They like their puddings sweet and slathered with cream, their mantelpieces doll-housed with bric-a-brac. For their curtains they like rick-rack, lace and ruffles, and for their music just the same. They like trills and cadenzas, crossed hands and flashy octave leaps, and they like improvisation, no matter how formulaic – a hit tune from the shows trilled to death on the spot. They bluster about Beethoven but they prefer Czerny and they prefer Thalberg playing it. Well, well. He can't change what they want, not overnight, but he examines it closely.

What he examines is Thalberg. Swiss-born, Viennese-bred, bastard aristocracy, aloof and beautifully turned-out, Thalberg is romance, decadence, civic loyalty and refinement in one tasteful pianistic package. He's not a clown or a pretty boy like Döhler or von Meyer; he is a sophisticate. In this city, they rate him above Liszt and while Wieck hasn't heard Liszt, he's read the reviews. The play-off in Paris some years ago now, when Thalberg played to 400 while Liszt played to 4000 – by God! the money it must have raked in! – the days when Liszt made no secret of his triumph, when he called Thalberg *no more tasteful than the diamond studs he wears in his own cuffs* were past. Thalberg was no fool and Thalberg had learned. It would not do to underestimate him now. For some time, then, Wieck, studies: Thalberg's stage manner, his technique, his method of programming, his compositions and his tailoring – Wieck studies the lot and he learns three things. First, Thalberg is *good*. He is splendid. This splendour of Thalberg's is an excellent thing, for it means Viennese taste is founded on *something* – and *something* can be understood. The second thing he learns is better still, for the second thing is that Thalberg is not, whatever the papers say, *inimitable*. His showiest trick – sounding like three hands instead of two – is easily taken apart: spread fast arpeggios with both hands as wide as humanly possible and snatch the tune with the thumbs in passing, and there it is. *Anyone* could do it. And Clara will too, if that's what it takes. The third thing is the best. Thalberg is not hungry. He is of a class that has never known worry about bread, skimped on hotel costs and costuming, borrowed and bargained and mended that it might put on a show. Thalberg's vanity drives him, perhaps, but not the certain knowledge of penury if he fails. And there they have him. Perhaps.

For now, though, if he programmes well, they'll stand comparison with anybody Vienna can throw at them. Bach, then. Bach establishes seriousness of intent. Pixis and Henselt, her own concerto and as much improvisation as she can stomach – a little dazzle is taken for granted. After that, Chopin. Then Beethoven. Before long Mendelssohn, even Schumann's newfangled stuff and they'll take it all. Not a parade of tricks and circus turns but something true, and who will bring it? He, Friedrich Wieck, Herr Wieck of Leipzig, that's who. The thought of his calling brings a lump to his skinny throat. He'll bring them his daughter and she'll give them *herself*.

She needs to be alone. She plays her dumb keyboard for hours, *études* and scales keep her fingers fleet but fill her ears with clatter. She plays, walks in the fresh air, attends gatherings, admires everything she is asked to admire. She is granted no rehearsal time with the orchestra and admires that too. Other cities: one accommodates. She is professional, unruffled and demure. At nights, however, when Nanny is still as death beside her, she hauls out the letters concealed under her bedding and the words are still the same. *Are you playing your concerto of your own accord?* What does Robert mean by it? What? That her concerto is *bad?* That she would not play it if she were not forced? That she has no will of her own? That *of your own accord* grates and won't stop. Until her first public appearance before the Viennese, that is. Then, she finds an answer. *Of course* she plays the concerto of her own accord. *Of course.* People ask for it — and *how* they ask. Applause in Dresden, in Berlin, even, is silence compared with this. They cheer, stamp their feet, raise their hands over their heads. They have Southern temperament, her father explains; they *express.* Meanwhile, his daughter, the orchestra at her back, stands up to address their approval, this deafening batter of Viennese boots, as though it is in no way unusual. In some ways, of course, it's not. But the scale of the thing! Its suddenness! The assault on the ears alone is terrifying, but she knows what to do. She focuses on individual faces, pairs of hands, the smiles tilted towards her. Then the noise is something else, something like warmth, like *glory.* She may stand under the snow of petals and laurel leaves, her white dress flickering in the limelight, and consent to be drowned in it.

Afterwards there is a noticeable tremor in her hands, gooseflesh bristling her arms. Some women tremble after they give birth, her father says and wraps her in a shawl. Shock and happiness. It is common enough. All night he crows, he barks his triumph, the routing of these Viennese cabals his sole theme till dawn and, despite the noise, she sleeps. For the first time in weeks, she sleeps uninterrupted, the night-mares go. In the morning she writes to her beloved, her tormentor, and is careful not to say too much lest she sound immodest, too proud for his liking or comfort. It gives her satisfaction, though, to tell him what she has learned for sure: that rare manuscripts are tumbling through the door, presents of songs in Schubert's own hand, invitations from the Emperor; that she has no time to eat and her gowns need taking in at the waist. By January they're fighting in the streets for tickets to hear her. They sell Clara-cakes in the cafés and people fight for those too. She plays the whole of the *Appassionata* – a whole Beethoven sonata in a public concert – and their astonishment is complete. No breaks between movements, no interludes for songs as they are accustomed; just the work as the composer wrote it, end to end. *Such audacity! Such concentration on such a delicate face!* they say. But they listen. No one has done this before, her father writes without a word of a lie. She is making history – and they stand for it.

A poem about her fingers makes front-page news. *A shepherdess*, it calls her, *an opener of treasure caskets, a child*. And eighteen. They whisper it, hoot it with laughter, raise glasses to it in pubs. Eighteen and never been kissed. She is a phenomenon and Wieck knows it. It makes him tender-hearted. *Dearest Wife*, he writes, *get rugs for our girls lest they be cold and look for a bigger house. As for those lazy boys, tell them their father sees what industry, what his daughter, can do and will hear their excuses no more.*

For her fourth concert, lest any doubters remain, she plays only Liszt and Thalberg, two hours of the so-called *inimitable* and the critics quantify, dissect and attempt to label her, are not put off by failure. What critic is? For now, she may do as she pleases. Herr Schumann has never been here, her father says. He has no idea of what we are accomplishing; no grasp at all. And it's hard to argue. How could anyone who had not witnessed it imagine this? She can hardly grasp it herself, this appetite they have for her, this vulgar lust. Strangers approach when they are out walking privately, some only to remark out loud how *ordinary* she seems up close. And she misses him, then in particular; she misses him very much. He should be here, within reaching distance, she thinks. And she pictures him walking through these streets, his necktie *à la Viennoise*, his arm under hers, firm and sure. *He should be here.* But he's not. Save through hidden letters, Russian doll envelopes, cloaks and pockets, codes. And Nanny, of course. He'd be absent entirely if it were not for Nanny, ferrying his letters back and forth without complaint.

In later years this fact, when she thinks of it, astonishes her. That

Nanny, who lit their fires in the morning, who ran errands for cheap bread and who oiled and curled her hair in the evenings, risked lodgings and living for no more than loyalty. Then, servants do. In Clara's houses, every house she ever lived in, the tact and discretion of hired people, of servants, has been called upon, been there. Between snatches of soup, listening for footfalls on the stairs, caught in the peculiar swell of fame that rose and fell, she knew even then. Still, she wrote — *forgive father* — *the storms of applause here* — *the Empress* — *forgive me* — *poor Miss Laidlaw* — *these tedious admirers of my own* — knowing whatever she said, however indiscreet, however foolish, it passed to safe hands. Not the hands of any member of her family. *Write to me*, she pines (he is so far away); *write everything* (so alone); *for ever until death* (so in need of reassurance) *Eusebiana*. She remembers watching Nanny from an upstairs window, the path she made through unfamiliar streets. Someone running, selfless, with secrets in her breast.

Letters! However they arrive, however they get written, he can't get enough. The programmes she's playing, rounding out like décolletage; even her handwriting stimulates him, tease his senses and imagination almost unbearably and the only cure is writing back. His time is not dictated by anyone but himself: he has his music newspaper, his composing, *these*; letters the size of novels, bulging with scraps and screeds, the contents of his days. It is the life he has always wanted. And yet, yet. *Child*, he writes, *Child of my Heart, I can hear you over mountains; I see you and you never know I am there.* How much he wanted to hurt her once! During that last terrible separation, when she wrote nothing, it occurred to him he should marry someone else called Clara, anyone called Clara, just from spite, but it passed over. The desire to kill himself passed over too. It always did. *It must be wonderful to know you have returned someone to happiness who has been tormented by the most terrible thoughts, someone who would have thrown his life away like a penny, who can still find the dark side of the clouds with a ruthlessness that terrifies him even now.* Nonetheless, he pictures a future: five rooms, blue wallpaper, copper engravings. They'll live plain, play duets by twilight and find each other's arms at the end of the day. What more does he need? Ha! What more does *she* need? Or anyone? No one needs more and anyone who says otherwise is a liar and a fool. Or the devil. Already Robert suspects who the devil might be. *Think Clärchen! Does the fame matter? Really matter? The opinion of the world? Every time you hear their applause ringing in your ears, their roars for more! More! — well. That's your father pushing me away from you — further and further. Think of that next time you hear it! Not that I grudge you your laurel wreaths — but a thousand of those won't make a bridal wreath, and I alone will place that on your beautiful black hair.* He does not edit or amend. As it comes to him, he writes. He reminisces, tells her things she can barely imagine or understand. He writes it all.

> In the Zweinaundorf Park, just outside Leipzig – do you know it? Very pretty. You have walked there too surely? – anyway, there, when I was just your age I heard a nightingale. It was the most beautiful sound I ever heard and I stopped everything to hear. Then – and this is just as it happened – I fell and trembled and thrashed my arms and legs for happiness that I was alive, and in this park beneath these trees with my whole life in front of me, I fainted, Clärchen! I passed out from beauty and sheer joy. And then I think I first imagined you. Now. Here comes the last secret – now you shall know everything.

Lord the relief of sharing it with one who will understand! Whether she understands or not, she will understand! This is the paradox of love, he thinks, writing feverishly, his head hot. *On the night of October 17th 1833, I was suddenly struck by the most horrible thought with which heaven can punish us — that of losing one's mind. I couldn't breathe when I asked myself, 'what would happen if you could no longer think?' I ran to a doctor. I often fainted —* yards of it, scrawled over pages, a story that would not be bearable if it did not lead to one outcome, this certain, sure thing his sentences rush towards. *Oh Clara! Since I have you again I've become almost completely free of it, that terrible sickness that grabs hold of me in the night and makes me cry out for help and makes me want to die! I am almost completely free.*

And this last, when she receives it, this last part, unpicked from his hieroglyphs one word at a time, unpicked over weeks, is the part she most readily grasps. Cure by love. *Her* love. They say it conquers all and it seems it may be true. Would he lie to flatter her? Not *lie*. But he might tell his story with a little licence. Like a play. He is a poet, and poets talk strangely as a matter of course. It can hardly be true, word-for-word true, this terrible tale — and even if it was, even if half of it was, now he's cured, does it matter? *If only I could tell you how happy your love makes me! But then language and sounds become immaterial and I see only two people embracing, and everything around me drifts away.* All that matters is his meaning and his meaning is glorious. He means that she, Clara Wieck, is the Dearest Thing in the World; that she is his own, entirely his own. He has forgotten this throwing away of rings and jumping into rivers, and whatever fault it was she incurred. He means that love matters more than — more than — more than even the audience at the Musikvereinsaal, which is not poetic, but the most *more* thing she can think of, and of course he is right. How could this not be right? He has finished the dances he's been working on, he says; they are full of *Wedding Thoughts.* She recalls her sixteenth birthday, the hesitancy of his footwork, the firm breadth of his back under her fingers. If only she were a poet, too. But she's not, not at all. *Forgive me,* she writes, ashamed of her practical turn of mind, at her clumsiness with words that seems to cause offence without trying, *something comes over me sometimes and I let reason rule my heart.* Yet it helps. For all she knows reason has had its day, is not the spirit of the New Age, it's reason that keeps her from foundering. Spontaneity, even at eighteen, is something she knows to treat with suspicion. When everything is healed and settled between father and lover, when another year or two have passed, when they are married, *later* — then might be the time for spontaneity. For now, even when she doesn't feel it, especially when she doesn't feel it, she must foster calm. And she does it very well.

Barely a week later, when the Emperor strokes her face, pins the highest artistic honour in Vienna on her breast, she barely smiles. She plays games with the royal children while her father weeps. Poor Herr Wieck! He bawls like a baby and blasts his capacious nose into his handkerchief, has to sit for support. A foreigner, a Protestant, a *girl* — he had thought every fibre of Austrian tradition worked against it; yet there she is, Royal and Imperial Chamber Virtuosa to the Austrian Court, glittering with medals, and his own, entirely, wholly, legally and morally his own. He pays the patent, orders headed notepaper for the joy of seeing *Royal and Imperial* on every page, the crest and letters for even their most fleeting acquaintances to see, and immediately books a carriage for Hamburg. There is no more to accomplish in Vienna. Charity concerts, a little holidaying, perhaps, but it's done.

For all that, the inevitable return to Leipzig is mildly depressing. Wieck has different standards now, expects a different level of *respect*. Another stab at Paris. London, Moscow, Warsaw, St Petersburg, the outlandish possibility of America, float in and out of his head. But whatever he has achieved, will achieve yet, there is his daughter to cope with, all the way home. She has played these new pieces of Schumann's obsessively, has been growing more stubborn and eccentric by the day. *I will never give him up, whatever you do or say.* It has been a long tour. Maybe he's had enough. Maybe he hopes to settle here for the next batch of concerts. Lord knows why. But he says something then, as they leave the gilded city and its cakes behind, and what he says is this: *If Schumann shifts himself to earn 2000 a year and moves outside Leipzig, if he manages to settle and establish himself in Vienna, if he proves himself serious in this way, if, I say if.* He sees this *if* registered in her eyes, filling them up like moons. *But he won't,* Wieck says. *He won't.*

Too late. Her head fills with pictures: a house with blue walls, copper engravings, duets at dusk. In Vienna she could make 1000 *thalers* from only one concert a year. Further, the place is weighted down with showy pianos, a freshly minted bourgeoisie desperate to dose their daughters with elegant, home-enhancing skills. For him, a professorship at the conservatoire would bring in enough – she can organise it herself. 2000 a year – it tabulates easily; her father's training is not wasted. She is tired of bland men telling her she is pretty and sending their tedious flowers, of having no time to rest, to think. She is tired of receptions and stupid people wondering whether the *Glorious Virtuosa* can even write her own name. Most of all, she no longer cares for Leipzig, its half-applause and sniffy, stuffy Northern values. Her temperament, she decides, has become *Southern* and Vienna is *South*. As soon as she is alone, she writes it all – no guile, just sums, facts, dates – she writes it clean so he will understand in one go.

Forget professorships! he writes by return. *An artist can only die of professorships!* But Vienna! He could *burst* even to think it! Vienna! Provided he doesn't have to wait there alone, provided his paper transfers smoothly to Vienna, provided he can get a publisher's licence, provided the Old Jew means it this time – *yes, yes, yes. You will pull your own weight*, he writes, warming to his role as adviser. That she is a woman out in the world while he stays at home, writing, is pure accident; things will fall differently when they are – he catches his breath even thinking it – man and wife. Not that he will stop her playing – not at all! She will play endlessly, he hopes, but suitably, appropriately, at home. And she will love him for the most tolerant of husbands! She will burn his eggs and undercook his steak, and he won't care. For marriage (by which he means the stability that marriage must surely bring, the domestic peace of home, hearth and garden by which he means *her*) he can tolerate a great deal. He has listened to his doctors, his heart and his purse. He has stayed in, finished mountains of work, saved his money. He has stayed sober. He has congratulated Mendelssohn on the birth of a son and meant every word. His fear of the dark, his terrible imaginings of living out his life alone and loveless, of opening pages of his music and finding the notes vanished inside, of losing his mind, are surely coming to an end. He has dreamed of his dead, dancing sister, her terrifying funeral outside the church gates, his mother's incessant, ruthless grief. He has despaired of Wieck and his cruelties, felt his evil spectre dog his steps, catalogue his every move. Now, however, he feels confident and light. *Your father will learn that love is not measles*, he writes, *not a child's complaint that will pass over and there's an end of it. Before we are done, he will know he cannot make me change.*

Outside, an April storm batters his shutters, the wind blows under his door. It won't rain in Vienna, he thinks cheerfully, and writes on into the night. He writes household rules, his thoughts on home decoration, his tips to preserve a happy marriage, how things will be, will not be, will fill their future days. He has revised the *Fantasiestücke* a little. He has finished the *Novelletten* — jests, Egmont scenes, weddings, families with fathers in attendance — mostly light. And he is finishing his *Kinderszenen* — she will understand him better and better when she knows *these* little pieces, nothing showy in them, a home of true feeling. A whole book of new things, *Kreisleriana*, will be his wedding gift since she, only she, is the theme and core of it all. None of these pieces exists without her, she is the heart of everything, and she will be their best interpreter. In such a short while, how much more deeply he has come to realise that his music is himself: his feelings, his thoughts and outlook, everything that affects him. Who can play such music without trying to understand his soul? And who best at that but his Clara? His own? *You*, he writes. *You with your secret smile will look fondly on them, recognise yourself inside the notes, for everything, everything comes from you.* That she might wonder what Kreisler, half-mad, half-genius drunken fiddler from a story book has to do with herself never crosses his mind: she will just play them and *know*. And he is right, his judgement never surer. He knows because she has told him so herself.

Last night — he writes on, he keeps writing on — *he woke in the dark and the candles were all out. He called her name and* — he hesitates. Is it something one should say? *And*, he writes. Whom else may he say these things to? *And — you answered back.* He can hear it now, if he stops breathing: a ghost over the flatlands. *I am not a knight of the moonlight any more, Clara. I can no longer call at your house as mere friend. I want marriage or nothing: to be able to call the woman I love mine — or see her no more.*

When the tears stop, it's darker. He needs more candles, matches. There is more to write. Outside, someone is shouting, walking alone on the streets. He hears blunt obscenities slice the clean night air and fade. Further off, the sound of horseshoes cracks on cobbles. He thinks of her carriage rolling northwards, coming home. The Royal and Imperial Court Virtuosa, with all she has seen and heard. The thought of Clara's lips against Banck's comes into his head, a crude hand that perhaps fumbled at her blouse. Too awful to contemplate! Then again, Liszt is in Vienna. Liszt and all his man-of-the-world tricks and ruses will seek her out and certainly want to kiss her. *More.* He thinks of Kreisler, sawing drunkenly on his violin, hammering at the piano till the strings break.

He wonders if Wieck can read his mind, if anyone can. And he writes, no longer able to stop himself, forty pages, more. In the morning he will wake with ink on his cheek and read, astonished, as though someone else wrote it. He will barely remember a word.

⤙═◉═⤚

After the last concert Wieck took his daughter back to their hotel rooms alone. He took the blooms from her hair himself, let her stoop to unbutton his boots. He told her then, as she knelt at his feet, that her brothers would not be there to welcome her home. What did they earn? he said. What, compared to herself, could they do? Clementine had found them an apprentice master in Berlin and they might return when they were useful citizens. When she said nothing, he tilted her face up to meet his gaze, and looked deep into her eyes.

Of you, however, I am proud. He swallowed. You are wilful, it's true, but at heart you remain a dutiful child. In spite of them. He sniffed. In spite of them all. I do not regret an hour of all my striving. A tear coursed down the side of his face and buried itself in his whiskers. Schumann is nothing to this, *Clärchen*. Gustav and Alwin, the two put together, are nothing beside you. You are my reward. His voice broke. After a moment, he seemed to recover his strength, feel able to look at her again. His eyes narrowed and focused as best they could on hers. Clara. I have taught you everything, given you everything. Do not forget. His hand gripped her chin so tight it hurt. You will never be able to repay me for all I have done for you.

Looking into his eyes, her face betraying nothing, Clara felt the most terrible pity, lurching her stomach, washing in waves. Her head, meantime, checked some arithmetic – 2000 a year, not Leipzig. Turning itself towards the future, elsewhere, away.

Next day, in Erard's salon in stifling, curtained half-light, someone unexpected confirmed it. Liszt, with his chiselled jaw and shoulder-length hair, his suit, stock, collar studs and boots in expensive, impeccable black; Liszt who took her breath away even before he touched the keys, and when he did, made her feel like a child, played *Carnaval* for her alone. For Mademoiselle Wieck, the Incomparable played the More-or-less Unknown, full of loops and glitter and rush, but not as well as she did and she knew it. When he turned to her, eyes green as glass in the sun, she could look straight back.

That is the best piece I know, Liszt said. And what of the heart that created it? A certain gentleman who lives not far from yourself? He spoke straight at Clara, her father for once merely someone on the side-lines, almost overcome with heat. You are acquainted with Herr Schumann? Knowing that they were a focus of attention, that her father might hear, that anyone might, that her voice might waver, she answered in any case.

I am acquainted with Herr Schumann, she said. And I am delighted to inform Monsieur Liszt that when we speak of Herr Schumann — sweat trickled at her temple — we speak of a very fine and singular person indeed.

A curl at the corners of Liszt's mouth suggested he knew as much, had heard as much; that he attended to gossip.

Her father saw it. He also saw the flush on his daughter's cheek. He saw Clara Wieck, Court Virtuosa in Ordinary to the Emperor of Austria, tilting her chin and allowing her hand to be kissed. She is like any other woman, he thought, pulling at his necktie, feeling the blood pulsing in the veins of his neck. The word *passionate* popped into his head unbidden. Then a woman behind him pressed forward with an autograph paper, pushing him aside. And Friedrich Wieck lost his balance, crumpled, fainted daintily as a girl at the tips of Liszt's chisel-toed patent leather boots.

⟡

Be at our window at exactly 9. If I signal you with a white cloth, walk slowly towards the old Neumarkt. I will come down to where you are soon after, since I have to fetch Clementine at her mother's. If I don't signal it means she hasn't gone. *For heaven's sake*, be careful.

Clara. The courage of the stage all gone. Who would have her, vacillating this way, unable to defy her father; like a child, a babe in arms? Rakemann with his moon face swooning over duets; Banck spreading innuendo to anyone who'd listen; Müller the cellist, still unmarried, the arrow-chinned Russian who lounged in their spare rooms, *dying* to compose with her and less than half the musician she was, that's who. Any one of two barons, two dukes, a prince and several sons of recently moneyed businessmen keen to make contact with *Art* in a manner more thorough than simple patronage; for sure at least a handful of those who threw indecently blown red roses at the stage and ambushed the house with calling cards, letters, gifts – *plenty* would have her, despite her talent. More pressingly, who would get her? Rakemann was a child and Banck was obsequious. Liszt was an oversexed Catholic, Thalberg was boring, and Chopin was a sickly, sarcastic snob, who despite his radical reform in so much else was incapable of acknowledging the charm of any woman born German. Döhler was a fop, Henselt was poor and Sterndale Bennett – Sterndale Bennett was *English*. Only one candidate remained: the hare-brained, overreaching, intolerably persistent mother's boy who walked along their street every night since they returned, looked up at their window, whistling, singing, watching the shadows pass behind their shutters, listening for fragments of her playing. And everyone, everyone knew. Wieck could complain, threaten, promise her presents of oranges all he liked. *I want to marry him*, she said. *Only him.*

What did she know of marriage? Her mother and Bargiel. Her father and Clementine. Fairy tales, opera plots, songs where people died of bliss or lack of it and poems the lodger told her a long time ago. But for *herself* – what did she want or expect? Asked the question, she could not have answered. To tell the truth she had no idea. One Other with whom to share a life, perhaps, One to cherish, protect and treasure the waking day. One Other to bring Light. And everything, anything, the world itself achievable through love, much love, an abundance of love.

What did she know of being a daughter? That it was a bond never broken. That a daughter given music owed double the duty for her father's extra gift. That it was no end of understanding, explaining, knowing that when he said awful things, when he railed and shouted and damned her to hell, he did not mean what he said.

What did she know of gratitude? That it was never, ever enough. *If you do not give him up you are an ingrate, a thief, a serpent at the breast. Go ahead! Drive your father to violence! Drive him mad! Then, when the extent of your treachery is apparent to all, then let him love you! Let anyone love you! Who that knew you as I do would have you, child? Who?*

What did she know of being a lover? That it was never enough either. *Do you know nothing about his lies and slanders? Lord, if you were to give me up on his account! My blood runs cold and I am sick, so sick! You must deal with me protectively, for I am not strong, not strong at all.* That even if they contrived to meet daily, by slips and sleights of notes and hand, her heart was torn for her father while it lasted, torn for Robert when they were apart. That if the course of true love never did run smooth, this love must be true indeed. What did she know of guilt? While they searched her after house visits from friends, while they locked her room door at night, while she read her letters, planned her meetings, skimped on practice, clung and wept in his embrace, fretted that Vienna would not suit him after all; while she lied and evaded and willed a peace upon a situation that would not hold, why, what she knew of guilt – *for God's sake, sweet Jesus* – was everything.

⋆──◦◦◦──⋆

He wore the same red coat with lengthened frock-tails.

The brocade waistcoat with silver fastenings for a second time.

He combed his hair, had Peter trim the lock that fell into his eyes again and watched her in the same white dress. Another evening in a packed Gewandhaus, himself at the back of the hall, she at the fore, sweat running on his back. Newer was his reaction. This time he would not despair. He would not feel queasy or fearful or held in contempt. He left the concert hall, went drinking for a short while, called his acquaintances by name instead of rote, and went home settled to write, smoke, drink a little more. There would be an end to this circus, and soon. Every bone in his body said so, the autumn crispness of the night air. Bent over his paper, pen in hand, he felt courageous enough to offer unstinting praise.

> You played magnificently. People here don't deserve
> you. You are too good for this life your father holds out
> – he thinks it will bring you happiness. All that work,
> these difficulties, for a mere few hours' triumph! This
> is not your future. No, my Clara will be a happy wife,
> a content, beloved wife. And when we are together,
> you won't lift a finger for an audience if you don't
> want to, for people who aren't worth even playing
> scales to. You can be an artist without that, can you
> not? My sweet one, my angel, my own . . .

This time, he was going to Vienna. Alone – and to no one he knew! Lord, how would he stand it! He who had come to hate travel and all it meant. Well, in truth he was not alone; he had Freise and Reuter – Reuter was such a good fellow! Nothing was too much trouble! – coming for company, and Clara had arranged that he be met by Fischhof, that he should have somewhere to live (not anywhere high, he had told her several times, he could not stay anywhere higher than the first floor) even an overnight stop with her friends in Dresden if he needed it, *which he did not*. A little too much arranging for the best preservation of his manly pride, but still. Vienna! This time the Old Jew would have to mean it, he'd see what Robert Schumann was made of. He packed copies of the *Neue Zeitschrift*, letters of introduction, lists of rental offices and his published pieces. He packed her picture, two fat books by Jean-Paul and a slim *Life of Schubert*. In the morning she would weep while he took the carriage, fret over whether this was the right thing, but it had to be. It was action, at least. He supposed that was how she endured, this moving that gave the impression of something happening, of life pressing on. He'd go from Leipzig to Zwickau, loop back to be with her for moments more when no one suspected, then go, leave with the taste of her still on his mouth and head east. Then he wondered. He wondered where he might find for them to live, what position at the conservatoire he might acquire, what the cost of cigars might be in Vienna, and could not sleep. He wondered till almost four, savouring what he knew. By Easter, the money would be found, all conditions fulfilled; by Easter, they'd be married. He could stand it, even welcome it. Torn between determination, tears and hope, he pulled his courage about him and chose the first. He'd done with tears and hoping, he decided, and sat up most of the night, fighting both. He was taking a carriage to Vienna, terrified, as a sign of his bond. They'd see, he thought. They'd see.

Wieck was furious, of course. Schumann was playing games with him – doing as he'd been ordered to do deliberately to provoke. Something like a thrill ran though him and he imagined Schumann laughing, drinking with his friends, boasting he'd thrown down a gauntlet, produced an ace from up his sleeve, called a bluff. If that was the case – in fact, whether it was or not – Schumann with his butter-wouldn't-melt face had another thing coming. And since Schumann was out of town, who it came to was Clara. Immediately, without compunction or explanation, Wieck revoked his consent to marriage under any conditions and made it his final word. As for the Paris trip, the trip to consolidate her reputation, well then! She could go, and – he sat opposite her in a chair with his nose pinched, his face set as a grate – since she was so stubborn, so ready to make herself independent of his guidance, go alone. Let's see how the Imperial Court Virtuosa does *on her own*. Let her plan and hire and beg at the printers that legible, affordable tickets should arrive on time. Let her book her own rooms and deal with the papers at border crossings, and bribe officials for concert space. Let her haggle for reviews and bully the tuners, work out the mood of each town and each crowd, let her choose her own programmes and her encores to suit, and do it all without a man behind her. Let her find out how little she matters as a woman – a child – alone in a cut-throat world, where all the officials, all the decision makers, all the serious players apart from herself sport suits and side-whiskers. A monkey in a dress without an organ grinder, let her learn the hard way. And, dear Lord, *let her fail*.

The letters from Vienna had sand in their corners, peppered and folded as soon as finished. She read one and another came, shifting its ground. Vienna was wonderful, the city of his dreams! All Viennese were snakes, intriguers, jealous and vain! He had never composed so freely or felt so at ease! Viennese censors were unbearable and they hated foreigners, especially foreigners with ideas of their own. Ideas, moreover, they wished to publish. It gave him pride to hear how honoured his Clara was, how held in perfect esteem, yet all this was tinsel, for all she wanted – was it not so? – was to be a happy wife. He felt free and he missed her. He missed the newly academically blessed Herr Doctor Mendelssohn and he missed David's, the orchestra leader's, caustic remarks and the chimes from the Thomas Church and the way they served blood pudding at the Coffeebaum and everything German – but he could not leave. He would not leave without making his name (a doctorate, too – Lord, another thing to win) and his income to a pre-arranged amount and *she knew why*.

Touched, not sure if she was being blamed but touched all the same, she wrote immediately that she would work *for both of them* if he gave her six months. We are young, she told him. It was nothing but the truth. He had told her himself that she was his best interpreter, and from the depths of her soul she understood she was nothing as a composer beside him. She would compose no more save to please him, and work at her sacred task alone, which was to interpret. To *play*. To be his support that he might compose all the more and be free from care. Had he not talked about symphonies? Had Liszt not begged him for trios, quartets, simply *more*? And Father would come round given time. *Let's delay the wedding of our own volition*, she wrote. *Let me earn good money while I still can. Wait, dearest, wait. It will all be for the good.*

Ah.

Looking back, it's obvious. Then – what is obvious at the time? There is only what one does, how one thinks on one's feet. Looking back, she knows her failings. There was inadequacy, she has no doubt, inexperience. She was hurtful, for he hurt so easily. She may have been, though she was never sure such a thing was possible, too devoted to her father and too ready to please. But her two main failings were one and the same, and indelibly in her nature. Robert sought change when he was fearful. A man who hated journeys, he looked for a new address, a new doctor, a new circle of friends; he wrote his music or found a fresh enthusiasm. He drew pictures or started novels. At the least, and even at his darkest, he hid away and plotted an altered state: what he would be, might be, would surely become. She, the seasoned traveller, sought stasis, a calm no matter how falsely induced, a semblance of *things exactly the same*. She did it like a cat-cornered mouse, without thinking, without wondering twice if it would work. When Robert's letter arrived, curt as a spit, the thinking had to start. *I know who is talking behind these moneyed words. By all means then, be a millionairess. I no longer want you.* Reuter knew when he was wanted. He came with smelling salts and selzer, pomegranates, pears. He exaggerates, he said, taking her hand, watching her pull it back. He is out of sorts, perhaps. He is occasionally volatile and not entirely judicious. He is not fully aware of what he's saying. He sighed. Reuter did not often sigh. He doesn't mean it at all.

Then how else was change to come but by these means, by overt threat?

Him or me. Perhaps she had willed it.

She said nothing, patted her scarlet nose with chalk when she left her rooms, but he noticed anyway. A psychic in his way, a mouser with years of practice, her father missed nothing and made his move. I am too busy after all to come to Paris, he said. You will manage somehow. He curled his lip. You have love to sustain you, after all. Some verselets from Vienna arrived two days before Christmas with warnings peppered through: two-line pairs, far too easy to remember. He forgave her *this time*. But he would not wait much longer. *Him or me.* It was not a choice.

One cracked glass pane, grimy from the inside; the horses barely visible through their own breath. A footman who looked her up and down before he lifted her bags on to the roof, tucked the largest trunk inside. The chaperone her father hired for her perfect scowl, who smelled of naphthalene and who spoke nothing of Clara's mother tongue, went inside first. Snow was making roadblocks at Bitterfeld, they said, gravediggers needed picks to break the ground. Altenberg, Nuremberg, Stuttgart and Karlsruhe. Father will come to Paris eventually, she thought, he will not spend all winter hidden here. Refusing to think, to feel the chill that stung her eyes, to acknowledge the stranger beside her, Clara pushed her back against the leather-covered horsehair and did the surest things she knew. Snow banks, flood water, ditches and drains could do what they liked. Such little heels, so stubborn. Digging in for siege.

⊷⇒◉⇐⊷

Well, then. Paris is not Vienna. What else can one say?

Clara Wieck's return to the French capital was not much asked after, even by her immediate friends. She earned money, certainly; she sold out, to be sure. But this was expected, almost normal, for Clara Wieck. Paris, a city of very particular tastes, was more astonished into admiration by women who shocked than women who merely excelled. They turned up and they listened, they applauded and liked her very well. Clara, they said, is special for the extraordinary dignity within her sound, her calm bearing, her subtle and deeply felt — there is no other word to use — *mastery* (the male form of the word is that which means excellence, after all; the female something less high-flown). Nineteen years old, she could no longer count as a prodigy. She was conducting no outrageous affairs, did not smoke havanas and never flirted. Yes, she could play quite astonishingly, she could move one to noble tears, but that was all. She had not Chopin's fastidious wit or exiled, bloody lunged romance; none of Liszt's sexual bravura or Kalkbrenner's disdain; none of their — what should one call it? None of their larger-than-life *celebrity*. The best celebrity, after all, the kind that radiated frissons was unfailingly masculine; women — let's be brutally honest here — aren't serious enough. Put charisma in skirts and it became somewhat less charismatic, at least in any meaningful, which is to say lasting, way; put genius-kissed talent in a dress and it invited only drollery — dogs walking on hind legs, etc. Women did not rise to genius, they rose to *allure*.

Clara was alluring, then, at least, alluring enough. Her doughy accent was nothing to an exotic Slavic lilt and her gowns were merely adequate. She had no snide remarks and no taste for them, therefore would never

166

be sophisticated. Paris, glutted with pianists, in thrall to gimmickry and excess, heard a magnificent pianist but saw a girl of nineteen, unmarried, without a father, a mother or even an aunt to accompany her or smooth her path into salon society – and could place her nowhere at all. How did she dare? By not knowing any better? By sheer force of will? By not being able to think what the alternative might be? By – was it possible? – enjoying at least some of the terrible challenge of going it alone? It took till after the Paris days were gone for Clara herself to realise it, but that time was less made of concert halls and salons than other things and most of those indefinable.

Paris brought to mind most readily something else, not the place itself, but a memory of ease, even freedom, in her limbs. At the time, she called it *learning* and it was that too. She learned to last out the journeys, the food, the grim city lodgings with a stranger lying next to her in a scratchy linen nightdress; to object when she saw fit. She learned that to be bored making her own arrangements was a reassuring thing, for boredom was not fear. She learned how to speak to hirers and officials in her own voice; to fall into conversation easily; to make laundry lists and haggle down hotel prices with blushless ease. She learned to play for paying audiences without the running stream of her father's advice, changes, last-minute lectures and fussing; she walked into rooms of strangers on no one's arm. She learned not to look for her father's face when the applause came, learned to stop it hurting that only strangers looked back. She learned who were worthwhile (few) and who were not (many) and that when they came together, she could learn the difference if she had to.

Henriette Reichmann, a student introduced by a would-be seducer; Henriette, fresh as apples, who wished to come to Paris too; Henriette, whose presence lightened the coach journey from Stuttgart and everything after, stayed with her and became someone – it gave her pride to say it – *loved*. And with this newfound accomplice, Clara formed opinions of Notre Dame and the Pantheon, disliked Herr Berlioz's frozen face and fretted for the absent Chopin, coughing like a watchdog somewhere in Spain; without prompting she allowed herself to sicken of concerts, at least as far as listening was concerned, if she pleased. Away from her father, Clara found plenty to say and most of it she said to other women. Pauline García taught her to make coffee and omelettes without scalding her fingers, Emilie List to make her stitching neater and darn lace; Henriette let her talk about Robert, to mention *love* if she wished; she might read her letters aloud without fear of what would follow. Barely two weeks after she arrived in the French capital, Clara learned enough to find her two feet, sack her father's chosen chaperone and spent her time not courting the Great and the Good, the career enhancers and titled sorts, but with — with one of the finest singers in Europe, the ambassador's daughter, a motherless angel from Stuttgart perhaps, but more. Her *friends*. For the first time in her life, Clara Wieck had friends with whom she might mix when she chose, share jokes and earrings, and make observations about the *opposite sex*. The woman Herr Chopin had taken as a mistress — or who had taken him for one, perhaps — the woman who called herself *George* had no female friends and Clara was not surprised. And the gentleman himself so *scrupulous* in all he did! Was Herr Chopin *very* attractive? Was Liszt? Women saved his tea dregs in bottles to keep around their necks on golden chains. Imagine! Were side-whiskers a feature best avoided, a danger as regards the collection of crumbs? More scandalously, did side-whiskers *scratch*? It got worse. *There is fluid*, Pauline told her. *The final excitement of men makes fluid*, and Clara could not begin to imagine what she meant.

Years later, however, she did not think of that time much, was not asked about it much, had no word to name it. Had she tried harder, been less carefully tutored in worry, panic and fear; had things not taken the turn they were about to take — but she did not, she was and they did. Making her own decisions, faring more stoutly than anyone would have thought or even wished, what she felt in her bones when she thought of Emilie and Henriette and Pauline, the thing she could not name, was *pleasure*. For Paris itself, the society of vulgar salons and stupid manners, its world-weariness and self-absorption, its gossip and clubbishness and back-scratching cliques, she needed no word at all.

⊷⊜⊶

She knew before she opened it.

She went to the Lists' garden and hid in the summerhouse, afraid of being seen without knowing why. Robert's writing barely disguising itself on the front, black-edged, from Zwickau. Eduard, the eldest, the best of his remaining brothers, was dead and Robert had left Vienna. Funeral processions, despairing people, ruin and rejection troubled him even in daylight, and he had been working on a piece he called *Corpse Fantasy*, sobbing aloud for fear, when the letter from Thérèse had come. He had heard, he said, a chorale, a beautiful hymn tune that no one else could hear and arrived too late for the funeral. The family publishing business was in ruins, Thérèse was a beggar and he – he was broken, failed, sickly and poor. So. He had come home in nothing resembling triumph. Vienna was no place for quiet souls like himself, no place for cautious or honest men, no place, put simply, for anyone not born Viennese. All he had to show was the pieces he himself had written, a story, a steel pen found on Beethoven's grave and a cache of lost Schubert – snatches of operas, songs, a whole symphony that had not seen the light of day since written, just there among the great man's papers, his family not having realised what it meant. It chilled him to think what would have happened had he not come, not seen: the fate of how many after their deaths? It chilled him to the bone. But the symphony – Lord he wished she could see it! A cathedral in music! – he would give it to Mendelssohn that he might conduct it first. If the art in Art was its capacity to spiritualise matter – and it was – this was Highest Art. Surely she would come home for that! For Mendelssohn conducting the dead brought back to life! Even so, he, who was still alive and moving through the earth as Schubert was not, was sometimes melancholy. He couldn't help but reflect he had found these things by himself, alone, as he now suspected he always would be. Was music to be his only life's companion? It was the case with Schubert, the case with Beethoven too, those to whom he had come closest on this journey. These were signs, surely, and terrible signs. Unless – could she, who existed so far above him in everything, could she care for a poor man? A man who would always need to be sheltered from the world? A man who had his pride nonetheless and wanted a true wife at his side, not one who earned the family income, who would not leave him ever, ever, because he loved her so much? He was composing, it was true. A *Carnival Jest* that might tax her fingers a little. Had the *Fantasie* arrived? She would find it dedicated to Herr Franz Liszt, but must bear in mind its subject.

The tone in the motto is you, is it not? I think it is. She should, he wrote — and his writing became more erratic here — recollect that the *Fantasie* was written during the terrible year of first separation, when he thought he would die without her. She must remember that when she played. She must be kind, always be kind. *I would be where Eduard is now if not for you, dear Clara. Darling girl.* Beyond the confines of the summerhouse wall, she saw trees in bud, showing ruffles of pale pink flower. *Zwickau is nothing but graves; what have I in the world save you?* The rose beds, however, were no more than puddles rimmed with earth, jagged sticks. Spring was late this year, they said. It was not too late for snow.

In the Style of a Legend, he had written. It was how it began. And it was music anyone would call mystical, strange. The thick chord clusters, suspensions pedalled over shimmers of running semiquavers, gave it something of the timeless. But Clara had only a Parisian piano. Rather than butcher the piece with it, she chose only to practise the march, the coda. So many leaps! And this perfect melody, its handfuls of spread chords!

It made her run hot and cold at once to play it, even to see it on the page. Its demands were fierce, but its result was sublime. This was virtuosity with a purpose, virtuosity as unlike the run-of-concert kind as one could imagine. Exactly as he had said. *The art in Art is to spiritualise matter.* She was the tone from which this glorious piece sprang and Robert, her Robert, had made it. He was not a poor man, whatever he said. He was a composer above all, she his interpreter. Their futures, their roles in life, had never seemed clearer. A fit of happy, longed-for clarity consumed her. She would play to earn their money. He would write. Apart from this, what mattered? What could touch them now?

Unconscionable manipulation!

He had read the first of her good reviews and been stung, that was all. That she could manage without him, succeed without him, was what caused it. He was a vain old man and that was the truth. So Pauline said and Pauline was not easily gainsaid. Then Pauline, as Emilie pointed out, was Spanish. Pauline was engaged to be married and her parents had offered no opposition. What did Pauline know?

Monstrous! said Pauline. Your own father writes to threaten you with disinheritance and legal suits unless you give up this man! Does he think you are a puppet? A servant? Is that what you wish to be? Why does he hate Schumann so in any case?

He doesn't mean it, said Emilie. Her father is a dear man and protective, that's all.

And he writes it all to Emilie! He knows she will tell you exactly what he wrote, that she will make excuses! How can you be so calm? said Pauline.

He writes to me because he knows I have your best interests at heart, said Emilie. He remembers my practical turn of mind, that what he says about marrying poverty is all too true.

Poverty! said Pauline. He threatens to keep her money and make her poor on purpose. He is a brute who would destroy his daughter to be right!

He loves you, said Emilie. He says so. He doesn't mean a word.

Get a lawyer, said Pauline. Whether he means it or not.

Henriette burst into tears.

Her father's second letter threatened nothing, it merely hinted. It hinted regret. It hinted the possibility of reconciliation, reasonability, some account of feelings other than his own. Hints, mind. But hints were enough. A teacher knows the value of a change of tactics.

I told you, Emilie said. I said he'd come round and it's beginning already. Here is the proof. What's the rush into marriage in any case? Soften him a little more, earn while you can, put his mind at rest. Invite him to Paris and he'll melt. If Robert loves you, he'll wait. He's a man, isn't he? Trust me, he'll wait.

I'll kill myself, you too, wrote Robert. Bring your father to Paris and there's blood on your hands.

Get a lawyer, said Pauline. At least draw up a will.

Henriette started weeping all over again.

Thinking him lonely, she had begged and confided – *Schumann is a good man, you will see! I will love no one but him! I have so longed to tell you everything* – longing for the chastisement she had missed and Wieck, it seemed, could not resist. By instinct, he did what he always did to something that made itself vulnerable, he attacked. Demands, impossible financial insistences, intrusions and harangues, judiciously spiced with complaints, injuries, spites and scorn – and why not? It had worked before. The mistake was not his tactics but his timing. His letter arrived in her hands the same week as a package from Schumann, and Schumann, for once, knew more than Wieck. In the first instance, he sent music, these *Novelletten*, in which, he said, she must notice herself in every phrase, every bar. He would never give her up – did she hear? In the second instance, she had to sober up! To realise that Wieck would never come round to persuasion, appeasement, offers, and that she must act without him or continue to insult the man she *claimed* to love. In the third instance, she must trust and obey her good Robert; after all, were not men above women? In the fourth instance – here his handwriting became larger, firmer – she must sign an affidavit. He was prepared to ask for her hand amicably one last time, then seek the courts' permission for a marriage instead. Fifth, he had written to her mother in Berlin, her *real* mother, the sweet and reasonable Frau Bargiel, and Frau Bargiel supported them fully. Sixth, he had put money aside, counted up more than enough in bonds, property, inheritance and was almost frightened at their wealth. Now! The rest was up to her. *Trust and obey!* he wrote. *Steel yourself! Sign!*

It's lovely, Henriette said, sniffing. Like a poem.

Expensive vellum, said Emilie.

Get a lawyer, said Pauline. She opened her purse, took out an address.

Next day, alone, Clara walked out past bonfires and stray hussars, past military police carts and broken glass to a place she had never been to meet someone she didn't know. There, in the tiny, green-walled rooms at Delapalme's, she signed three papers before witnesses, watched the affidavit stamped, paid in cash and walked back by the same route. Planks of wood were scattered over the roads and shops were boarded. In the distance, the Tuilleries were banked like a fort, smoke rising from the far-off gates. Only the week before there had been riots and revolution on these self-same streets, fifty people shot. Some musicians from the smaller orchestras, they said, were already begging. Then, Paris was always volatile. And she was not Parisian. That it might start again gave her nothing to fear. What frightened her was the stuckness, having only lessons to teach, these tedious Englishwomen with false hair, rouge and watches, even if they had not run away; that the salons and halls were closed, that Pauline was packing for Spain. Clara Wieck was finished with Paris. That much was clear. As she turned to cross the street, she saw a man watching her from an upstairs window. He watched her to the end of the alleyway, her sober German face and thin coat, the speed of her. Over the tatters of barricades, blown rags of paper, her boots, he observed, barely touched the ground.

❖─◦◉◦─❖

He had had crow's feet since last she saw him, he said. How could he help but age with such a scandalous girl for a bride? *I know everything you do*, he wrote, *and have thought through what you have not provided.* Rosalie would be chaperone. *Don't take the three o'clock, take the one o'clock or nothing. And wrap up warm* – these dear German states were not France, or had she forgotten? Altenberg! He could hardly believe it! Altenberg, Schneeberg, Zwickau, Leipzig! Was not her heart filled with joy? He could see her, picture her now. *Never forget*, he wrote. *I see you always. I know everything you do.*

Her father had always said the same. Her father and Robert. Two men were pissing against cartwheels as she folded the paper, not caring who saw. He knows everything I do. She thought of Father, just as he would be thinking of her. She could picture him quite clearly in his armchair, a man in his own home; Clementine at his side, with writing paper, ink. As the horses picked up speed, she recalled signing the affidavit, watching it fold inside his efficient ledgers for copying, setting in motion. He knows everything I do. He would know she was coming home, by which route, when she would arrive in Leipzig. *Her piano, her clothes, her two little sisters.* She imagined herself waiting at her own front door, knocking, the shutter bolts clicking, the sound of locks turning from inside. It wouldn't matter how hard she knocked. Her diaries. Her letters, dear Lord, her letters. Henriette offered a pastille from a figured tin, her hands shaking with the rattling of the coach. Even before Clara reached, they tumbled, poured like pearls on to the dusty floor and under seats, into corners, behind travel bags and cases, rolling like worry beads all the way to Mainz.

❖─◦◉◦─❖

Lawyers at dawn, then. Who would have thought?

Conditions

1   The couple, if they marry, may not live in Saxony.
2   7000 thalers in savings from previous earnings of Clara Wieck forfeit.
3   Schumann's statement of income to be guaranteed by the courts.
4   Schumann must have no communication from Wieck unless Wieck expressly wishes it.
5   All inheritance rights pertaining to Clara Wieck rescinded.

Leipzig was worse and it was not worse. He had begun the business of not being there already, packing for Dresden as he always did, this time for good. She would not see her house again, her things where she had left them. It was terrible and not terrible. Sometimes it seemed absurd. She was not destitute, after all, she had a mother who took her to Berlin, aunts who tided things over, Robert offering every help. For the first time in years, she could see the man she loved openly, freely. They had their health, after a fashion, and they laughed, did they not, at his arrogance? She could play her *Romance* for him, hear him play the *Novelleten* back – and was not everything merely a diversion en route to an inevitable conclusion? And when these terrible, terrible court proceedings were over, would they not reconcile, mend what had broken, heal into a family, a family where fathers and daughters might be in harmony with each other once more? But.

But.

Renewed conditions

1   All personal profits from past seven years of concert touring gifted to her brothers.
2   1000 thalers for return of piano and effects.
3   8000 thalers (two-thirds of his total capital reserves) from the account of R. SCHUMANN to be set aside as marriage settlement to accrue interest in preparation for eventual (inevitable) failure of marriage.
4   Three-month concert tour in the company of her father for

a guaranteed sum of 6000 thalers, and the agreement she postpone marriage until she is twenty-one.

The Bargiel children watching her with their wide green eyes, Bargiel himself coughing and sighing into the night, the stink of sickness and boiled fish that clung to the very walls. Walking in the Tiergarten for hours, visiting the Mendelssohns ceaselessly, not wishing or willing to go back to the house that Bargiel owned, her mother paid for. Planning programmes in her head to find capital – there was the necessity of earning, was there not – to find her own dowry if nothing else? The bride who provided no dowry, even if her father had run away with it, provided no respect for the husband. And Robert understood that, for all his talk of settling and *hausfraus*; he knew what she meant when she told him *I must play*. She meant Stettin and Stuttgard, crowds and applause, a set of Berlin dates and 450 *thalers* profit. By *play*, she meant *work*, which was what *play* meant, had always meant. But.

> Questions
> 5 Do these young people possess the financial means for marriage? and
> 6 do they have the personal capacity for their marriage to last? Clara Wieck cannot cook, clean or run a household. She was not raised to it. She has a temperament that requires constant support, ie the temperament of an ARTIST.

But. Her father followed her everywhere. Though he packed up their house, her house – her clothes, her piano, her money – rather than meet her in the streets, he followed her relentlessly nonetheless. He followed her in letters to other people, in hints to hirers, organisers, sweet heaven to *newspapers*. He followed her in her room at night, when she wrote to Robert, how much she pitied him that he was brought to this. He followed her even on to the stage and whispered over her shoulder that her notes were sick without him, that her bows were graceless, that nowhere would she be acceptable without the blessing of her father, that everyone, everyone would know how badly she had turned out. Flyers and bill sheets, letters and rumours, everywhere she was due to play.

Timely Information

7   Clara Wieck is travelling without the consent of her father.

8   She knows only stiff English Broadwoods and will ruin any instrument she touches.

9   She is sorely in need of lessons and is not playing well.

10 The noble mind of the King of Prussia will surely forbid her to appear or to profit from her defiance, and tickets bought for her concerts will be money wasted.

11 She is on the verge of bankruptcy and will return, penniless, a beggar at my door.

He knows everything I do — what's more, he had made every intimacy, every plea, public, turned his daughter into a parade of faults for all to see. *He has read all my letters to you, Clärchen. He knows everything, he will do anything.* Horribly, his words, or something like them, slipped into Robert's mouth, surfaced like drowned heads in Robert's letters. *I may come to your concert, I may not. I am busy, however, so don't expect me. Never expect. And when your father starts in on his lies, don't you defend me at all? This is your loyalty! Your constancy! Well, then, play the Good Child if you must, but I am an adult man and I need a wife. And quickly! My rooms are in a terrible state and certain things prey on my mind that only a wife can — alleviate. When I say wife, however, don't assume I mean only you.* And she could not account for it, save to wonder if he wished her back in Leipzig again, if he meant that she did not behave as a wife should, and wept for hours alone, afraid to tell her mother. *Camilla Pleyel invited me to her rooms the other day — I could hardly refuse, even though she was in bed, a dark shape reaching for me. I should not say any more, but this is fair warning. Return to your father if that's what you want. I won't stop you.*

When Robert's letters stopped altogether, when she learned that her father had turned up on stage to turn pages for the same Miss Pleyel, and that Friedrich Wieck, the proudest man in Leipzig, had fawned over her like a lover, kissed her hand, all but swooned at La Pleyel's feet, only then did the face-ache, the throbbing in her shoulders, the hectoring pain in her head force her to cancel that evening's concert and go to bed. She lay but could not sleep. Her eyes watered effortlessly, not like crying at all, but oozing, overloaded sponges, puddling in her ears. I should give up touring, she thought, I have not the strength. I should give up composing, I have not the talent, no woman has. I should give up this terrible life and marry him now. The same piece of lace in her hands was dotted with blood and poor stitching, no use to anyone. This was what came of darning without a thimble. She had no thimble. She had not the simplest of things. With winter coming, she had no thick cloak, for her father refused to send it. *I should* — she hesitated, thought of omelettes and bad coffee, Robert thinking this should be amusing — *I should learn to cook.* And so she could. She could stop playing tomorrow if she chose. She had a room in Berlin at the Bargiels' for as long as it took, a room with dark-green shutters, a white cut-work shade, a rag rug at her dressing table worn clean through. *Five rooms*, he had written. *Blue wallpaper, copper engravings. Think, Clärchen! Does the fame matter? Really matter? No! For my Clara is to be a happy wife! I have a premonition, a vision from God!* She stayed in her dun-coloured hotel bed, her pictureless room, postponing her opening date two more days till the letters came.

The first was from Robert saying he had been sick, so sick, he was aware he had written oddly. *Pray for me! My head is like lead, so I can scarcely stand up. I am dizzy, eaten into, all but finished! You don't know how much, dear girl, I want to embrace you; how much I depend on you! O Lord, to depend!* To weep in someone's arms, to fade away, to cling. How glorious to *depend*, she thought, and for pity's sake, for the very notion of it, she leaked all over again.

The second letter, however, was from Ernestine. Dear Ernestine, writing to anyone who'd listen. Ernestine was widowed and Ernestine was penniless. There were legal complications, she wrote, no will, in-laws who had taken everything, a father who could not help. What should she do, she wrote, the ink fading already on the words, the fold marks on the paper stronger than her florid cursive. Perhaps, she wondered, Clara knew of a position? For someone who had never learned to teach? Who had not touched a keyboard the past few years? Clara sat up on her pillows, nose swollen as a tuber, and recalled Ernestine's teenage face. She had white-cuffed wrists, the rose-backed comb with which she had brushed her hair, a laugh like a child. She recalled their playing Schubert duets as though it were a game, how Ernestine knew how to sit, how to tilt her profile to look pleasing. Now, here was Ernestine, with her big eyes and her slim waist, learning something new – how to offer her desperation as prettily as possible. This was what her years of kindness, of pleasant disposition, had fitted her for: for begging and wringing her hands in the hope she appealed.

Clara pressed the heels of her hands into her eyes and squeezed till she saw stars. Perhaps she thought it would push her courage back into place. She squeezed till it hurt. And when her vision cleared, she got out of bed. The sun was watery in the sky outside and children were running. A man at the edge of the road was selling sticks and chestnuts, his gloves raddled with holes, a dog at his feet. She watched them for a moment, no one buying, then turned to the jug on her dresser and began washing her face. This shutting oneself away was a poison. It made her weak and helpless. Clara Wieck would not be helpless. They could gossip, stare, whisper, cut her in the street if they chose, but she'd be presentable while they did it. After that, there was a tuner to hire, notices to arrange; people to see, people to play for. No one's beggar, no one's burden, Clara Wieck was going to see her dear friend Herr Doctor Mendelssohn, his wife Cécile, to see Emilie or to see no one at all. The main thing was to keep moving, it didn't matter where. Clara Wieck, Royal and Imperial Virtuosa in Ordinary to the Court of Vienna, was choosing a bonnet, pulling on her best gloves. Chaperone or no chaperone, she was going out.

Some said Wieck was finally crazy. Others thought he already had been for years. Most could not have cared less, but they talked, how they talked. People are always saying something, he bellowed at Clementine, issuing open letters of his declaration to the court. It's what people do.

Declaration

1 The Court should realise that Herr Schumann is incapable of supporting himself.

2 Herr Schumann is lazy, conceited, unreliable and spendthrift.

I present letters from his own mother (received some years ago) attesting the very same.

3 Herr Schumann has let his newspaper founder, squandered his talents and the goodwill of others, and is further a mediocre composer whose music is not only unclear but impossible to perform and unintelligible to rational people.

4 Herr Schumann has damaged his own hand through ruinous self-will.

5 Herr Schumann is alcoholic, a drinker in secret or with one other person in wine houses and at home. He has a mystical and dreamy personality and means to exploit Clara Wieck (proved by his treatment of his previous fiancée, Ernestine von Fricken) for his own ends.

6 Herr Schumann is incompetent, childish, unmanly, and incapable of social adjustment. He will hamper her career and destroy both the happiness and reputation of Clara Wieck as a performer.

7 Herr Schumann will be unable to keep his family and Clara Wieck will need to keep their household to the detriment of her happiness and security. Clara Wieck is unsuited to a life of piano teaching yet Herr Schumann would demand this of her. Clara Wieck is unsuited to housewifery and wholly unprepared for its demands. Clara Wieck does not know how to run a house but only how to practise Art.

8 Herr Schumann is sexually promiscuous and mentally unstable.

9 Herr Schumann cannot speak clearly.

10 His handwriting is hideous poor.

What did she do? Nothing. What did she feel? Nothing that showed.

Invisible bruising isn't invisible for ever. It appears. If only to the sufferer, it appears. Her bones creaked from being torn in two. She had blackouts and fainting fits, numbness in one arm, in both, in her neck and shoulders, difficulty in concentrating, sleep problems and tremor in her hands. No one noticed a thing, certainly not audiences. They applauded, though she could not remember whole stretches of being on stage, whole *études* from beginning to end. She stood at the finish, they applauded – and it racked her wondering if she had deserved it, if they should have stayed silent instead. It racked her when Alwin came, carrying his violin in a battered case, asking for money for his upkeep, his lessons, his continued apprenticeship. Father would not pay if she could, he said. Why should she not pay? And it was Alwin who cried.

Is there nothing he will not do? Schumann asked, his lips white, and Frau Bargiel opined there was not. Wieck was a creature made entirely of will: if he chose to be deaf, dumb and blind, then that's what he'd be. The picture in her mother's words haunted Clara, turned itself over and over like a tongue on a toothache. A creature made of will, like a genie, perhaps, a demon from the sands of Arabia who could make terrible things come true. Deaf, dumb and blind, was he not pitiable? Was it possible, truly possible, to lose one's senses by choosing to do so? Was it possible too, then, to kill someone if they chose to die of it? If they chose *ingratitude* as the name of its cause? He had always said so. And how did you appease the unappeasable, even stand up to it? How did you make it stop? She wondered what the boundaries of filial duty might be, what the boundaries of paternal duty might be, whether they even existed. When she read in her newspaper he had championed Camilla Pleyel as *The Best Virtuosa Yet Known*, she stopped wondering and collected herself instead. She collected her things. One duty she was sure of, never doubted at all. Through Hamburg, Bremen, Lübeck; a first sight of the sea, a monstrous, shimmering silverness that stretched further than all sight of land, that seethed with mist all the way to Travemünde; nursing her memories of Clementine, round-faced and pop-eyed, who had never counselled her, never given a word of soothing or advice, never given her anything, not so much as a cherry or a plum, nursing her memories to hatred for one must hate *something*, she played. She played.

What did he do? Dear Christ God Almighty he thought he would *implode*. He had thought it before but this time was the worst. That such ignominy, such shame existed, that one could feel so conspicuous, so hateful and ground-down simply from *words*. How many had read these dreadful letters and bills? How many thought them true? Now he had received his prized doctorate, how many more eyes were upon him, waiting to judge him for nothing at all? If he drank, he imagined people looking, checking if he would stagger, if he would mutter to himself like a madman, if he would stumble like a child. If he spoke, he thought they'd make judgements on the very tone of his voice; if he did not speak – well. They'd say he was an idiot. If he smiled they would think him heartless, uncaring; if he braved it out despite them, the name he'd get was *callous*. If he wept, they would think him weak, unmanly, self-pitying and, probably, drunk. Herr Doctor Schumann was lazy, conceited, unreliable, *mediocre* – was that what they said? These things Wieck accused him of, said made him an *unfit husband*? It was unbearable. Insupportable! And what was she saying to contradict him? Anything? By God how he would like to strike something, anything, anyone. But he was not the kind of man who struck, and this was the price. Anguish. Ghastly tearing at the soul with no escape but drink.

Wieck's vile adjectives circled in his head like flies, nipping into his peace of mind as though they would never stop. Perhaps that was Wieck's idea: to undermine and destabilise him to the point of madness and *wild!* – prove his point. Perhaps he was trying to re-create a Schumann of his own making from sheer bluster. Perhaps, and Schumann's blood ran cold when he thought it, perhaps Herr Wieck really was the devil, an evil monster who knew how much this tore at his victim, who cared nothing for the pain he caused, who meant only Not to Lose Face? And in the course of his evil, whom would he persuade by his hideous public rantings? Surely no one would believe these dreadful things? These *lies*? Becker, romantic despite his years, told him no one could judge harshly one who *wrote* so affectingly, while Reuter, reserving judgements of anyone, anything, dosed him with tea and silence, nothing else. Increasingly that silence alone was preferable.

He stopped answering the door to Reuter, kept to himself, burned his candles, and read. He read Shakespeare and Burns and Heine, Chamisso and Rückert, Eichendorff, Goethe, Byron and Lordknew who, wrestling their words into other shapes as he paced his rooms, spoke them aloud. *Madness churns in my soul and my heart is sick and sore.* And, reading, he almost forgot about Wieck and got lost in syllables. He began to make something whole from their broken bits. *In the depths of my* soul, an image. He almost forgot that a group of Dresden lawyers would decide his happiness, that a spiteful old man against whom he might not protest should hound him like a wild animal, for wishing properly, whole-heartedly, to love. He remembered Florestan and Eusebius, running poems over his tongue — *You are like a flower* — into his fingers — *I look at you and I tremble* — refashioning them into something beyond themselves, something of himself, herself, something — *in my dreams I saw you last night, your gentle face as pale as death* — filled with sound.

Every morning I rise and wonder
will she come today

My heart is sair, I daurna tell,
My heart is sair for somebody

With myrtles and roses, bright and fair,
I would make this book a shrine

You are my heart and soul, my bliss and pain
The world I live in, the paradise to which I will come

You are like a flower, so fine and pure and beautiful
I look at you and a sorrow steals into my heart.

I am sending a greeting like the scent of roses
I am sending it to one with a face like a rose

Father and mother are long dead
no one in my homeland knows me now.

My love is like a red red rose that's newly sprung in June

Poor Peter staggers past as pale as death
Surely he has climbed out of his grave?

The waves whisper and murmur over her silent house
In the quiet moonlight, a voice is calling: Remember me!

Remember me!

What did he do?
He *sang*.

Dearest Clara,

Something new. Since yesterday morning, very early,
I have written almost 27 pages of music, weeping and
laughing aloud, as I wrote

| *Liederkreis von Heine* | *Myrthen* |
| Song cycle with words by Heine | Myrtles |

	Widmung
Morgens steh' ich auf	Freisinn
Es Treibt mich hin	Der Nussbaum
Ich wandelte unter den Bäumen	Jemand
Lieb Liebchen	Sitz' ich allein
Schöne Wiege meiner Leiden	Setze mir nicht
Warte, warte, wilder Schiffsman	Talismane
Berg' und Burgen schau'n herunter	Die Lotosblume
Anfangs wollt' ich fast verzagen	Lied der Suleika
Mit Myrthen und Rosen	Die Hochländer-Witwe
	Mutter! Mutter!
	Lieder der Braut
	Hochländers Abschied
	Hochländers Wiegenlied

	Mein Herz ist schwer
Sag' an, o lieber Vogel mein	Rätsel
Dem roten Röslein	Leis rudern hier
Was soll ich sagen?	Wenn durch die Piazzetta
Jasminenstrauch	Hauptmanns Weib
Nur ein lächelnder Blick	Weit, weit
	Was will die einsame Träne
	Niemand
	Im Westen
	Du bist wie eine Blume
	Aus den östlichen Rosen
	Zum Schluss

Six books of songs and ballads! I can't tell you how
easy it has become for me, how happy it makes me feel.
I write while standing or pacing my room – not at the
piano at all. This is a different kind of music, one that
does not have to be born through the fingers first –

Die beiden Grenadiere   *Dichterliebe*
Die feindlichen Brüder   A Poet's Love
Loreley
Der arme Peter   Im wunderschönen Monat Mai
Ich wandre nicht   Aus meinen Tränen spriessen
                                         Die Rose, die Lilie
                                         Wenn ich in deine Augen seh
                                         Ich will meine Seele tauchen
                                         Im Rhein, im heiligen Strome
                                         Iche grolle nicht
Liederkreis von Eichendorff   Und wüssten die Blumen
Song cycle with words by Eichendorff   Das ist ein Flöten und Geigen
                                         Hör' ich das Liedchen klingen
                                         Ein Jüngling liebt ein Mädchen
In der Fremde   Am leuchtendem Sommermorgen
Intermezzo   Ich hab' im Traum geweinet
Waldesgespräch   Allnächtlich im Traume
Die Stille   Aus alten Märchen winkt es
Mondnacht   Die alten, bösen Lieder
Schöne Fremde
Auf einer Burg
In der Fremde
Wehmut Zwielicht
Im Walde
Frühlingsnacht
                                         Die Löwenbraut

Der Knabe mit dem Wunderhorn   Die Kartenlegerin
Der Page
Der Hidalgo   Die rote Hanne

And this spring, it takes me by surprise to see how
suddenly everything is in blossom, how profuse everything is. I can't calm down.

I am composing so much it frightens me. But I can't
seem to help it. I am having to sing myself to death
like a nightingale

Frauenliebe und -leben
Woman's Life and Love   Sonntags am Rhein
                                         Ständchen
Seit ich ihn gesehen   Nichts Schöneres
Er, der Herrlichste von allen   An den Sonnenschein
Ich kann's nicht fassen   Dichters Genesung
Du Ring an meinem Finger   Liebesbotschaft
Helft mir, ihr Schwestern
Süsser Freund, du blickest   Märzveilchen
An meinem Herzen   Muttertraum
Nun hast du mir den ersten Schmerz getan Der Soldat
                                         Der Spielmann
                                         Verratene

The old ugly songs, the terrible, tormenting dreams; let's bury them!
Bring me a coffin.
There's a great deal to rest in there – I can't say what.
Bring me a bier made of solid timber, longer than the bridge at Mainz.
Bring me twelve giants, even stronger than the Cathedral at
Cologne on the Rhine.
They are to carry the coffin, sink it deep in the sea
(such a burden needs such a grave).
And why is the coffin so heavy, so vast?
I am burying my love, my pain.

What did he do?
He bought her a new piano. He sued Wieck for slander and won.

Juchhe! Victoria!

He sang.

When judgement came she was elsewhere, in Jena, Muses, Leibenstein, Erfurt, Gotha, earning, in case. He was waiting at the courthouse door. Reckless, he took the coach and, when she opened her door, he was there, his red coat, his green waistcoat, his necktie scented with violets.

I am come for a concert, he said. They say Clara Wieck is to play her last. She stared at his face, his button collar, and he let her. For a measured eternity, he let her.

After this, he said eventually, the public must learn she has a new name.

Orange lilies trembled in the crook of his arm, staining his sleeve with pollen.

Little wife! he said, laughing. With no idea of what it means, the courts have pronounced on happiness. We may be married, little wife.

Little wife.

It was true. Some Henselt, Liszt, Schubert, a great deal of Thalberg and a short *Romanze* by Clara Wieck and it was all but done. She would have her own name no longer. Her person, her money or her lack of it, her worries, sickness and health were for another to share. And after all this time, so abruptly! So wholly without recourse to change. She recalls sleeping like a child, waking to an awareness of difference, of something having happened, something unquantifiable, not able to be wholly grasped. She must have played the piano, the usual three hours' practice still unremarkable and expected. It must have been that afternoon, then, that afternoon that he took her walking till they found a stream, the water sheeny with summer light and dragonflies. It was hot and they talked in fits and starts, almost embarrassed to be so unobserved. He asked again and again about the time he first came to Leipzig, what she recalled and did not recall, what he had worn or said. He capped what she said with quotations from letters, and sang little fragments of their game-playing themes. He told her tales about his family and their stuck-in-Zwickau thinking, their disbelief that with a family publishing concern for the taking, he should wish to study music, of all things music, how confused they were that he read so much despite it! Did she recollect, he asked, that he read poems to her? That she had had not the

187

name of one Shakespeare play in her head? And now she knew so much, so very much. He held her hand.

Near five in the evening, doped with his stories and carefully selected reminiscences, she brought him back to her room to rest. He might sit with her, she said, read a poem if he liked. He liked. He would read Heine, who was not the cynic everyone thought him, if they had ears to hear. He would like very much to read Heine, Rückert, perhaps, as he would when they were married. He pulled the shutters half across for shade, the light catching his hair so it flared white. He sat beside her on a blue sofa that belonged to neither of them, opened his book and read. *You are like a flower, so pure and beautiful. I look at you and I tremble. I tremble.* And his voice petered to nothing. He didn't move, just stood, looking at her, sweat sheening his brow. He was, she realised, nervous. There was nothing to fear now and it made him nervous. *A flower*, he whispered, half coughed, his face suddenly drawn, uncertain.

What would any good woman do? Any woman with pity in her heart? She reached out a hand and stroked his cheek. Deliberately, carefully, he caught and held her there, close to him, pulled her by the wrist to bring her closer. *Pure and beautiful* — drew her nearer still. She heard him close the book with his free hand, saw him place it gently on the sofa beside her as the circlet of his grip about her wrist tightened. His lips touched her temple, her cheek. She felt his fingers weave gently into the hair at the nape of her neck, his weight and warmth pressing towards her. No longer Clara Wieck, not yet someone else, in this place that was not a place; somewhere on the outskirts, rented, full of concert flowers. *One night*, Emilie had said, *you will not miss my company for one night now Robert is here.* The man she had imagined in her Paris bedroom, conjured for Pauline while she combed out her hair, was here before her, where he would always be. She would, she realised, heartbeat flooding in her ears, undo the dress hooks herself. She would allow some dignity, the space for definiteness and decision. She might ask him to look away, but she would not resist this. She would never resist this. The scent of sun-slackened roses, his mouth closing over hers. She eased back in his arms, felt the momentary hesitation before he held her firm, an embrace close as drowning. *The final excitement of men makes fluid.* Pauline's words whispering in her ears. Clara Wieck could not cook or run a home, but some talents, it seemed, were already anticipated. They were wholly, abundantly, ready to bloom.

⊷⊶⊙⊝⊷⊶

The tiny church at Schönefeld; few guests.

A blue dress, a handful of white flowers. Mother and Bargiel, coughing like bones in a butcher's bag, Becker, Reuter, the Krägens, the Voigts and Emilie – the merest scatter of friends. There was music at Aunt Carl's house, some dancing; nothing riotous. He said almost nothing at all, sat pinkly in the corner, a glass tilting in his hand; overcome, Dr Reuter said, and he was right. Dr Reuter was always right. *Heavens, Clara!* Madame Voigt said, one eyebrow arched, *that tonight your Robert should show himself so shy!* Clara, the myrtle wreath still pinned in her hair, opened the window to the evening air. A tinker was calling his dog to heel, knives and metalware clattering at his back. Behind him the streets of this unknown part of Leipzig, and beyond that, the slope towards Grimaisse Strasse, the *Mountain Lily* where she had been a child, the steeple at the edge of the square where a man had been beheaded. *Think of me on your wedding day.* Mad Woyzeck in his white shirt. *Think of me.* But Clara did not think of Woyzeck, not then. She watched only the street, faded it into her reflection, the spread of her fingers on the pane. Slowly, she saw him doubled against her; for a moment, a dizzying split-second, thought he was someone else.

Robert, chalky against the window's night-black sheen, was standing behind her, his hands reaching for her shoulders. The reflection of his eyes stayed keen, watching her, knowing she was watching back. Slowly, his mouth began shaping words without speech, a message from his mirror-self to her, only her. *Eine Blume.* She watched it form and fade. *A flower, a flower.* She saw her own reflected smile make a ghost over his, the shadows of leaves in her hair. On the window clasp, her wedding ring, glittering like a blade.

FIVE

Helft mir

Help me

Number 5 Inselstrasse, Leipzig.

Apartments in the Friedrichstadt district, where all the houses are new: small rooms but pristine, cosy. The house of the Leipzig Virtuosa, the one whose father left for Dresden under a cloud. Clara Wieck. Her house. Not on the upper floors, but *near the ground*. The requested rooms were quite specific on that score. One day-maid hired at 14 thaler per annum, five rooms, one piano, thin walls.

She was twenty-one. What did she expect of marriage? Here at its outset, what did she think? That marriage must mark people, and mark them for good. That it ennobles those who live righteously and rigorously within its strictures, woman as helpmate and man as master, if only in name. That his cares are now her cares, his sickness hers to shoulder, his worries and dreams the critical subject for her concern. Two hearts as one, lives shared and troubles halved, the commencement of a *family* with children, worldly goods held in common. And everything, anything, the world itself achievable through love, much love, a boundlessness of love.

CLARA
- valises, chests and travelling bags
- two pairs of stout boots, two pairs of dress, five pairs evening slippers
- maps, pens, a collection of letters, a quantity of music
- her wedding piano
- a decorated wooden box of French souvenirs
- very little jewellery, a watch, a gilded clock with a matching key
- a handful of pictures

- a small sewing chest, needles and silks
- what clothes remain from Paris, Berlin, the Thuringian tour
- what savings remain from Paris, Berlin, the Thuringian tour
- an edition of songs bound in velvet (her husband's wedding gift!)
- a cookery book detailing cuts of pork, beef, mutton and fowl (as above)

ROBERT

- tables and chairs, cups, pots, saucers and kettles, glasses and bottles
- the music bureau
- account books, boxes of newspapers, manuscript
- pebbles, ribbons, leaves, wax seals and locks of hair in a glass box
- the book chests
- many books
- more books
- portraits, pictures, paintings, etchings
- more books still
- an impressive copper kettle and stove
- spits and roasting pans, ladles, a handful of blunt knives
- shirts and trousers, stocks and tiepins
- pomades and colognes, a shaving razor strop and wash-rags
- cigars, lamps
- everything else

JOINTLY

- a fireside rug, vases, flowers, vials of rose-water
- the marital bed
- a great many sheets

This diary.

~⇥◎⇤~

My dear, beloved young wife

First let me kiss you on this special day, your first as a wife, the first day of your 22nd year. This little book begun today has an intimate meaning: it will be a diary about everything that affects us both in our household and our marriage; our wishes and hopes shall be written here. It will be a book for requests from one to the other when spoken words are not enough, one of mediation and reconciliation when we misunderstand each other – in short, a good, true friend in whom we may confide everything. What is written here may be read aloud, what has been forgotten added, the whole week weighed to see if we are building our lives aright and perfecting even more our beloved Art. Entries for the week shall never cover less than a page, and whichever of us fails to write as much will receive a punishment! (Anecdotes and jests will be by no means excluded.) All the joys and sorrows of married life will be truly written here so it may give us pleasure even in old age. If you agree, wife of my heart, sign your name here under mine.

Robert

Your wife, who is devoted to you with
her whole heart
Clara

What did they do?

They studied. Shakespeare. Beethoven. Jean-Paul. Bach. The right way to sear veal. The copying of quotations from *Hamlet* and *King Lear* regarding the beauty of music, the study of harmony at the fireside, the

Well-Tempered Clavier open on the desk. *It is not so grand as your house but it is all our own. My wife has worked this napkin, these beans for supper she chopped herself. She studies fugues with her husband in the evening, he smoking cigars while she stitches a collar. Is this not the perfect life?* What was it made of, this first settling into the married state? What, when her children ask, does she remember? *She has played already and then against my wishes. You may not tire her, for she is mine now. Mine. A husband and may not be denied!* Teasing at his expense, her expense; *the same expense now,* Becker said. Robert, his mouth hidden behind his hand as he laughs, Herr Doctor Mendelssohn smiling his driest smile.

I hear you, dearest, working from the other room.

She wrote this sentence, lovesick as a schoolgirl, penned his name on the blotter's edge. She would merely sit and listen as he played or repeated a phrase, honed its harmony, astonished at this thing that had come about. Man and wife. A bed, a diary, this house. One piano. Thin walls.

The deliberateness of her former life, its careful schedules, rosters and planned moves, the solid paragraphs of duty cautiously punctuated by crowds and applause had never struck her so fully as when it was no more. She had, she realised, expected it to return. Living with her mother had been a mere interlude, after all, a necessary and terrifying hiatus on the way back to something she might recognise as *my life.* Now *my life* was *our life,* and what that meant took learning. A great deal of learning. She had been in different surroundings, in different countries and ramshackle hotels; different preferences and sensitivities were nothing new. Troupes of visitors and musicians to her house had been commonplace, almost routine. But to play the hostess, to choose the food and ensure it was cooked and plentiful, to have no one else to blame for a lack of potatoes, shirts, coal in the scuttle; to know Agnes would do exactly as she was bidden but would not look in Robert's direction but hers only *hers,* as though she knew, as though Clara must know by virtue of being *Frau Schumann* what that bidding should be. Ash that came out of a morning fire grate could be sold or used for cleaning-paste, windows needed vinegar to keep a shine, fat on the surface of mutton seeped beneath the fingernails when touched – there was no end of detail to the part.

She imagined what *real* wives did, *real* women, those whose effort she had hardly noticed until now – her mother and Aunt Carl and angel-faced Cécile Mendelssohn, Clementine in her hideous matron's bonnet and droopy aprons – scouring her memory for clues. Should she ask? Not at all. She could not have borne the shame. *Clara Wieck does not know how to run a house.* But if they knew, if they suspected, they did not mind. Robert's friends came anyway, Clara's too. Verhulst the Dutchman and Hauptmann, Becker and the Voigts, Emilie List and Sterndale Bennett and Reuter and Krägen and Mendelssohn, their dear and doggedly cheerful Felix, who insisted she play and do *nothing else for she is peerless, and stolen from my ears under my nose.* He told them stories about the Scottish mountains which, he said, resembled nothing else, the English Queen who had held her husband's hand and not cared who had seen, how brazen they were despite their constant fog. *You must see for yourself, Clara,* he said; *England would approve of Clara Wieck.* And they laughed that he had not her name upon his lips yet, that Clara *Schumann* was still somehow a stranger, an unknown creature who had no past behind her to speak of at all. They laughed, of course they did. They smoked cigars and drank champagne, they made few judgements.

And when they left, when the door was drawn for the night, Robert and Clara Schumann were alone with the oddity of each other for company, the vague and persistent prickle of surprise. The sound of him, singing in another room, the sight of him searching for a mislaid pen, the scent of tobacco that meant he was near – someone called *my husband*. She peeled him apples and burned him stews to watch him eat, his fork poised in mock suspense against the perils of her cooking. She brushed nothing from his lapels, traced her fingers over his books, his litter of papers, his writing desk, the man-shaped coat hanging on a door hook when no one saw, and in all of it, this pleasure in his very presence, was the sensation of freedom, of boundless *permission*.

He looked wholly at peace with the place, with simply being there: he had no need to run his hands over its polished surfaces, to speak the words to himself to believe these four walls were *home*. He smoked at breakfast, spilling ash in the milk. He closed the shutters at night without asking, left a lamp burning all night at the end of the hall, heedless of the expense. *We will have no hours of darkness in our house*, he said, *only twilight, the promise of dawn.* And in that twilight, between winter-weight sheets and woollen bedding, was another life still. Half seen in half-light, its only music their patterns of breathing, this life that happened between pieces of themselves. What they had done before was hampered and fretful, and she had not known. Now this spaciousness of night-clothes that shifted so easily, covered so loosely; the textures of skin and cloth blending, the animal brush of hair. That a man might touch her with more than his lips, his hands; the involvement of her own body in this business, these sudden whispers and murmurs that were her self. That her mother might have done these things, felt these things with her father seemed unbelievable, that Clementine had done so less credible still. The thought was dismissible, proof only that other ways existed. What she and Robert enacted, one to the other, was surely unique.

He began with his mouth on hers, this light press of his kiss changing to something fuller, repeated. He held her shoulders and turned her face aside, running his kiss towards her neck – always this. Then he moved on top of her, spreading his weight over her chest, lifting his nightshirt, reaching for the hem of hers. She learned the patterns quickly, easily, with no difficulty at all. What surprised her was his cry, the muffled sound of something like pain, stopping his breath and how tender it made her feel. What surprised her was how much she wanted this thing that happened between them, the bewilderment of excess, its repeated lessons; how much *liquefaction* was involved and wished for, gloried in. She learned to rise to bathe, to return to bed again; to sleep cupped into his body, to lift her hair to allow his breath to fall on the nape of her neck. Sometimes they lay awake, neither speaking, watching the flicker of lamplight from the crack-opened door, the sheen of flame on each other's eyes. Sometimes she lay awake alone, watching his face in sleep to know that he was, after all, as contented as herself. He talked in his sleep, nonsense words, and she was young enough to find it funny, to think this her secret. That others had heard it before never occurred. She heard sounds outside the window, people passing in the street, singing, and lay in the dark, feeling herself alone and not alone, the single object of consummate love, the *only* love. The year turned scarlet to grey as she learned it, Agnes carrying washing bowls, more sheets, the emptied piss-pot, saying nothing; lacing the mistress of the house more securely with every passing month.

Shakespeare. Beethoven. Jean-Paul. Bach.

The copying of quotations. Mendelssohn and Becker touring her kitchen admiring the drawer of cooking knives.

> Every beginning is difficult, dear wife. I swear that you agree with me. Again and again I have seen in you the most unpretentious, loving, solicitous wife, and every day I see new accomplishments. We quarrelled only once because of the way you interpret my compositions, but you are not in the right, Clärchen. The composer alone knows how his work is to be presented, no other. It is as if you wish to paint a tree better than God made it. Now do as you're told and give me a kiss.

They ate overcooked hake, played trios, she, Mendelssohn and David; they sang. Robert sang the part for the absent soprano. When Becker and Krägen asked if she would play again, Robert opened another bottle.

My wife will not play if she doesn't wish it. Her playing is for old friends, certainly, but at her discretion. The tours are cancelled, thank the Lord. A war with the pasha of Egypt, and who would have thought that a godsend? A new husband has no wish to leave his warm nest and go to Russia. He wishes to go nowhere at all.

And the new wife? What does she wish for herself? Felix asked. He asked in play but she could not read the look on his face.

A new wife has other things to do, said Cécile, and there was none to say otherwise, not now.

I am a poor traveller, he said. The paper will not run itself.

No, Becker said. And I will not run it for you.

Besides, I am prone to homesickness.

It's true, said Krägen. The very mention of Vienna makes him think he's coming down with typhus.

And Clara might not travel alone, Felix said. You may play for the German public, I hope. The Gewandhaus may still invite Mlle Wieck?

Madame Schumann, Clara said. She was aware of saying it quickly, almost angrily. I will play again as Madame Schumann.

Cécile Mendelssohn laughed. Of course you will. My husband thinks musicians are not normal people. That they are not subject to the rules that govern the rest of us.

I love her the more for it, Robert said. Listen, this will suit you better. We are writing songs together – I select the poems – and every day we read from *Art of Fugue*. You would laugh to see the labour that must be endured!

You should not list our failings, she said, blushing, hoping it didn't show.

I may be nothing short of excellent with such a wife beside me. And she is, she is! His face lit, his eyes shone. To hell with Russia. Play Beethoven, Clara, the C minor we have been studying together. This surpasses anything you may have heard from Mlle Wieck. Daily we grow together and learn more, see more. See if I am not right. Only hear her play this Beethoven, a sonata entire, something the crowd would not understand and tell me whether I am not blessed. Dr Mendelssohn, tell me – am I not the most blessed of men?

Afterwards, he went out drinking with Felix and Becker; Krägen took Cécile home. He returned some hours later when she was already in bed, and had sex with her as immoderately and repeatedly as he had earlier praised her. Do not play so much, he said abruptly when it was done. The soul sickens of too much. If it had not been for my eyes willing it to stop, you should have driven me from the house. The less they hear, the more they want. You need not give in to it. Then he stood.

The library is full of poetry, he said. It won't wait. She did not see him again till morning and did not sleep. He was happy, that was all, testing his husbandly authority. She had teased him and now he responded, that was all. She imagined Felix's face as he had stood at the door, Cécile in her fussy little bonnet and gloves. *Farewell, Virtuosa*, he whispered, a joke for an admired friend, a colleague whose sex had suddenly become something to consider, notice, take account of. We will play the next time I come – but only for each other. If you wish it, of course. Only if it is expressly what you wish.

✦✦✦

First Christmas. He said it as though there had never been Christmas before. Almost blasphemous.

First Christmas.

The tree came from Berlin on a wagon and she baked gingerbread for it herself. Iced stars and white crystals. She gave him three songs, settings of his precious Burns and Heine, and he almost wept. I have written nothing, he said. You bring me the best of gifts and I have nothing of this kind for you. They played for Krägen, Becker and Emilie List in the evening, and Clara sang. Mother did not come from Berlin because the roads were bad, and Bargiel was sick and needed nursing. Bargiel was dying, she suspected. She suspected it was what she was meant to suspect. But they stayed put. We are quiet, she said, us two, and her saying it gave him acute, almost excessive pleasure. He repeated it several times, smiling and whispering to himself. We are quiet indeed! He opened champagne. This quiet and my wife beside me – these are my chiefest joys. He handed her a glass, kept the bottle by his boot heel. She did not drink much, however. The bubbles made her queasy.

By the first week of January she was surer, by the second she told him. *I have hopes*, she said, these very words. She would not even whisper the word *baby*. From these *hopes* he formed his own. They must write a book together, an album of songs that none might tell where one of them begins and the other ends – a joint creation to arrive *some months from now*. Pleased at the joke, he picked out poems the same afternoon.

Rückert – all Rückert. He went out drinking in the evening and danced with her on his return. In the morning she woke alone. Robert was in his rooms playing the same note in patterns: F♯. After ten minutes of the same, F needle ♮. He would not open the door save to shut it again; there was nothing he wanted, nothing he needed save the piano and peace. He was perfectly self-contained.

Clara tried but could not work. The sound of him in the other room drove thinking away and in any case she had visits to make, calling cards to respect. She might lay out the ink and manuscript, pattern the ruler and pencil on her table, but that was all. How could she work? The intensity of his concentration seemed to filter through the walls, staining into the colours of her own, not yet ready, thoughts. And how could she compose with these *other* thoughts picking and picking at her like birds? Since her mother could not come, she called the doctor. He pressed her, asked her embarrassing questions, but confirmed without hesitation. No, he was not sure how long, but she was certainly *expecting*.

Robert was beside himself. He sang. He picked her up and stood her on a table, apologised and brought her back down. He drank their health, his, the health of the town and spent the night with her, one long caress, a hundred kisses, counted one by one, on her arms, her neck, her hands. Thereafter, he returned to his work with more vigour, more fever than before. His head burned, he said; he was racked by pains, nausea, a swollen gut. He had an ache in his jaw, his back, his feet. He could not swallow. She must forgive him if he stayed alone, understand it only as the requirement of a Creative Spirit. He was writing a symphony, and a symphony, he said gravely, was a test of greatness. It also meant wider audiences and he must not fail. Was it not what he had always wanted to do? What she had encouraged him to do when his confidence had flagged? And now, here he was, on the brink of joining the ranks of the Serious! But it had a price, this turn of events. A price he knew she would understand. It pained him that she must repeatedly ask, he felt wretched, but what was to be done? She might not play. *How often you must purchase my songs with invisibility and silence, little Clara, but we love each other truly* – he ran his hand across her still concave belly – *and that must be enough.* Did she see?

She saw.

He would not eat except in the Coffeebaum, came home to write afresh. He looked dishevelled, distraught and would not be embraced. The same week that her morning sickness started in earnest her mother wrote to tell her that Bargiel was dead. Bargiel, who had shepherded her across the street when she was small, speechless, who had offered her cake. One less to rejoice in my pleasure, she thought, one less good man on this earth. Unexpectedly, it made her tearful at times of the day when she found herself alone. It is my condition, she thought, it makes me volatile. She thought of her mother often; hoped vaguely, without expectation, her mother might need her. Then again, her visit would take more than need. She sent money in an envelope, aware she had not earned it, Robert's money. But money nonetheless. She must send money from now on, and more often. And when she earned it, so she would. For now her husband was writing a symphony. The first! Something stuck in her chest just thinking it, mixing an indigestive pain with a queer, elated trepidation. This was a new marker on the long road before them both, full of God knew what pleasures, what shocks. Poor Bargiel! He would have been so proud of Robert. So very, very proud.

Thalberg came to see the Schumann couple: his very phrase: *The Couple.* Thalberg has such beautiful hands, she thought, watching him play, hands like someone in a picture. His scales were strings of pearls, his octaves beyond description. No technique could be more perfect, she said, and Robert agreed, his eyes not on their guest at all. He had work to do, he said, excused himself and Clara sat with Thalberg without knowing what to say. He had not known it was Mendelssohn's birthday; no, he had never met his children; yes, the spring was slow in coming indeed. Her acquaintances in Vienna were as she left them. He did not know the sonatas of Beethoven particularly well, but understood why she studied them. No, she had no concert tours planned. No, the trip to Russia was cancelled: there was fighting in Egypt and Robert disliked travel. A pity, he said. She would like Russia. He admired the wallpaper, her china cups. He stood. Tomorrow he would leave for Dresden, Breslau, Warsaw. *Soon*, he said, *there will be no city I have not played in at least once.* She watched his carriage leave from the upstairs window, the dust of its wheels gusting east.

His sketch was done in four days. Then came orchestration, correction of ranges, marking up of parts, dealings with copyists, Mendelssohn's advice to be asked, David, the leader of the orchestra, to be quizzed, Reuter and Becker, Lordknew who else, to express an opinion. She asked him gently in the marriage diary, implied as if amused, that he had left her out. She left notes for him, themes they had shared when he lodged with her father, pieces they had worked on in tandem. She left the diary open with her handwriting, page after page, gaps to show the absence of his. A rebuke. A wifely thing to do. One day, returned from visiting, a bunch of snowdrops in her hand for the maestro, she found a note open on the hallway table, right beside the lamp, his handwriting pinched and faint. Her fingers rusty from the icy outside air, from lack of practice, she picked it up and read.

> The symphony is all but done. I can only thank the good spirit that guided me through – this joy and anguish mixed! – and in such a short time. Now I need to rest. I am so tired I can scarcely stand – exactly the way a woman must feel after she gives birth, happy yet sick, sore to the soul. You are an angel of forbearance and because you love me, because you are my wife who understands me best of all, will know what best to do. Let me kiss you, Clärchen, gently, when I wake.

He was in their bedroom, an empty bottle beside the bed, one glass. The shutters were drawn, the air sodden with his sweat. Clara kissed his forehead, found it salt but cool enough. Not fever. She slackened his collar anyway, unbuttoned his shirt-front. She undressed him out of his trousers and washed his face with a flannel cloth, put fresh water beside the bed, his flowers in a vase, then went to the piano room. She found a soft shawl and unhooked the facing from the action, damped the strings with the material, tucking it into place neatly so it would not slip. She listened for a moment, but his breathing stayed steady, loud, deep. It would for some time. Without sacrificing the pressure of her fingers, imagining the grandeur of the sound that should have been there, imagining perfection, she played. She worried and listened. As long as nothing came, she played.

Unannounced, unescorted, her piano rolled up at their door one afternoon and demanded admission. Paid for with her own earnings, begged for, bargained for, now out of nothing, her father had sent it on as though he had become bored with keeping it – and without her other belongings, without any sign of sorrow or conciliation: just a piano, speechless, the hasps on the stand flaking more varnish than she remembered. One single inlay, the lower A, was chipped.

Since he has been served sentence – his eighteen days for slander – he sends back your rightful property, Robert said. He hopes to cheat justice by offering this.

It is my piano, Clara said. *Mine.*

He expects us to look upon it as generosity, Robert said. He is slippery as a viper. And Clara said nothing more. The whole wretched past in that wooden casing, filled with her father's absence, his guidance, his correcting hand. Her heart bled for him, the losses he had endured, that she guessed he had endured. It made no sense and irritated her husband, but she felt it nonetheless. They housed the brute with its face to the wall, the only way it would fit, and Robert took to his bed with the symphony. One section for horns was entirely in the wrong register and required correction. He needed to think, he said, but his face was flushed, his blood boiling. She played the prodigal only once in four days, crushing in against the wall to reach; stopped when he wandered in, following the sound, to wonder what was wrong.

When her mother arrived from Berlin, it could be contained no longer. She wept aloud, ashamed for her helplessness, the reversal it demanded. Freshly-widowed Madame Bargiel, who should be comforted, was required to do the comforting: in the end it was much the same thing. What Clara spoke of, however, was not her father. It was someone else. Robert, she said, was sickly. He had not been wholly well for more than one day since they were married – his digestion, his eyes, his interminable nervous fevers – she hesitated, bit her lip – might she be to blame? After the separations and letters and longings, this disappointment, that she could not care for him well enough to make him content, was bitter. She had expected a great deal, it was true. But surely it had not been too much to think he would come at the end of his day and show her what he had written, ask her advice and praise, wonder with her at his great luck in their being together, their winning through? Instead, he sat alone in his room. He worked. He smoked and worked some more. He brought nothing, showed nothing, needed nothing but the odd page of transcription and this she did alone. Sometimes he looked at her – she was sure she did not exaggerate – as though he wished she were not there at all. And the walls! Sieves! So thin she might not play even when he slept and sometimes he slept where he sat, over the keys. And what did she do? She fretted. She complained. She got headaches and tremors of guilt. This was not how she wished to be. It was not how it was meant to be.

If only I did not get so far behind. She sniffed. Every day without playing is a burden and I am ashamed. Not one hour in the day for myself, the merest scales and exercises!

Her voice was sticky in her throat.

It's selfish, graceless, and I am ashamed for this too. But reasoning doesn't force it to stop. I am dependent on his moods, which is weakness and pitiable, and I cannot help it. I am – she swallowed till it steadied – a Bad Wife.

Marianne Bargiel, twice a wife and once a widow, took her time. When she spoke, her voice was calm and definite. That her daughter should turn to her like this made her ill at ease and the episode would end more quickly if she strove to be definite. Well, then. You may only improve.

Clara looked up. Marianne was looking straight back. Her black bonnet, its lacings loose under her chin, made her face seem almost transparent and her lips were pale.

You are married only a short time. Bear in mind that you have years ahead, and there is a great deal that can be learned over years. With marriage there is always a great deal to learn. Before was all waiting and guessing. Now there is only being a wife, managing from day to day. This is what marriage is. Her hands, spread out on the black linen skirting of her dress, were speckled as farm eggs.

How might I improve? Clara asked. She felt this exchange, after all her effort, was in danger of closing too soon. This had not been easy to begin and she would not close it now without something gained, some little thing at least.

Her mother waited, looking at her nails. Eventually, she spoke. Wives must be practical people, patient people. You will play, teach perhaps, soon enough. Few husbands are sanguine if their wives are conspicuous, child. Then again, husbands are more various and inexplicable than generalisations, and there is no telling how things will turn out. Except to say they will change. People change and circumstances change. That is always true. She straightened her back. And while they are changing do not sit idle. Find answers, don't question. Blame God for nothing. Don't rake over old coals, wake sleeping dogs, or seek what is not to be found.

She smiled, a limp smile that looked something like apology. She gave her daughter a kerchief from her sleeve. All that troubles you is this one thing. It is preparation for motherhood, nothing more. You fret, you leak. Everything changes. It is the best grace to learn that everything changes. She looked at Clara, her eyes level. A look Clara knew from her father on this other face. And you'll do, she said. You'll do.

Honed on Bach, sharp as a fin.

Whether she understood or not, not knowing what good it would do, Clara listened, learned, dried her eyes. Her mother had endured this long enough. They should move on to other things, now. Advice already paying off. A Good Wife after all.

A concert by the *Couple* was Mendelssohn's idea. No, a benefit for the orchestra pension fund was not the most romantic of trysts, but think how well the orchestra would play! Look on this as a business enterprise, he said, an investment of capital in resources to hand! Practise, Clara; you and the symphony both carry the Schumann name – there is family pride at stake!

She wondered whether to be offended, chose not. What he said was true enough, meant only to tease her, tease Robert perhaps. He meant to earn her time at the piano. Two hours a day at least, then, while he hovered wordlessly at the back of the hall, checking the orchestral parts, finalising his work, she might stay at home making noise, blessed noise, at least two hours a day without question or difficulty.

On the last day of March, the *Wunderkind* and her husband made a triumph in the town that had known her all her life and knew it. Her appearance on stage made them jump to their feet, applaud till their hands hurt, throw flowers even before she sat to play. Mendelssohn crossed his arms, letting the baton wait. He turned his eyes to the roof, as if expecting to see it rise, and the orchestra laughed, good-humoured, as delighted as any to see her restored to this place. And she played well, this much for certain. Scarlatti and Thalberg, a handful of her own songs; Chopin and Schumann certainly. In the four-hand duet with Mendelssohn, she found herself closing her eyes, the better to hear. Simply to experience the pleasure of making music. *They are clapping loud enough to hear in Dresden*, Felix whispered, *see the pride on your husband's face!* For the first time since she was a child, it seemed, a concert was all pleasure, all reward. For Robert too. That Leipzig took to the symphony from the first was clear enough. The opening fanfare made them sit up.

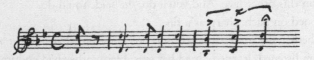

Her too. To hear a whole orchestra under the command of his imagination, finally to hear it entire! In the peculiar gravity of the third movement her heart wrung for him, how anxious he would be. Her heart wrung, she realised, from the music, from spring, maybe, for he had written spring into the symphony in moods no one else might imagine. Even so, what touched her was more than this. What touched her was the oddness of someone so close, so publicly on show, without her as his mediator. Without her collusion *at all*. She watched her husband's face as Mendelssohn shaped the phrases he had forged alone, saw his head held to one side that he might listen better, saw him almost smile. Not her husband, *the composer*. Someone else.

At the close, Mendelssohn took his hand, led him to the stage. Robert, neither Florestan nor Eusebius, it seemed, stood before the lime-light, awkward, unable to speak, face flushed as a rash. He remembered almost without prompting to return Mendelssohn's embrace, shake the leader by the hand. He glanced at her, leaving the podium, almost shy, then left the hall. People came to press her hands as they always did, ask for autographs. They wondered aloud where Herr Doctor Schumann had gone, turning this way and that; had he gone to a reception, some fine celebration with his friends? Would he not come to join her here and speak? No, she said plainly. She thought he would not. Herr Schumann was tired, that was all.

She found him in shadow behind the orchestra curtain, turning a loose cuff button, a worry bead, over in his hands. Despite the chill now the hall was empty, he had loosened his collar, was musky with sweat. She watched him in silence for a short while, making a context for this moment. How many times before had she not been able to approach him afterwards? How many times had he left halls without more than the public's glimpse, without so much as a kind word, hearing applause for Henselt's music, for Thalberg's without hearing a note of his own, no one knowing his special place at the heart of everything? Now it was past, done with. What she had wanted had finally arrived. Now her freedom was complete, she did not know what to say. She picked words badly, could not describe how the things he had written made her feel. But he knew that. Surely he knew that.

He turned, then, and saw her, breathed out. He let his shoulders drop. Thank heaven, he said. I have been waiting an eternity. Come, *Clärchen*. Fetch your coat.

Oh, Robert, is it not everything we wished for? Our good conductor says the symphony is —

He kissed her lightly, stopping her mouth. Come, he said. Tell me at home.

But we are going to the Mendelssohns', she said. Felix and Cécile will celebrate with us. He says I am playing better than before, that marriage agrees with us and the whole world knows. He says we might plan for more together, that we might —

Mendelssohn is a Jew, he said.

She looked back at him, suddenly puzzled, ashamed, and not sure why.

You pay too much court to these things. The applause of a crowd is a fearful thing, is it not? A terrible sound.

She looked at him.

You played so beautifully, so perfectly! Now play for me. Some Beethoven, Clara, for your husband. My head aches with people, with too much music. Ideas are fighting in my head — an overture, a second symphony, this time with your name. Five notes falling, flutes and harps! His fingers turned the stray white button from Lordknew where over and over. What will you say to your composer then? Eh? What will you say?

She looked at him. She remembered not to raise questions. She found an answer instead. I will say I am a foolish woman with the best of husbands. She kissed him. And I have much to learn.

My good wife, he said. He nodded, smiled with his lips pursed, his eyes turned down. He stretched his hand as if to touch her hair, drew it back again. Come, *Clärchen*. She heard something like a sob in his voice. I am sad, suddenly, in this place. You play so beautifully and it makes me sad — I can't tell why.

She looked up, saw the dark colour spread in his face, the rims of his eyes pink. She kissed his cheek and took his hand. Come, she said. Take me home.

Stifling. That spring was hot and colourful, May blossom bunched in clusters chokingly thick. The Rosenthal filled with pink and scarlet buds, children, wet-nurses with tight black bodices and babes in arms. For what seemed the first time in her life, Clara noticed. And what she noticed most were pregnant women. Not that she stared. But occasionally, neat young women, their waists thicker than their wrists would allow, melted in and out of the crowd. More terrifying were those she had never seen before who yet had no option to hide: a flower seller wearing her flowers side-saddle, impossibly huge in a smocked coat; a livestock owner tying geese by the feet, arching herself backwards like a fish, this swollen mass not one self but two. Clara knew how this thing resolved itself, or knew enough. But knowing did not suggest understanding, insight. The horror of watching their bellies, wondering if that stretching of the skin caused pain, how much pain there might be to follow. Childbed. Something that sounded like rest but wasn't. Labour. Snatches and whispers. Pauline whispering in French when no one had been there to hear, Emilie scandalised to death and not wanting it to stop.

It was Henriette who knew most, her father's housemaid having had her baby almost under their roof. The weeping and tight-lipped silences, everyone sorry for the girl but certain she must leave. *She wasn't married?* Clara asked, her eyes popping, and even Emilie laughed. What happened after that was mystery entire. Henriette knew something of blood and something of weakness: having babies made one weak. Emilie knew the pains of Eve were punishment and were dreadful pains indeed. Pauline said it could not be so bad for people survived, in the main. They survived and, what's more, they did it all over again. And they had laughed and looked at Clara, the affianced party, suspecting she knew more than her butter-cool mouth was prepared to say. Even now, when the mechanics of sex were satisfactorily comprehensible, how a baby was born without splitting the mother in two seemed, at the least, unlikely. Some, she was sure, it did. Some of these women her eyes lingered upon in here would certainly die. Their time would come and take them with it and they would not work on the Neumarkt corner or walk in the Rosenthal any more. Some, God help them, would be taken to hospitals if they could not protect themselves, hospitals being last resorts, resting places on the way to an infective end. The jolts and shocks of alien limbs that came from inside her own body gave her pleasure only by theory. *My baby*, she told herself, deliberately testing her heart for tenderness. Yet it terrified, this kicking and gouging: it scared her to death.

Whom might she tell? Who might offer advice without her having to find the words for herself? The doctor, the same Dr Jörg who had assisted her mother, who had held Clara first, the same Dr Jörg gifted from aristocrats that the people who played the music they loved should not stoop to a midwife, had work to do. Besides, a stranger, a court physician, a *man* – it seemed shameless to ask him anything so intimately, horribly female. Aunt Carl, given to drifting over to Inselstrasse in the mornings as the ninth month approached, said only not to worry. She said it worryingly often. Her mother had barely mentioned it in what letters came and her father remained silent, dumb as custard. She had sent birthday greetings, word of his impending grandparenthood, but if they touched him, if he thought of his first-born daughter, he did not let it show. He made no answer at all. Who else? She recalled Clementine, her face puffed up like pastry, the frilled collars she had thought becoming when she had carried fat little Marie. Had her father been soft, yielding? Someone in whom she might confide? That yellow stick with his well-water spectacles, Reverend Fechner? One idea was as absurd as the other. And Robert? Not Robert. Certainly not Robert.

No one. Not one.

This slow stretch of cloth over her abdomen, the tough mound of muscle swallowing up her waist. A woman inside this body after all, a woman who would certainly pain her and who might put her in mortal danger. Outwith her control. It hardly felt like herself. Whatever was begun would finish somehow; that was the only certainty. She played songs for Robert's birthday, lightning forking the sky at her back. Beside this, the Sinfonietta, the Overture, his sketches and memos, more songs. Robert sleepless, restless as a bear. He drank wine and water mixed, like a Frenchman, his little room sweltering in the summer heat. Out of bed in the early hours, he announced that he would walk to Connewitz while the air was fresh, demanded that she come. He put on his shoes, lit all the lamps as though it were day. *You wake me, little wife*, he said, bright as birdsong. *I find I can't be still.* He brought her a plate of buttery bread he had cut in the kitchen, trailed patterns of crumbs to his room, ravenous, incessant; 3 a.m. How often did he wake at 3 a.m., polish her shoes and fetch her bonnet? How often did he go out himself, singing, return within the hour and work some more? The symphony, the *Fantasie*, the Overture and Scherzo all for Clara, he said, all for my wife and our first year together. And all in seclusion. Fragments of melody, like weed through water, wove through her fitful sleep, the English clock chiming the hour. Beneath her top sheet, under the canopy of her own flesh, a separate life tugged on its anchors, fighting back.

Work is the saviour of the confused.

Someone must have said it. Someone wise.

She finished four songs, the Rückerts, after six months and was settled enough they sounded well. Six months to write what he would have finished in fewer days but no matter. This little triumph was something. She had finished and that was a good sign. Now came the task she set herself. Walking was cumbersome but she walked. The hall was too hot but she sat. If the new *Fantasie*, a scatter of fireworks in notes, the most beautiful melody imaginable, was really to be *hers, only hers*, then that's what it would be. At the Gewandhaus, stopping rehearsals while the brass players tipped out spit and the fiddlers flexed their wrists – anything to avoid watching Mme Schumann as she arranged her skirts neatly over her own vastness – she played the whole thing twice while he looked on. Pushing down on the pedals made her belly hurt, but her fingers were in good enough form. Something else to fret about did that, it made the notes themselves come easier. That it was not entirely seemly didn't matter; precedent was already set. In this same hall, twenty years before, her own mother had sat playing Mozart, bloated as a marrow with Alwin. *They see only a vessel for music*, she told herself, unaware of any joke, any glaring proof she might offer to the contrary. *Music has no sex.* More to the point, Robert was pleased with it. Not as pleased as she had hoped, but pleased enough. The episode was cheering.

But then it was done and her body was undeniable again. At nights she could not breathe without sitting upright, her back propped by pillows. Her stomach gurgling with acids, her throat dry as paint, she prayed open-eyed and soundless – *may heaven protect me, may heaven make it soon* – while Robert paced, smoking cigars, drank glasses of watered porter, talked aloud. If she fretted, he calmed her. He soothed her with poetry, read her stories when she lay awake. *My good genius, my best of friends; we have nothing to fear.* By day he went out walking, met friends, worked only fitfully. He ordered champagne they could not afford, filled the kitchen and house cellar with the best of wine. He sketched notes to his brother, to Becker, to Bennett and threw them all away.

On the last day of August, at five in the afternoon, he went for the Court Physician. That done, the social niceties attended to, he went to the tiny piano room. He lit candles and a cigar, and sat before the keys. Among his neatly ordered files and books, in one place, a familiar place, the place that was most like home, he filled his mouth with smoke, watched the keys forming and re-forming in the slow release of his breath. Hazily, he heard Agnes running for water jugs on the stairs, the low buzz of the doctor's voice coming through the ceiling. He had a tremendous urge to write to Verhulst, Bennett, perhaps, someone who lived in another country to whom he might be open. But he couldn't sit still enough, collect his thoughts. Thunderstorms were coming, wild, unpredictable weather. Only a week since, forty-two windows had been broken in their street, right here in Inselstrasse. Gales from Russia, they said; freak storms tearing down from the east. Two ships had been lost at sea, possibly lives, about that he was less clear. There may have been lives. Robert Schumann closed his eyes, his head full of sails cut to ribbons, shattered panes of glass. When the sound of footfalls began in earnest, creaking back and forth overhead, a low moaning that might or might not have been the trees outside, he prayed. Like all good husbands, he fought a terrible, heart-seizing impulse to run.

◀▬▬◉▬▬▶

Dear Mama!
You are the grandmother of a charming, well-made
little girl. There is great rejoicing in our house. If
only you could be here with us! Clara herself is as
though reborn. Dear, gentle mother of my Clara,
grandmother of – what on earth will we call her?
What?

Marie. An easy choice. Named for her mother's half-sister and the
Queen of All Heaven. Marie who fitted into the crook of one elbow, the
black sleeve of her father's jacket masking half her face, who endured no
end of picking up and placing down again, of turning her this and that
way under the light. They said she looked like Gustav, like Alwin; like
Marianne Bargiel and Robert's dead mother, like his long-gone father or
even Aunt Carl, while Clara thought she resembled no one but Robert,
she was exactly and only like Robert. It wasn't true, of course. Her
hands, at least, were her mother's – the only part, or so her mother
claimed, that anyone would wish. Good-natured, more astonished than
they could have imagined, they held a christening party where guests and
godparents cooed and coddled her, offered charms and keepsakes and
money and rings. Agnes made her a sucking rag and Reuter gave a silver
bracelet with her name inscribed. *Marie.* Already a woman with jewellery,
she had lavender in bowls near her crib, a room with fresh autumn
flowers, rosemary sprigs and heather.

Who understands, looking at a first child, what is to come? How
little say one has in any of it? Wayward Elise. Sickly Julie. Emil, God rest
his soul. Troublesome, troubled Ludwig. Ferdinand, shy and clinging
to a fault. Fretful, wistful Eugenie. And Felix, *heaven help him*, Felix.
But before them all, Marie, the instigator of eight letters, eight passing
deliriums of one kind or another: born in September, with her mother's
birthday, a wedding anniversary and a christening to add to the general
joy. Robert was a man come into his own, a *father*. He repeated it aloud,
wished his own had been there to see. *I am*, he said to the mirror, who
knew how often, *a father and a found man*. His gift to his wife –
Mendelssohn had given gifts to his wife when their children had been

born and Robert thought it showed beauty of character — was straight-forward: a new bound edition of his own piano pieces and a manuscript. *What else, after all, might I offer her but my music,* he wrote so she might see and approve, *which she receives with every tenderness. How proud I am to have such a wife!* Now they had everything, he said and she agreed entirely, though of course she understood very well that *to have everything* was a figure, a pretty line. One thing they did not have was more than plain. He did not come and sent nothing, not even a note. The one person whom no one hoped the child resembled: Grandfather Wieck. Then, no pleasure is unalloyed. A fresh presence, a conspicuous absence; the smell of roses and sulphur together; this, or so she understood, was the nature of family. And now, from this day and on, they had their own.

⋯⋯⊙⋯⋯

Childbed. It sounded like rest and wasn't.

What did she know?

She might weep, she thought, she might call to Jesus. The rest was beyond imagining. She had felt pain before, certainly, but this pain would be different. And so it was. When it started, the low burning in the pit of her back, something like the festering complaint of bad food, she said nothing. That she had made all the fluid that flooded the sheets and papers upon which he had placed her seemed impossible but she did not remark. And when the pain came back, widening out so it lost all sense of source, coming and coming again like knocking that would not go unanswered, she clasped the iron bed end between her hands and held it tight, as though it might prevent her from being swept away.

The doctor smiled. This is only a beginning, he said. This pain would go on for some time — he fished a pair of pincers, jars, a long leather strap out of his bag — intensifying at the same rate, and he could not say for how long. Only God knew how long. But she was a brave young woman, he knew. He had heard her play. Now, he said. He repeated the word like a chant, pressed his hand into the small of her back. She wished, she realised as he prised her loose from her grip of the

216

wrought-iron rail, she wished to seem — what? Less ignorant, maybe. More *rehearsed*. But there was no time left for wishes and the performance had already begun. He began walking her up and down on the rim of carpet, its plain green weave seeming to seethe under her feet, and Clara fretted that no one had brought him coffee, no one had offered him a chair. When he laid her back on the bed and covered her from the waist with blanketing, towels, layers of cloth, she remarked the recent rain had been uncommonly heavy for the time of year. When she could no longer focus on his voice so clearly, no longer hear or speak, she pulled the pillow to her mouth and held it there, hard. When the pain made her think she might howl aloud anyway, made the shame of this sodden, pitiless business immaterial next to the struggle merely to draw breath, she took the strap the doctor placed in her hands, for a moment imagining her father looming towards her, holding out a sugarplum. Then she imagined nothing else. She put the strap between her teeth and bit. Hard. Increasing the pain all by herself, succumbing to nothing, she bit. When something cried out, then, it was not Clara. Not that first time and certainly not afterwards. Not from pain, at least. Clara Schumann gave birth as she had hoped, without much complaint. She took warm water and sips of brandy as they were offered, gathered the offered baby, her baby, into her hands and lay perfectly still, watching the room right itself into stillness, the quiet coming down like snow.

White and red.

Bleeding for weeks, a thick, steady spill pouring out of her and into the cloths bundled at the raw space between her legs. Other times the blood would be thinner but lumped through with thick drops. Sheep drained from the neck, calves upside down for veal. Her rags looked like a consumptive's handkerchiefs, but worse. Much worse. Their copiousness, the silence of this draining away of something so vital, fascinated and disgusted her at the same time. It was her own doing, this mess. Agnes didn't even look, just took them to the boiler room in the linen trug, a cache of roses. She empted the night soil and changed their sheets, and this was merely more of the same. Another unremarkable part of all the rest. Things moved on. It was what things always did.

Ten days, twelve and the visitors were less frequent; the repetitious, frenetic slowness of early motherhood took their place and everyone agreed this was exactly as it should be. Marie the first-born: *Angstkind*, worry-child. Everything unexpected. That her baby smelled of apricots; sucked like needles through the heart. That her every cry brought a form of fear. That this scrap of life had its own name and preferences, a startling capacity to deny. She croaked and spat and would not feed. Her eyes crushed against it, her mouth clamped tight while the oozy hardness of her mother's breasts grew more painful every morning. Robert went back to his notes, his pens, his fragments of fleeting sound behind a closed door and left her to it. What, after all, was there for him to do? He might take the child and rock her, carry her, croon to her under his breath, but all else is mother's task, mother's joy, mother's body. It was isolating, shocking, in its quiet way. What else had she expected? Asked bluntly, she could not have said. Something like this, but less solitary, perhaps, less relentlessly, tirelessly, unavoidably *hers*.

Afraid of milk fever, certain of insufficiency, she sent for Dr Reuter and he gave her advice, sound advice, as Reuter always did. The same advice, in fact, that Agnes and her mother and Aunt Carl had given her even before the baby had been born and which had seemed far from imaginable then. A wet-nurse: wholly respectable, wholly convenient, risibly cheap. Agnes knew someone herself, a good woman, she said, in Sittel — hardly any distance. Sittel, dear Lord, not at all, Sittel was far too far! But after another week she found herself asking again, wondering about the woman's name, whether the woman would come to Inselstrasse, knowing as she said it the decision was as good as made. A wet-nurse was a woman more likely than not with burial costs to find, a professional of sorts; she would come if she was paid. Set a schedule, Aunt Carl said, follow it to the letter, the very letter, or you will become a turnip, a mere vegetable lump. Good mothers do not cling. Clinging leads to spoiling and spoiling is the path to hell. Babies are Gifts from God etc etc but if a woman is not to be a drudge, she must hire some other woman to be it for her. So they went to Sittel in frightful rain,

Robert silent and dour as dirt, and in three weeks — less, perhaps — life was almost recognisable again. Almost. There was less cramping in her thighs and belly, the terrible bindings mummifying her chest could be peeled away, the bleeding all but stopped.

Her concert dresses did not fit in the same way, however. Her figure had shifted, subtly but definitely, but there was no immediate demand for concert dresses, as Robert rightly pointed out. She might sew, a good domestic occupation, and one she might yet master if she tried. So she took to threading needles, her baby fattening daily with another woman's breasts to thank. And as Clara healed and altered, so she dreamed. She dreamed someone was crying and woke to the sound of nothing at all; she dreamed of dead children, Viktor, maybe, Klemens, come back to life and hiding under the floorboards, watching; she dreamed her mother was young again and playing at the Gewandhaus, Mendelssohn claiming that he knew of no *Frau Schumann the pianist*, there was no such person at all. She started upright in bed, listening.

One evening, maybe following such a dream, she found Robert at the foot of the bed, pacing. She thought the baby had wakened him, but there was no crying in the air, nothing but his own soft bare footfalls on the hemp rug. When she asked, he looked at her, peering as though she were far away. You know very well what disturbs me, he said, half puzzled, half indignant, when she asked. Your father. *Your father.* In the morning, however, Clara wondered if she had dreamed that too. He did not return to the subject or even mention it, and it seemed petty to force. She turned her attention to letters, then, to friends who had been neglected and certainly missed. Letters from Mother, and from Carl and Pauline in Schneeberg, from those she regarded her friends and acquaintances, from people who had been kind to her on tours, and contacts, admirers, flitters and drifters to other countries, something valuable, or so she thought, in each one. Letters, as she had been taught, as she had learned for herself, were lifeblood. No matter what her circumstances or distractions, no matter the tide rising all around, a Good Human Being paid painstaking attention to her letters, the friendships folded inside their paper skins. She let the household resettle around the baby, dreaming, everything reluctant to return to its former, tighter shape.

One morning a post-boy came with three replies. One from Emilie, one from Pauline, one on official paper from Weimar and all for *Madame Schumann* alone. Three had surely arrived all at once before, but this morning was particular. Clara remembers the stream of winter sun falling across her face, the crackle of wax under her hands. Marie was a breathy white weight draped high on her shoulder, warm and limp as dough. Clara opened the letters one-handed, their seals cracking and falling away without effort, and read.

In the first, Weimar offered concerts to the Schumann couple – this expressly – principally through the expectation of concert dates agreeable to Madame Schumann. This she put aside.

The second, awkward to unfold, was Emilie's: handwriting cramped as gout and all gossip. Liszt was playing an endless round of concerts in Berlin, Vienna, Copenhagen and London, a slave, he complained, to public demand; an eleven-year-old boy rejoicing in the name of Rubinstein was the rage in Paris; and Chopin, thin and strapped for cash, was concertising whether he liked it or not in Pleyel's salon and causing crushes and was it not wildly exciting and these were the times they lived in and goodness she had heard nothing of Robert recently then Clara was always his chiefest champion and so few others played his work and she had been so *busy with other things* on the subject of which, heavens! her father the good Herr Wieck was running all over Dresden speaking to anyone who would listen, calling the new baby girl – well – *being unwelcoming to her arrival* etc etc for ever. Clara read to the end, though it made her almost dizzy, then waited for a moment, still. Still. Liszt; well then. Liszt was Liszt. But when had they last seen Chopin? When at all? She kept a review, something Robert had found and cut from a newspaper, hoarded like a jewel in a box upstairs. And she read it several times, letting it fire and shame her, both at once.

> In Monday's concert, he chose works that were not a concerto or a sonata or variations, but preludes, *études*, mazurkas and the music of his nation. Speaking to a society, not a public, this master may reveal himself for who he really is: a poet. He had no need to shock, he

sought merely sympathy, not acclaim, and from the first, found it. An artist, an original, and more. He is *Chopin*. Two *études* and a ballade had to be repeated – they would have demanded the whole concert again if it had not been for the exhaustion already apparent in the pallor of his face.

A sick man. Chopin was a sick man, yet playing in public. And for all of his battered, lost homeland by the sound of it. He composed, she had heard, scattering blood on to his manuscript sheets. Well, then, who would have thought? This Chopin they said was so fragile, so delicate of spirit, had endured. He more than endured. Clara finished the letter, watched the paper collapse into its own pinched shape again without much encouragement. Emilie's edges were nothing if not sharp.

The third letter, Pauline's, was quite different still. It was brisk and bright, and Pauline herself. Pauline said she would be in Berlin soon. She wanted to see her good friend Clara Schumann (Frau) and hear everything she was playing. She wanted to hear about everyone she was astonishing. *Some say you are retiring here, imagine! They don't know you as I do!* The ink was scented with eau de cologne.

Clara pressed the letter to her face, inhaled deeply and looked out over the rim of paper. The trees outside were leafless. The baby snuffled in her sleep and the house was quiet. Only her father's voice whispered in her ear – *in two years you will be forgotten, mark my words* – but she pushed him away easily, without guilt. Unfocused, staring at the light, she conjured a different possibility: pages of Chopin, Spohr, Henselt, her husband's work, of course; the map in the parlour library with Weimar, hardly any distance at all, clearly marked. She swayed the baby, flexed her fingers against the warm woollen shawl. She sang under her breath, kept her eyes on the shapeless sunlight outside. Weimar was not so far. A nursery rhyme. Not so far at all.

Leipzig was wild.

Not as wild as anywhere else, mind, but wild for Leipzig, alight with tree candles, whispers, the ticket-buying public. Liszt — *the* Liszt, was there any other Liszt? — was coming. Mendelssohn, who couldn't stand the sight of *another* spoiled darling, or so the rumour ran, had already left town to avoid him and the orchestra were a froth of anticipation, bitchiness and over-rosined bows. This little town that loved books, when it loved anything at all, that housed 150 bookshops and fifty printing establishments and thirty newspapers and no fine dresses or princesses or lavish parties of the kind that Herr Liszt favoured, was prepared to be as sycophantic and bubble-headed as Vienna now it had the chance. Moreover, Herr Liszt offered moral improvement. A concert free of charge for the poor! For the orphanage and insane asylum, a benefit for the Hospital for the Blind! But first, and most particularly, a concert for the fee-paying at the Gewandhaus — Liszt the Demonic, the Indefatigable as Added Attraction at the concert of the Upright, the Lyrical, the Magnificent! Whom else did they mean? Who else could play beside the King of Music but the Queen? Clara, their Clara. Clara Josephine *Wieck*.

Liszt, so Robert thought, looked wonderful. His hair was longer, darker, the colour of wet sand; his mouth had taken on a proper aristocratic thinness and, when he lifted his hand, he looked as though he expected it to be kissed, not shaken, and why not? Even Rellstab, Rellstab the critic who hated everyone and everything that the public could make up its own mind about, called him a king. Henselt was pretty as a girl with his blond hair, his smooth-as-wax skin, but Liszt was a Greek, a masterly statue in solid marble, and their playing mirrored the same. Indeed, he looked more youthful, if anything, since Robert had last seen him, and this despite what one read in the press. His household was broken, his retreat at Nonnenwerth was up for sale, his paramour clinging to his legs and weeping as he left for good. He had kept her hidden long enough for fear she would scent him with ruin, but everyone, everyone save the most cloistered, blind or wishful, knew. An aristocrat of some stripe and he left her as excess baggage ha ha. Well, think of it! He had a thousand neckties, a retinue paid for from his own earnings — these days, what did he need a rich introduction-brokering ladyfriend *for*? Then again, the things some papers were prepared to write! The affrontless *schadenfreude!* Truth to tell, Robert felt sorry for Liszt. The man had no privacy and had thrown his domestic life away. He had no real peace. Had Robert been indiscreet, then, to mention his own happiness? Surely every man wanted marriage, children, the love of a good wife? Liszt had the children part and that was something, but the rest, well! That catalogue of mismanagement could not even be mentioned in delicate company.

Don't be afraid you will wound M. Liszt's feelings, Felix had said. From my observation, M. Liszt's feelings are remarkably resilient. Well, then. Liszt irritated Mendelssohn and that was an end of it. Liszt's handsomeness, his fair hair and fairer skin, that fine long nose — of course that would irritate Mendelssohn. It seemed likely, also, that he had never forgotten that Liszt had called him *a player who means well, no virtuoso*, then beaten him hands-down (wrists up) in some ghastly virtuoso sparring match when they were both too young to know any better. Mendelssohn's memory was long; he bore grudges. Also, Robert was sure, Mendelssohn said things to please Clara. They sided, conspired, shared glances and thought Robert could not see. He saw all right. He also knew Mendelssohn's former opinion of him — a critic with aspirations, someone without enough grasp of his craft, a *late starter* — while Clara had been *the bringer of musical light*. Ha! He knew all sorts of things and he wouldn't forget them. Even Mendelssohn had his faults, then, and his opinion, for once, Robert chose to discount. Besides, Felix hadn't been there, hearing Clara play a perfect sonata, hadn't heard the Weimarians applaud as much as Weimarians ever do, the fine Symphony — the *Schumann* Symphony — that Chélard had wrung from the orchestra. Even the horns note perfect! Robert had, and he was content.

He watched his wife at her work and was pleased it was not his. Lord! they expected a good deal for their hire fee! They crowded the halls, trouped backstage, demanding autographs, a smile or a touch from the artist's still-trembling hands, and so many of them: politicians and local clerks, members of the aristocracy, officials from musical societies, those seeking lessons, stagehands, girls, especially girls, and God knew who else looking for her, always *her*. And he watched her deal with it, the manner she assumed apparently without noticing. She did not look lofty yet tender-hearted, as Liszt did; she did not make witty remarks like Henselt. She took the scraps of paper, programme notes, little gifts where they were offered; she signed their books. Her slickness, her *enthusiasm* for work and its trappings, made things easier for him and he was grateful. He had not even minded hotel living, the receptions and gatherings, the incessant snow, his tiny daughter elsewhere, not at all.

When Liszt came, then, straight to their hotel room with mud still on his boots, Robert welcomed him thoroughly and ordered champagne. Since Liszt paid, lots of champagne. Still writing songs at fever pitch? Liszt asked, embracing him like a bear. Still a bachelor with a lawsuit on his hands? The firebrand of the Davidsbund? He is teasing me, Robert thought, oddly pleased; he is teasing this old married man. They stayed up late, kippering themselves with fancy-import tobacco and alcohol, Liszt telling anecdotes for hours. Yes, he was far too famous and in thrall to glamour, a name dropper, an opportunist and an egoist, a flatterer of anyone who might resemble a *contact* – anyone could see it. Yes, it was questionable, this mass swooning of nubile and not-so-nubile women (men too, do not forget the men) that broke out every time Liszt stepped on a platform to play. And yes, the worst of his compositions – crashing, overscribbled nonsense! – were not to be endured. But he was kind-hearted and a genius of sorts, and that was surely good enough. A face like a god, a heart open and unassailable as an alphabet primer, an enthusiast – put simply, Robert *liked* the man. He appealed to something that could not be reasoned away, and was not one of those who would denounce a man behind his back or cripple a rival career for the sake of his own, unlike *some*. A sincere and generous soul, as Liszt seemed to be, was not to be turned away.

Next day, however, they didn't have to. Nowhere to be found at his morning engagements, Liszt rolled up in the afternoon only to play table tennis with that flop-wristed friend who had come in tow, the

Prince of HeavenKnowsWhere, whereupon the two had gone off to his estate.

The following evening, at the Schumanns' farewell to the Weimar court, Liszt was not only late, but abominably late. Arrived, he drank, smoked, caricatured his own eccentricities, drew attention to his new velvet jacket and made pretty remarks in exaggeratedly Frenchified French. Did he apologise for his lateness? For even one of the four hours he had kept everyone stewing? Did he even mention it? Did he hell! That Liszt had turned up at all was meant to be enough. Clara, saddled for most of those hours of tedious talk with two horse-faced women who spoke no German and had the effrontery to try to hire her, had other ideas but Robert swallowed a fishbone and the moment slipped past. The fishbone was a godsend. Robert could not be heard above a whisper – not much different from his usual voice, but permissible as a medical excuse and therefore an escape. Clara spoke the farewells for both; she voiced the invitation to Liszt that Robert insisted should be made.

They left just as Liszt sat at the keyboard, flicking his coat-tails so they should not crush, tilting his profile to the light the better to look like Christ on the cross when the moment came. As it would, it would. It was one o'clock in the morning and the last day of November. The palace gardens were glittering with ice and horse breath clouded the coach path. A scatter of notes ricocheted from the open doorway, spiralling wildly, as they climbed inside. Clara reached out to pull at the driver's sleeve. The carriage was paid for? He was certain? It seemed he was. As the carriage lurched and turned, they drew together, huddling from the cold. A hurtling cataract of music was audible as far as the palace gates. *Grand Gallop Chromatique, indeed,* Clara muttered. *Grand Gallop Abominable.* Robert smiled. He took her hand, shrugged himself under the coach blanket feeling wholly sleepless, alert to the brightness of the night sky. Halfway home, Clara asleep on his shoulder, Robert fancied he heard the spiral of notes again, an afterglow perhaps. A shift in time. When he shut his eyes, it came louder; expanding, contracting, turning in on itself and back again. He shook his head, laughed softly. Clara did not stir. He turned his gaze to the sky outside, a porthole of black through the frosty window. He heard it quite distinctly.

Wednesday, 1st December: Liszt arrived from Weimar. We rehearsed the *Hexameron* together in the afternoon. It is fierce and brilliant and exhausting. We were happy to see Liszt in our own house for once, and to have at least a time alone. On Thursday 2nd, a dinner in his honour – my first test as a housewife! The Freges, the Härtels, the Davids all came, Liszt conversing the whole time as though no one else had anything witty to say. He also played a little, enough to show off his best and remind us he plays like no one else. Prince Lichnowsky came with him and was a silly old woman all night. What a ghastly man. 3rd: Liszt to Dresden. I meant to practise for my concert but hurt my finger and couldn't play a note all day. 5th: Liszt back to rehearse. 6th: concert. Well, then. The public. They could have roared the roof off for Liszt alone, so the pair of us were a sensation. Applause in the middle of one piece meant we had to repeat it there and then before they would let us play the rest. I wasn't happy at all: that kind of applause is stupid enough to make me depressed. Also Robert wasn't pleased with anything, not my playing or the symphonies and how they were dealt with – the whole evening was one mishap after another from the rattly carriage that kicked it off to Liszt's incessant fidgeting on that creaky piano stool. And the crowd noise! All too much. The hall was hellishly full – 900 people. Liszt handed me a bouquet, which the audience lapped up – he is such a panderer. I did not play well. 7th: Liszt stayed in bed all day. Wednesday (the 8th) he went back to Dresden. Dinner Schletter's on the 9th. My God the most tedious event of the year. I could have

CRIED I was so BORED. Sunday 12th Liszt came back to David's celebration dinner and they played the Hummel Septet with some others, then some pieces of his own, things so horrible as to beggar belief. As a composer I could almost hate him. But as a player, he sweeps everything in his path, even if he makes stupid faces. His concert on the 13th was astounding. The *Don Juan Fantasy* popped like corks and we played the *Hexameron* again, same reaction etc. At dinner afterwards, two women almost ate him and he made no effort to stop them (I'm a gossip, I admit it – dear Robert, give me a slap). Thursday 16th: Liszt's last concert – the Beethoven E♭ concerto, then a revolting fantasy of his own. Sitting listening to that was the hardest part. 18th: Liszt left, thank the Lord. We were supposed to accompany him as far as Halle but were so pining for quiet by that time we simply couldn't face it. Liszt is too restless for comfort. If it's not acolytes, it's him running everywhere, burning the candle in the middle as well as at both ends. Festive upheavals: no peace at all till the 24th when I sat down and tried to compose something for Robert's present and – wonder! It worked! I can still write songs. A beautiful Christmas, even more so than the last. How Marie liked the candles! We are very happy, very happy indeed, aren't we, my Robert? Very happy. Say yes, dearest. Yes. Yes.

January. February. March. The awful advance of spring.

So. What could he bring to account for these empty bottles? The slowness of the clock? This overbearing, heartsick spite? The thought of Weimar, noises from Agnes and the baby in another room, the ghastly news from Becker of his bloodstained coughing – these were mere distractions. It was more than these, the sum of these. He needed something to blame. He poured himself another glass and picked up their marriage diary. The light was not good and his eyes were sore, but what else was there to do? Her handwriting, inscribing the months, then his, only his. He did not want to read his own words, he knew them too well already, and reading hers, his corrections and edit marks scattered here and there up the sides of the page, a habit she never minded, only made him miss her more. But he read anyway, looking for clues or comfort, a salting for his wound, not minding which he found. Feeling something, anything at all, would be a relief. This numbness, a creeping paralysis of the mind and heart, only wormed itself deeper in. Where were the last things he wrote? There! *Only the luckiest man alive could have such a wife, such a pretty little daughter.* To see in this light, this drunk, needed his nose almost touching the paper, but the words were plain enough, and true. He wasn't going to argue. The very sight of the child, of Clara with her, had thrilled him so much his nerve ends twitched and he overheated. He had come out of his room and there they were, co-joined. If they were not, he'd fetched the little one from Agnes and made them so. He thought he would never tire of lifting his daughter, of squeezing her sponge-fingered little hands; of parcelling her squalling, struggling bundle to Clara so she might play something pretty and soothe her fussing. She had favourites already! Mozart! Felix laughed when he had told him but it was so: Clara played, the baby stopped crying – what further proof did anyone need? In addition, he had his wife back, her body healed and whole again and how molten she had been inside! She was remarkable, this woman, and he was remarkable too.

His own body astonished him, the stiffness of his sex impressed him as much as when he was just a fluff-chinned boy. This piece of himself that put seed inside her, that made them one flesh, and led, *dear Jesus*, to . Another Being. Thinking about it made his eyes moist, especially after sex. Then, his penis still sticky, his nightshirt bare at the throat, he might watch her unashamed; this Clara, his wife, the mother of his child. He watched her turning in the lamplight, trickling water from a jug, sponging final traces of blood from her gown and almost could not bear the feeling of satisfaction that came over him. That he loved her as only a husband can love went without saying. Almost completely without saying. Surely she knew? he thought to himself. Surely – surely she did not. Why else would she come, worried and white-faced sometimes, looking for reassurance, for the *words*. And the words – the tender words he had so often asked for himself in letters too – would not come. They lumped in his throat, refusing to be spoken and, truth to tell, he did not fight much to make it otherwise. There had been plenty of tender words when they had been apart, they had poured from him, a torrent. But that was all courtship, it was what *before marriage* was like. Now what was the need? The very thought of saying things like that *again* made him feel foolish. Not liking the feeling – he was thirty-one years old, good Lord, a man in his settled prime – he let anger and coldness, a kind of chilly embarrassment, overtake him instead.

Alone in his room, he read through scores, puffed cigars, sent Agnes for wine. After a short while he suspected this had little to do with Clara. It was the music. It was always music. And him. He could no longer compose. After the songs he had found easy as breathing, the great outpouring of a whole symphony, another on its heels, it had simply given up on him. He sat in his room looking busy, editing his paper and taking notes, but when it came to music? Only purposeless scribbles, half-themes going nowhere. He found himself drinking more, brooding more, his head aching whether he drank or not. Nothing helped. Even concerts made him faint. He dragged himself to the Gewandhaus and had to watch a great fuss over *her*, the pointing and nudging as she took her place in the front row only to watch; then the music – a new overture of Mendelssohn's, something Scottish and limpid and beautiful, made him so spiteful he thought he would weep. It was only to be expected, Clara said; stasis was rest, preparation for growth. But Liszt's coming and going at shotgun speed, Verhulst's sudden marriage (who would have thought? Verhulst the imperturbable Dutchman?), Becker's slow illness, like Schunke's before, told a simpler truth. There was no such thing as stasis: there was advance and there was decay. Nothing more. If he was not advancing, which he clearly was not – well. Well indeed.

At the same time he noticed his taste buds getting numb, nicotine and ethanol taking their toll, the damnable Russia Question poked its nose over the horizon and leered at him. Damn it to hell, Russia, and all Clara's fault. *The value of the rouble, our finances, the prestige of St Petersburg, my strength and youth, the second time they have asked me, such invitations may not come again*, her logic impeccable, chilling to the bone. Besides, he had promised. The day after their wedding, his birthday gift to her as he held her hands: a Russian tour for certain. What was he to say now? Russia *dear Christ* in February! He would die. He would fall into the ice of the Moskva in full flood when their sleigh skidded off track, crack his head on an iceberg, inhale ice water and turn blue. They would fall foul of bandits and be robbed and mashed to pulp with clubs while an assemblage of peasantry looked on, smiling, hideous gold teeth glittering in the low light from their torches, keen to loot the Germans for all they had. Horrible pictures haunted his waking hours and he was afraid to sleep.

As he was on the verge of praying for malaria, Mendelssohn, an angel dropped from the sky, made it all go away. Liszt would be in St Petersburg at the same as Clara's intended tour it seemed, and Liszt – well. Felix shrugged his shoulders, rolled his eyes. Russians were not *subdued* people. Given the choice between a crystal glass of brandy and a bucket of potato wine, Mendelssohn reckoned the Russians would plump for the bucket. Moreover, the concert-going public in such far-flung places tended to read *critics* as though they made any sense. And what did critics do? They *pitted artists against each other*. They compared and contrasted, hurling everyone alike, so many comestibles, into the same vile stew. It made his blood boil even to think of these third-raters, the sort who played so badly they could make way for their own cacophonies only by damning their fellows under the guise of *review*, sharpening their nibs for such as Clara. Bad enough to bear it at home, this contagious disease of published, pointless sniping. It was an art form of its own in Paris! But in Russia? To be weighed and measured against Liszt throwing his hair and grimacing and striking poses in that Hungarian hussar's get-up? It didn't bear thinking about. Not only would Clara's box office takings suffer, her dignity and confidence would be compromised and – *well*. What more could he say?

Quite, quite, Robert muttered gravely, hoping he looked disappointed. One may not argue with Mendelssohn. He is always right. And when she had come to him as her husband afterwards, looking for something of sympathy, when she fretted she would be forgotten and shelved, when it looked as though there might be some call for tender words, he had turned cold and guilty at the same time, and had hared off to find the baby. He held out Marie, now cleanly weaned and frocked in white, a kind of present instead, and Clara cried. Even so, even so. He was ashamed of his duplicity and wished, somehow, to make amends. When the letters from Bremen and Hamburg came, how he might get this wish became clear. The letters, moreover, came the same day as fresh call-up papers and he took it as a sign. Signs had been appearing lately – they came in batches at particular times – and they at least were something he might trust. Reuter – thank the Lord for Reuter – got busy with a requested further exemption letter (high blood pressure, possibility of stroke, poor eyesight etc all to some degree true), marshalling a second opinion from a certain Dr Brachmann, and orchestral parts were parcelled in bulk. Silver lining, Clara said; investment. The money from one tour might last us a year.

Silver Lining. Sea air.

Four weeks, she promised, kissing the baby again, again, again. Carl and his new wife, a woman who looked nothing like the now long-dead Rosalie of his heart, took the baby at Schneeberg. Robert's last remaining brother, grown suddenly grey and broken-veined, held up his niece's fat little fist as they left, making it wave. Clara held a handkerchief to her eyes, catching overspill. After that, there was only sniffing. Sniffing and sniffing like a bloodhound tracking scent. Sniffing for miles.

So. Not Russia but as far as he could stomach for now.

Magdeburg. Braunschweig. Neustadt. Hannover. Bremen. Hamburg. Councillors and clerks, petty aristocracy and officials from musical societies, stagehands and girls in frocks, *again.* Parades of strangers even backstage, leaving her no peace, demanding more for their money. Clara in a travelling cloak, gathering the orchestra parts, organising accounts, sending advance letters and delivering invoices; fetching bread, organising bags, hailing porters, settling bills, finding the right coach at the right time. She had done all this and several times over, after all; he had not. He was managing, however, no one could say he was not, till Hamburg. Till Oldenburg and the invitation from court for the Royal and Imperial Court Virtuosa, an invitation for her *alone*. An invitation for a man's *wife* without one for him! It was dreadful, she agreed, an affront; a pianist elevated before a composer, a wife before a husband – dreadful on more than one count and she would certainly complain. But she would attend nonetheless, and he knew why. Musicians were not free agents. For all the fine words about *the freedom of the artistic spirit*, the only kind of musicians who had it in any secure degree were gypsies. Of the rest, all, even Paganini and Liszt, were dependent upon invitation, official permissions, letters of introduction and orchestras, which meant dependent upon the nobility, or patrons or commissioning bodies, which more often than not meant dependent upon the whimsical, spoiled and frequently ignorant rich. If they chose to be boorish, what was to be done? Nothing. He knew full well. Nothing at all. It rankled, though. It made him bitter so he bit at her. *As well wear livery and be done with it,* he said to her retreating back, watching it flinch. But she had kept going, brought him back pastries, a plate of sugared sweets, assured him he hadn't missed much. He was sure she was right.

Nonetheless, things had shifted slightly. He was pleasant enough and liberal in his enjoyment of the good northern beer, but the eye problems, hearing loss, difficulty with his windpipe and pain in his chest gave a truer picture. He disliked the orchestra and the cow-eyed sorts that hung around her. The newspaper needed him, he said. He could not work in these suddenly ghastly conditions. After Hamburg, the last playing of his symphony, he spat it out. He was going home. Letters lay there on the hotel side table, the roster of planned engagements requiring to be addressed. Dumbfounded, she pointed them out. A woman might not travel *alone*. Did he mean her – she could hardly say it – to *cancel*? Not to fulfil her concert dates and deliberately take back her word? To pay compensation costs, travel costs, hire costs and hotel deposits out of only what they had so far earned? Humming and hawing, marching up and down. *Of course* he didn't mean her to cancel.

That was an unfortunate by-product of his *perfectly justifiable* disinclination to continue. The booking letters lay there. She just let them. Eventually, he lost patience with waiting for her to give in and said what he should not. *Go on if you must. Get a pupil or a chaperone or some other hired stranger and go to Copenhagen. Why not?* Never anticipating, not really, that there and then she would burst into tears and simply accept.

So. His own mouth, his doing.

His fault that Clara sailed on an ocean-going ship, Clara who had only seen open sea once before; his insistence that he turn back for the train, his newspaper, his piano, their daughter. His fault, this utter, abject misery. Or hers. Now he allowed himself to think it, the fault might well be hers and certainly would be if he worked on it. Concerts at home, he had thought. For a hand-picked circle of musicians and close friends, he had thought. *My Wife's Career* something he could tell their children about, and be proud of in the abstract and in the past. But this was not how it was. He was thinking too much, getting a headache. Also, thinking made him angry and anger was terrifying. Lord alone knew what anger, given rope, could do. Well, then. He would strive not to lay blame at all. He would write it all down instead, clearly and fairly. He poured another glass and found the bottle almost done. Upstairs, the baby cried again, the floorboards creaked as Agnes fetched her. He lifted his pen.

It really was the most stupid thing I ever did to let you go. God bring you home. Should I have neglected my own work to be your companion in the trip? Should you have left yours unused when you are at the peak of your powers? No – we are a Modern Couple and hit on a way out, that was all. But what will the world say, Clärchen? What will Leipzig say? Your father – I can hardly write for rage – is running all over Dresden already saying we are *separated*. He is an evil and vicious old brute. But that and the loneliness have taught me one thing. It will never, never happen again. We won't give him the opportunity. There is only one way we can work together, side by side without my dignity being compromised or your conduct being called into question. America. It would mean leaving our friends, our child, I know. A horrible prospect in some ways, but two years would earn us enough to live on and then we might live as we choose.

America. Christ! What was he saying? Was he writing it to frighten her into realising that home was where she really wanted to be? Did he really mean what he had said? For a moment, a terrible, bewildering moment, he truly did not know. Everything he had written down, everything he had thought and felt over the past terrible, lonely, drunken weeks, came together and he thought he might fall to his knees, howl, call her name out loud as he had when they had been forced apart by the man she still called father. Bad days, bad days. And here was the old bastard doing it again. Sometimes he wished he could simply die, slip away from the horrible complications of other people. And when he felt that way, he found a kitchen knife and started prising corks. His clothes smelled of wine; his hair and his fingers. His teeth were turning pink. He dozed sometimes on his study floor, breathing in the smell of hemp fibres, woke with his face a herringbone map. What Agnes saw as she paraded around with the little one, what she suspected, he had no idea. But she said nothing. In all likelihood he looked merely studious, or like a man missing his wife. That was it. He was a Man Missing His Wife. And he had written songs, had he not? He rubbed his eyes, tugged his fingers through his hair, forced himself to remember the songs. Not another symphony, not yet, not even close. But something. Well. He might write more, even now, a piece for her. If he could bring himself to think about the piano. And after he was done with this damnable book. Well, then. A conclusion. *A quiet Easter without Clara.* The quill tip was beginning to split. *What will those of the future be like?*

Three weeks. Three weeks and his wife would be home.

He thought about Clara waiting for him at the dockside, the ribbon on her bonnet streaming in the sea breeze. He thought about Copenhagen, its being across water. America, further still. He thought about his coming medical examination to satisfy the call-up board he was not fit for service, the screwed-up paper that was all he could show of an opera, the evil black cloud called Wieck that sickened him to the heart. He thought about the three weeks still to come. Well, then. There was lots more booze in the cellar. Lots more. He chose some of the best, gave Agnes the night off, turned up the wicks on the paraffin lamps and settled back in his chair. The diary was still open. He pulled the first cork and, on impulse, picked up the pen.

Drinking too much, he wrote. *Stupid ass.*

He closed the book. He almost smiled.

⟡⟡⟡

Kiel, Lübeck, Hamburg. The astonishing sight of the sea.

> Dearest Clara, do you recognise this handwriting? I am an idiot for having let you leave by yourself. Reuter looks at me as if I were a criminal: *why did you let her go alone?* his eyes say. It is so sad in our house. Everything, even the flowers at the window, seem to ask, *Where is Clara?* I am sick as sick as can be.

Copenhagen. Storms, fog, water. Interminable delay.

> Have you forgotten me yet? Yesterday I could hardly bear the solitariness in this house, this emptiness. Nothing tastes right or good. This loneliness is oppressive as death.

Tears. Soft-shouldered Madame Hartmann, her kindness.

> I read your letters three or four times over, learn them by heart. Oh, but I don't blame you for wanting to use your beautiful talent while you can. Not at all. What else were you to do?

Andersen, Gade, Queen Caroline. Writing letters on eggshells.

> I can't write and it's your fault. You have robbed me
> of all my ideas and I can't manage even a simple song.
> I don't know what's the matter with me. Only that
> you did this to me, *you*. And you write so little about
> yourself – what you're playing, whether they treat
> you well. Write more. You don't tell me anything.

Inflammation of the fingers. Overplayed. Underslept. Yearning.

> Are you on the sea yet? A ship with a gigantic sail!
> Heaven bring you home safe. Listen, people have
> been talking about us, saying that I left you sick and
> all by yourself in Hamburg, all sorts of terrible things.
> You must put a stop to them when you get back, put
> them right. Oh, but I can hardly wait to see you! You
> have no idea! I can hardly sleep for thinking you are
> coming home.

Kiel harbour alight through the morning mist, the house filled with
garlands, ribbon, roses, baby's kisses. America quite forgotten and far,
far away.

And was it worth it? All the anguish and isolation of selling her playing
abroad, of leaving her spouse and child, of braving storms and ships and
the ghastly business of organisation all alone? Was it? No one would
have asked Liszt such a question. Or Thalberg or Henselt or
Mendelssohn. No matter. No one passed up the opportunity to ask
Clara Schumann, and they asked her for years. What's more, she could
answer. It had nothing to do with the inexpressible longing for husband
and child, the terrible tearing at the heart she sometimes felt, the fear and
difficulty and loneliness even in groups of people, especially in groups
of people, that had marked so much of her time away. This was what
one expected, what had to be endured. What it had been worth, as

directly as she knew, she brought home on review sheets, penned its benefit in full in the household book herself: *1155 thalers (100 louis d'or after expenses); enough to keep us comfortably for one whole year.* Why should she not write it down? Was he not proud of her, her triumph carried home in visible, spendable packets? Did he not say so? Of course, of course. She saw the pride in his eyes, in the way he kissed her wrists, stroked her hair, even as he whispered in her ear. *Never,* he murmured as he crushed her tight. *Never, ever again.*

⋆≕◦═⋆

HERS   The chopping of cabbage. First teeth.
         Hire of new housemaid, interviews, checking of references.
         Listing of all household stock.
         Local concert for Hamburg fire victims.
         Accounts. And silence. Much silence.

HIS   A minor. F major. A major.
         Three quartets in as many weeks.
         Three children barely born, yet beautiful.

She was home.

⋆≕◦═⋆

They were, he thought, themselves again. The relief of her presence and skin and sex against him, his life, his peace and continuity, back to its centre. Then again, Robert's centre shifted from day to day. Soon after the return, as little as three days, if she recalls it right, he threw a fit of temper about someone who had slighted him in the street. Someone he didn't know.

Herr Doctor Mendelssohn is in London, she said. Whoever didn't speak to you, it wasn't Felix.

It was Mendelssohn, he huffed. Imagine! his mouth twitching with rage. You cover up for him but I know all too well! Imagine! He sat awake all night, glaring, saying nothing. There were days of pique and

237

brittleness, of shutting himself away, one whole evening of unannounced disappearance, a kind of punishment for something she could not pin down. Another time – it was morning, early morning when the stars were still out – she woke to find his eyes immediately in front of her, watching and watching with an expression of terrible pity and longing on his face. She saw him get out of bed sometimes when he thought she was asleep, listened to him stumbling to another part of the house, the ominous silence that invariably followed, that went on and on. How was one to know for sure this was in any way unusual? Whether questioning him would merely irritate, even make things worse? On the other hand, what if this was discontent, some disease of the soul or spirit, a corrosive, self-poisoning thing that should not be allowed to go on in case, in case. What on earth should the Good Wife do? Lie awake, it seemed, trying to control her own anxiety. Recall old advice. Husbands were more various and inexplicable than one imagined, she had been told and there was no arguing. Maxims in imagined voices, listening for his footfalls coming back.

Summer in Bohemia made a change of air, the two of them almost reacquainting. She had connections there, friends who would not crowd but simply help smooth things and allow the quiet of the countryside to do its work. They stood on top of a mountain outside Prague, their legs sore from climbing, embracing the vista. *Look*, he whispered. *How high we are.* He kissed her cheek. *Yet I am not in the least afraid.* They visited Metternich who held out his hand, and held it out for nothing. Robert would not take Metternich's hand from unworthiness, he said. A room full of paintings twelve feet high, marble columns, open first editions; Robert's face crimson as a plum. For all that he said he was sorry to come home so soon. He was a man who enjoyed travel, he claimed. It restored the spirits. Clara said nothing at all.

An E♭ quintet and
alcohol
quartet
for piano and   *eye strain*
strings
fragments   *sluggishness*
fugal exercises   *nicotine*
Visit of Herr
headaches
Wagner   *dizzy spells*   the Fantasy
Pieces
feverishness   *hangovers*
loss of sleep   night-
sweats   complete
and   utter
halt.

That the music was maturing was not in question. Everyone whose opinion mattered said so and Clara would certainly not quibble. Even Mendelssohn, who made cat's faces at the pieces he called the *Miniatures* in that mealy-mouthed way, who spoke of *Kreisleriana* as though he might catch something from it, was moved by the quartets, the dedication to himself, the perceived development of abstract form that so recently had discovered itself, and so beautifully, in Herr Schumann. But compliments seldom encouraged him. She might tell him the most heartfelt thing that someone had said and watch him fly into a sudden fury. Meek as a milk jug in Felix's presence, he might snort with rage as soon as the visitor had left by the front door. That they should speak down so, that they should think themselves so superior! At other times the irritation was momentary on the way to tears of gratitude that they finally counted him worthwhile. Without praise and recognition – and Mendelssohn's was the highest kind – how was he to keep going? Creating work was hard enough, but to create work that was misunderstood, foolishly objected to for its uniqueness – sometimes she believed him when he said such slights would kill him. Or at least kill his spirit.

Mendelssohn's endorsement moreover, meant sooner publication and sales, the promise of commissions, contracts and performances, and without that, who would hear any of it? Who would care at all? Only a young man with no idea of his own frailty could scorn the encouragement of his peers; only a young unmarried man or an arrogant fool. And Robert was neither.

With his chamber music, music that fought its way into the light in only days, even Clara, only a pianist as she said herself, a simple pianist, understood that Robert had composed something particular. He had found a way to push at the edges of these strictest of rules – four instruments only, all the colour, the richness and harmony to come from that – and made something new and rooted and wholly fine. But it cost, dear me, it came at a price. By December, Robert's headaches found a life of their own. They made him tired, he said. They forced his eyes to pinch and made his food tasteless. They made a dark, hollow singing noise in his ears here, he said, jabbing the lowest F$\sharp$ on the piano; this sound here. He heard it in his sleep and it wakened him. The very sight and sound of his daughter laughing was like mockery, a horrible howling in a tunnel and no, he would not see Reuter. Or Brachmann. A homeopath, perhaps, but no one with drugs or any other pill or poison. He had suddenly become aware of the Great Truth that the chief preoccupation of all doctors was poisoning and none of them, not even Reuter, understood the soul. In any case, he suspected Reuter. To be blunt, he suspected the way Dr Reuter watched Herr Doctor Robert Schumann. He suspected the way Dr Reuter watched Herr Doctor Schumann's wife. The only thing he wished help from was light. Not doctors, he said, but light, more light. And singing! Why did nobody sing in this house? He bought quantities of candles, fresh wicks for the lamps and, whether it had to do with light or not, a crate of champagne and damn the expense.

After a week, maybe two, of this irritability, he calmed again. Another week, and there was the now almost-expected opposite extreme. When, for three days running, he was so lethargic – or hung-over, it was hard to tell – that he could not stand or get out of bed without coaxing, she washed him where he lay. A walking child being more difficult to contain, she sent Agnes off with Marie and felt easier. She changed his sheets, cut his toenails and put a fresh cover on the pillow beneath his head, unobserved and almost free. She rearranged his tumbled books and refreshed the lamps. He had been under great strain with his composing, after all; such work was more onerous, more of a burden, than most people imagined. Those three days and nights, however, she wondered if he did not — she hesitated, but the thought was certainly there — if he did not love her any more. Might that be why he fell sick, why he so often stayed alone? Was it — she almost hoped it — something to do with her? The thought tugged at the corner of her thinking, so she had fetched a whole barber shop, the lathering soap, a razor, a clean towel, a bowl of warm water hot enough to scald before she realised. She had no idea how to shave him. A neat line of implements shone up, their faintly medical glitter suggesting only one thing: Reuter. Reuter would know how. An old friend, discreet and trustworthy, Reuter was, she felt sure, a Good Man. And who else — she racked her memory, all her ingenuity — who else was there?

As soon as her note was irretrievable, however, this note with its clumsy roundabout wording, she was frazzled with guilt. No doctors, he had said. Not even Reuter. And since Reuter was loyal and reliable, there was no hope, none whatsoever, that he would simply not come. And what would she say? How would it sound? By the time the bell sounded, her heart was ticking with nerves, sure that whatever she did would be feeble or worse. But she answered. She couldn't not answer. She took his coat and stood, leading him nowhere at all. Robert had been having headaches, she explained, that was all. Headaches and what he called his *nerve fever*, a little mild malaise. Now he was asleep, and the good doctor had come for nothing and she felt foolish. But he would understand, would he not? He would — she fidgeted, looked at the floor — understand.

Should I not see him, then? Reuter asked.

Ah, she said. Ah. It might be better if he slept. He had not slept well recently. Indeed, he had slept very poorly. She would rather, perhaps, the words fading into a murmur, he simply slept.

Reuter looked at her.

Besides, she stumbled on, he has lately taken a dislike to doctors and doctoring. He – it took her a moment, but she spat it out all the same – he does not know you are here.

Ah, said Reuter.

Ah, she said.

Well, Reuter said. He whispered. I have retained his friendship all these years by never behaving like a doctor if I can help it.

Clara almost smiled. She did not invite him further into the house, but the awkwardness between them, stuck in the tunnel of the hallway, lightened. I'm sorry, she said, to have called you here for so little.

No matter, he said. No matter.

And to fill the silence she asked how he was, how his practice fared; how well Marie was advancing for her years, how different everything seemed now they were married. How different for Robert, in particular. How very different. Maybe too different. Her mouth was running away. It was possible, was it not, that he might be disillusioned, that he might find it burdensome to be a father, a husband? Perhaps the married state itself, a state he had expected so much of, was not what he had hoped and this had somehow caused him, it had caused – what it could cause she did not articulate. She had already gone too far.

Reuter tilted his head to one side, looked at Clara's face reddening, her hands twisting and lacing together, as though seeing her for the first time. He shook his head, incredulous. No, he said slowly. He did not think Robert's malaise – if it was the malaise he began to recognise from what she had already said – was attributable to any such thing.

So, she said. She seemed as crestfallen as relieved.

Your husband has suffered a periodic – malaise as long as I have known him, Madame Schumann, and I have known him a long time.

Well, she said. If I may not alter myself, then –

Then? Reuter asked.

Then – how do I help it? What else can I do?

If I earned enough money, if we went to America, if. If. Words already filling her head so quickly, she bit her lip to fasten them down. He could work as he so often said he wanted to, free as a kite, unhampered by material worries, if they had more money. She could earn in months what it took him years, free him from everything that took his time, used him up and made him fretful. She would be his buffer to the world if. If only he were more agreeable to it. If only he could work without her being there. *If.* But this was not something to say to Reuter, to anyone. Not even Robert. She knew already it was not something Robert wished to hear.

Suspecting part of what she wanted to say was missing, suspecting a different part entirely, Reuter spoke again: He will not take medicine?

No, she said. He will not take medicine.

Then he might try mineral baths. They are calming and restorative. I have heard stories of great success with humble mineral baths.

She nodded.

As for yourself, you might read to him. Read. Play. Be near and not near, not intrusive of his thoughts. I am sure he would like to hear you play.

How could Reuter know that noise, any sound, grated at his nerves so he snapped at her, shut doors, became more distant still? That if he wanted to hear her play he asked. That she had no time to practise in any case and her playing might well alarm as much as please him these days. How could he know at all?

What he wants is to work, she said. To compose.

And when he feels a little better, said Reuter, stubbornly missing the point, *he will.*

It is when he cannot write that he is (what was the word? What sounded reasonable?) he is – downhearted.

She could not mention the constant depletion of the wine cellar. Or that she found him, sometimes, awake and bathed in sweat, afraid because the candle at their bedside had gone out. Or that he had pains and noises in his ears already and she could not, in charity, add to them. Or – well. None of this. This was all one and the same thing and the substance of what was secret between husband and wife.

He is, she explained again, explaining nothing, very downhearted.

I see, said Reuter. But when he works, when the ideas carry him along, he stays awake and thinks too wildly. That is my own memory of things, Madame Schumann. And if this is the case, it will lead only to more malaise, another bout of his melancholia. That he should accomplish more work does not seem to me to be a true answer.

Yes, she said, though what she was agreeing to she was not entirely sure. Not then.

I know this melancholia, Reuter said. He said it very gently. It is nothing new. In whichever shape it comes, it is the very thing that drives his work and his dearest ones away. Not the other way round.

Clara looked at him, his steady brown eyes.

I am certain, he said, he means no lack of affection. He coughed. I must ask one thing, however. Something delicate.

Clara waited.

Is he ever — Reuter took the best word he could — threatened by gloomy thoughts?

He works intensely, Clara said, apprehensive of where this was leading. He feels things deeply.

Yes, said Reuter. He does. Well. He sighed, shrugged. When he is cold, warm him. Enthuse him. Talk to him about the world outside his own door, outside his own imagination. When he is overheated, cool his heels.

She looked at him. Reuter thought she did not understand.

For once, he went on, Robert Schumann has a home, not a new address in lodgings every half-year. He has settled surroundings, a wife with a gift from God in her hands. A wife, moreover, who will move heaven and earth to comfort him. He has peace if he will take it, a pretty child. And another to come, is it not so?

Clara could not speak.

These are great things, Reuter said. And you are to thank for them. Understand that. You are to thank.

He took his coat, opened the door and made to leave. Your husband has a strong heart, Madame Schumann, a courageous spirit. He comes through. His habit, whatever the fight, is to come through.

He thought, as he left, that he had spoken something useful and something true. He thought he had left her consoled.

Dear Jesus sweet Lord Jesus Christ she was frantic. Reuter had meant it kindly, and she saw it, she was not blind to kindness heaven knew. But mixed with it was something terrible, unbearable. She had not wanted a handful of life-enhancing tips or advice about how to best adjust while merely watching her husband harrow his soul as a matter of course. She had wanted to hear how to make it stop and had heard no such thing. What she had heard, however kindly put, was that this thing that happened to him, that happened to both of them, was simply what happened and had to be endured. There was no avoiding and no cure, none even hinted. And this as a picture of their future shocked her to the bone. Of course she had known, as well as she could, that he had – what had he called it? – *suffered* before they married. He had told her so himself; said he had been so sad he had sometimes thought of – of something she could not even bear to recall at this moment. But she had thought, they had both thought, things would somehow get better. And get better as a direct result of – of what? Of their being together? Of marriage itself?

She forced herself to sit, to be still and think. What was she to do? What had Reuter said? She forced herself to think of Reuter, the sound of his voice. *Read to him.* Well, then. When Robert felt calmer, when he could bear it, that's what she would do. She would read aloud. Slowly she stood and walked to his study. She had something to do and accomplishing that alone would help. She would find a book, the right book. One that would remind him he had a purpose too. Some sheets of translation he had recently been poring over, reading and reworking as though they held some significance, these were what she wanted. They were not hard to find. He had kept the pages like treasure, writing obsessively and letting no one else see. Now she would read them too.

These eight months at home, eight months of house concerts and little more, Clara had read a great deal. Not just scores, manuscripts, the harmony books they worked on side by side, but words: bits of Goethe. Byron, Walter Scott. Shakespeare's *Tempest*, something vile about a hunchback in French, even a little of Jean-Paul, the last of which she had not understood and been afraid to say. Poetry she liked best and this was poetry. He had written it out in his own hand. She sat by the window and read.

One morn a Peri at the gate
Of Eden stood disconsolate.

A peri was an angel. She knew this much already. And this angel was locked out of heaven. She was found weeping by a Great Spirit that held out one hope. *The Peri*, Clara read, she read it all, *The Peri yet may be forgiven who brings to this Eternal Gate the Thing most dear to Heaven.* With no clue, no word of encouragement, the angel flew across the sky to a ruined India and found a drop of a young martyr's blood, a martyr who died for a noble cause. She flew to Egypt to catch the fading sigh of a maiden dead for love. Such suffering! Such pitiable things! And still they did not melt the heart of heaven. What, she wondered, would be enough? Anxious, she reached the close and found her answer. The tears of a penitent caught in a vial: an offering of pity, of terrible grief – that was what heaven wanted. Clara read it twice before she put the pages down. Her face was wet. This *thing of great beauty* that Robert had chosen as his own. And what it said was something she could not bear to know. She sat for a long time, bracing herself.

At eight o'clock, Agnes brought the baby to her mother. Clara asked Agnes to settle her and gave her a list for tomorrow. Then she went round her own house, closing doors, dowsing lamps. She went to bed as a child might, because it was time. She folded her clothes, washed her face, loosed her hair, scrubbed her teeth with salt and mineral paste, and laced her nightgown at the neck. After that she lay beside her sleeping husband and held her face to the pillow to weep so the shaking of her shoulders, her sharp intakes of breath, should not disturb him. And all the time her mind saw the angel, its worthless gifts. Its hard-won knowledge that the gift of love alone was not, would never be, enough.

SIX

Süsser Freund

Dearest

*R*oses and sulphur. Life, indeed, held no end of surprise.

> Daughter
> My wife encourages me write, but it is my own pen-
> manship you read. In view of my genuine love for
> Art, the work of your gifted husband is something
> that may no longer go without remark. I hope you
> will come to visit us in our little home in Dresden, the
> music rooms of which I also offer for a performance
> of his Quintet if you will bring the parts and also play.
> Offered music, drink or food, Dresdeners will come.
> It will be heard. The new railway is not unpleasant
> and babies travel free. I will go so far as to meet you
> at the station. If you will not come, I must have the
> opportunity to hear in public some of his newest
> works, and would come to Leipzig deliberately for
> this purpose.
>
> Your husband and I have hard heads, but we have
> stuff in us. He cannot be surprised if I wish to do
> justice to his capabilities. We need say nothing about
> the past four years – we have other things to talk
> about. Your husband will agree with me. Come to
> Dresden soon. And bring the Quintet. I remain your
> best and noblest, your truest etc.
> Fr Wieck

Their first meeting in four years. And she can't remember. Not whether he turned up with his hat on and kept it that way, whether he had knocked or pulled the bell, whether she had answered herself or let Agnes fetch him in. She could not even remember whether or how long Robert had stayed in bed to avoid him. Was that shocking? Had he looked at her belly and refused to let his gaze linger, refused to ask for the absent Robert's whereabouts as though there were no master of this house, as though he did not really exist? Had he picked up his only grandchild, held her stiffly at arm's length, tried to converse with her in far too loud a voice so she cried? Did he give her anything that showed he was family, regretful or glad of this reconciliation? Anything to show he was a grandfather or a father at all? The second time, however, the day she gathered her skirts against the dirt and noise of the train to sit alone all the way to Dresden, that day she recalls clearly indeed. A vision of her father walking through a cloud of steam, a face half hidden and floating in a cloud; his calling a porter to lift her bags and leaving her to pay; that neither of them spoke a word. She recalls they walked. Of course they walked. She recalls his door.

His door. She had not anticipated such a thing. The setting for the occasion, what they would say, do, feel; what her sisters would look like, yes, but nothing as physical, as horribly *real*, as this solid, green, glass-windowed door. A memory of the door he had closed as she left for Paris, only a girl it seemed now, knowing nothing, the door he had refused to open to her again, rushed solid as a wave as she stood there, waiting. But she forced it to pass. What did it matter now, after all? What did it matter? For there was Clementine, the girls in pretty dresses, Alwin, his hair à la Liszt and still a fool. And how the girls had stared when she took off her travelling cloak, the size of her a revelation, though everyone waited for her to say it. A new baby, and soon. She hoped a boy. She had a girl, as they knew (did they know? had he told them?); a dear little girl with cheeks like a cherub in a picture book. Her half-sisters did not smile, however, and Alwin, trying to seem distracted and aesthetic, looked only as if he had toothache. Clementine was no help, but then Clementine had never been a help, and the air turned sticky and stayed that way until Clara herself found the cure.

Music. Concert dates and the content of subscription series, instruments, visitors and acquaintances. How Berlioz the Frenchman ate *stewed fruit* when she had met him; how Mendelssohn was conducting even more with a baton these days; what David's funny remarks at the start of last season might have been. Orchestra gossip, old haunts, who was sick and who had died. In half an hour she was Clara again, someone who had something to say. Over the days of her visit she found herself inventing who had asked after him to keep him sweet, discovered she had forgotten how difficult that could be. She made a full list of Robert's new work because he asked and played when he insisted. Yes, she agreed, she might certainly play. And sitting in front of this familiar piano, this teaching instrument from the music rooms that had also been hers, her father at her shoulder and breathing down his nose the way he always had, she chose. She chose to forget Robert's wariness, the court case and her father's fabrications, his angers, embezzlements, maliciousness and snideness, his attempt to taint, wound, or ruin both her and the things she loved. In the split-seconds as the music faded she chose, without choice being much a part of it, grasping the only way to bear the sudden hellish emotions that threatened to overwhelm her: she would forget. A storm, a drowning, a terrible fragment of her life swirling before her eyes. She would not even think of it, save in silence. When she turned to them, then, her face was exactly as it had been before, the best face, increasingly, to turn to most things. Blank. The girls clapped. Clementine's dough-face looked slightly less kneaded. And her father, his hair completely white, his expression stiff as a terrier's, nodded. He was, she understood, pleased. *You'll do*, he intoned. His lips did not move but she heard him plain. *You'll do*.

She passed the week. The little sister who could hardly look her in the eye played neither well enough nor poorly enough to be intimidating, and the *soirées* went tolerably well. She played every day, not caring who heard, and he let her. Not till the night before she left did Wieck engineer being alone with her, wait up, gathering her music as he always had before. She only recalled when she saw him do it. He had been the one who fetched and carried at her girlhood concerts. *Look*, the gathering up said, *look what cherishing you threw away.*

So, he said. So. This quintet – he looked down at the copies in his arms – is particular, you think?

It is particular, I think.

Then we are in accord, he said. He finished gathering. You like chamber music now, it seems. This is a gratifying change.

He walked ahead of her to the sitting room and offered wine, poured it slapdash into a glass. Far too much.

So, he said. He sat, his back arching away from the cushions, a camber. So. Mendelssohn has set up his conservatory.

Not his, she said. Not Mendelssohn's alone.

Three years of his energies spent on finance, lobbying like a politician. A man of his wealth and background arguing for money like the rest of us! It has its humour, I think. He took a snuffbox from his waistcoat pocket, opened it carefully. Mendelssohn the banker's boy is teaching there himself?

Herr Doctor Mendelssohn is teaching. And David and Pohlenz and Hauptmann and Becker. And – she felt the hesitation in her mouth, fought it bravely – and Robert. Of course.

Becker not for long, the Old Man said. He spat phlegm into a handkerchief. I said, Becker not for long. He is coughing too much.

She waited till the whispery laugh subsided, watching the dark well in her glass, the pattern her fingers made on its side. Robert will teach for seven hours a week. When the time comes.

Seven pupils? Wieck asked.

Seven, she said. Seven hours, seven students. Piano and composition. He will teach both.

Piano! What is to be said? Ha. Piano. This is amusing. But tell me about the place itself. He shrugged, curled his lip. You did not learn like this, like choosing from a market stall. You travelled to the best I could find and for each subject. A conservatory is – what? A box of plums! Poor specimens of teachers in with the good, students served up yesterday's cold cuts – there is no real freedom of choice in an institution. There is merely what the institution provides.

They have the best of teachers, she said. The best anywhere.

You think so, he said. Well. Then that is what you think.

Aware something hung in the balance, that her answer might hurt this frail peace, she chose her words again. They do not have you, she said. This is admitted. But they have the best in Leipzig, and Leipzig is not nothing, Papa. It will be a benefit to have all the disciplines in one place. To have composition and technique and harmony, to have –

Benefit, he said. She saw his mouth curl downward. Benefit to whom?

Her mouth was becoming dry, her throat constricting. He can still do this, she thought. To my discredit he can still make me feel like a child. It will be a benefit for all music and anyone who comes there, she said.

Will they teach many girls?

Clara nodded.

Your sister? You advise this *conservatory* for Marie?

Marie has you. It came out sharp. She steadied her hands from fidgeting. She has everything she needs.

Ah, said Wieck. He seemed pleased. Everything she needs. Well! He settled back for the first time, it seemed, since Clara had arrived. Well! And you? For the finished menagerie of Leipzig's musical curiosities, will they have you?

She did not need to look down at her shape, her buttoned-up bulk as they sat here, father and daughter, in the low light, but thought, even hoped, he might. He didn't, of course. In his life, pregnancy had not complicated things unduly. Beside him again, a girl again, it didn't bear saying that anything else might be the case. And perhaps it wasn't, not ultimately, in the grand scheme of things. Not when she saw the world, as she could so easily sitting beside him, through his eyes.

When the time comes, she said. I will teach there soon enough.

So hesitant! he said, as if he found their whole exchange suddenly foolish. So tentative! This caution I hear in you is new too. And gratifying. It is all very – he paused just long enough, turned his gaze upon her, eyes sore as needles – gratifying. So. You will teach playing, of course. Technique.

Of course.

Composition, of course.

She hesitated. She changed the subject. She brought up Herr Wagner and his horrible opera, the *Rienzi* nonsense he had taken her to see. She spoke a little parable about Mendelssohn's goodness, the excitement of the times through which they were all living, the blessed rewards of duty. She said Robert's thoughts were turning to oratorio, that he admired *Elijah* so and he had a perfect text in mind. And how well his work prospered! How little time he had for anything else!

Her father's eyes stayed upon her the whole time, not shifting. When she was done, he waited. He fished a snuffbox from his inside pocket, allowing silence to reclaim its territory while he did so. I confess it was my vanity that tempted you into thinking you might compose, he said. Well. He opened the plain silver lid with painstaking slowness, filtered a pinch of the contents between his finger and thumb, and turned to look at her. Marriage roots out the true nature of a woman after all.

She said nothing.

So. Your husband is the composer of whom we speak. An oratorio, you say? Not opera. Well. He settled the black grains on the back of his hand, rocked suddenly backwards as he inhaled, flourished a handkerchief from his pocket and dabbed at his nose fiercely, repeatedly, noisy as a turkey. He sneezed twice and his eyes watered. He looked for all the world as though he were laughing. Good, he said. And your husband's health? He is — he sniffed — well?

Yes, she said quickly. He is well. He is very well indeed. Perfectly well. We are both — well.

Excellent, Wieck said. He flashed the crumpled white linen over his lips for a moment, blinked hard, his eyes red-rimmed. I salute your husband's health and the price of duty. He wiped his nose, patted his temples, snorted and honked like a horse. You are my daughter still, Clara. Folding the finished-with handkerchief smaller and smaller. I discern your training. It runs deep and that is gratifying. Very — he said languidly, restored to himself as he stood to go — *gratifying*.

He walked her to the station again the next day without words and no need for them. They were, she understood, still finding their way with each other. Three months later, on her own home territory, a new baby to show for how she had spent her time, she grasped the fuller truth of the matter. Wondering if her hair was neat, if she should have worn something else, if Robert would allow himself to appear, if the children would pull at his coat-tails, cry or vomit was all unnecessary. As soon as he arrived, her father went to his room and didn't come out till morning. After that, he spent the week testing pianos with Marie, arguing and harrying her, and Clara hardly saw him at all. What's more, she did not much care. The fear, fear suffused with terrible love she once thought would finish her off, was not gone but it had changed somehow. He was Father, but Father at a step removed. His white head a shock, his oblivious face scrutinising maps, he was planning someone else's career. *Marie will not take a bow as she is meant to, and these dresses! Fortunes!* One daughter at her feet, the other, days-old Elise, twitching in her arms, her breasts bound and leaking under her plainest spring dress, Clara understood for what felt like the first time. He was Herr Wieck, piano teacher, of Dresden, and she – she was Frau Schumann. Someone else's, now. Wholly a wife.

When they left the house was quiet again. No sound from his room. Part curiosity, then; part searching for his company and part – what other word could there be for it? – part apprehension, even then. And these parts together, the babies fed and set to sleep, had led her to fetch a plate of supper to Robert's room. It was not something she did often, though it was simple enough: bread and sausage, an apple, beer, an arrangement on a blue plate, nothing rich or grand. And she had stood a moment, listening outside the door before she knocked. And with no answer, no answer twice perhaps, she had gone inside. She was all the way to his desk before he noticed her and wheeled abruptly, his face sharp, the whites of his eyes almost luminous. His reaction was so extreme, so nervous, that she looked over her shoulder in case someone, or some-thing, else was there.

Behind her back came his voice: *someone has been stealing wine.* She almost laughed. But the way he looked when she turned back, the intense set of his body hunched over his pages, stopped her. She merely placed the plate on the table near him, cleared some papers away in case of crumbs. He was working, after all; perhaps he wanted no interruptions. Then he put down his pen. He lifted his face to look at her directly. Stealing wine, he said. And do you know who? The clippedness in his voice was unfamiliar and intimidating. It was more than a question. No, she shook her head, gaining time to think. No. She couldn't imagine. *Your father*, he said. The tightening in her stomach said this was not a joke. She looked at him harder. His face was shiny, his top lip slick with sweat. His mouth looked as though it belonged to someone else. You have admitted him on purpose, the mouth said. Your father and all he has done. Exactly — this word like a whip crack — *exactly* him and no other. She half opened her lips to say something, Lordknew what, and saw him raise his hand, a flat slab, towards her. Don't talk, he said, though she had said nothing. Not a word! Don't deny. He leaned forward, his face very close to hers, and his breath smelled tangy like metal. *I know everything you think*, he whispered, a snake in her ear, *everything you do.*

At that moment, a sound like bone cracking under a coach wheel rang out. The supper plate with its blue mountains, its vision of Dresden, lay broken on the floor. Whether he simply did not hear it, or did not wonder what it was, she didn't know. He was, she realised, too intent upon her. Now, he said. He took her hands in his, looked at her with a face full of barely restrained pity. Despite what you have done, though it is hard, so very hard — all of a sudden, shockingly, his eyes filled with tears — *I. Will.* — every word articulated clean as bites — *Forgive. You.* And knowing somehow that this forgiving would last for some time, feeling the feverish heat of his skin on hers, she understood what to do. While he intoned the same things — *you are a good wife at heart, Clara, despite the bad places in your soul* — absolving her for some terrible sin, whatever that might have been; while he shifted his pace and read her the *Peri* poem aloud as far as the rubies in Chilminar, then read it from the beginning again, over and over; while he told her to *Listen! Listen!* laughing incongruously at the look that must have crept from time to time across her face; through all this, she understood not to draw attention to herself, not to show her growing fear. She knew to stay calm, stay quiet. To stay very calm and very quiet indeed. *This is the most beautiful thing your husband has written*, he said, repeating the poem for the fifth, possibly sixth, time, handing her a treasure he wished her to keep safe. *And God, God himself –* a pebble, a simple, sea-washed pebble – *is on his side.*

It was the early hours of the morning before he lost his appetite for God, repetition and forgiveness. He stopped in the middle of a sentence about the meaning of angels and his eyelids drooped. He allowed himself to be taken by the arm to the bedroom, still explaining something the drift of which she had long since lost, and there he fell to reading. She left him with the lamp turned up, helped him loose his collar buttons and covered his back with a blanket. For all she knew he did not sleep. She walked carefully, soundlessly, back to his room and stood in its echo of his absent voice. The slip of a moon was already fading outside and, by the last of the wick-frayed candlelight, she got down on her knees and gathered up the fragments of broken plate and tumbled bread. In case Agnes saw, perhaps, in case – what? In case something. It simply mattered to do this alone. Fragments of glazed earthenware, every one a razor edge, she counted till they were done. She held one piece up to the window, checked her hands and wrists in case they bled. Watery sunlight was beginning somewhere, shading the spaces between her fingers red. But there were no visible cuts, no marks of any kind. Nothing to account for this pitiless, deadening pain.

He did not mention it later that day or that evening. He didn't mention it the next. After a week of diligent silence, she began to wonder if she was the only one who knew it had happened at all. Maybe, the thought occurred, occurred again, maybe not even that. Maybe she had dreamed the whole thing, dramatised something explicable, read things wrongly. It was possible, after all. Anything was possible. Even so, she found herself drifting to his room now and then, standing in the open door frame and casting her eye over his pens and blotters, looking for something she could not name. She sometimes touched the things that he had touched and left to wait for his return. Their diary, the reading glasses he paid for and did not use, a circlet of cigar stubs, a new, bound edition of *Faust*. The household book with its neat additions and expenses, more recorded going out than coming in. Then there were sheets of the *Peri*, there on top of everything, the word *Chilminar* bringing back the truth. She had never been a fool and would not begin to be one now. It had happened. It passed. That was all. *A strong heart, Madame Schumann, a courageous spirit.* It was, she believed, so. She turned his manuscript away so she should not see *Chilminar* burning on the page, its bright red rubies. Other than that, and in every detail, she left the room to itself, exactly as she had found it.

My dear Verhulst

Domestic and other news! First, I have finished *Paradise and the Peri* last Friday – the biggest thing I have tried so far and I think the best. I wrote *Finis* with a full heart and thanked God He'd helped me through it. Now I know what it must have been for Mozart to write eight operas in so short a period of time – it exhausts me even to think of it. Do you know the story of the Peri? Part of Thomas Moore's *Lalla Rookh*, and just made for music. I will give a concert of it this winter, I hope, and maybe even conduct. You must come! My other news is that there has been a reconciliation between Clara and her father. If he persists in trying to reconcile with me, however, he will show himself for a rank hypocrite. After what he has done! He would be bereft of all decent human feeling. If things are better for my wife, however, I am glad. She wrote some songs for my birthday, more tender than anything she has written before, but children and a husband with his head always in the clouds do not allow her much time. She complains so little, but I know every pianist needs to grind through the mechanical exercises if their fingers are not to rust, and even this is difficult to make room for just now. But she is happiest as a wife and a mother, which is just as well. The new little one is hale and Clara so restored she is transcribing the *Peri* already. I see her in the evenings, head bowed over manuscript, her back framed by our little sitting-room window, and am humbled with thanks for the good angel that brought her to me. Sometimes – this is only the truth – I think I am the luckiest man alive.

❦

Chilminar. Right there. A sudden sink from A to A♭, his three neatly inscribed sharps melting into four flats without much announcement, much fuss. India and blood, Egypt and plague, Syria and repentant tears. His dispensing with the notion of recitative, no real divisions between arias and choruses; his exotic, erotic harmonies. Whatever the reason, the first outing of *Paradise and the Peri* was found more desirable, more *gorgeous*, by the Leipzig public as no piece of Herr Schumann's music had before. Certainly she had written the piece out and certainly she had versed the choruses, but in isolated pockets, phrases and bars requiring to be worked to perfection. She had heard it while tapping on the stands to quieten the choir, between outbreaks of score-checking, place-losing, snappy little inferences about which section was rushing the beat. She had heard it piecemeal or from reading on the page. But when she heard it as they did, in the Gewandhaus, with the orchestra and choir all gowns and coat-tails, with Livia Frege arching her voice into perfect, sorrowful cambers as the Peri, it surpassed even Clara's expectations. And Robert in the midst of it, a *conductor*. That Livia Frege and David, his violin still under his arm, exchanged glances as they took their bows, their faces faintly astonished, did not concern her overmuch. That the Voigts wished to negotiate a second performance, perhaps even a third but with another conductor, she took as enthusiasm to conserve his health.

Others, a handful of students, were more blunt, as students are. The piece! Heavenly! But his *conducting* – they hooted, slapping each other on the back – haha! His conducting! They talked about his teaching at the conservatory too, but what they said or did not say, Clara did not wait to hear. Students were students, by definition ignorant and envious. They did not know what they did not know. Her husband had been a success tonight. He had, as he told her himself, earned a place in paradise. Whatever anyone said to the contrary, David or the Frege, or all the students in hell, she knew some things they did not. She knew he was himself again and happier than he had been for a long time. She knew that anyone who expressed negative opinions about her husband was wrong. To seal the matter, a letter came almost immediately from Dresden, furred around with Latin homilies that Clara could not understand but on her father's best paper, and in his most legible hand.

> Tempora mutantur et nos mutamur in eis. With Clara and the world to think of, we can no longer remain distant. You are a father too now; need we have long explanations? We were always agreed about Art – I was your teacher once – my decision decided your career. I need not assure you of my approval of your talent and your work. There awaits you in Dresden with joy, your –
> Father

How could they decently refuse with Christmas coming? They packed, left the girls behind and went to Wieck's green front door with presents and music in their arms, Robert's face poker-stiff but his feet at least willing and walking in the right direction. And Wieck was waiting for them, framed in the window with the Christmas tree at his back, the picture of a prosperous patriarch set to receive his dutiful children, the face of his daughter mired in content. How else should she look? Her life – family life, the truest concern of the female sex – was healed. How else should her father look? The champagne was already chilling, cigars and a map of Russia were laid on the table, his head was flea-bitten with tour plans. Robert removed his hat to fit under the door frame, just as he had when he had come for lessons, a young man, years ago. He remarked upon it. Clementine almost smiled. Business as usual.

So.

He would go. He would not go. He bought a fur coat with a high fox collar, then took it back. The newspaper needed him, the *Peri* score had to be tinkered with, his students etc. You might compose, she said, echoing her father. You might write for the *Zeitschrift* as we travel. We might earn. Yes, he agreed. He had made a promise and he understood the value of a promise. They would go to Russia! A man should see Russia! And that same afternoon came migraine headaches, spots before the eyes, a sudden ghastly rash. What choice could he make? The coat went back all over again. So she ran to Felix, fretful as he had never seen her before, and knowing it could not be the subscription concert programme that ailed her, he *asked*. And Felix took himself to Inselstrasse and invited Robert out to the Coffeebaum and – and what? To this day, she has no idea what it was they said to each other. They merely went out drinking, afterwards smoking themselves into a companionable conclusion. What they talked about, if they talked, Clara has no idea. Maybe that Count Lvov had already secured the venues and promised performances of the symphonies, or that he, Mendelssohn, had stood as guarantor, or that she, the Royal and Imperial Court Virtuosa Clara Wieck Schumann, at the age of twenty-three, would rot like a tin box left in the rain if she did not play for the public and that she could not, could *never*, manage that without a husband in tow. Maybe he reminded him of Copenhagen, how terribly he had missed her; that between a devil and a deep blue sea, that to go was the better option.

Whatever it was, it worked. Court composer in Berlin, a Prussian now, *Felix Meritis*, little knowing what he was beginning. Two fur coats this time, deposits paid. The furrier insisted. As a gesture of good faith he ordered boots and mufettes, scarves, gloves and hats, 804 *thalers'* worth of clothes and boxes and belt-tied trunks. Pauline and Carl arrived for the children, Marie screaming, her little face purple with misery and rage as soon as she saw them, already aware what the appearance of these relatives meant. Unbearable, her resistance; Clara lifting her daughter while the child kicked and struggled, held the sides of the chaise door; maddening to the point of tears that she would not stop. Robert watched all from the window, his expression unaltered, unaltering, as though it were a play. He waved, smiling, Clara recalls. As though nothing untoward was happening. He waved. But this was the cost of Art, there was no help for it. Clinging was spoiling etc, as Aunt Carl had said. Aunt Carl, however, seemed entirely to have forgotten. The whole street can hear, she said, pink-cheeked with embarrassment; what will they *think*?

It was Wieck himself who silenced her, who hurried them to the station on time. Robert, suffering from dizziness, could carry nothing, but porters were plentiful enough. Wieck snorted and huffed and shouted at the handlers, gave Robert the hefty shove that pushed him inside. He started to say something too, but the engine shudder, the steam hissing, the yells of the train crew drowned it completely even before the carriage doors banged shut. Robert put his head between his hands, made a show of being deafened. He did not like the train. He said so under his breath all the way to Berlin, over and over, rocking as the sleet-grey sky and barren trees rolled implausibly by. He looked down at the sleepers on the track, at how far below, how dirty and distant, they seemed. No. He was certain. The train and Robert Schumann were not in accord.

So. Berlin to Königsberg: 48 hours' travel/two concerts. Königsberg to Tilsit: 48 hours' travel/two concerts. Tilsit to Tauroggen: 48 hours/border guards, passport complication/letters of introduction/no transport/no food able to be ingested/no bed without vermin – in sum, Russia. Tauroggen to Riga entirely by sledge so their faces froze and ice formed on their teeth. This was Russia. *Russia*.

She had imagined white, some granite-grey. It was cut in vivids. Glittering, almost garish. St Petersburg's houses green and yellow against the slate-blue sky, the 1200 rose-tinted spires and cupolas of Moscow scattered with gold-leaf stars, and Tver like a monument in deserts of barren flatness, a ghost risen huge in a graveyard. Between the cities countless villages, some no bigger than three huddled dwellings, bristling with cold, dogs and lice. Ginger-pink chickens and piebald horses, sledges stamped about with bright blue hearts, people broad- and raw-faced as babies, with knife hilts glinting at their moth-eaten, flea-infested fur-bound waists. And everywhere, over everything, smothering trees and footfalls and the very air they breathed, snow. Snow made the streets they stood upon, the roads they skidded over; it made ice walks of rivers and shivered the stars into pinpoints: constant, muffling, scraping the skin and the memory raw as a graze. Blizzards came overnight and made whole landscapes new: flurries and drifts of it filled corners, animal prints, eyelash roots by day. Against this backdrop, forests seemed bluer; water, where it burst from beneath the carapace of ice, more sparkling and the painted walls of the cities came stark and clean as pictures in a story book.

Everything, looking back, the very language and its lettering inscrutable as hieroglyphs to someone who had no Greek, seemed to have happened to another woman, someone she read or dreamed about, and not her anxious, literal-minded self. A woman called *Madame Schumann*, someone finished, accomplished, grown. Not *Clara* and never *Wieck*. A woman who had commandeered transport, argued with pistol-armed Cossacks and border patrols, negotiated for better food or bedding and haggled down prices specially trebled for foreigners assumed to have money. She had looked different, too, wrapped in layers of fox and bearskin tucked up in a *troika*, her eyes and nose shiny with cold, her bitten fingers nonetheless able to meet the demands of Thalberg or Chopin within hours of arriving at the next concert hall, the next stop. Needs must when the devil drove. How things were. To tell the truth, she felt more fully alive – rubbing her face with alcohol so the frost did not eat it away, looking sideways into the slicing wind for glimpses of wolves, sitting on her hands the whole journey – than she had at any time for months. And she played, every day without halt or hesitation, as matter of *priority*; how she played.

Mitau to Riga: three hours' travel, two concerts
Riga to Mitau: three hours' return travel, two concerts
Mitau to Riga (again): one concert
Riga to Dorpat – *three concerts of breathtaking brilliance*

The newspapers, she admitted, did not lie. The tour into its stride and Clara with it was too much for Robert, however. He noticed the roaches in the rooms more, the poor quality of the sheets and the water, and he took sicker, sicker than in Riga, sick enough to risk her concert schedule and the money that went with it and took to his bed, suffering pains and fears he could not describe. This rushing does him no good, she thought. Perhaps his age makes a great difference. Perhaps he will compose if he rests here, perhaps he will write. But he did not compose. He wrote numbers in his notebook – he was thirty-three. He wrote it in full. She had played three three-hour concerts in this city, had received three gifts of brooches as presentations from royal sorts. Eventually, swayed by subtle omens, he allowed himself to be seen by three doctors from Dorpat University Medical Faculty who applied three leeches and three sharp incisions to treat what were undoubtedly haemorrhoids (unnumbered), then rested for another week in bed. Off and on, he read *Faust* and *Corsair*, Goethe and Byron, ate the candied gifts of sympathetic aristocrats sent direct to their hotel marked irritatingly *for Clara Schumann's husband*.

She piled his bed with other gifts, brocade-trimmed quilts and fur cushions, fed him jellied wine from her own fingers, offered pickled herring to his lips. She hired rooms to practise so there was no hardship, not really. But still this waiting brought him no joy. He is bored, she thought. He would like something to see and do, something to stimulate his mind. St Petersburg, she said, she said it to cheer him, is full of paintings. They say it is magnificent. A man such as you, she said, stroking his hair from his eyes, will appreciate St Petersburg.

And so he did. If magnificence resides in art galleries and palaces, buildings both elegant and beautiful to the eye and streets wide as concert halls, it was magnificent too. He went walking immediately, absorbing Nevsky Prospect like a blotter. He found bookshops and music sellers and much absurd iconry, but the hotel was happy enough, a more fitting place to stay in bed if the need arose and it would, he felt it certainly would. For despite his efforts, and she saw them, even in the middle of the distraction that concertising brings, she saw a gloom was coming upon him that he could not shake off. He did not wish to be a

burden, he said repeatedly. But he could not work. He could not compose or write articles or edit. He did not want to socialise with strangers
and who else lived here? He did not want to accompany her on the
endless round of visits that went with the whole business of touring. He
hated being grateful and being expected to talk all the time, and that was
an end of it. He went to the Hermitage and the Winter Palace, and
inspired himself with Rembrandt, with the linear lines of St Petersburg's
statuary, but nothing, not really, took away the edge of his melancholy.
More and more, he lay in late. Books piled by his bedside. He watched
the St Petersburgers from his window, followed solitary people with his
eyes. That was all.

The St Petersburgers, in turn, followed the Schumanns, which meant
mostly her. Pauline Viardot-García had recommended her, after all –
Madame Schumann sings at the piano better than I do – and the St Petersburg
concert crowd *loved* La Viardot, so word got around. They read up,
subscribed to Herr Schumann's newspaper, overdosed on her reviews.
And then they came. They came to see this queer, sad-faced German
woman player (not a novelty exactly, but they hardly grew on trees) and
having come, having expected not a great deal, they found Madame
Schumann more to their liking than they'd imagined. What's more they
came again; her audiences increased with familiarity, unlike Liszt's.
People swooned for Liszt, of course, they posed at street corners
afterwards in notional dreams and reveries, and the more affected told
everyone they were bewitched, but they went once. More than once and
one risked the whole experience, somehow: it was always possible the
glitter might not be quite so brilliant a second time around. For Madame
Schumann, however, one might go twice, even more. She could play fire-
crackers straight out of the box if she chose, for who does not like a
show? But *then* she served Weber and Beethoven, her own variations and
those perfectly *yearning* little pieces of her husband's, and all this, more
often than not, *alone*. No circus of assisting performers and acting
troupes, no singers to sweeten the load. Who would have thought
that those little *nocturnes* of Field's, a *presto* by Scarlatti or a Bach *prelude*
echoing through a packed hall, could sound *this* way? Who, before her
appearance, would have heard them to the end?

For all the sobriety and demands of her programmes, one came to Madame Schumann to hear something profound and, having heard her, one acquired it. Included in the ticket, it seemed, was the most delightful challenge, the most fulsome compliment: she trusted her listeners to *listen*. Well, then! Let those who liked Pasta and Liszt and Thalberg and the like prefer concerts of ever-decreasing circles. Who remembered such concerts two days after, could name one piece they had played? She did not astound or take the breath away. She did not set out to. What Madame Schumann did, undoubtedly, was far, far more. She touched the deepest corners of the heart. And how dignified she looked! How erect at the keyboard, her gowns never coquettish, her big moon-size eyes using up half the space of her face! To the concertising public she was a marvel: an *Artist* and also a *Woman* (they spoke both with capital letters), a *Woman*, moreover, who turned down the advantages of her sex and did not seek to please or even smile much at an audience. She ennobled, she dignified one's ears, she – she *played*.

Then, of course, there was the opinion of the aristocrats and their support machine, officialdom. Napoleon or not, without the approval of artistocrats, the private orchestras they could afford, their patronages and permissions, the player's life was, at the very least, stunted. And to this set, the givers of bracelets and letters of introductions rather than fees, she was a marvel too, but a marvel with – how might one say it? With *limitations*. If Madame Schumann had a failing, they said, it was not her refusal to maintain a steady grin. Heavens! People who toughed out Russian winters could certainly understand the practical economy of not opening one's mouth if one could help it. The failing was perhaps that lumpy Saxon accent that reminded one irresistibly of a governess; an accent, moreover, she made no attempt to hide even when she spoke French – *how funny* – and so earnest that she was often droll without knowing it. Then musicians were not, after all, one's friends. *Artists* formed a separate class altogether, one that could not be easily contained or boundaried, one that often had a less pleasing side than one might at first believe possible. Some were coarse, some were drunks, some were rude, some downright *political*. The *poseurs, aspirants* and lunatics – every cache of artists had a fair dose of *those* – were tolerable enough but as for the rest, the sincerely gifted but somehow difficult, what could one do? Nothing. Nothing but put up with their flaws and eccentricities, and a certain amount of ghastliness, to obtain their gifts. It was the gifts that mattered and that was a saving grace. Artists *themselves* might come kissed with greatness of a kind, but few were well-bred and Madame Schumann, as if wearing a torn petticoat, let it show. She moved prettily among the malachite tables and gilded palms, she understood which fork was which, but when she opened her mouth – alas! There was the teacher's daughter they knew her to be. Her husband was a bookbinder's boy and almost entirely self-taught. As hired entertainment went, however, Madame Schumann was superior. She would not have spoken so much in any case had it not been for *him*. For *Dr Schumann*.

And *what* was to be said of Dr Schumann? Some had heard he was prone to illness, that he felt the cold bitterly, that he was delicate, melancholy or homesick. A few had seen him at the Wielhorski *soirée*, conducting Wielhorski's orchestra in his own symphony, a pretty hymn to spring. And the symphony had had charm and breadth, they said, and St Petersburg could have had a place in its heart for him if he had wanted such a thing – but given he was also morose, sullen, narcissistic and prone to huffs, perhaps he didn't. Also, he seemed – what was the word? Dumbly *aggressive*. Nothing overt, nothing so *déclassé* as brawling or shouting, but it was there. His unwillingness to accompany his wife to receptions, the lips that pursed like a dowager's, his blank stare and cut-off silences suggested it. Also, he did not encourage conversation. Nothing drew him: not Pushkin, not discussion of Metternich, not Swedish foreign policy – *nothing*, though he mumbled to *her* now and then, expecting her to relay what he said.

Others noticed a temper occasionally, unaccountably, rising to the surface, a black bubble on what seemed a glass of sour milk. *Your conduct!* he had hissed at his wife one night, there at her own reception and dressed to the nines or as close as he could come. *Your conduct!* glowering at her as she handed him wine. And this after she had won a clapping and cheering and hat-flying ovation, after she outshone an orchestra and a half and every man within outshining distance, after she had raised the painted quasi-Michelangelo ceiling of Wielhorski's concert rooms with applause. Others again said he was quiet, that was all; they'd bet he was a *darling* at home.

One thing all agreed upon was his conducting. Unless it was the fashion in Germany these days to beat time badly, to bring in the soloists not at all, and not to notice if the players seemed adrift, he was a conductor of truly epic awfulness. The man, they began to whisper, was a liability. Or a genius! Or an idiot – the two came so close, did they not? Or perhaps she led him a life of private hell and torment, and this was his only revolt – who knew? Who indeed? What did it matter? Gossip, rumour: it went with her territory, that of being *in vogue*. He was only the husband, after all. (Splaying of feather fans, smiles and nods.) The pianist herself, the one they had paid for, was wonderful. She would certainly do. When Madame Schumann left Petersburg, then, it was with tears in her eyes, a deal of jewellery and a doll's house in her luggage. She was, she said, sorry to go. Her husband didn't even blink.

St Petersburg to Tver – a gruesome journey!

Potholes the size of canyons, the horses skittish and skidding on rivers turned to ice! Three days of bump and hideous grind! But Robert's uncle, gone to Tver some fifty years ago, had written and Robert wished to see him. His mother's brother, with his mother's virgin name of Schnabel, a last link with all that had gone. Refusal was not an option. So they bounced to Tver before they made for Moscow, lasting out in the hope of finding Uncle Schnabel still alive, and so he was. Barely.

Almost seventy, a man who looked like his mother so much Robert thought he might faint, Uncle Schnabel greeted them in person. He managed an interest in his lost sister's darling, never missing an opportunity to tell Robert that's exactly what he had been. *All her hopes rested in you*, he said, embracing him and almost tipping over. *You above the others, and look! Here you are!* Undeniable. Robert had Russian cousins, Uncle Schnabel said, and since Cousin Carl was on to his third wife already, many Russian second cousins too. But the family were prone to early death, were they not? Only Uncle Schnabel himself had outstripped them, and that would hardly be for long. He coughed. He hadn't been a surgeon for fifty years without being able to see that much! His liver was packing up, his kidneys were worse than useless, and his heart – ha! His heart needed a thump now and again to remember what to do! Now, he said, ignoring the whiteness of his nephew's face, he should like to hear what they had to say about being musicians. Especially the young lady about whom he had read in a newspaper. She must tell him everything, everything. And though Clara had liked Uncle Schnabel, Robert, after all his journeying, wanted to be on his way. With barely time to freshen the horses, it seemed, they started over again. The snow buried houses, the sledge hit buried roofs and almost turned over, the driver swore incessantly, but the outskirts of Moscow came. Eventually. From the heights of Petrovsky Castle they stood where Napoleon had stood as the city burned, looked out over the domes and grass-thick needle points of churches, the thin spread of country houses and hovels, the dull glint of the Moskva. His eyes stung with cold above the bearskin travelling rug, a look of weary astonishment on his face. Moscow. The word whispering in his ear had woken him from nightmares, and now he stood before it, it was beautiful; raw and bitter and cold-bloodedly beautiful. The redness of the Kremlin and all within and beyond it, Saint Basil's nine different tulip towers, women with no bonnets, only scarves, and men in leather-belted Cossack gowns. He felt, he said, as though they had come to the end of the earth. He would not visit *strangers*, he said. He wished to keep to himself and look at this city, to watch it from his hotel window as the snow turned to mud in the streets beneath. And when he wanted more he went out, mostly alone. Now and then, if the outing risked people, he took her too: one visit to a gallery for the paintings on the wall, two trips to the opera for music he did not much care for, a museum that smelled of cabbage and linseed. He stared at the mammoth, incensed by its tusks. *A vile beast.*

When she played for the orphanage, however, she played alone. He waited outside, refusing to see the children who were far too quiet, far too thin, children who applauded only when instructed to do so. The rest of the time he stayed in their room, propped on pillows, writing poems: poems about Napoleon, Easter time, the Veliky bell. Poems about angels. He took her to see a spot overlooking the Kremlin where he thought this bell might have been. It was flawed in the mould as they made it, he mumbled. And because it was flawed, they cast it aside. Then it sank deeper into the earth each year. Drowned by its own weight! By neglect – after all the time it took to fashion! Now see – see! Who can tell it was ever there?

Clara looked at the spot. A mud pit.

We will know, she said, not understanding the question, not sure it was posed to be understood. She had thought it was only a story, the tale of the Veliky bell, but perhaps she was wrong. More and more these days, she found it a helpful thing, a reliable thing, if she prepared to assume she was wrong. People will read your poem and they will know too. This reasoning fitted any eventuality, surely? But he didn't move or speak. He didn't turn his head. He stared only at the caked earth, the place he supposed a bell to have fallen, the breeze blowing his hair over his face. He hadn't heard a word. By the time the pains in his eyes began, Clara understood it was time to go. In four months, they had made 4799 *thalers* clear profit. The concert season was done.

Berlin

Schneeberg

Leipzig

Leipzig was merely itself. Elise clung to her refound mother's skirts and Marie was wary of her own room, her own bed. Mendelssohn was still in Berlin, Reuter was off in Vienna, a new maid needed hiring. Robert went to his room, touched his paperweights and inkstands, opened his window and breathed in the fresh May air. For two days he was merry as a boy. He considered, he told Verhulst, a trip to Holland. Perhaps he even believed it. Those same two days, Clara wrote everything from the travel notebooks into the diary. She worked at the big oak table in the sitting room. She copied very neatly.

> On Friday, dreadful thirst drove us to a dive selling beer. Two men singing horribly out of tune. I think they were coachmen. Dinner at Fischer von Waldheim's.

It was what he had written. She had some difficulty penning the same words, but that was her task and she stuck with it. Duty was duty.

> Here Robert has written *My suffering was barely endurable – and Clara's dreadful conduct!*

The mix of feelings as she read these words, something bitter and sharp at once, held also a tinge of fear. Certainly fear. She told herself she would speak to him tomorrow, the day after, maybe, find out what he meant. For now, she was tired. She picked up the pen and wrote what she could.

> I can't think what this means, but I notice while reading these notes that I seem often to have made Robert angry enough to speak ill of me. Whatever I did was surely not meant. I am slow, perhaps, not tactful. I sometimes fail.

Then more. There was more to go. She copied till her arm hurt and her eyes watered, and she reached the last page of their diary and stopped because that's what it was. Though she didn't know it at the time, that's what it would stay.

The headaches and dizziness he had hoped were the hangover of travel and thought might clear by June did not clear. They got worse. July and August brought lethargy, feebleness in his arms and legs, unspecific anxiety and foreboding, sickness and a dire, unshakeable, melancholic state. Not long after, colic and trembling and a vigorous terror of heights. He would have no doctors till constipation seized him up with pain, then permitted Reuter to offer an opinion. No drugs, no pills, no bleeding, he insisted, and Reuter agreed. But he needed something. That much was plain. What was left? Reuter racked his mind and his colleagues. Despite the odds, he came up with an answer. Mineral baths, he said, wondering if his patient would bite. Bathing in spa water. Simple hydrotherapy. And the bathing worked, it worked very well till it suddenly didn't.

He knew she was pregnant again almost as soon as she did. He had been keeping a note of her menstrual dates, planning his sex life with meticulous care. He also knew that bloom on her skin, how pretty it made her, how *young*. Was it true? he asked and it was true. A third baby on the way. By their anniversary in mid-September, he was weeping fearfully, at times unable to walk for sadness; he shouted in his sleep. Eventually, he consented to speak to homoeopaths, for at least homoeopaths were not poison traders; and by her birthday — twenty-five! Could his wife be truly twenty-five? — they arrived, keen to test him for toxicity, to fill in their puzzle books about his moods. Reuter again, someone with a beard, even Carus, Mendelssohn's physician. Who did not come to advise him? Word, it seemed, was travelling. Then, God knew from where, the idea of Dresden, its air unindustrial and its surroundings fetching, Dresden that was far enough away to avoid the grisly question from students and staff alike, a question that became unavoidable, of *How Herr Doctor Schumann was today*, wormed into their thinking and did not shift. It took root like a creeper, holding on till it was almost choking, the notion of Dresden as salvation, Dresden, somehow, as exactly what was required. Elise took a fever, news was confirmed that Mendelssohn was giving up the Gewandhaus directorship for Berlin, Agnes resigned. The new blank book that should have been purchased never was. The marriage diary, their little book of wishes and hopes, their honest record, fell unnoticed into disuse.

Well, then! Was he a man or was he not?

Was he fit to make decisions or languish at their mercy?

He needed to occupy his mind with something and this was it. Autumn trees and pigs and windfall apples; hideous clouds of steam through a grainy window. For four slow hours. One had to think of something. He had brought some books of poems but couldn't read them. He had forgotten his glasses. In any case, the awful complexity of the journeying — checking the bags were still there, that the train was going in the right direction, keeping pace with the seemingly independent migration of tickets from pocket to pocket – made concentration impossible. Everything about trains was hateful, hateful and extreme. The gates and flag-waving and whistles, the awful gruffness of the machine itself, and after the initial frenzy, no relief. Only this airless, horseless stuckness, a malevolently slow watch. Trains were brutes, ugly black beasts raging over the landscape, tearing everything aside for the sake of something as banal as speed. He wondered what Bach would have made of it, but gave up that game quickly. Speculation of that sort was not only trivial, it was old-maidish. Fearful. Whether one liked the signs of industrial progress or not, it went on. A wise man must come to terms with his world, and nothing, as he knew very well, stayed still.

He flexed his gloved hands on his thighs, staring at the movement they made under the leather, the stitched seams straining, releasing, taking up the tension once more. He needed to calm down. He had something to accomplish today and needed a clear head. Lately he had been a little – *overwhelmed*. Let him be gracious enough to admit it. But the glances in the street that he had attracted, the murmurings behind hands at the conservatory – that had been unexpected. What did a man do when his colleagues went whispering behind his back? Saying nothing to his face? Were rumours of some kind at the bottom of his being overlooked by the Gewandhaus, not even considered as replacement for Mendelssohn's post? It grated to think so, but what else accounted for it? They had gone straight for a foreigner instead, and Gade was a fine enough fellow, but. But. No use asking Mendelssohn if he knew what was behind it. These days, Herr Doctor Mendelssohn lived in a world of his own with his persistent tours and obligations. It was just how things were. And if that was the case, then let it be. The last thing a man such as Robert Schumann needed was a tether; he needed peace and quiet and his own devices. Too much excitement was no good. Worse, it was bad. Too much excitement added to an orchestra (which, as anyone who had been anywhere near one knew, was an internecine rabble of gossips and slanderers) with the continual demands and pressures *that* implied – well. Thank God they foisted the burden on Gade. Realistically, he knew, he knew; past the demands and wounds of ego, it was a huge relief.

This past short while – he should make no bones – he had suffered the torment of the damned inside his own head and had battled that torment with work as far as he could. It came back, however. No matter what he did. It came back till he was afraid of the very pages he had written. The words' fault. Faust. Devils and sorcery and the horrors of growing old, and such power! Whole dramas unfolded in his head when he read them. Then again, the words were not solely to blame. The thing itself, the feeling of brooding darkness inside his own skull, had been – was it possible it had been worse? Certainly noticeable even on the outside, to tiresome rounds of people asking after his health. Then, of course, the doctors with their quiz sheets and infuriating concern, not able to understand anything. Had they no notion, not even for a moment, that all their questioning was at least misguided? That it was potentially incendiary? What did they think they were *doing*? Was it outwith the reach of the medical imagination that some thoughts, deep, vivid, sudden thoughts from the back of the mind, might be better not sought out, not spoken aloud? Even in the darkest of his dark days – and he could conjure them if he wanted to, make them dance like skeletons before his eyes – he knew that much. He was sure that *what the darkness hid* was ten times more terrifying than the darkness itself. Sometimes he wondered, watching them peer at him, poking at him as though he were a chicken in a market-cage, what would happen if the blanket of his restraint slipped. Dear Christ, it would free a behemoth and what might it do? The very idea made him sweat.

There was a mountainous force inside him, something literally unspeakable, that only silence and his own self-control (how often he had chanted it to himself, to keep away from excitement, upset, heights?) kept contained. Was it anger? He supposed so. The very idea of Wieck, that arrogant pinchedness of his petulant face, could claw at his hard-won peace of mind for days. So he would not think about Wieck. Or his own father, an invalid with books under his arm who wouldn't say boo and died too soon for his pains. Or – the train slid past lakeland, shiny and wet as cow eyes, underwater eyes, the eyes of a sister who cried a good deal and who finally – no. He would not think about Emilie. Emilie or water. He pushed till his knuckles and temples hurt, then opened his eyes once more. He would not think of *anyone else*. He would not allow this morbidity its head by thinking at all. And Brachmann, the Müllers, even Reuter, always pushing him to do the opposite (what do you *think* is the cause of this concern/this fear/this unexplained pain in the joints, Herr Schumann?) knew nothing. Further, they knew nothing about the fact that they knew nothing. Indeed, none of them, from Kuhl and Otto to Glock and Hartmann, not one from the whole medical sideshow that followed his life, had had a glimmer of insight into the complexity of the evasive, infinitely gentle, infinitely duplicitous ways of the Schumann mind. Still, he liked to know that doctors could be called upon, that *someone* would come if asked. If *Clara* asked, which was better. Then it did not seem merely his own weakness. His own foolishness perhaps. Doctors — ha! Men who could not swim called to the aid of a shipwreck.

He watched his fingers move like the missing animal muscle under the flayed hide skin. Ships and water, leave-takings. This train. He was on the train and going to Dresden. That alone was something. Reuter had said not to go. Müller senior was ambivalent and negative in one phrase — *not in his present state. Not in his present state.* As though he were a child with an attack of croup. It was debilitating, emasculating and he had wished in silence they would go to hell. Out loud he told each side the other advised Dresden as an excellent idea and that was that. No more opposition. Doctors. To hell with them. To hell with all of them. A man had to shift for himself and where this man was shifting to was Dresden. The old letters appearing from nowhere as he had rearranged the books on his bookshelf had been sign enough: letters from the terrifying time when he had worn a black armband for his mother while begging Clara to be his bride. Dresden was restorative and picturesque. Its opera house was where the great Weber had lived and worked, building something fine for German music. Dresden was where he and Clara met in secret to spite the Old Man and where they'd spite the Old Man all over again just by arriving. By being unafraid. To be unafraid, that mattered. It certainly mattered. How did he know? By *suffering*. And if suffering was learning, he had learned.

And everything he had learned and suffered through told him the same thing. So did Jean-Paul and our Lord Jesus Christ and *Hamlet* and

Faust and everything else he picked up that attempted the profound, and the thing they all said was this. Courageous Confrontation of Great Fear Was the Only Path to Salvation. This was the deepest thing he knew and he held it as sacred and true. Courageous Confrontation of Great Fear Was the Only Path to Salvation. How did he mean to apply this knowledge? One step at a time. Listen.

For years now he had been fearful of the *physical corruption of the body*. It was not the thought of cessation but the thought of death's discolorations and suppurations that made him tremble. Listen more.

When Beethoven lay dying, Luigi Cramolini came to his bedside to sing *Adelaide*. By the time the song was done there were crowds outside the door demanding to see the remains. He might have heard them! Think! A public display in death, dear Christ what an end! And Schubert had come in a coach to pay his respects and what had he seen, lying there in sordid state among its own bed sheets with the skylight open and the flies gathering? A soul gone to heaven? Radiant light shining in a halo round the fallen god's cranium? What do you think? He saw a bloated blue hulk, the chest cavity already seething, a stink that made half the waiting queue retch into their collars. Thereafter, there were 30,000 lining the streets, a funeral of music and interminable speeches, horses fainting in the crush. But what did it prove? What did it *mean?* God was nowhere, and under the cloth-of-gold and pyres of flowers the stench remained. And Schubert knew it. Beethoven, even as he was dying, had known it too. Who, then, was Schumann to disagree?

Now, given this unavoidable fact, and few facts are more unavoidable than putrefaction, how could it be argued that Immortality and Transcendence attached to the act of dying? Answer: it could not. Immortality and Transcendence — it was hideously clear — were achieved only by death's opposite, ie by *living effort of will*, ie by *Work*. Work alone endured. It was blasphemy and it was terrifying but it was the truth. Confrontation of Great Fear = Salvation: hand in hand. Christ, the inexorability of ageing! The decay already apparent in his own body! These broken veins blossoming on his own cheeks, the doubling at his waist and chin! He had banished mirrors from Inselstrasse, but had to endure official portraits, watch Mendelssohn's receding hairline and worry lines. As a youth he had had a great rambling circle of friends and an ability to be charming despite himself, and the naivety to think life moved at a leisurely pace. In short, he had had *Time*. Now, there was not a day that passed without his awareness that the time in which to attain Transcendence in any shape or form was melting; not a day without feeling he would die unannounced and unattended, without having written his best, that he would die believing his suffering had meant nothing after all. Lord, it was so difficult!

His eyes were hurting, threatening tears, and his throat was tight. He looked away from his gloves, whatever fascination they possessed, and rooted in his pockets again for his watch. Ten minutes. Dear God. Ten minutes. And still ticking. Well, then. He took a deep breath in, sighed out. Dresden. There would be Dresden, sooner or later. He must calm down, focus and prepare. If he arrived in one piece and not mad, if he got his bags to the hotel address, he would count it a success. The rest would follow from there, and he was, after all, doing the right thing. The Leipzig circle, his teaching in particular, were too much. He would sell the *Neue Zeitschrift* for any money he could get. He would walk, one step at a time, and find lodgings. He would not stay with friends. He wasn't looking for friends. Whether the doctors liked it or not, he was doing what any man would do: finding a new home for his family.

Ah. Ah indeed.

The gap between intention and accomplishment, the holes that yawn between will and deed. And forgetfulness. He had his tickets and his purse, his bags and his music, and a set of directions. He had spare gloves and stout shoes. But there's always something. There is always something, on a journey, that one forgets.

He had not reckoned on the vastness or the horrible echo of the railway station, or the sight of children begging. He had not reckoned he would not hire a porter since he was sure the man would walk too quickly, confuse him further with sheer haste. He had not reckoned there would be such crowds: an autumn market day, men with ducks and hens in cages, hurdy-gurdies, pot and jug sellers, the too-close crushes of people.

He had not expected the sheer sprawl of Dresden itself. He knew only the countryside and this was definitely city, all hysterical rococo fascias and museum walls high as battlements, the blind eyes of statues seeming to follow him wherever he went. The name of his hotel on paper, written out in neat print by his wife, was tight in his hand. He read it several times to be certain and walked on. Once he almost dropped it, but the crisis passed. All of them passed. Till he reached the bridge. A towering, tri-arched bridge making great white bounds across the water, the far side distant as another town. He stopped and looked at it, at the river beneath. He had forgotten about the Elbe.

Of course he knew Dresden was built on the river, *of course*. But he had not expected to see it, somehow, or that it would be in spate. He had not expected the bridge would be so terribly high. His task now – he folded and unfolded his piece of paper to keep it from harm, steeling himself to begin – was to cross. He had come this far. It would not be too terrible a thing, surely, to cross. He stepped out, keeping his eyes ahead. The bags were not difficult, but his legs hurt from sitting and he stopped halfway. Hearing blood in his ears, he put both cases down, caught his breath. The sound of the water was nearly benign. Almost by accident, he looked over the edge. There it was. The Elbe, pounding and churning, thick and brown as mud, and far beneath. If he studied the waves and eddies, coiling in on themselves, they seemed almost alive. Wild enough to carry a dog away, he thought, hungry enough for a child. For a moment he saw an arm rise from the tangle of currents, fade back beneath. But it was only the branch of a tree. Surely that's what it was. His heart shuddered. He felt faint and loosened his collar. He remembered falling to his knees, covering his head with his hands. Was he in a park? A park he had visited a long time ago? He could hear the trees rushing overhead, a nightingale singing. Zweinaundorf. He was in Zweinaundorf and at any moment he would start laughing. Was that not how it went? His legs were shaking. Shaking terribly. After that, colours, shadows. No narrative to speak of.

It was blustery when she arrived, the leaves of the lime trees turning. The sky was very blue. In her pocket, the letter begging her to come, lay flaccid as cloth. She knew Dresden well enough to direct the cab and the last few yards, she ran. Interminable form filling, signing of names in the hotel register; another gentleman brought him Frau Schumann, no no they couldn't say who. But her husband – *Herr Doctor Schumann*, there was his signature, just *there* – was certainly here, a very pleasant gentleman, very quiet and polite. Goodness no, he hadn't seemed unwell and certainly hadn't called for a doctor. He seemed to study a good deal in his room. Yes, he had given them a letter to post to her, but had made no other demands: an *extraordinarily* uncomplicated guest, if only there were more like him! She might certainly have another key, certainly. The desk clerk's voice fading, the silk of her travelling dress rustling as she walked upstairs. She held the handle, knocked, spoke her name.

He was in a corner of the room, sitting the wrong way round on a flimsy boudoir chair, his day clothes crushed, feet bare. He wore no jacket and his sleeves were loose, cuffs hanging wide at his wrists. His waistcoat, she noticed, was his best and buttoned. His face, however, was grey; his eyes and nose running, swollen, his mouth a thin line. He said nothing, did not touch her or even look in her direction. But he closed his eyelids, he sighed as though a weight had been lifted from his shoulders. He knew she was there. If he knew nothing else, had no hope or expectation, he had one sure thing. She was where she should be. Here. *Here.*

Number 6, Waisenhaus Strasse, street level, one month in advance.

It took two days finding, two months thereafter packing up affairs, hiring and firing and settling accounts, and stuffing of life into trunks and bags. She brought Robert back to Leipzig too, the better to ensure he rested and sorted the rest herself. The upheaval! Pianos and children and manuscript in enough boxes to build the Tower of Babel, and in the middle of it all, Robert incoherent with misery or frenetic excitement or angels, snapping at her whatever the mood. *Listen. It's perfectly loud. Singing and singing. Who would have thought angels to be so wilful?* Why on earth did they persist? She looks back and wonders it herself, can find no real answer.

Because things had been set in motion, perhaps. Because there was no overwhelming reason to stay in Leipzig. Because they needed to see something, anything, through to a conclusion after months of lassitude and wasted time and pain. Under circumstances of consistent awfulness, there was only one rationale. Because they did. Because they did. Because they did.

She played the *Emperor*, a great sprawl of Beethoven, for the first time in public that December; for reasons unspecified, it mattered that her farewell at the Gewandhaus should be something difficult and grand. The last concert of all was a domestic affair, something for friends alone and their obligations were done. Livia Frege sang her *Peri* aria, and Joachim, a protégé of Mendelssohn's, a strange little boy who had left his parents behind in Hungary to follow his heart and his violin playing, played. Joachim without the jawline or the breadth to his hands; the same Joseph who would come to mean so much. Had he really played for them? and on the same violin he would use all his life? Her diary says so, but Clara can't recall. She recalls Robert, however, that he had stood to listen and that he had lasted. Without mishap or panic, he had made it through to the end, given every appearance, even, of enjoying himself. He stood with Joachim and told him so. *Do the angels know how beautifully a little boy here on earth has been playing the violin with Mendelssohn?* And while Joachim watched, his fiddle under his arm, Herr Doctor Schumann pointed at the sky: a father, one might have thought, with a son. He was not overexcited, unhappy. Not this time, not at all. She remembers these two profiles, a man's and a boy's, tilting up at the stars, their faces almost pitifully at peace.

Carrier carts and coaches, trunks, wardrobes, books, linen, children.

Pianos: two grands, one pedal effort like a baby church organ.

Like moving an army, Reuter said. Only harder.

Despite the cold, the sun shone. And someone else arrived to share it. A someone who preoccupied the entire capital, it seemed, or at least its musicians, its opera officials and court sorts, which in Dresden meant a great many people indeed. Weber. Carl Maria von Weber, the founding father of German opera, of any opera worth the name, the Great, the Mighty and the Good, had come home. Back from London to the city he had called his own for so many years, and the opera panjandrums he had served were waiting in a fancy procession. Only Weber did not take the train. He arrived by ship in a sealed box and a very particular hole in the Dresden churchyard was already waiting. Eighteen years dead, and they still loved him; they had begged for his return from foreign soil. Getting the English to give him up had not been easy. Someone Great and Dead was a fine catch and the English were famous hoarders of treasure not their own. But he belonged elsewhere. Now, triumphant in repossession, the Dresdeners wanted Weber's Dresden Burial to be Grand Indeed. The Schumanns caught sight of the hearse, the six plumed horses, the slow march with a misshapen little man in black at its head, slithering darkly past the river, and only then knew what it was. Remembered snippets from newspapers clicking into place. All this grandeur and desperate significance and they had simply forgotten. Then, family life can be preoccupying. Once things were in order again, once life was back in place – not long, Clara had no doubt – everything would soon be set to rights.

No welcome note from the orchestra.

Not a word from the opera house.

No one came.

At Christmas Robert went walking to the graveyard alone, to the Great Man's new grave drowned under winter flowers and little mementos, and came back in a state. The weather turned muddy and chilly. The children grizzled for Agnes and did not take to Martha, the new nursemaid, and the kitchen flooded twice. On either side of this, a deal of nothing. No music press, no musical paper, no *Zeitschrift* for the purposes of distraction or relief. No subscription concerts, no friends without effort, no Leipzig. What did they do? They read. They studied the proper rules for the solid construction of eighteenth-century fugue. They went to the opera house, of course they did. Dresden was nothing but opera house, it seemed; opera and Rubens on its gallery walls, all histrionics and flush-pink nakedness. Not having thought much of *Rienzi*, Clara thought less of *Tannhäuser* (histrionic music and the stupidest story, full of love goddesses and popes) and she and Robert argued. Over *Tannhäuser!* Imagine! It was the place's fault: bitchiness hung like moisture in the very air. No chamber music, no quartets, no unofficial gatherings to hear new music, no lending library of musical books, no conservatory or teachers worth the name, except for Wieck and he was not the teacher he had been. Even the attempt to be dutiful children, shuffling single-file with the babies in tow to Wieck's house at the other side of Dresden, failed: the routine roster of cabals and intrigues and People-who-Resented-his-Genius was more than flesh and blood could stand. And when they stopped going altogether, pleading bridges and vertigo and pregnancy again, Wieck ferried himself to them instead, an unavoidable inter-ruption, a running sore.

Increasingly, there was only Staying at Home, fairy stories and cautionary tales for the children (*be careful what you wish in case it comes true*), studying at the same open book in the long winter evenings by the low-lit fire. He corrected her harmony with the children nearby, no other occupation but to compose ahead of him, no travel as far as the eye could see. A Family Home indeed, one that should, by all his calculations, have been Sweet. But. But. There had to be earning, and earning meant music and for that music, diligence, ideas, self-belief. And none but the former would come. Or if they came, would not develop. Or he gave up, or he could not think. Or any one of a number of things.

As a young man he had thought composing – to live always in the world of sound! – would be blissful. And so it was. Sometimes. In odd moments that melted like snowflakes as soon as they were seized. And even these grew fewer. His young-man fantasy had been that having found a way to write, a voice, it could be relied upon as well as a spoon to eat stew. This was merely untrue. The voice, he discovered, had to be refound now and then, reclaimed as his own, and retaught how to sing. And, of course, his demands of himself, what he expected from what he put on paper, were so much greater. And who was there to shore him?

Only Clara, the Wife. He knew he would miss Mendelssohn, but not that he would miss him so dreadfully. And he missed David and the Gewandhaus and the orchestra news and gossip, and the possibility, even if he did not take it up, of musical camaraderie that he now realised was Leipzig. He missed Leipzig. Lord alone knew how much Clara missed it too.

Hiller came, of course. No longer the fresh-faced boy she had met on her first trip to Paris, but a lot of water had passed beneath all manner of bridges since Paris. Eleven years, as Hiller reminded her himself; dear Lord, the thought of eleven years! But he had come, a huge man with a face-consuming beard, the conductor of his own orchestra now, and though he was not Mendelssohn, they both thanked God he did. Thank God also for Professor Bendemann and Herr Hübner and Madame Schröder-Devrient and little Joachim. But most of all thank God for Hiller, his dependable, gentle brightness in the enveloping Dresden drizzle.

Herr Wagner had come too, of course. It can't be said he didn't. A big-shot at the opera house while having nothing good to say about the place, Wagner certainly showed his face. Their paths had crossed only briefly before (and he had borrowed books from Wieck's lending library and owed *fortunes* in overdue fees) but he came, resistant as fungus, *every week*. Wagner, with his head like a wormy potato and his ludicrous French hat, great slabs of libretti under his arm so that he and his monstrous opinion of himself could barely squeeze through the door, swept into their home and talked enough to stun a cow before leaving, invariably abruptly, in a huff. Always and only, he came for Robert till one day he didn't. Then they heard he spent his time complaining that Herr Schumann was backward and eccentric, and had nothing to say. Not to Herr Wagner he didn't. And if silence kept him away, hurray for that.

Well, then. Perhaps this isolation was part of the cure. Great Fear and Salvation, lasting out etc. No one had forced this, after all. Against advice, they had chosen it for themselves. They were voluntary residents of the city of choice of King Frederick August the Beloved, and they knew they had better get used to it. This one orchestra that dragged its feet at the proposition of one extra concert a year; this forest of spires and the fierce Frauenkirche, the grand scatter of museums and art galleries and official residences, the palace and the town guard house, the opera house and its short-sighted, tight-arsed, jumped-up, snotty-nosed administrators – administrators, Clara fumed, who would not have recognised a creative pulse if it jumped off a flea and bit them – were all theirs in a parcel and no one else to blame.

Between not-work and study, poems and household maxims, what did they do? She hired maids and a good girl to take the children out for walks and play in exchange for lessons. She answered letters of invitation saying she might not come, worried about their finances, and thanked God for the Russia money and the exchange rate. She strung her own beans and made passable soup. She found pupils. She taught. She cleared a table in the evening for their joint education and sat with him when he did not like to sit alone. She even composed. A little. Now and then.

And Robert? He turned to his ledgers, his diaries, his correspondence collections. He had composed a little and ploughed over old ground, and drank and damned himself to hell and bored himself to literal tears. He called the new doctors. Let it be said: if Dresden's musical crowd made a poor showing at the Schumann house, Dresden's doctors, from the very day of their arrival, made up for it. Carl Carus, Helbig (dug up from God knew where), the tireless Reuter, a handful of locums and medical apprentices one after the other; and Robert found a fine new collection of symptoms, panics, trepidations and turns for them to argue over.

To Carl Carus, the star of the ensemble, a natural philosopher, author, authority in obstetrics, gynaecology and patient-centred psychiatry, and physician to the royal court, Robert offered soreness in the neck and shoulders, visual disturbance, forgetfulness, ringing in the ears, rushing pains in the head, high blood pressure and melancholia. To Dr Helbig, a specialist in phobias, Mesmerism, regression and talking medicine, he confessed a fear of heights, fear of mortality and illness, fear of poisoning and horseshoes and most things made of metal including keys and music stands; fear of boredom leading to a *rash act*, fear of loud noise, crowds and fear itself, and melancholia. To the others he donated facets of the above, the odd aural disturbance that could not strictly be deemed *rushing*, bowel disorders, stiffness of the hands, lethargy and the various coughs, fevers and as an extra, the childhood rashes of his daughters.

After a short while, assured there was no guarantee of improvement, he threw Carus's and everyone else's pills away and settled securely on Helbig. *His* treatment, Helbig explained, induced hypnotic trance and a state of calm. It was not assisted by pills or purging or even seltzer and salt bathing treatments. It was — here Helbig's nostrils flared triumphantly — entirely passive. Robert signed up. Clara watched them go together into a room, and thereafter knew only that they came out again at the close. After two sessions of Mesmerism, the effects began to show. Robert ordered champagne for the cellar two days in a row and fainted four times playing chess. For one whole afternoon (though Clara had the uneasy feeling he was merely pretending) he claimed to have forgotten his own name. Sometimes he started talking and could not stop, and Helbig took notes to match. *Obsessive and fixated,* Dr Helbig wrote; *moody, irritable, prey to pompous, deceitful or spiteful outbursts, resentful, secretive, evasive, withdrawn, agoraphobic, self-preoccupied, suspicious, sentimental, gullible, incapable of relating to anything but music, and melancholic.* All these words of description, pages of remarks! Clara read them twice but there was nothing new, nothing helpful. Had he, Clara asked, putting the sheets aside, some suggestion for alleviation of same? Ah, Helbig said. He did not expect anything curative in Doctor Schumann's case, but hoped Mesmerism might be more of a *diagnostic tool.* Ah indeed. Perhaps — here his eyebrow arched superciliously — Madame Schumann had missed the point. Perhaps not.

They got shot of Helbig and his Mesmerism without regret, and only one thing remained: bathing. More bathing. Only bathing. Even Carus would not argue with him. *Do you mean to imply,* the patient asked shirtily, *that I do not know my own mind about my own mind?* And since the patient was this beginning-to-be-distinguished gentleman, somewhat on his dignity and with some *knowledge of the law,* who would? Besides, he had not harmed himself, had he? Not recently? Not seriously? Not so far as anyone would admit.

Reuter and Clara, especially Clara, kept their mouths tight shut.

What else should she do? He never meant his threats. They came *in extremis*, a by-product of overheating, of hypochondria or any other explanation he chose to suit his mood, wounded and angry if she did not trust him. And always behind closed doors. He didn't need a doctor, he said, his voice brittle; he needed only quiet. Of course. Until he demanded the contrary. Of course. Until he did not speak at all or whispered to her to pass words on for him, or the doctors, not able to hear his responses, asked her outright to make things plain – or any one of a number of dizzying shifts. *Look, Clara. I have a disciple watching out for me. John the Baptist has no fear of poison.* A game with no rules.

And if he changed his own rationale from day to day, who was she to say? If he spoke in peculiar, inexplicable metaphor, she understood that she was slow. He was poetic. *Volatile.* It was a part of his nature. She was his wife, no less and certainly no more. To assist their continued closeness, perhaps, she developed headaches, watering of the eyes, stiffness of the fingers, premature contractions and anxiety, and found him almost amused. *We are devoted as can be,* he wrote to friends. *Why, we have even developed Hypochondria as a couple!* Hypochondria. How gentle it sounded! The broth of symptoms and phantoms that came and went, that seemed mere eccentricity to those who did not live with him, who could not chart them or cater for their rising and falling in his constitution as a wife could, all *this* turned to a one-word joke: *hypochondria.* And if it helped, why not? She was his helpmate and strength, better and worse, whatever her mother might have said or done to the contrary, till death's parting shot. Whatever else was yet to come, she would always be his wife.

> Marks and markers, new Life, two hearts as one.
> His cares were her cares.
> *Worldly goods held in common, love, much love, a*
> *boundlessness, etc etc.*

When she cast her mind back over what she had wished for, this marriage was not, in essence, so out of tune. It could not truthfully be counted less than she had wished. It was *more*, though what had to be learned to deal with that *more* was almost too terrible to bear. And what had to be learned was this: that sometimes all the trying one could muster accomplished nothing at all. She had seen her husband weeping, crying out for relief from the rushing in his head, for escape from the wild pictures that tormented him. She had seen the brokenness he could not shake. She had seen him rant about her treachery, shaking with fury because a coach arrived late or she had been delayed on a visit, or because she had not understood him, or for her apparently tireless knack of suggesting the wrong thing at the wrong time. She had seen him open a hotel room window, throw the catches wide as a crucifix, wondering aloud if he should End Things Now, if she would not be better off. She had heard him wonder if she *wished it so*. She had seen him drink himself into loquaciousness, becoming more and more slack-jawed into the night, and sat with him as he told her stories she did not understand, about sisters and mothers and angels and devils, devils and angels, and she had followed the line of his finger as he had shown her a star in the corner of the room — *a planet, tiny, shining bright as a flame!* — and tried, for all she was worth, to see it too. And afterwards she had seen him sit in silence for days, refusing everything but his own blackness.

And there was no altering these things when they happened, no amount of protestation or bewilderment or gentling or outrage or humouring or tears; they merely came and had to be stomached, digested, somehow absorbed. If they had to be learned the hard way, perhaps the lessons would last. Some things, however, were not a matter of learning: they were beyond all control. Other things, other people, the randomness of things. The worst was the day her father had come to the house so sure of his welcome that he never knocked. And he had found her in the bedroom, trying to coax her husband back to bed. A man in his nightshirt with his hair in his eyes, refusing to speak or sleep, barely able to stand. Her father had begun to help, declaiming and pointing with his stick, sure if he spoke loudly enough his orders would be obeyed. And when they were not, when Clara tried to usher him away, he — what other word was there? — he *kicked* Robert where he sat. From nowhere he reached and began hauling, pulling Robert's arm and *screaming*. Manliness, Self-respect, the need to Pull Oneself Together, a great jumble of words formed in bites, bursts of horrible meaning. *Will you have them call you a madman? Have you no shame? Will you make yourself and your wife a laughing stock in this city too?* And she had stood and been able to think of nothing, nothing, to make it stop. *Madman!* The pattern on the rug whirling, pulling in on itself as the cane beat down on it, the tumbling folds of her husband's nightshirt as he had fallen, his hands over his head. Then Clara turned, knowing somehow by instinct, and there was Marie, not the height of the doorknob, watching. A cold-water rinse of shock poured over her skin to remember it, the sight of her daughter in the open door frame. What had the child seen? Or understood? Nothing. Clara decided there and then — *nothing* — scooping the child away and carrying her to Mathilde, Henriette, whoever came first, and nothing of the incident, thereafter, was said. Not to Marie, not to Robert, to her father least of all. To say anything would merely waste breath and time. But it rankled. It rankled to the white knuckle ends and back just to *think* what he had done and said. *Madman!* That he should call Robert by such a name! Refinement, culture and aspiration, great gentleness of soul such as marked Robert Schumann was a world away from everything to do with *madmen*. Madmen howled and tore their clothing. They were not *thinking people* at all, but beasts, beasts unwilling but beasts all the same and pitiable in the same way. Liszt had played concerts in asylums and been so heart-torn he had faltered, unable to go on. The sounds that came from such buildings only confirmed it. Madmen, when all was said and done, were something less than human and everyone knew it. But *her father* had said it. And *she* had said nothing at all. Well, then. What might this be called? Slow-wittedness. Cowardice. The mark of a Poor Wife indeed. In short, failure, and allowing herself to dwell, to brood, or to breast-beat did not change that failure one bit.

The only thing that might mitigate this dreadful shortfall would be to ensure it did not happen again. She would think of something, something sound and sure. It would begin with stout locks, new keys; an order to Henriette that no one but herself should allow her father through the door. Something better would come too, but since she was slow it would take time. And since she was a coward she must pass that time building her own courage. *He comes through,* she told herself, repeating the words like a rosary chant, *his habit, whatever the fight, is to come through.* Reuter's words were on her side, the sound of his voice speaking clear. And Mendelssohn too. Pages of Mendelssohn, playing the pieces he had written for her, would be a consolation. Playing the best she knew. Scarlatti, then. Bach. Chopin till her wrists hurt. And Weber, who had come to her rescue before, the very manuscript still by the piano, its gold leaf faded to nothing. Most of all, she would play *Schumann*; his name on the frontispiece as though he was someone else. Every night, then, when he took his evening walks, she filled the house. She played *Carnaval* for the exercise of technique, *Kreisleriana* for exorcism of demons, songs for the rigorous discipline of poetry. Most of all, she played his concerto.

An especial thing, this concerto, and made particularly for her hands. Music that became more intricate and well-fashioned with every playing. And what was it? Scraps and leavings, things plucked from the air. He had taken the *Fantasie*, written for her as long as four years ago, for her and only her when she carried their first daughter, and to it he had added more. He added fragments from the early days here, their most cold-bitten, fearful time, odd jottings from the times when he could hold a pen, when he could bear to note them down. He had saved everything, waited, begun again, again. And what had come of it was one seamless flow, as tender and far from shadows as music could be. Even the *look* of it thrilled her: the bar lines looped over and skirted and duped for melody's sake, effects that might be seen only on the page, not heard in their full subtlety at all. It was clever and beautiful, but it was more than that. It was proof. Proof that sheer effort of will could construct a wholeness where none existed. Proof that music and those who made it could confront chaos, and find in it what was tender and fantastical and clear and true. And this was her purpose: to play such music; music that made everything, everything, come through.

Some weeks later, she played the concerto for the public for the first time, fat as a barrel, stretching for the keys. Robert being indisposed, she had gone to Leipzig herself and not cared who remarked. Her hide, she understood, was toughening. Weeks later again, there was Julie, skinny as a bow-string and twice as nervous; less than a year after that, Emil, restless from the first and his cry was weak, but a boy *thank the Lord, a man should have a boy*. One month after that again – she could tell immediately, the sensations were familiar by now and quite clear – another baby on the way. She had no knowledge, it struck her, none at all of how to hinder her own fecundity. Such things were possible but there was no one to ask. That some means existed and was something that men understood and attended to was all she knew. And Robert? Either he did not know or did not care to and what was to be done about that? The possibility of abstinence did not occur.

Clara was not built for abstinence, anyone who listened to her play knew that. Only tone-deaf or myopic sorts could have read that by-choice restrained demeanour (as some tone-deaf and myopic sorts certainly did) as *cold*. A word she had certainly heard and read in reviews, the word *cold* used of herself never failed to astonish her. Others too. Liszt with his huge blue eyes, looking at her directly; that ghastly prince of somewhere who pursued her round a table in Moscow; the oily Rakemann all those years ago, saying things from the other side of the room, loud enough for anyone to hear. *A thin shell of ice over a volcano, a Dark Horse indeed.* And she had thought he was only trying to unsettle her, to unseat her concentration in the hope he would sound less awful by comparison when they played duets. At any rate, whatever anyone said or did not say, abstinence was not an available option. Besides, even to mention such a thing might have caused upset or irritation and what that almost invariably led to.

The last thing he could afford (by which she meant he, she and the entire running of the household could afford), was *upset*. Treading on eggshells worked. It had worked all her life. And though his nervous attacks, inflammations of the head, irritations and exhaustions still came and went, it was the case, more noticeably as the weeks and months of diligent mood monitoring went by, that it worked still. Something more like *himself* was returning. He was working again, colouring sounds into some symphony sketches he had made before his work stopped altogether; a symphony he thought cheerless and in an off-the-peg key, but still. Better. He was orchestrating, reading texts and talking operas, chamber music, *plans*.

How long had it taken, this turning point? Two years? That much? But whole weeks could be counted upon at last. And they would stay that way. She had made up her mind. Like a general, someone to be reckoned with, she had learned a set of tactics that would stand this marriage, this stability upon which all else rested, in solid stead. And the tactics were these. If he was excitable, she would engineer that they withdrew from company; if he was moody and withdrawn, she would ensure they surrounded themselves with books and home; if he was melancholy, she would sit it out, be patient, wait and see. If they ran out of money and she could no longer work at all, and when the new baby came – well. The tactical set was not complete yet, but it was begun and that was something. Containment and fortification. One might survive on such things. And only one of them could ensure both. On the strength of her new wisdom, they shifted to Reitbahngasse as fast as a house fell empty. Somewhere bigger, she said, somewhere further from the noise of the city centre, somewhere less expensive but with a garden, flowers, trees. Somewhere, with no angels and devils sucked into its very wall-paper, a place where the mirrors had not yet reflected the past. Somewhere to be braver, perhaps. Whatever its function, it was somewhere *else*.

That spring, the spring Emil was born, she was a different woman. People remarked upon it – that roundedness in her chin, the mature tilt of her eyes – and she did not contradict. She had weathered the worst things she ever hoped to face and understood what mattered. Love was not kisses or children or even what was commonly called happiness. It was the protection of what one loved best of all, at whatever cost, and on that score she had no doubts. *Him*. Without him, no family, no happiness at all and what else followed from that? Nothing worth having. Ergo, what mattered was him. All she had to do was offer some necessary shelter.

When her father burst into the quiet of the nursery at Reitbahngasse, then, roaring his thoughts on Jenny Lind – All his pupils wanted to be Lind! Everyone was to sound like Lind, even the pianists! What singer could be as good as they said? And a Swede! Whoever spoke of the Swedes and music in the same breath? Damn this fever for Jenny Lind! – what did she do? She let him have ten minutes, called for Henriette and organised an exit. Henriette with his coat over her arm, her father's face a picture. But he went. Furious, but he went. And she had raised herself from pillows with the baby in her arms, shielding him from the sound of the slamming door. *I am a fortification.* Those very words under her breath. *A shield.* Perhaps she believed it.

Not long after, when Robert's work ground to a stop and he took to fretting afresh, it worked again. She found someone for the babies, a few weeks in the suburbs at the Serres' house in Maxen, a place he had always liked. And when the view from his window there became more hindrance than help, when he pointed out to her that every morning what he saw was Sonnenstein, a madhouse on the hill, Sonnenstein and only Sonnenstein, she took them somewhere else instead. *There is always something one can do,* she told herself, a fount of resourcefulness. And the something was Norderney. There, in a spa town of quite terrifically unmitigated tedium and stolid little boarding houses, no friends or acquaintances to interrupt the sluggish pulse of the day, they lasted out a month of sea bathing, a month of dutiful recording of temperatures and water levels, a month of nothing at all to work its monotonous trick. And it did. Upon Clara too. The effect of the hot springs was not wholly unexpected. A doctor was called in the middle of the night and he gave her teas to drink and particular pills, and that was that. Peace of mind, he said. Bedrest. But she was rested enough. She was rested to distraction. As for peace of mind, not everyone obtained it in the same way and Clara – Clara wished to play. Sitting on inch-thick towelling and a constant slither of blood-clots, her face white but composed enough, she played a concert as soon as it could be set up for some local hall, and for not much more than the asking. She would have worn black in case of staining but had brought none, so maroon served. Maroon, she decided, was practical. She did not examine what she felt, did not think she might *feel* anything. *Feeling* did not alter facts. Miscarriage happened, the will of God was the will of God. This was the form of avoidance of more children that women took on, that was all. And their lives, if she were to count her blessings, were less hazardous again. The calmer days she had promised had come and that was a satisfaction. Clara Schumann wished to be a woman who kept her promises. A performer, skilled more than most in flawless concealment, she could congratulate herself on that. Another city, another house, another set of medical practitioners certainly helped, but uppermost, she was in no doubt, strength of character had ensured that as far as Herr Schumann's health and dignity were concerned, *hardly anyone knew.* The word *madness* had come too close. It would not happen again if she could help it. She played *Carnaval*, taxing her fingers, imagining the merriment of dancing. Something with the feel and size of raw goose liver slicked out of her on the final chords, her stomach swilling. Maroon was certainly the sensible choice. Dizzy, gripping the piano lid for support and finding it, she turned, smiling, to her applause.

SEVEN

An meinem Herzen

Here, on my Heart

*I*t took longer than she would have imagined.

But it was done. A trio entire. Her first true piece of chamber music, the music Robert had always said was the mark of a finished composer. This time, the composer was herself. It was for no particular occasion, this piece, merely to mark time. With her own room, her own table at which to write, what might she not do? Meanwhile, however, this trio was something, and her father wished to judge its worth. I will not fault its structure, he said, casting the manuscript to one side. But it's no concert draw. That sombre stuff will never put arses on seats. Minor keys have no appeal to the public at large, Clara, and it has no bravura, no show. Whatever your husband has led you to believe, chamber music is mere filler – something for a domestic *soirée*. The fugal section at the close is too intellectual and expansive and peculiar. It is not sufficiently womanly: it is too clever. You will get no reward from this thing. They will think – he sniffed in triumph at the close – they will think *he* wrote it.

Enough. Her trio would come with them to Vienna. Robert insisted. No matter what her father said, her trio would come too.

Vienna. What possessed them? And Robert, who had always been so reluctant to travel at all, suggesting they take the children too. The invitation for the symphonies or the concerto, the possibility of escape from another winter in Dresden? Money? Defiance and the possibility of difference after the awful, mummifying stillness? A fit of foolish over-confidence and bravado? All and none of these things. Lordknew. All the way to Vienna when mere months ago he could not even cross a room! But he was hearty. He was keen. So they packed the sets of scores and the collated string and woodwind parts, and the books of songs and the ferryload of travelling gear, and damned apprehension. At least Vienna was familiar. They had friends. They might even, they fantasised as they travelled, Marie and Elise, a five and a three-year-old, bouncing on the wooden train-seat slats, *move* to Vienna one day. *Come birdie a-flying.* Robert sang with his children on his knee, the countryside from Prague clipping past in the window; Marie pressed her nose to the grimy pane. Elise wore white gloves, each fingertip grey. Why should they not be happy? Why should they not entertain the prospect of being happier still? Nothing tied them to Dresden, after all, least of all gratitude. No one had offered him work there. No one had offered *her* work, come to that: the pupils that allowed her to earn a little every day she had found for herself.

Vienna, on the other hand, city of Beethoven and Schubert *etc etc*, was also the city of Clara-cakes and effusive applause. The place where her father had burst a waistcoat button from sheer inability to contain his ego from swelling to twice its normal size. The city's Royal and Imperial Court Virtuosa was better known and loved in Vienna than anywhere else in the world, quite so, quite so. For what they were worth, she recalled the reviews and the confectionery and the medals in velvet boxes very well. But she had forgotten the Viennese and their penchant for sensation. She had forgotten the nine-year gap between then and now. She had forgotten *herself.*

Vienna.

The beauty of the Austrian capital was there, but grown garish, some-how, blowsy. The applause was there, but not wild. And the praise was there, Kolb and the others effusing efficiently, but. But. Madame Schumann was *stately and measured*, she was *possessed of soaring technique and profundity and clarity* and lots of other things as well, but. But the candle power of the place and her being there, of the people, of the halls and − and *everything*, really, was not so bright as it had been. Nine years. She had been eighteen. *Eighteen.* Did she not in all honesty grasp the difference? That the tight fit of her dresses would no longer be so exciting now the dresses themselves were not white muslin? That married-lady plaids and bottle-greens would temper the rapture of her reception? That what had titillated this titillation-loving city at least in part – a girl with the power of a man, a child with the artistry of maturity, the delicious shiver of *for sale* that somehow ran up the spine when a virgin mounted the stage for public display – was gone, irrespective of what else she had brought to show?

There was the music, of course, very good music, all that Bach and Beethoven was probably very good for one. And her husband's stuff, a great deal of her husband's stuff, which they understood was modern and difficult, and therefore probably very deep, but *really*. Some loyalties could be carried *too far*. Also, she played rather too much Mendelssohn. But then, any was too much Mendelssohn. They hadn't liked him years ago and they didn't like him now, however popular he was *elsewhere*. Still, she played it, if someone had to, beautifully, nobly, with insight and finely honed power, and a lyricism that was never sentimental and so on, quite, quite. She was, quite possibly, unique. But. Liszt could break piano strings and faint from sheer rapture – imagine! – when he played. Lind was a full-voiced coloratura who, even at twenty-six and unmarried, looked juicy as a pie and *smiled*. Thalberg played so fast his fingers blurred, and those diamond studs he wore on his shirt were the height, *my dear*, of grand. Then there was Meyerbeer, his operas as florid as something by a Real Italian, saucy and *all in French*, which made one feel so effortlessly *entertained*. Who with this on offer, after dressing up and hashing through town in a hansom, wished Only Music as one's Night Out? Some did, thank heavens; small audiences that lasted out through the husband's symphony to get to what they had come to hear, and what they had come to hear was her. Their applause was something to be grateful for but the applause of half a hall just the same. When the papers extolled her intelligence, she despaired. Who, in Vienna, would turn out for *intelligence*? The answer was as she suspected: not many.

And for his symphony, with Robert himself conducting and no Clara on stage at all, even the faithful failed to respond. She watched him walk off stage to the echo of scraping cello spikes, coughing, a scatter of clapping that sounded like a mistake. And how it tore at her! That they should insult him like this! She paced up and down in her dressing room, damning the Viennese and their ruination by everything Italian. She blamed Italians, herself, the programme, the orchestra and the weather.

They care only for novelty, she complained, near to tears with frustration, embarrassing herself and not able to stop. She tried, she was sure of that much. But this feeling of being on tenterhooks, of waiting for thunder, of – what other word was there? – of *apprehension* would not go away.

Fischhof, grown much fatter with the intervening years and twice as irritating, tapped his nose and twitched at Robert, man to man, whispering loud enough for the opera stage: *Your wife is much agitated, Herr Doctor Schumann. Perhaps this touring is a little too much?* Dear God, she could have hit him. Perhaps she should have. But it was Robert who acted; who, when he found his voice again, spoke to some effect. Who soothed her. *In ten years*, he said, *it will all be different.* And left her ashamed, silenced, with Fischhof staring as though she were a temperamental coach horse.

Two days later she found Marie and Elise, left with their father for the afternoon, huddled together and alone in the middle of St Stephen's Square. There was no mistaking them, the same blue winter coats, their hoods down. Elise's gloves were missing. Papa had left them, Marie explained, Elise howling at her elbow, Papa had left them in the cigar shop. He had gone away. But he was there, in their hotel room, unaware of any dilemma. Safe, altogether safe. He had simply forgotten, she told herself. A lapse of judgement, momentary, something anyone might have done. Perhaps he assumed they knew their own way. Perhaps. And she said nothing, did nothing to suggest anything was out of kilter. Why should she? What good did it ever do? But she watched. Carefully, distantly, without his being much aware. Who knew what anything was a sign of any more? Perhaps, as her father always warned her, as Fischhof suggested, she had lost her nerve.

As if to test it, her father, in town for nothing but to push unready pupils into the public eye, turned up to state the obvious. You are making a loss, he observed.

She knew.

Unheard of.

She asked if he was done.

Food prices here, he said. Potato shortages! Unaffordable.

He straightened his waistcoat front as he rose. You will never feed yourself playing his music. Pack, Clara. He sniffed. Go home.

Then Lind appeared. A lady is come to ask for Madame Schumann. Like a fairy with a bow-tied basket of apples for the children, Lind, the box office breaker, the toast of anywhere she fancied, had come to ask if she might sing. She wore a plain wool dress, her hair in braids like a child's.

It would be an honour, she said, her voice ringing, a lesson beyond price, to sing for Clara Schumann.

No fee. She meant no fee. And Clara was glad they had met in the quiet of this hotel room, for all it was small and flowerless. She was glad of the distraction of Marie on her lap. She couldn't speak.

We might walk, her guest said. The Prater is pretty, even in this cold.

She fetched coats for the children, fixed their buttons herself, lifted Elise as though it were no effort. With her other hand she gave Clara a handkerchief from her pocket, flapped it open with a wave of her lace-gloved hand. Madame Schumann, she suggested, might care to blow her nose.

One week later, in one concert, with one song of Mendelssohn's, Jenny Lind had done what Clara could not. She sent them on the road back home in profit, winter apples in their children's hands.

⋯⊶⊙⊷⋯

A bare turn on the heel, a matter of days. No sooner back than they went to Berlin. Yes, there were performances and people to visit, and the chance to see Mendelssohn on his home turf was not to be turned down and, and, *and*. But what was it for, looking back, this running? Merely greed for activity, a little excitement, before stasis crept smotheringly back? A kind of desperation, a castle built upon his slightly more settled sand? Opportunism, even; casting for work somewhere else, *anywhere* else but Dresden? Or something as tawdry and likely as avoidance of the sight of Emil's chest tremor, the wheezy, never-enough sound of their little son's breathing? Carus told them, Reuter confirmed it: the boy would not live long. They certainly knew. And they certainly kept moving. It could not be denied.

And what did this running achieve? Three small chamber concerts.

One *soirée* stuffed for aristos; an evening where she could not bring herself to sit in the antechamber, separated off from the assorted toffery like a bootboy waiting for business, while Robert, waiting in the audience, endured the King asking loudly to his face who *that queer, silent gentleman* might be waiting for. After that, his two great outings for the *Peri* in the city of Mendelssohn, both falling to pieces with infighting, complaints and tantrums; one performance crumbling into silence while singers lost their way and Robert conducted unswervingly, helplessly, hopelessly on. The critics were not hard on him. Not at all. They ignored him by and large, and as for Clara, they opined that despite her flawless technique and effortless interpretation, she was somewhat – how could one put it? – *over-refined*. Madame Schumann should *steep herself less in Bach* and smile a little more. Was this meant to mean anything? Could it ever, in any circumstances, *mean* anything? And Mother, pointing out that Chopin had been criticised in much the same way only without the smile part, succeeded only in making her more furious still.

I invite you at last to meet my sister, Mendelssohn said, vastly amused. There is nothing that entertains her more than a polished show of indignation.

And for what seemed the first time in months, Clara laughed. After a while and despite herself, but laughter all the same.

Was that why she recalled this visit? Mendelssohn's brightness of spirits? His face finding a smile despite his recent agitation and nervousness, his desperate overwork? He had not been the same in Berlin, she had heard. He had headaches that drained the colour from his face and these days seldom joked. She could see it was true. But with her a few hours, in her company over the days, his face eased out and he seemed less prone to jump at every noise. In short, he seemed more the Leipzig Mendelssohn he had been. He talked of his childhood, told her he could test the pitch of window-panes by tapping them with his nail tip, was surprised to find she had not done the same. And he took her to his sister's, a house in whites and buffs, muslins in cascades at the towering windows, the cornice picked out in eggshell-blue. *Madame Hensel's rooms are the picture of joy.* She recalls saying it, though not to whom; she recalls, momentarily perhaps, but clearly, wishing for a room of her own such as this. Clearest of all, she recalls the Pleyel near the window for the best illumination; Madame Hensel's Pleyel since she had been a girl. She had played duets with her brother here, sitting on a double stool. And there was nothing to choose between them, Felix said, save that his hair had been longer and prettier.

Not any more. She laughed. In either case.

My sister is an excellent pianist still, Felix said. And composes against all advice. Speak to her, Clara, make her realise this is no hobby for a woman.

And he sat at the keys, playing phrases and fragments, complaining about the tuning, the sticky pedal, the candleholders that were not to his taste.

Forgive him, she said. It is a habit to point out my shortcomings when I especially wish to make a good impression. Now, Madame Schumann — she leaned forward, looked Clara full in the eye — tell me what music you have brought.

She wore a flower in her hair, a cluster of little white bud heads like the tips of matches. Forty-one years old and only one child to show for it, her face still completely fresh. On the chair beside her, a love seat or something preposterous, was Joachim, the *protégé* no longer. His sober little man's face was furrowed and he sat with his feet barely reaching the floor, all the buttons on his monkey suit fastened tight. Feminine surroundings, she thought, watching the boy squirm against silk cushions. These are wholly feminine surroundings.

I am sorry my husband could not come, she said. He is —

He is busy, Madame Hensel said. I know. It is the nature of gifted husbands and part of their fascination. My husband is a painter. They are, all of them, busy men.

She composed, she said. She played a little. She confessed she had published songs. And she held concerts, but only for family, those who could bear to hear. What she wished to set in place, more than anything else, was a concert here and now and, having said it, she meant it. She rounded up chairs and set things in their places, rooted stands from corners, organised them to play. Yes, she had heard Herr Doctor Schumann's trio at Madame Schumann's concert, but she wished to hear something else. She wished to hear *Madame Schumann's* trio, if Joachim would assist. Which he would, she made it quite plain that he would. And it had been easy to play there, in this unannounced, almost assumptive way that was her brother's too. He had done the self-same thing at evenings in Leipzig, had brought her on stage at concerts where she had gone to listen, brazen and incorrigibly favouritist and loyal to the last. This time, it was he who let himself be steered to perform despite himself, told to pick out the cello part because someone had to, and he had stood without fuss at the piano beside her to play or sing or busk in some wise the necessary line.

Clara thought of Müller, the cellist who had declared himself in love with her in Hannover; a time when she had played every day without thinking twice and had not known the Herz Variations were the most terrible nonsense. When she had not known what she knew now. But this was not Hannover or anything like. It was a corner of Berlin, a house she could never afford as long as she lived, and Mendelssohn, Felix, with grey showing in his whiskers and his hairline receding, filling in; *singing*. It refreshed him, perhaps, this little concert for his sister, the room with portraits of a family who resembled each other so well watching from the pallid walls. And how much pleasure it had given Clara, even if the work was only her own. Scotch snaps! Counterpoint that Bach would not have disowned!

Joachim could not contain himself. He asked, wide-eyed, if Madame Schumann had really written this music by herself. But how is it when one composes? he asked. What it is like?

A fourteen-year-old boy with earnest little lines between his brows, searching her face for answers, almost irritable in its desperation to *know*. One had to say something. But what? How *had* it been done? No one had ever asked her such a thing. Pianists improvised, they composed: it was What One Did. One learned *how* in much the way that fingering, phrasing, the rules of harmony were learned. Time had been set aside every day and she had filled it: Variations and a handful of Romances, the queer little concerto, songs. Pieces appeared on the page because they appeared. Because her father set her to write them. Because Robert set her to write them. Because she wished to please. Not *this*, however, this complex and infuriating thing that had made her bang her brow in frustration. A trio that she had taken upon herself merely because she had. There was no one's birthday, no one's demand to blame. How was it she had written *this*?

Like – writing a letter, she said. She heard her voice, distant, saying it. A letter to someone whose face you have not seen for a long time. Exactly that.

But how is your composing achieved, Madame Schumann? That is what I mean – how is it *created*?

The assemblage of paper and ink and enough nibs to last. A knife and blotting sand. The finding of somewhere to sit that gave adequate light and the rolling back of sleeves – tight cuffs and not white, it paid not to wear white – to save them from smears. Ensuring the door was closed. Trying to sit still. To think. Blocking out the piano from the other room, the flat-footed toing and froing of Henriette on the way upstairs with fresh towels. Wondering if Mathilde had been told what to order for the kitchen, if her husband would need the cellar key. A lamp somewhere near, a deal of clock watching. Slowness, tedium. And from it, occasionally, very rarely, moments that turned into an hour or more, swallowed by one idea and its working out into a timeless state of self-forgetting. Sometimes they lasted mere minutes. But they came. Till a child with a hurt finger, a drawing, a wish for a kiss appeared at the door or something caught the eye or someone came to the door to be taught. More often, there was the *stuckness* and the desire to be elsewhere, doing something else, anything rather than trying to force some order out of the random pieces that refused to go further without a fight. It was achieved despite her, somehow. Despite everything. But this was not anything to say. It was not instructive, or illuminating, or grand.

Writing music is a matter of patience, she said. Patience and persistence and reading. I have studied a great deal. Herr Doctor Mendelssohn will tell you how important it is to –

But inspiration, he persisted. *Inspiration*, Madame. Schubert said he heard the voices of angels. Is it like this?

The little man-boy held his violin like a sword, waiting. Felix's eyes lit upon her, the corners of his mouth twitched. And all she had in her mouth were plain things, and he knew it. Practicalities. Apologies.

You might ask my husband next time we meet, she said. He always knows what to say.

And Felix could no longer restrain himself. He snorted. He threw his head back and laughed out loud, looking wholly restored, himself again. This is one reason we are busy men, Joachim. We must speak for our womenfolk as well as ourselves. If we do not work ourselves to death with explication and necessary work, if we are not torn to pieces on the teeth of inspiration, we may rest when we are forty.

Like a sick man made well again by a trick of the light. His sister, beside him, raising a glass of Rhenish. The Best of Men.

⋅⊷══◉═⊷⋅

My husband would wish to sketch you, Madame Schumann. When you next come to Berlin you must call. I should wish us to be friends, great friends. Visit us often in Berlin.

The same day she knew for sure, had braced herself against Robert's insistence that another child was a blessing because all children were blessings *and so they were, they were*, the note from Cécile arrived at their door. Cécile's handwriting, the fine black edge on the card. A seizure, it said; a haemorrhage from within the brain itself. A matter of a few hours. Madame Hensel had risen from the piano and walked to another room, complaining of feeling unwell and before the physician had arrived it was over and done. Madame Hensel was dead. Her husband and son were beside themselves and Felix sat like a stuffed doll, even his children unable to rouse him to speak. No flowers. The family wished no flowers.

Imagining another family's grief: a fearful thing to do.

What did she know of death? Schunke, Robert's mother and Rosalie, half-remembered faces. An idea of Viktor in his shawl. And when Emil died, as they knew he would, she thought she knew little more. He had lain in his cot, making painful little cries till they had stopped, his breathing labouring on while Carus advised them to prepare. To *prepare.* The sketch Robert had had made, something to show when visitors called, an offering of paper, inky lines behind glass, he turned to the wall. God's will etc. For the best. *The smallest are nearest God as the smallest planets are near the sun.* Quite so. Yet Clara could not bear to utter her boy's name. That she should feel this reduced, so numbly and persistently bovine, might have surprised her if she had felt capable of surprise. And when Robert shut himself away to work, she arranged the funeral. If she had not, her father would have come and she had no desire to see her father. None at all. To know that much was something.

But when she heard that Mendelssohn was dead, had bled away invisibly in exactly the same way as his sister, groaning so loud in his agony that two streets distant could hear, her heart had all but stopped. Information, piecemeal and salted with rumour, perhaps; the essential fact, however, remaining. Felix Mendelssohn was dead. Lordknew how many had gone to his door, rattled the bolts, requested their rightful last glimpse, and Cécile would not have stopped them. She would have gathered the children about her, made a wall of supporters and sympathisers and family, and bided her time till the crowd had looked her husband in the face, and they pleased to look at him a while. A Great Man is the public's property and the public know it. On the day of the funeral they hemmed in the coffin with palm branches, pressed their noses to the windows as the procession passed the Gewandhaus and on to the Thomas Church with six clergymen for company, none of them a Jew. There had been Bach and Handel and a fleet of chorales, and Cécile had come at the last to fold herself and her skirts about the coffin, a spectacle the public doubtless enjoyed as added atmosphere. Had they given her ether, Clara wondered? How had she remained so dutifully *calm?* But calm was what everyone, with evident satisfaction, remarked that she had been. As a finale, they trooped her with the casket to the train station for the whole show again in Berlin before the ride to the family vault, his barely cold sister. Robert missed that part. Of course. Leipzig had been enough. Having seen what he went to see, he came ash-faced, unswervingly home. His features, however, were altered. He talked a great deal. Incessantly. That he had been there. He, Robert, who had been too harrowed by the thought to attend his own mother's funeral, who had run away from terminal glimpses of those who had once been his dearest friends, who hated travel without an orchestra to conduct at the end of it, had boarded a train and gone to Leipzig to find Reuter – a friend, a man could do with a friend when he was afraid – and view a *corpse*. He had been to see the body in death of a Great Man and a Great Colleague. And this by himself and for himself, while she could hardly shift. She should have seen, he said. The great swollen veins of Mendelssohn's forehead, the mottled blueness under his translucent skin! That he had been there and she had not – was it not astonishing? He would write an opera, these texts he had been sifting and checking through, he felt a requirement to write *something*. And he laughed, a laugh that faded as soon as it began. He put his hands to his face. He ran to a mirror and stared. Clara, the baby kicking, juddering her body as she stood there, watched him do it. His eyes shining, this inexplicable upturn to his mouth as he looked at himself. Frightening, for a moment, this face made of dissociated pieces. For a second, a stranger.

This same frightening thing happened again at Hiller's farewell, only two days later. *Düsseldorf*, Hiller was repeating the word *Düsseldorf* and being tedious. He had no regrets leaving Dresden, he said, or something very like, if he might write to his old friends. Whatever, it did not lodge in the memory. Very little of the evening did. She had no real wish to be there and in some ways, doubtless, was not. But she showed her face. She played. She played Mendelsshon's *Frühlingslied* and was not overwhelmed. Of course not. She barely felt her fingers on the keys. In this warm place, the candles and magnesium lamps burning fit to raze Moscow, she was cold. She played again, watched Joachim managing his bravest, his most lost expression, but this terrible sensation of frozenness, separateness, did not go away. This room, these people. That man who was her husband there in the corner, checking the veins at his temples in a glass of something, anything. Glass after glass. Her baby turning over, a fish against a tide.

After all his wrestling and elbows in the bladder, Ludwig arrived on the coldest day of the year, the coldest January in living memory, without much fuss. Dark and spiky as a hedgehog, so ugly that people tried not to notice. He looked – *healthy*, people said, and hoped it would do. Whatever he looked, he was not like the blond and blue-eyed and long-dead Schunke whom Robert suddenly wished to name a child for, but he was strong. Carus confirmed it. Ludwig was constitutionally sound. And after the christening, Robert went back to his opera, his *Genoveva*, an *Othello* with a happy ending, while the rest of the world fell to warring with itself.

The French started it, of course. The French, it seemed, could not help starting things. Then the Russians, the Prussians, the Austrians, one after the other, rolling like logs off a pile.

There will be more red tape before there will be less, her father said. Metternich's castles were crumbling in the air.

Shooting in Berlin, in Vienna. In Lombardy and Switzerland. In Warsaw. In effect, revolution on all sides. What a terrible word it was, *revolution*. And the press more shut-down, the whole of Dresden more speculative, every day. Some people, the rich, left the city *in case*. With some, the threat of a workers' holiday was enough to provoke that and besides, they had somewhere to go. Musicians followed work. *Ipso facto*. There was simply nowhere that wanted the Schumanns. No matter how much the world needed music, an art worth the name at such times – and they unquestionably did, Clara had no doubts – there was no future in running. In the middle of all such political froth and bubbling, the only option was more of Dresden. More choral society eye scratching and pettiness and trap-faced spites. Home. A great deal more of home.

Ludwig who never slept. Marie with lessons of her own every day, Elise headstrong and Julie small enough to be taken for a baby and rising two. Manuscript paper in a feathery pile, the daily work of transcription. These were her days. She tailored his overtures and choral pieces, his symphonies and chamber work to ebb and flow, and suggested their colours for one pair of hands at a keyboard so they might sell, and that was something. Piano reductions earned money, therefore Clara

Schumann transcribed. And trained his choir and versed the sections and edited what needed editing if he asked. But there would be no touring, no playing much. No composing or staring into space, which activities were certainly joined. There was only home, its huge and torpid self the middle of everything, while enough fear and trepidation in the air to frighten drays in the street came closer. Metternich had resigned and the King of Prussia had permitted – *permitted* struck Clara as a droll choice of word – the students and the marchers and the rye-starved farmers to talk openly of confederacy.

Her own mother arrived from Berlin, with terrible tales of Swedish conscripts and trigger-happy home-grown hussars content to shoot farmers' boys like so many rabbits. Clara gave her money and a listening ear, but could not stop her from going back. Of course she went back. Berlin was at least alert to change. Berlin, under its hail of bullets and bought-in soldiers, was – the word struck her neatly – *alive*. Better the danger than the awful nothingness of Dresden, where snobbery and denial and arrogance were daily passing themselves off as forms of Patient Saxon Wisdom. Did Madame Schumann not understand what Union and Nationalism would unleash? That without an aristocracy, *a strong guiding force*, a strict set of censorship rules and military policing of the rabble, *anything* might happen? Dear God, how patronising they were! Even the Hübners and the Bendemanns, people she thought she knew. *Then Madame Schumann can afford to be a revolutionary*, Bendemann said. *No fear of enlistment is a great inducement to romance.* Robert said nothing. Why should he? He had no need to argue his ideas with anyone, let alone Dresdeners. So why – the question crossed her mind even then – did she?

She, who had never expressed a political enthusiasm of any stripe before now, was suddenly impassioned. She played Chopin at charity concerts for the dispossessed Poles. She opined that the function of Art was profound, and its function was consolation, pattern and meaning in chaos, the restoration of the value of beauty and to hell with their mealy-mouthed notion of music as anything else. She sent money to soup kitchens and argued with her neighbours. She called the director of the opera house, to his face, a *Klutz*. One must do something with one's emotions, after all, and these were better things to do than most. Passion for the sake of passion itself will do.

If Robert was surprised, he gave no sign. His Clara had always been a thing of passion, if not perhaps *in this way*; and he had always been a creature – of what? Ha! That was nobody's business but his own. A creature of keeping himself to himself. Until, of course, he changed his mind or his mind changed him, and he became a wit, a froth of hypochondria and complaint, a child refusing to play. And there was more. Whatever was turning in the sky, this present charge in the air that provoked countries to fight each other and Clara to develop politics like a rash, it stoked white furies in Robert. He had always been *intense*, dear Lord, she would never have denied it. But now? What had trembled beneath his skin came to the surface. He tore up papers and clenched his fists and – it might not be denied for so many had seen it – *he threatened Liszt*. And at a dinner in the Great Man's honour, the invitations for which she had sent with her own hands. It had not helped that Liszt was two hours late, or that he interrupted the music that Robert had arranged to have played, that he called Robert's quartet *Leipzigish*, hooting the 'L' down his nose as though he scented shoe-borne shit a little too close by. It hadn't helped that Liszt had drunk two glasses of champagne, then played so affectedly, so head-tossingly badly that Bendemann swanned off without a word, leaving them to whatever spectacle the guest of honour cared to unleash next. When Liszt tumbled from the piano stool, however, offering yet another toast, this time declaring *One Berlin Meyerbeer to be worth Two of these Leipzigish Mendelssohn sorts any day of the week*, everyone knew that even for Liszt, Liszt had gone too far. Even so, Robert startled her. He startled everyone. Spilling wine and forks, capillaries bursting in his cheeks, he rose from the table like Zeus on a mountain and Clara thought for a moment he meant to strike her. Then she saw he was looking past her shoulder, directly at the man behind. At Liszt. *Dear Christ*, what had been more shocking? That her husband, a byword for stolid citizenship and clam-faced reserve, might roll on the floorboards with Franz Liszt? That the impeccable Liszt had made a drunken affront of himself in this way? That she had felt so vulnerable, so cluelessly, shockingly *female* in the presence of it all?

In retrospect, when she tried to reframe, imagine what others had seen, had it been so bad? Schumann grabbed a handful of velvet nap, Liszt's shoulder somewhere beneath. He had held on tight till their eyes met and then — then he spoke. That was all. He hadn't hit anyone. Of course not. He certainly had not, as Wagner later told half the town, making an opera plot on the spot, shouted. He had hissed, perhaps — *Who are you to speak of Mendelssohn? Who are you?* — but no more. It was not what he had done at all that shook her; it was his manner. This dark unexpectedness, the electricity of violence that crackled in the air around him, were, to Clara at least, terrifyingly out of all proportion. Liszt himself said the same, scarf in hand as he left the house, taking his time to show he had not been rattled. He was, however, suddenly sober. *Herr Schumann is not himself, Madame. If I did not know him I should feel insulted.* Wagner, his pockmarks ticking, making his infernal notes.

Who would know? she asked herself. Who would care what Wagner said? Very few and none who mattered, surely. From his letters there was no telling anything had been out of sorts at all. He wrote miles of them suddenly, mostly to Verhulst. The last time he had seen Verhulst had been God knew when. An Absent Friend. He could tell a man whose understanding of late rested only on paper anything he damn-well liked. *I am lost to anything else, and happy as a sandboy. I do not know when I have been so cheerful.* What did he cite as his reason? *Genoveva.* Genoveva and her famously insulted fidelity preoccupied his months. No libretto was good enough so he wrote the words himself, no musical idea was too demanding. If he lost sleep, did he care? Not at all. He would invent a German opera that Weber would be proud of if it finished him, he said, and Meyerbeer with his Italian and French fancies could fry in hell.

Immediately after that there was *Manfred*, Byron's madman clinging to a cliff-face, recreated in an overture and a set of matching scenes. And since all the Russia money was long gone, since their income was not as secure as once it had been, there was only one cure. He would write some more. An album for youngsters, choruses and dramatic scenes, songs and piano suites. He wrote chamber music and fantasies, and pieces for cellos and clarinets and horns, and oriental fragments and Republican marching songs in red, black and gold.

And when she told him she was pregnant again, weeping in a way that was not suggestive much of joy, he buried himself head first in the wild woods, filling pages with forest scenes for the keyboard as quickly as penning a letter. The *Waldszenen*. What was she to say? He asked her to play, to settle them under her hands. Some pages seemed full of darkness, malevolent turns and twists that made her blood run cold and, after the first, she avoided playing them. Even *he* avoided them. But the pieces kept coming and with them a wandering mass of verbiage, written-out notes and diary pieces and Rules for Household Life, filling shelves. *My imagination is inexhaustible! It boils in my head so much I swear I can see ideas, floating in the air like ectoplasm. See, Clara.* His finger, its nail bitten down to the quick, pointing at nothing. *In the corner! A cloud!* Eyes bleary, moods rocky as a ship's clock. What did he do? What should a composer do? He composed.

⋯⊷⊙⊶⋯

It was the month Carl died. Or not long after. He had sent a letter with his farewells and, by the time they received it, was being bled to death by the best doctors in Carlsbad, keeping his word. An Easter with no rye flour for the cakes, a great deal of rain. Coming home for the evening from Lordknew where – she recalls a garden quite clearly but not whose – coming home together and looking out over the trees in early leaf, the threat of blossom, they saw smoke. Distant at first, and hazy, no more than a light column of dusty grey. But from the centre of the city. There was no doubt. A straggle of people were running along Reitbahngasse, their faces edged with reflected yellow from torches, the occasional flickering lamp. Someone carried a cleaver, its edge a clear glint in the low light. They were home before the bells started, the drums and alarms and the downpour of footfalls. When the shots started, he fetched a bottle of wine, two glasses. The fighting had begun at last.

Kings have much on their conscience, he said, much to answer for. I have only you.

She recalls the texture of heavy green curtain cloth in her hand, the taste of wine on his mouth. They stood there at the window till the early

313

hours, growing colder, watching for shapes in the darkness, lights in the sky.

⟵⊶═◉═⊷⟶

Barricades.

The city had been molehilled overnight; paving stones and sewer lids, planks and wooden boxes, poles from carriages and cart axles, a wardrobe with a carved wooden face. There was more of the same all the way to the market, handcarts piled with debris and men shouting, clattering about on top of the growing pyres and shouting. The King had made a run for it and left his cast-offs in charge at the town hall. The Neustadt was full of soldiers with six sets of orders; thousands of them, Prussian bastards, hand-picked. The roads round the castle weren't safe. She caught the word *cannon* here and there; the word *hospital* though the conjunction made no sense immediately. She saw someone catch Robert's sleeve, no more than a boy with an axe at his belt, a little sister by the hand, warning him to turn back. And he did. He took Marie up in his arms and they walked back to Reitbahngasse, alone. And because she wanted to or needed to, in the guise of finding goat's milk for Julie or someone she knew or *news* or some other such, Clara kept on walking. Surely Mathilde had been with her? A basket over her arm and jumping at every corner? Surely she had seen someone she recognised all the way into town? She can't remember. Only these men on the barricades, staring at her as she walked, things in pieces, the dust thick on the toes of her boots, sewage in the gutters. And the hospital. It was true enough. What they had done was there in the forecourt, on open view to everyone.

Bundles of cloth, she had thought at first, carpet, perhaps; something sodden and left out in the sun to dry. Until she looked again. They were men. Fourteen men, no names, no uniforms, no weapons. Laid out, she realised slowly, quite deliberately as show. The nearest no more than a boy, one fist gripping a broken branch, his hair and half his face matted with what looked black enough for tar. A pool of the same had flooded from behind his head and congealed there like afterbirth, a feast for flies, while his eyes gazed up, astonished. Beside him, a man with a missing shoulder, drenched brown to the waist. The other side of his jacket was rough but clean still, his knuckles cut about to the bone as though he had been struck by a knife. A hussar bayonet. Clara recalled Frau Nussbaum, Frau Nussbaum who had lived in the Neumarkt all those years ago, her apron over her face. *War drives people to madness.* This looking at corpses, gawping as she was supposed to, appalled her suddenly. She had no wish to see it any more. With or without Mathilde, she went home and stayed there, listing provisions, waiting for the sound of gunshot that never came.

Dried bacon and bread flour, dried apples, eggs.
    Salt fish. Pickled cucumber. Wine, cigars.
    Three scores as single copy hidden beneath the floorboards.

It was very early. There was the sound of running, the crunch and cobble of men's boots at the gate. Even before the hammering started, she knew what they wanted. So did he. He ran upstairs and, she hoped, out of sight. No, Dr Schumann was not at home. He was not fit to join up in any case. Did they know who Dr Schumann was? But he was not at home. He was emphatically not at home. She closed the doors and pulled the storm shutters after, but she knew they would be back. She had to shift him, and now. What choice was there? The children not even dressed yet, not even out of bed? Robert had time to fetch what he could and she lifted a cape. A cape, money, a handful of bread. Marie, playing in the kitchen, a wooden spoon in her hand. The clothes they stood up in. She made a sweep of the hallway, told Mathilde to look after the children till nightfall and did not wait for a reply. *I will be back,* she called over her shoulder, keeping going. *We have things to do. I will be home directly,* opening the back door, walking, walking. They walked, wanting to run with their hearts fit to burst, hushing Marie at every second step and trying not to think of Elise, a child who asked questions, the house and the road receding behind them. She held her husband's arm, her daughter's hand. The railway station lay on the other side of the field and the grass was spongy, treacherously uneven. They would not stumble.

The trains would be running. They would not be overcrowded. She told herself again, again. Whatever happened, they would not stop walking.

⊷══◎══⊶

Mügeln   Dohna   Maxen

Two trains and two miles on foot between. Marie marching, with her pigtails undone, saying not a word. Less than twelve miles, almost as many hours and there was Maxen, the familiar gardens of the Major's house with its cherry trees in bloom. And more than the Major come to greet them. The place was full of refugees; well-dressed, but refugees nonetheless. Robert sat in the main hallway, the stairs behind him, and tried not to look out of place. Marie sat beside him, her face streaky from mud and smoke, her eyes closing. A room and some privacy, Clara said. You will not let us down. And neither he did. The Major knew Robert, or thought he did. He could be relied upon to find a quiet room, organise a tray of beer and sausage, suggest that Marie sleep. She had no doubt at all he'd set things to rights without her. And they knew Clara, had known her, indeed, for most of her life. They would put up no resistance if they thought she had made up her mind, and she had. She most certainly had. She had no need of sleep, food or quiet. She wanted a carriage and someone to share it with, another woman with the same idea. It took almost a whole day but she found them and didn't think twice. Now that her husband was in good hands, there was only one thing Clara needed to do. Go straight back the way she had come.

The journey, bumping through the pitch-black, tasted of smoke. Frau von Berg rocked slightly, patting the other girl's hand. Frau von Berg was a surgeon's wife, the girl an estate manager's daughter, Lordknew on what errand. The girl's face, her name Clara does not retain, only her shoes – a peep of blue kid with wooden heels destined for ruin – and her youth. Her extraordinary youth. Three women together who had no desire to exchange stories or family histories or amusing anecdotes. They had no desire to speak at all. In the sound of the coach wheels, clattering like a bridge on the point of collapse, through the 3 a.m. chill

316

in the air, all three listened silently to the sound of shot and cannon fire, trying to gauge how near, how heavy. And lavender. The scent from the other woman's gloves, the glint in the other woman's eyes, for a moment meeting hers. *Your baby is soon, Frau Schumann.* An observation, not a question. *Let's be thankful that loud noise need not, in reality, precipitate such events.* And when the houses began to crop up ahead and the coach could go no further – for houses meant barricades and the barricades were shoulder-high – Frau von Berg helped her down the carriage step, lifted her lightly to the ground, her lace-gloved grip about Clara's waist secure as a man's. Three hours, she said. The carriage would stay here three hours. It would wait no more. And she started walking.

Across the fields, each in their different directions, guessing as much as knowing the direction of home, their hems dragged at the heavy grass, soaking and sticking to their boots. Though dawn was coming, the air filtering to thick grey as Clara walked, kept walking, the bursts of light on the horizon serving only to make the surrounding sky and this interminable marsh ground darker still. Now and then, another soul appeared out of the smoky gloom and walked beside her. A battalion of men emerged from the mist, scythes and poles in their fists, a consignment from the suburbs ready to fight hussars with farm tools.

As she reached Reitbahngasse, every house with its face shut tight as though for sale, the noise of cannon, noise that had blocked and filtered everything else to the point where she no longer noticed it much, stopped. Entirely. Dear Christ, what a ghastly ringing the silence made! There were shots and cries from the city, the scatter and cracks of rifles, but the cannon, except for this ghostly metal-edged echo in the head, was gone. In this kind of peace, then, a peace that chilled her till her hands shook and her legs trembled as she walked, she found her own garden, her own door. It was unlocked. A crate pushed back, but nothing more. And there was Mathilde, Mathilde in her apron at the foot of the stairs, the clock ticking on the wall beside her, slumped over carpet bags, asleep. She held a ribbon in one of her hands, the baby's shawl tucked under her thigh. Clara leaned forward, touched her arm. I am here, she said. Her voice was firm, unhurried. Mathilde. We have things to do. We have a great many things to do.

They made Maxen by early evening, the sunlight full on the trees. Ludwig was feverish, Julie was fretful and threatening to cry, and Elise carried a pebble. All the way from Dohna she had turned it over and over in her hands, refusing to let go. Robert had gone walking, they told her. He had been restless. But he had left her a note, they were sure he had left a note.

Upstairs, in the scent of camphor and cigars, she found his jacket, an opened book, a scrawl of papers littering the desk, the floor, the table beside his bed.

> Are you well, my Clara, are you strong?
>> can do nothing while you are absent, and no peace
> anxious, suffering the torture of a soul in hell, while
>> my good angel has deserted me and I may never more
> God preserve you dear soul for the husband who
>> anguish that floods through my veins that

Pages of it, zigzagging the paper, his handwriting heavy, black.

And set aside, in a space of its own, a single sheet of manuscript, a furl of clefs and notes describing something cheerful and open and limpid as light. Something beautiful. She heard the melody herself as she read, the notes wavering through saline, saw that morning's date in the corner in a legible, strong hand. On the desk itself, one letter scored again and again into the polished wood with a blunted knife tip till it sank like a carving, its single runnel filled with powdery varnish. C.

Kreischa. High summer.

For a short while there were lilies of the valley, ferns outside their door. Ludwig started walking there, holding his sisters' hands. Elise climbing trees with a rip of lace at her hem. Julie with leaves in her hair. Marie like a nun over a notebook, writing prayers. And Robert? Robert read newpapers with holes cut into them by censors, then read them again, though what he absorbed was anyone's guess. From his writing, one would never have known they were in exile of a kind, that their possessions were buried below their own floorboards somewhere else. He wrote songs, pretty catches for children, the whole of tiny Kreischa outside his window, calm and warm as a stupor. On the other side of the hills, the world was upside down, but not here, in this valley. Here, so near Maxen, in the cottage the Major found for them to hide in, all they did was read about war, not live it. The heat's fault, Robert said. All that fretfulness and shortness of temper, the blood overheating. If Romeo and Juliet had met in winter, who knew how the story would have ended? The evenings were quiet enough to hear rabbits, their snapping at grass blades with yellow scissor teeth. Something dug at the plants she put in the window box, uprooted them whole, and smoke over the Rächnitzer Höhe drifted south. Too far to be real. Their sky in the morning stayed stubbornly blue.

How long had they lasted? Three weeks? Almost four?

Then he could not sleep for the quiet, the hollow call of cuckoos, the insidious trickle of water tumbling over rock. Despite all poetry, there were places one belonged, places one did not. Robert pined for his house. Besides, she had read the newspapers too. There were civilian casualties, random shootings. She wanted to see her father *in the flesh*. Mathilde complained the whole journey, (little Julie's constitution etc) but minds were made up and rightly so, rightly so. Back in Dresden, they found Henriette cured of chickenpox and nothing burned to a crisp; things, in short, better than they had hoped. The beds were not ready but they slept. Next day, the bags still buckled, only her bonnet changed, Clara went to see her father. It was her own choice, no one else's. Hers alone.

Well, then!

Wieck was keen to engage. What fairy tales have you heard?

She watched him lean forward, catch Minna's eye. It was important his students notice when he was about to say something he thought witty.

What did he mean, *fairy tales*? She looked at him.

Who was witness to these *sights* you mention? This ghastly shooting of an innocent musical instrument in the streets?

He could barely contain the derision in his voice. It was a voice she knew well enough, but it threw her nonetheless. She had said nothing contentious. Visiting her father, after these years of practice, avoiding contention was a habit. Why should he choose to deny what everyone knew? The Prussians had looted the place. What was there to argue with in stating the obvious? All it took was looking. What wasn't black with soot was black with dust, the gutters off the town square swilling and festering with pipe-burst shit. The opera house was three sides rubble, the gas lamps intact on its single still-standing flock-coated wall. Outside, the auditorium chandelier lay tinkling in the gutter, a mere draggle of crystal drops. Glass crunched underfoot everywhere that feet were capable of crunching; the big houses in the Zwingerstrasse were crazed with holes. Huge chunks of twisted shrapnel, big enough for paperweights or murder weapons, could be picked up on any street corner. In one backstreet a French-polished piano, tilted on its side and shot to splinters, its keys scattered in the road like slaughterhouse ribs, was plainer than day. Dear God, what manner of people would shoot a piano? That was all she had said. *What manner of soldier would shoot a piano?* Now she wondered why. A shift of subject seemed in order.

There are warrants for Herr Wagner's arrest, she said. I have heard he made inflammatory speeches and had to hide at Liszt's house, and everyone is treating him as a hero and Liszt has –

You exaggerate, he said. He looked offended. If Herr Wagner has gone to Liszt's house, it is because he has some plot afoot with Liszt. Do you think the Prussians have nothing better to do than chase a puffed-up little toad like Wagner and take pot-shots at pianos? What foolishness!

There are bills posted on every second corner.

Counter-propaganda, he snapped. Insurgent trickery. And you are dumb to believe it.

And the atrocities, Papa? The report of –

What atrocities? He narrowed his eyes.

Clara looked. The girl beside him, a spoon-faced singer blessed with no opinions beyond those that pertained to herself, stared hard at her nails. The students, she said. Her voice sounded weaker.

He cocked an eyebrow.

Twenty-six boys, Papa.

He shrugged.

Twenty-six boys with not one gun between them hiding in the smoking room at the corner of Schefelgasse. The soldiers tore the place to pieces till they found them.

He would not look at her, but she kept going, not stopping to think what for. Except that it was true. She wanted him to admit what was true. They took them to the window and shot one after another, and hurled the corpses out of the open window – twenty-six boys, Papa! You know very well!

He snorted. I know nothing of the sort.

Clara took a deep breath, controlled her temper. He was doing this on purpose. Why, she had no idea, but it mattered to hold her temper, to talk to him as if he were a child. Frau Hirsch told you outside this very house. I was there. Her brother –

Well, Wieck said. *Frau Hirsch.* If Frau Hirsch said it, it must be gospel. Frau Hirsch, and Frau Hirsch's brother. He owns a pub, does he not? Selling beer on the back of stories such as these, and against such sitting ducks as the Prussians, he'll draw in every student and Republican for miles, all keen to buy Frau Hirsch's brother's beer. It's clever, eh? You can't say it's not a clever way to grow rich.

How dare you, she said. She said it before anything rational could stop her. How dare you mock such terrible suffering? Dear Lord, her voice. You make honest people into liars by defending the indefensible.

Had she ever spoken to him like this? Exhibited such lack of self-control? But it was done now. And in front of this desperate, cloying Minna, Minna who, in the hope that this teacher at last would give her a career, was rolling her eyes like a circus pony at such filial ingratitude.

Wieck, however, merely looked at his daughter. Long and cool. And only when her eyes met his, when they stayed steady, did he speak. What do you know of lies? he said. Or honesty?

The tone he had chosen, had polished for this moment. As if he had been expecting it to come. Frau Schumann who ran away at the first sign of firing? Whose husband startles at the sound of a coach-horse fart and who has no notion of military justice past avoiding conscription? This is a husband, indeed. This is a public embarrassment, Frau Schumann. He has ruined Hiller's choir, conducting with hieroglyphs and signs, never saying so much as a word and still he thinks he will take the place of Mendelssohn! Is there anyone in Dresden who doesn't know what an apology he is – except you? Who between us, defends the indefensible as a matter of daily course?

He looked at the pregnant mass of her, the obvious restitching on the bodice of her dress. Once, you might have presented yourself anywhere, before anyone without shame. And what has come of it?

He lurched towards her suddenly, repeating what was not a question: What has come of it? Exactly what I said has come of it. Don't fear for my perspicacity, Clara. Attend to your own. A country-wife in Kreischa sewing aprons! Attend to your own.

He was having trouble breathing. Even he could feel it. She watched him exhale deeply, force his skinny chest to deflate. Then his face began changing, shifting into something like indifference. He was trying for detached. Urbane. He had not forgotten how.

Well, then. He neatened the front of his waistcoat. Exciting stories doubtless make a dull life more bearable and you will listen to your neighbours, your maid, your – *confidantes* – whatever I say. Your mother did the same. She imagined cruelties. Can you believe such a thing, Minna? An embittered woman is an abomination. She stains and taints her children, for something has made her bitter and we must not ask what.

Minna nodded, chinless, her eyes bulging. Clara looked at the Old Man, his mouth moving.

Be that as it may, he said. He coughed. The Prussians are a Force for Order – a surge of emotion shooting the last word up an octave – whatever Frau Schumann's husband or neighbours might have led her to believe. As I am still your father and a man, not a coward, I tell you that order is what matters, not sensational stories. *Order.*

He sat down abruptly as though he had forgotten the chair was so near behind him, fished a handkerchief out of his pocket. Order, he said again. He dabbed at his temple and reached for the water jug on the side table.

Minna here is a daughter to me now. That is how I think of this girl. She is very dutiful and deserves no less. I have posted her name on the new programmes for Vienna. Minna *Schultz-Wieck*. It sounds well, don't you think? *Schultz-Wieck*. We need have no secrets before Minna. She is loyalty itself.

Minna, her face a perfect weekday saint, looked pityingly at Clara. As though Clara should know better. Sweet Christ, was I like that? Clara asked herself, fighting for her face to show nothing. Was I ever such a ridiculous, self-satisfied, simpering prop?

Not knowing or caring what she was thinking, her father sipped from his glass, refreshing himself. Concluding Remarks. She knew his habits well enough to understand he was preparing what he thought were Concluding Remarks.

You are become suggestible, Clara. His hand that held the glass trembled, sending little waves rippling across the water inside. Perhaps even sour. Who would have thought?

Minna sniggered. Lightly.

Now! he said. The word was a handclap, and his features settled into smug formation. He thought he had smoothed things over admirably well. Now! Clara — you will play so we might hear Minna sing. She is well trained, if I say so myself. We have been working on Spohr. Later, Minna, you will be interested to see my fine letter from Spohr. He was a Great Man when he wrote this letter, and I was as yet Unknown. I was most moved. To be gracious in one's dealings, he said. He stared at Clara without subtlety. That is a something we must *all* strive to attain.

Minna tangled up her eyebrows as though Wieck had said something profound. In fact, she was trying to remember the right page for the Spohr, the words to the second verse. She was trying so hard, she hardly noticed till it happened that Frau Schumann had left the room, that Herr Wieck had followed to slam the door and forgotten to come back, forgotten, indeed, that he had just asked her to sing. She stood at the piano, his *Other Daughter*, a matter of no importance at all.

He is old, she told herself.

These streets, their walls pitted and spiked through. The damage that had been done to good families.

Some people do not believe what is difficult for fear it brings them pain.

The linden trees in bloom, their leaves showing white skeleton hands through the green.

And truth is painful. The beauty in truth follows its necessary pain.

Prussians were lounging on straw at the Altmarkt, smoking, playing cards, eating their stolen food. Some of them had bandages, their fingernails black. She walked past the Frauenkirche, stuffed with prisoners, down the alleys where barricades had been and were no more. Past bills ordering the arrest of Wagner, the forbidding of red, black and gold as colours, the extreme punishability of engagement with certain texts, certain poems, certain songs. People must be careful what they sang, it seemed. The city was in complete disarray, in pieces. And with it, any sense of what mattered any more. She sat on a low wall that had once been part of a shop, perhaps, a storehouse, and caught her breath. A brackish taste was rising in her throat, the heartburn that went with her condition. A married woman pregnant as a cow and all alone. Unseemly. The idea almost made her laugh. Unseemly.

But what is to be said when what is solid counts for nothing? What then?

What then? Was it possible that something could be made false by sheer insistence? Was truth a matter of numbers? Something one could be hectored or ridiculed into? Was it just *opinion*? Had her father said those terrible things, those dreadful things, without knowing what he had done? It was not a new question. But for the first time the answer seemed less clear. It had taken some time, but she was beginning to grasp something, something barely endurable. Her father said dreadful things and said them *on purpose*. He ridiculed truth and suffering, love itself. He ridiculed — it took some admitting but she pushed the new-found insight as far as it would go — he ridiculed *music*. Not, as he had always maintained, to seek the best, but because it gave him the last word. Because causing anguish silenced her. Because he *did*. Had he no notion at all of Robert's value? Arranging concerts for that stupid girl, dragging out his tired old letters from Spohr — as if these things mattered *now*.

And this in preference to — to what? What alternative had he ever adopted?

This man who knew pieces of her past that no one else, not even herself, could know, who had trained her to be all she was, was, after all, not who she had supposed. He was not merely difficult or stubborn. He was — it struck her cold, a moment of horrible clarity — *alien*. Her father by default, but *not herself*. One might spend a lifetime trying to please such a man and nothing would alter it. It had to be faced. He was treacherous. He was monstrously selfish. Had he asked after their welfare? After his grandchildren? After *anyone's*? He was — the words popped unbidden into her head and she let them — a *wicked* old man! He would devour all meaning, all loyalty and, it seemed, *all his life* for reasons she would never understand. For no reason at all, perhaps. And this broken city, ordered this way by its own administration as revenge, this city full of back-biters and hypocrites and opera managers was the city her father had chosen as his own. He would die here, too, most likely. And quite content. Quite at peace. Well, then. Well, then. Well.

She stood and stretched, leaned into the pain in her back. She started walking. He had made his choices. As she would make hers. And she would begin by knowing what she knew, whether her father liked it or not. People *had* been maimed and wounded, warrants for arrest issued, whatever her father said. And her own father was, after all, a hateful man. Robert had been right. Her husband, who built beautiful things as truthfully as he could despite the sneers of those who thought music, and all affection, *everything*, a trivial game; despite his own self-doubt and the ridicule of critics who knew no better, despite his family and hers, *especially* hers. He had been right all along.

An abandoned handcart at the edge of the road. That meant the corner of Reitbahngasse. She had walked all the way back, her feet choosing the path of their own accord. This was *their* street, strange, and scarfed up and silent, but theirs nonetheless. For better or worse, this was where they lived.

In her own house, a light was burning. A yellow edging showed round the edges of the music-room shutters, flickering. Someone at home, pacing. Crossing the floor and back again. There was only one person it could have been. Their bags had barely arrived, and in all probability he was working, sound shifting in his head. Making music. And waiting for her, waiting patiently. As surely as he always had. *Don't you defend me at all?* Words he had written in a letter, more than once, enduring her father's slanders. *Don't you defend me?* This tightness in her throat was choking. Her fingers were wet. A chill spread on her shawl, on the hand that held it closed. Tears were dripping from her chin. In case anyone was looking, hidden somewhere in the shadows, she did not wipe her eyes. She sniffed and started walking. Her back hurt and her belly felt heavy, terribly heavy. Her face, drawing tight and sore as the salt water dried on its surface, felt papery, old. But walking was curative. And making lists. Devices, perhaps, but they worked. Turning the mind to the practical was, she knew from habit, greatly curative of self-pity, and the cure for self-pity was a great thing indeed.

Soap, then. Bicarbonate, two good pots, a box of writing sheets and ink, at least three bottles of ink. She would fetch what was missing from the pantry. Mineral salts and collar stiffeners, studs and buttons. Stay in a good deal with the children till the street, at least, was whole again. Thread, sugar, Goethe and Shakespeare, both diaries – everything must be unpacked. A country-wife maybe, but one with a good husband. A husband, moreover, who would not deliberately cause her pain. She saw his faults, certainly, but Robert Schumann was an honest man with a stout heart. She repeated it with every step towards home. For such a man Frau Schumann might do her duty where she owed it most. The flame in the window wavered. She saw the shutters open a little, his face appear briefly, looking for her outside. She called his name, watched him search for the source of the voice in the half-light, her heart filling fit to break. Nothing, she promised, would injure him again.

In a matter of days the dust sheets and boxes were cleared. In a matter of weeks, with little ready at all, there was Ferdinand.

I birth your boys, Carus said. This is my best use.

Lifted to see his baby brother, Ludwig screamed. Then, Ludwig always screamed. Ludwig, Carus reminded her, had been carried during *difficult times*. Ferdinand, on the other hand, had been ferried across open fields to the sound of gunfire. Ferdinand, he predicted, would be an adventurer. The idea! her mother said. As though any such thing might affect an unborn infant! Children were empty bottles, waiting to be filled. Only from the age of eight did they exhibit anything like feeling, understanding. Eight years was the age of reason, or so Rousseau said. The memories of small children and babies were poor to non-existent. Surely you retain nothing of being a child, Clara? Anything otherwise was beyond imagining; the capacity to absorb an atmosphere, to *feel* before birth – that was a fine one! Even Carus laughed. A joke after all. What he had said, however, stayed.

Feeding her new son from her own body that night, she wondered. To hear her mother tell her she remembered nothing, and that she had pieced things together only from stories, seemed likely enough. Children came. They arrived with not much by way of invitation, certainly whether they were welcome or affordable or imaginable or not. Children were mere facts of being. Sometimes, however, she fancied she remembered a great deal. Voices and songs, snippets of music through walls. A man with his eyes staring, standing deadly still on a stage. She thought of Robert with his daughters on his lap, whispering, producing pennies from behind their ears. *I have been travelling to Arabia*, he said, tipping sugar into their open hands. *Look! I have sand in my pockets.* Ludwig, screaming.

Empty bottles or no, her older daughters had been filled with enough music to play a birthday march that September and Robert, reeling from the fact that his wife had turned thirty, got drunk. With nothing to stop her and everything to encourage her, so did Clara. They had something to share. The Prussians had finished eating everyone out of house and home, and celebration was certainly called for. Robert's three *Faust* scenes, written in a matter of days, would be played in Weimar, Hamburg, Leipzig. The transcriptions were selling, the albums he had written for children too.

I am popular, he said, surprised and not surprised. Everywhere but in Dresden. Everywhere but here.

It was true. Scaffolding made tunnels all through the city. Pupils had come filing back under unlucky triangles of builders' ladders, the choir had regrouped and the theatres were reopening. Berlin, they said, had opened its arms to more democracy but not Dresden. Here it was business as usual, a dour determination to cling to older, harsher ways. The opera house refused him a *première*. They refused him access to the orchestra. They refused him tickets, preferring free handfuls for the court circle that turned up for the booze, then slept through every third act. They refused, *may God forgive them*, a memorial service for Chopin. Herr Schumann had not the authority, it seemed; his suggestion of such a service was *inappropriate*. Besides, Polish sympathies at this time *could be misconstrued*. Protocols, princely sensitivities so soon after all this revolutionary business. The whole of Paris had turned out to watch the *cortège* pass, *the whole of Paris* or at least enough to take it for such, and in silence. Pauline had sung and angels, they said, would have wept. Here in Dresden they wept over nothing but demotion from the *right* circles and asinine opera-house protocols: Chopin could go to hell in a handcart for all they cared. What Chopin had been, would continue to be long after the name of every administrator in Dresden was less than dust, they had no idea. To them, he was merely a dead foreigner, no country to his name, whose memory was revered only by *inferior people*.

Clara's rage was towering. This Dresden that fancied itself refined was a vile place, full of mean-minded, money-grubbing, arse-licking, gossip-mongering high-borns. What's more the orchestra were time servers, dough-faced, terrified little jobsworths and viola holders *to a man*, and she hated them all, all, *every one*. Telling her husband afforded a little relief and it pleased him to hear it. Telling tales to each other cured nothing, however. They had to act and to act meant to leave. They knew that. But where, in these unsettled times, would have them? Hiller's letter brought the answer, almost without delay. An orchestra for the taking: secure money, half what Liszt earned in Weimar, maybe, but income. No audition, no references, Hiller's say-so alone would do it. But it was not Vienna. Not Berlin. Not Leipzig. Not, *thank God and damn them all to hell for it*, Dresden. Somewhere neither of them had visited or imagined. It was Düsseldorf.

What did they know of Düsseldorf? That it was not Saxon. That except among writers and sculptors, perhaps, it was not a *name*. That it was almost all the way to the Belgian border, two days by train more or less non-stop – and that with five children, two pianos, a library that took up an entire wall. It would mean a house, new schools and teachers, a new maid, a cook, a nursemaid, students to find all over again. It was no small thing to leave a crop of loyal, hand-picked pupils; the money, the baby minding and sitting that came with them. And Düsseldorfers, they had heard, were so frighteningly garrulous, not to mention bibulous, back-slappy and (every student knew, whispered behind their cuff), closer to the French in more than terms of physical geography, viz they were brusque, volatile and – ahem – *sexually free*. What they knew. Nothing useful at all.

My dear Hiller

I am a regular froth of indecision. Düsseldorf seems so far and strange. Mendelssohn's opinion of the place was poor enough, and Reitz wondered why you had gone there at all. Was it for better money? Are the orchestra, as I have heard, a rough bunch? Even if they are, I have put up with more than enough in Dresden, and know very well how to deal with difficult people, especially players. You would have them primed that I'd take no nonsense, wouldn't you? Now, the rest:

1 Who is on the board of directors? Are they idiots?
2 Are you sure the salary is 750 thalers? That's all?
3 How good are the chorus? The orchestra? *Be candid.*
4 Is Düsseldorf expensive? How much are you paying for your place?
5 Will they give me somewhere furnished?
6 What are they paying for moving expenses?
7 Does the contract let me change my mind if I'm offered something better?

8   What are the holidays? And are they paid?

9   What's there for my wife? She can't sit idle. *Please* find something for her. If you can't, we won't come.

Funny thing, though – I was looking through an old geography book, trying to find out a few things for myself and read there are three nunneries. Is there also an asylum for the terminally insane? It might sound odd to ask, but a few years ago now we took a short trip to Maxen and I found that the view from my window was of just such a place. I saw it every morning and every night and grew to hate the look of it. A madhouse. It makes me shudder even to write the word, and I need to guard against anything melancholy if I can help it. Maybe the book is wrong, though? Maybe it's a hospital, something perfectly normal. Check and let me know. This is most important. You see how good I have become at issuing orders? I am trying out the trappings of conductorship! See if I do not show my true colours if – and I do say *if* – we come to Düsseldorf.

Yours most faithfully

Robert Schumann

Frying pans. Fires. How was one to know? On the other hand, what terror could the unknown hold when the *known* was such a disappointment? Vienna had disgraced itself, Berlin was too dangerous and even Leipzig had been putting off the opera in favour of Meyerbeer – *Meyerbeer* – for months. These days, I wouldn't piss on Leipzig, Robert said. He said it quite distinctly and in company, and Clara didn't turn a hair. He said a lot of things in company. He argued with concert organisers and conductors and audience members, spoke too fast, complaining everyone else rushed him. She was playing poorly, he insisted, whatever the reviews said. If young men waited outside the theatre gates and autograph hunters pursued her, she was shameless; if they didn't, it was proof her playing was going to the dogs. On tour in Berlin, some fool left a package of music at their hotel hoping for a free critique, and Robert sent it straight back, postage unpaid, ranting. And though they came home with 800 *thalers*, enough to last a year at least, his mood did not lift. He snapped at nothing, imagined slights from those who spoke to him and from those who didn't. Elise has a headstrong look to her face, he said. Ludwig watches me all the time. Nerves, she thought. Indecision. Delays. A bullet needing to be bitten.

Dear Mother

These Leipzig rehearsals are relentless! Then, for an *opera*, we must expect to suffer a little. Marie and Elise will be back tomorrow — collect them at the station at 2.30 *sharp*. A big case with laundry will arrive too, and money for sewing and starching etc in with this note so you have enough. Can you send me TWO things? Go to my room and check the top shelf of the bookcase for a YELLOW paper-covered book. Forward THE BOOK ALONE without the spare sheets. THEN go to my husband's room, sit at the piano and put out your right hand at full stretch to find a package tied in brown paper. Six copies of the *Album for the Young* are under it. Choose a CLEAN one and pack it so it won't get tattered in the post. That and the yellow book. Don't forget. Also, before my head turns to jelly, let me know if you're coming for the first night. If so, *Monday*. The orchestra will not be truly played in (and the singers will never be at the rate they're going) but it will do him good to see you. Monday, *please*. LOCK EVERYTHING UP before you leave. And could you carry some things back? I have a doll for Julie and little tin soldiers for Ludwig if he will promise not to chew them. And a book. They will like these things, won't they? I am in such a panic at the thought of what needs to come together.

Robert is very apprehensive: the thought of the first night is making him restless. Everything irritates him, even the colour of the walls. Pale green, he says, is the colour of disease. He doesn't mean to be sharp – it is the frustration of everything but I am ashamed to say I am sometimes concerned how bad it might look. I try to be encouraging, but never say the right things, or try too hard and he is angry with me. But I am here. For whatever I can offer, I am certainly here. Do express your own admiration for the piece when you come. This, more than anything, is what he needs. You will be very proud in any case, without my advice. It is merely to remind you to express that praise *fulsomely*. I am fussing. Be patient with me.

Kisses to the little ones and tell them there are ducks on the pond fighting for the same crust of bread. Is Ferdinand's tooth through? I will send him a horn spoon, in case.

Your obedient

Clara

On the opening night, everyone came. Liszt and Spohr and Gade came. Moscheles and Kuntsch and Joachim and Hiller, Pauline thin as a bootlace in head-to-foot black. And mother. People had travelled miles; that should not be forgotten. Her father, moreover, would know. He would read the papers to know exactly what he had missed. May it bring him joy, she thought, without hope of any such thing. May it console him that we have such friends.

It was the third night, however, before the composer chose to show himself on stage, and then mostly to strangers. After the closing chords, the applause for everyone else, he forced himself at last. A lone black figure without a set of tails to his name, his frock-coat unbuttoned, he stood with his face in shadow. Then he tilted his profile to the light. He chose his moment, if Clara was not mistaken, and *rose* to the applause. Applause that had taken three performances to reach much of a pitch, for a piece that was averagely reviewed, for a performance that had its flaws, but no matter. That was how opera was: a leaky ship. That it sailed at all would do. Not that she would say such a thing out loud. She admired his opera at length and unstintingly, and would hear no one who did not do the same. It wasn't that he didn't know how much she admired his work, not at all, not at all. It was that here and now, his head imagining slights and intrigues and with plenty, Lordknew, to feed itself upon, he needed her to be clear. To be unreserved. To be, at times and behind firmly closed doors, almost overwhelming. She wrote florid tributes in her diary, surprises for him to find by contrived accident, a better healer than her tactless mouth. She bought him armfuls of flowers. And she had seen it work. She was sure it worked.

Now, as he stood with his back straight, drawing applause like strength, the evidence was there before her eyes. He looked, she thought, like a boy who jumped on a table to claim he was two people, both keen to set the world to rights. Fuller, florid and forty, perhaps, but in the reflection of the stage lights, standing on the boards she had once made her own, he was a poet and hero all over again. Hydrotherapy be damned. This was what he needed. If she had not been clapping so hard, she would have wept for sheer joy. That night, buoyant and certainly as drunk as he was, she watched him make their decision. No more beating about the bush. Henriette could be served notice, Mathilde should order boxes. He could knock that west-side orchestra into shape in his sleep. Was he a man? He shouted it so loud, she thought the street would hear and didn't care. Well, was he? Was he a man who could rely on the utmost devotion and from his bride, his Clara, his wife for whom he had endured so much, so very, very much?

He staggered slightly and his glass tipped, spilling a seething puddle on to the rug. There was no need for her to say anything, thank the Lord. He hiccuped suddenly and caught her about the waist.

He would tell her exactly what he was. He was *A Man whose Hour had*

Come, and he was taking no more damned insolence, impertinence, cheek or lip from anyone. *Anyone*, did she hear?

She heard. She knew what he meant. She kissed him, felt the room tilt under her feet. As soon as they got home, as soon as they had sent the right letters, as soon as they had packed, they were going to Düsseldorf.

❖──◈──❖

Well! Trumpets and flourishes, laurels at the door and flowers in every room. It's only fitting, Hiller said, taking them to their room past plaster cherubs and windows the size of walls, for a Man in what is now quite certainly Your Position. And for Madame Schumann, he spluttered, face redder than ever. For our dear Madame Pianist, too. No time even to wash, however, before he rolled them in front of dignitaries, no time to get rid of the grime of the road. And such a road! Dresden to Meissen to Leipzig. A sharp climb northwards from Leipzig via Halle and Köthen to Magdeburg, Braunschweig and Hannover. Hannover to Osnabrück to Münster before countryside disappeared completely. Thereafter, the train chugged to Essen so slowly they might have walked, the children peering through the windows and blacking their noses with soot. Thirty-two hours, almost to the minute, from the start, with Hiller on the platform, an entourage in tow, duty had begun.

Robert, she noticed, looked unsurprised by the committee, the gifts, the fact that he could still walk after such enforced sitting. Even by the gilt and marble on their way upstairs. Robert, it seemed, was *a man in his position* from the start. When Hiller and the orchestra committee and the boy who brought the bags and everyone but the children were gone, she tracked down the expenses letter herself and checked it twice.

What is Hiller doing? Robert hissed. Bringing us here? A second floor room? I sent a list of very specific requirements and a second floor room is out of the question! He sighed. Ask them to change it, *Clärchen*.

We'll move, she agreed. Rooms first, then house-hunting *immediately*. What was the point in delay? She hid the expenses sheet, but knew what

334

she knew. Whatever the room's elevation, one thing was more than clear. They couldn't afford this damned hotel.

⊷≈◎⇐⊷

People in their position. What did it mean? Mayoral salutes. Interminable speeches with nothing to eat but dry *canapés*. Delegations from the orchestra appearing from behind curtains to play the overture to *Don Giovanni* when they sat down to dinner. The choir singing under their window one morning, almost a shock. And on the day of their tenth wedding anniversary, the very day, a grand civic reception, applause, a ball they were too tired to attend, a panoramic excursion (likewise); a great deal of nodding and looking benign. All this respect, she thought, would finish them off. By the looks, it was already exacting a cost from Tausch, the assistant conductor. A man with a plucked-chicken neck and a too-tight collar; his eyes, Clara thought, unnervingly small.

Frau Schumann, he said, chewing. She did not offer her hand. Our dear friend Hiller will be sorely missed.

Herr Tausch has taken choir rehearsal faithfully, Hiller said. He will be your husband's greatest ally. Ask the good Dr Müller, or Hasenclever, here. The committee think very highly of Herr Tausch.

Hasenclever, plump and soft-faced, waved a fork and went back to his plate.

Indeed, Clara said.

I have heard it is your husband's preference that you act as *répétiteur*, Tausch said. A pianist of your standing – I am very surprised.

Let Tausch take it back after things settle. Hiller tapped his nose with his finger. It is onerous and unrewarding work. Herr Tausch here – he smiled and nodded at his colleague – is used to that.

I studied under Herr Doctor Mendelssohn, Tausch said. Rietz also. In Leipzig. Herr Schumann, unfortunately, had left the conservatory by the time I arrived.

Clara smiled and said nothing.

Hiller clapped a hand on Tausch's shoulder. This man is an asset.

335

You will value him as I do or he will die in the attempt. Is that not so, Tausch?

The assistant conductor was still looking at Clara. Peering. I met your esteemed father once, he said. In Leipzig. He had a great deal of interest to say.

Hiller perked up. Hasenclever inched closer, ready for a pleasing story. Clara felt a flash of anger, perhaps shame. Whatever her father might have said to this man, she did not want to hear. Please resist an anecdote, Herr Tausch. I dislike anecdotes extremely.

Hiller laughed. So did Hasenclever. They thought she was being funny. Well, he said. Well.

Well. Tausch drained the last of his tea. We are a little orchestra but a proud one. Enthusiastic and, I hope, of a standard that is not unimpressive. There is our former conductor to thank for that.

Hiller made flustered noises but seemed pleased enough. From somewhere close by, Robert's voice drifted like scent. *But my wife.* Explaining something to Lordknew who. *My wife understands my methods.*

I am sure we will prosper ever more brightly now you and your husband are here. My heartfelt welcome to the famous Frau Schumann.

He raised his cup, his little finger cocked. Pastry crumbs dangled in his moustache. Hasenclever stood beside him, shoulder to shoulder. Close enough, she thought, to scratch each other's backs.

Welcome, they said. One voice. Welcome to Düsseldorf.

⁂

Three house moves in seven months. Eight concerts in six. Even the houses were strange. How are we to stop making war with our neighbours with such huge windows? she complained. Every sound will carry. And so it did. Street hawkers woke them at five, and cabbies' iron-wheeled scraping kept them open-eyed till late. Every maidservant was sour, every cook smart-mouthed. On the positive side, the string section was good. The strings were very good indeed. The brass, however, were borrowed from the town military band and turned up as and when; woodwind soloists played part-time for the theatre across the street and thought nothing of rolling up half an hour late. And the chorus — well! The chorus *talked*. They swapped recipes, jokes, anecdotes and sandwiches, wondering when tea would arrive. *We have stumbled into a social club*, he said, *and I must conduct it*.

They had God on their side, however. God and Wasielewski as orchestra leader, the best violinist who'd take the job. They had a new first cello. Better still, they had Beethoven and Schubert, Bach and Handel, Weber and Haydn and as much new music as Herr Schumann himself could write, which was a great deal indeed. Music by the best and brightest must be staged here — why not? As a conductor, a programmer, he had a duty. Here was power to enlighten and bring joy — another Davidsbund, if he could find the recruits to make it work. Moreover, they had the divine Mendelssohn whose piano concerto Clara would play as the first of the season. If that didn't constitute an education in the way Herr Doctor Schumann meant to do things, he was a Dutchman. The name *Schumann* would be synonymous with integrity. With *taste*.

That was the idea. The reality followed suit as best it could, which in the beginning was well indeed. The Grand Opening was a Beethoven overture to consecrate their house, an advent song and two fine choruses, and Clara playing better than she had in months, perhaps years, like a girl again, from memory. His first concert as conductor was, so she thought, a splendid success. He stood on the podium with such gravitas, did he not? Like no one else! Hiller hummed and hawed a bit, but that was what Hiller did. Herr Music Director Schumann's approach is unique, he mumbled. And the band will fall into line. Or he will. One of the two. Tausch nodded his head like a puppet on a pole. It is certainly, he said, a revelation to witness Herr Schumann's — *distinctive* style. And afterwards, if Hiller had proposed a toast to Clara and only Clara — merciful heaven, the embarrassment of it, the collective blush that bloomed round the table to hear a soloist elevated before her conductor and *in his presence* — it was surely a slip of the tongue? Hiller, she said, she said it repeatedly, was hardly the most intellectually graced of men.

The concert was what mattered, and the concert, as everyone knew perfectly well, had been magnificent, remarkable, *worthy of Mendelssohn himself.* Quite so, Robert said, his mouth a nipped-in line. Quite so. And how congenial the place was to his work! After only four days, the beginnings of a new symphony – he even let her see. This, he said, peering over a fresh cartload of packing boxes from Dresden, was proof enough. He had settled. He was ready to do what he had come to do, ie. be the Servant of True Music and earn money for his family. His face was grave and quiet and clear. With this orchestra as his own, he said, *thank God and just in time,* he had finally come home to roost.

Near Christmas, three concerts to the good, the settling seemed sure. Even Tausch said so. And was he or was he not composing, a cello concerto and a new symphony to his name, the shapes of fine solo and chamber pieces; an oratorio fizzing like brewer's yeast in his head? He was and he had. New pupils were coming in ones and twos, old friends were writing letters, the children were remarkably, stolidly well. And so was he. He insisted. An overture in two days, a chorus, six songs. He had never been better and had written to Verhulst to prove it. In the New Year they would go to England – imagine, England! Where poor Chopin could hardly breathe for damp air clinging to what was left of his lungs but no matter – following invitations from dear, long-lost Bennett. He lit Christmas candles, the taper spitting in his hand, played blind man's buff with the girls and pretended to faint from exhaustion. *Fetch brandy, Elise. Papa must be given brandy when he is faint.* He played chorales and read aloud from the Bible with Ludwig struggling on his knee before he went back to his room for the evening to work some more, his face thunderous if anything threatened to stop him. He was – might she say it? – happy. As happy as he got, that is. Happy or, in fits, furious, but the latter did not dilute the former.

She put herself out on a limb, wrote the sacred words in her diary with only a passing frisson. *He is happy.* She watched him carefully, keenly, willing it not to go away. It didn't. It intensified. More overtures, choral stuff, sonatas, fantasies, an odd little floral cantata. He took the new symphony touring, not far but touring nonetheless, and everywhere, *everyone,* approved.

Until the someone who didn't spoke up. Spoke up, moreover, in the local newspaper, anonymously, regarding the recent slide in the orchestra's standards, the sameness of its programmes – too much modern stuff! Too much Bach! Too much Leipzig! – its *wholly ineffective conductor*. Tausch, Clara said. If not Tausch himself, someone acting with his knowledge. Someone in the choir, Robert said. He had shouted at them only last week. Betrayal certainly. But from one person, one with a twist in his sorry little mind, and such a person would not ruffle the fine plumage of Herr Music Director Robert Schumann. He didn't buckle either when he walked off stage to the sound of only his wife and pupils applauding the new overture at the last concert of the season. But he flinched, dear me yes, he felt the blow. Overtures to tragedies never went down well at first hearing, Clara said. It was a known fact.

The progress of his forty-first year, however, her reassurances, *something*, had made him, almost, mellow. Poor receptions had happened to him before; they doubtless would again. That was the price of trying something new. He had expected a little more faith, perhaps; a little more respect for his years and his hard work. Ah, well. If not now, it would come. And if he could suffer things now that would once have felled him for months, who was she to argue?

Pregnant, again, quite sure of it, the last thing she had any notion to do was argue. Every pregnancy was weakening, they said; after so many children, the body could suddenly give out, lose all power of recovery. Or perhaps the mind just stopped the fight to maintain all notion of – what was she to call it? Of *career*. The English tour would be cancelled, of course. And when she was sure, the ticked-off days in her calendar past, when the familiar queasy tightening of her belly was no longer merely indigestion, she felt only bone-weary misery. And this time, she made it plain. She held her head in her hands, clenched and unclenched her fists as she told him. Another child, wholly certain. Another child.

He said nothing for a week, two maybe; he kept to his study, playing phrases and writing. Till one evening when she was sewing with Marie by the sitting-room fire, he appeared in the doorway. He stood for a moment, like a suitor with a hat in his hand. He set two glasses on the table, poured wine from a kitchen jug, then sat next to his daughter. Would she play the *Arabesque*, he asked her. He would like very much to hear her play. She didn't question. And when she had finished, he sat back, peering as though his eyes hurt. I will make some amendments, one day. It is too fanciful. As I thought. He turned to Marie, pointed his finger to his nose, whispering. Though my Old Clara plays well, does she not? She plays it very, very well.

The novelty of it. That she might dislike things, turn to him for reassurance. He was mellowing, surely. *This Düsseldorf*, she wrote, *suits us very well*. That summer, in Switzerland for nothing but rest, they sat by the banks of Lake Geneva watching a lightning storm fade over the city, the sky turn from grey to pink. He read to her, as he seldom did these days. And in English. A foreign tongue.

> The lamp must be replenished, but even then,
> It will not burn so long as I must watch.
> My slumbers, if I slumber, are not sleep,
> But a continuance of enduring thought
> Which then I can resist not.
> In my heart there is a vigil, and these eyes but close
> To look within . . . Sorrow is Knowledge.

Byron. He wrote these very words in this place. *Sorrow is Knowledge.* Is it not beautiful?

And though she had not grasped much of it, her English being poor, though she was not sure the sentiments were entirely comfortable, she wished to agree. Something beautiful. It suited the distant sound of goat bells and the swathes of fading flowers. It suited their being there at nine o'clock in the evening with the clouds turning lilac and the lakes far away, mirroring nothing at all. They sat on till it was almost nightfall, coatless, quite sure the storm would not return. They did not discuss the children's schooling. They did not discuss finances or the rent for the new house. They did not draw up plans, or schedules, or lists of engagements, or mention those letters remaining on the dresser, demanding replies. They did not even reminisce. They merely sat together, the two of them quite alone on the hillside, watching the sky, the starless dark and the silence crowding in.

EIGHT

Nun hast du mir den ersten Schmerz getan

Now, for the first time, you have
caused me pain

*P*roblems, battalions. What comes.

Even before they came back from Switzerland, the headlong rush of the Herr Music Director's expected activities cranked back up to speed. House concerts and Lordknew, the judging of shocking French choirs singing claptrap. A public figure must judge bad competitions and bad singers that would never set the world on fire and *gratis,* knocking days off his life with travel. It went with the salary, Tausch remarked. He shrugged.

Liszt arrived from nowhere in a newfangled carriage and thumped the piano — *their* piano — so it popped its top strings. He looked, she thought, like a marionette. His thick-waisted mistress wore ludicrous *décolletage* even in the afternoon, ungraciously expensive frocks. They were certainly a pair. After their limp applause, their even more limp excuses that they could not arrange a concert in his honour at this late date, he pulled gifts from a velvet bag and embarrassed them all over again. In fine form, he strode to the fireplace, hooked an elbow on the mantel and beamed. He was happiest, he announced, now he had retired from playing. Being a conductor was a freedom, was it not? The orchestra at Weimar meant labour and anguish too, of course, but beyond that, this conductor's life was a joy. It was a clear invitation for Robert to speak, but he did not. He said nothing at all and for once, Liszt looked lost. His eyes showed the first signs of lines. He drained his glass of the nothing that was left in it and rallied a little.

A freedom and a joy! Liszt said again. He sounded tired. His baroness clacked her teeth. Robert said nothing. Eventually, indeed, he fell asleep. After Liszt and his fleshy fancy woman left in a flurry of ghastly effusiveness, she went back into the parlour to find him gone. The sound of opening and closing drawers led her to his study and there he was, fishing out manuscripts, sorting sets of parts, tabulating possibilities on his brow. Within the hour, he started work on a new overture, transcription, some re-orchestration. Freedom and joy were calling, he said, arching an eyebrow. They would need some music to play. She might shut the door on her way out.

He composed. He composed poor pieces and things of such pathos they melted the solar plexus. He composed through the night and every afternoon until the rehearsal season started. Then the signs began. Retrospect sharpens. At the time she did not understand them, but the signs were there. And the signs were absences. Gaps. Three members of the choir didn't turn up the first day, all tenors. Five absconded on the second, two on the third. One formal letter of resignation came to roost. Perhaps if she had been there, it would have been different. She might have seen, done something, sorted things out. It's unlikely, but self-blame is easier than regret. The fact remains, however: she was *not* there. He was. He grumbled to her over breakfast, wishing pupils and pregnancy had not kept her away. You know how to talk to them, he said. They are less – *unruly* when you are there. They need constant direction, like sheep. The next routine committee meeting of the orchestra's board of directors had nothing ovine to recommend it. On the contrary, it was an ambush. She wasn't there, but she heard. He came home in a dudgeon.

Herr Doctor Schumann might well have been tired in his first season, but things could no longer go unremarked. His voice was seasick, swirling with all the sarcasm he could muster and his cheeks were fiery.

I am told I must *change*, he said. And what must I change? I asked.

He took a deep breath before going on, inflating his chest. Where do I begin? I am told I take half an hour waiting on the podium before starting. I am told I ignore good ladies and gentlemen of the choir when they ask questions. I am told I am – these exact words – *vague and uncom-municative*. I am *further* told that at one rehearsal I allowed the choir to fall into such disarray that only Herr Tausch was left playing at the keyboard – and that I went on conducting regardless! This is their reproach, he said. He looked like a startled owl. I went on conducting regardless!

She waited. He marched about with his hands clasped behind his back, looking a picture of affront.

What, she asked, finding her tongue, what on earth did you say?

I told them exactly what was so, he said simply. That I have no hesitation on the podium. That I gather my thoughts, that a man must gather his thoughts – it is not unreasonable for a man to gather his thoughts!

He glared at her and she wondered if he needed an answer. No, she said quietly. Not at all.

He nodded and began pacing again. I told them that the ladies of the choir come late to rehearsal and no one calls them to account! I told them, furthermore, that certain members of the choir might at times *fail to take into account a person's absorption in the beauty of the text.* He spoke the last part as the climax of a magic act, the silk scarf flourished from a sleeve. There was more, however. It came immediately and in a rush. I also told them, in words of short duration, that I realised the choir had stopped singing, *of course* I realised. But that it is a conductor's employment to conduct. What else should I do? *It is a conductor's duty to conduct,* I told them, and to notice the beauty of the score laid out before him. The *beauty.* I said exactly that to Tausch. I called him to the lectern and showed him. *Look!* I told him; *this bar is beautiful!* And he was forced to agree. There was no unpleasantness. *You are rascals,* I told them.

His voice remained quiet but became more clipped, edgy. I argued with the choral secretary – that is the reason for this affront. What more is to be said? They are rascals to insinuate what is not true in this way. To Doubt Me.

He stopped abruptly and looked out of the window. The tremor of his breath was quite audible.

Was there more than one who made complaint? she asked.

She regretted she had spoken at all. He turned sharply, stared at her for a long time. Clara did not move. She didn't lift or lower her head. Her eyes flickered, drawing away and coming back to meet his gaze, finding it steady and cold. Bitterly cold. She tried to speak and nothing came. This look, she understood without knowing why, transfixed her. It made her, somehow, afraid.

Will you not defend me? he said, almost whispered. Will you – you – add to this collusion? He shook. His eyes filled up, glittering with awful tears. You will suffer most dreadfully, Clara, when you understand this thing you have done.

Doors banged in a series, leaving nothing but empty ringing behind. She understood, her heart thudding in her ears, that he had left the house. A lump, like unchewed bread, sat clogged in her chest and acid climbed in her throat. She sat till it felt more containable, rocking on the edge of the sofa, her eyes tight closed. It was important to remember he did not mean what he said at these times. They had happened before. But it hurt, dear me yes, it hurt. And would again. Things might be contained within their own four walls, but there were always Other People. Other people who didn't know how much they didn't know setting about the dismantling of a precious, fragile, construction. The committee and the choir, *damn them*. It mattered to remember it was not his fault, but the fault of those who had jarred his confidence and made him forget himself like this. *Other people, damn them to hell.* And what, in God's name, *for*?

His first season had gone well, there had been no difficulties. Now, dice cast and bridges burned, their commitment to this place assured, they chose to upset him, and with these petty accusations – what more did they expect? He had never been talkative. From the rehearsals she had attended she had seen nothing untoward. Nothing to those who knew him. She had been right there at his side to see. It was she who set out the music on the stands, organised the choir and disciplined them for silence; she who stood next to him sometimes to help him find his place again on the open score. The way he had conducted in Berlin and Hamburg and Zwickau and Leipzig, he conducted here.

Certainly, there had been an occasion where he had stopped and stared at the music and a whispering, a rustling of waiting pages had grown around him. He had been *thinking*. Once or twice, when the choir had been so restive as to be insufferable, she had stood to conduct from the piano herself, but this was not new. This past month when she had not been there, had things become worse? Was the necessary support entirely beyond Tausch? *He had gone on conducting silence.* The very thought of Tausch made her shiver. Tausch and his wormhole eyes. *Conducting the sound of nothing at all.* She'd not be surprised if he had begun this, exaggerated it for his own ends. He wanted the post for himself, and that was the truth. And if Robert had argued with some bigwig in the choir, Tausch might well have seen and seized his chance. *He waited on the podium, whistling soundlessly, his arms raised on an upbeat that never fell.* That he had missed her presence at the piano during rehearsals had doubtless made things — more difficult. And they still hankered after Hiller. Robert was not Hiller. Not at all. *This bar is beautiful.* But to criticise him in this way — these *amateurs* who had fallen over themselves to get him here! Who dared to give him such hope and who now brought this trouble to her door. They had made him angry and Robert's anger took fearful, unexpected shapes. What they might begin with their petty complaints and annoyances they had no idea. If she let them get away with it. Somehow it came down to this. If *she* let them.

What had she done before? The difficulty of it, remembering through veils. She had hidden them both away on the outskirts of Dresden. She had taken him to Norderney. She had waited, watched. She had made sure the children were with people who were cautious and wholly trustworthy, who would not leave them alone with Robert for longer than moments, which meant looking for a new nursemaid. This at least. And she had let him know she was there. To suggest they leave work behind, even for a few weeks, was impossible. The new season had just begun, and how would it seem? In this mood, too, he resisted every-thing as plots and intrigues, a *betrayal* and *treachery*, and she couldn't bear it. What was left? Patience. Obedience. Her bravest show of loyalty till the season was done. Then he would rest. She would see to it. And he would get better. He always did. It was something to remember all over again — that he always did.

Lord but the crawling in the pit of her stomach! The intensity of unease, this woozy, nerve-spangling fear exactly as before. She had almost forgotten how terrible it felt. But that would pass too. Patience. Obedience. A new window needing to be replaced in the hallway, a sheaf of moving expenses were waiting to be paid. There was certainly plenty to do. After that, rehearsals. After that, the baby would be born. After that? After that. Her breathing began crowding again, a sudden inrush making her slump forward. Unexpected, frightening; the weight of flesh that hung oppressive on the bones. If only she were not so tired, so dreadfully weak. She tilted her head back, her neck stretching till the muscles hurt. Not so young now, not so resilent. She stared at the white ceiling, this room that she had had painted to her own specifications. White and eggshell-blue. *Madame Hensel's rooms are the picture of joy.* Clara sat very still for a long time, watching the reflections of shadows turn on the walls, the flatness of the stark, bright ceiling.

The first of the angels was Bertha. Bertha came almost by accident: a suggestion from Hiller in a letter. Reliable and rational, and blessedly almost dumb. She signed and laughed and the children liked her, all except Elise who liked no one, so was disregarded. This much at least, then, was attended to. With no regret at all, Clara dismissed the bat-faced misery who had been hovering in the corners of her house too long and hired Bertha for a good rate. The difference was immediate. Of course it was. Everything, as her mother always said, was related. The children were quieter, Clara less guilty. Someone sure to care for one's children was surely the most precious asset a woman could have. Next to a loving husband, of course, but that went without saying. Bertha was the means to greater efficiency, and that was not to be underestimated. She wrote it in her diary lest she forget, and felt better for it.

And whether it was Bertha's influence or not, the rest of the season went unremarked. Perhaps Tausch had sobered up a little, seeing that Robert Schumann was no soft mark as he had doubtless supposed. Seeing that Frau Schumann knew his game. In case he was in any doubt, she glared at him fit to set his hair on fire, seldom gave him the time of day. Tausch's fault. More every day, everything was *Tausch's fault*. It was Tausch, however, who helped him from the podium and steadied him in a chair on the last day of the season, Tausch who brought him back to his own front door.

Herr Music Director Schumann, he told Clara, did not wish to socialise with dignitaries tonight. Or with the singers or with anyone. Herr Music Director Schumann was unwell.

She said nothing, merely took her husband's arm. Herr Tausch

was not invited in for chocolate. He was not invited in at all. He waited
outside as the rain started to fall, uncertain, then left with his hat still
between his hands. He had news for Frau Schumann, but it would wait.
There had to be a better moment. Nonetheless, there were things she
should know. Dr Hasenclever had been asking after her husband's health:
people were — *talking*. Wasielewski was job-hunting elsewhere and so was
the principal oboe. At the corner of the street, he stood a moment in the
rain, looking back. He saw movement at an upstairs window, the curtains
shutting everything back inside.

Tausch received no invitation to the christening party. Hasenclever
brought the new baby a silver spoon. Eugenie, he said. A pretty name
indeed. Eugenie. Like a Russian. He lifted her, chucked her under the
chin and handed her to Bertha. Evidently, he had things other than
babies on his mind. He drew Clara from the rest of the company
towards the fire and settled his glass on the wooden side-table. He
hoped, he said softly, that he was not speaking out of turn. But he
wished to make it plain, as a member of the orchestra committee himself, that he thought the *unpleasantness* over Herr Schumann's conducting
had been unnecessary. His friend Dr Müller thought so too. He
coughed. He wished to make it plain he was a great admirer of Herr
Schumann. And Frau Schumann too, of course. He wished them both
to know they could depend on his good self. And Dr Müller too, come
to that. Those words exactly. Bertha slapped Ludwig away from the
christening table, cake spilling from his open mouth as he yelled. Frau
Schumann might depend on Dr Müller.

⊷≡◐⊂≡⊶

He snapped if she suggested rest. He hid his work, slipped past her
as though from something contagious. He re-orchestrated a whole
symphony, scribbled two complete sonatas in the space of one week
and saw miracles in his beer. *The bubbles rise to the surface and plough under
again, carrying pictures of my face with them. I am an infinite cycle of life!* But
it passed.

How magnificent is a mind like his, with all his power and incessant activity, and how fortunate am I to be the one who understands and shares his life and work. A terrible anxiety comes over me when I think how I, among millions of women, should be so blessed, and I ask heaven if I have not too much of happiness. What are the shadows of everyday life compared with the hours and years of bliss that have come to me through my dear husband's love and work?

One way or another, it passed.

He planned an oratorio, sketched a cavernous mass with forces enough for a symphony. Latin text. He insisted. *A Lutheran may attend to the needs of his flock in holy Latin — the language of angels, surely, when they do not speak in music.* He ploughed through his scheduled concerts without much in the way of event, or much in the way of good reviews, and read Shakespeare between times, as though trying to memorise it, his nose marked from rubbing against the print. And soon enough, his face settled back into its own shape. Less hunted, freed from behind his recently permanently narrowed eyes, his face was thoughtful, she observed, and her heart filled with tenderness. His face, when he allowed it, was beautiful still.

Well.

Leipzig looked very well. Even if the place had forgotten the passing of the years, had organised concerts and *soirées* and appearances so thickly that there was no rest to be had. *They will kill me with music,* Robert said, almost pleased. And how well they enjoyed his new pieces, how well they played them! The Gewandhaus has a *Good Orchestra,* Clara said, with feeling; one that knows which way round the music should sit on the stand, *unlike some.* And how well they liked her, their own Clara, come home! Liszt, there for his own event, was enthused as ever with everything she touched. No one played so nobly, he said, all aquiver, as Clara Schumann. How so, when she is Leipziger through and through? Robert asked. We are, are we not, *Leipzigerish, Clärchen*, and if Leipzig has no quarrel with that – and here he smiled, made it clear he had been teasing Liszt, trumping him all along – *then neither do we.* Moscheles came too, to hear his own concerto from her hands, and was delighted enough for three. He could no longer manage the octave passages, he said. But he had heard a goddess play them in his stead.

Robert could not take his eyes off the old man's fingers, the knuckles grown bulbous as tree knots.

With Frau Schumann on my side, he said, clutching his stick for steadiness, I will not be forgotten.

Mother complained they had not brought the children, confided she sometimes forgot how many there were. Life passes more quickly as one ages, she said, mildly surprised. Things tumble over each other and one is reduced to spectatorship. Emil, however, she recalled very clearly; how like Viktor he had looked. Clara did not know what to say. As for the rest, there were no surprises. They slept poorly, ate well, they drank a lot. Swiss champagne – as cheap as beer. Months of living crammed into three days, the shock of reluctance at the need to return. To make it easier, Reuter, dear Reuter who had outlasted all the Schumann brothers but Robert himself, turned up to see them off. He did not look well and Robert said so. A little indisposition, Reuter said, nothing more. A doctor may not mend himself, however – it goes against the grain to offer a cure without the fee.

He sat with Robert while Clara organised the bags and tipped the porter, with Clara when Robert strolled the length of the street and back to stretch his legs. Not far, she said. No more than fifteen minutes. She had no idea if he was listening. It was noisy, luggage loading.

Things go well for you in Düsseldorf, Reuter said. Some respite after Dresden?

It's not Dresden. She let her eyes meet his. It's not paradise, either.

Nowhere is. He smiled. Though Robert tells me he is still searching. He has become enthused by God, I hear. By Things Spiritual, at least.

He is writing a great deal, Clara said. And hard work with little reward only makes him work harder, whatever I say. Nothing has changed in that direction.

Reuter nodded. He has always been headstrong.

She said nothing. Buckles and brasses clinked behind them, shouts and flurries of running feet.

He tells me he is filled with music. With Great Thoughts.

She kept her eyes on Robert, his progress back to the cab. He is sometimes a little overwrought. As he has been before.

Reuter inhaled deeply. Well. He is doubtless in good enough health. Or you would tell me, would you not?

She said nothing. Reuter was ailing and these past months had left her unsure of her own judgement. How many times had Robert told her she was foolish? Treacherous? Even if she knew he did not mean it, it had an effect. And here, in the coach station on the verge of departure, was hardly the place. Short of time. Always so short of time. Visit us in Düsseldorf, she said. Perhaps you will see for yourself.

He caught her eye, let his gaze linger there a moment, testing the meaning of what she said. Robert was coming closer, carrying his gloves in his hand. I will come when I am better. You have babies I have never seen! I will need my health and wits about me, but I will come. Robert, my friend! My comrade-in-arms!

Robert opened his mouth to speak at the same time as the coachman, closed it again and let him roar.

Your visit has been a great joy, Reuter continued. A great joy.

Robert opened his arms wide, like a dancing bear, his mouth pursed in a silent whistle. He kissed Reuter with great deliberation, clasping him tight.

Reuter coughed. The force of it was quite visible. He waited on by the station till the horses had turned, till the first jolt of the journey started, and raised his hand in farewell. Courage, he wheezed, waving. God grant you both safe!

Clara shouted at the window space – *Come and see us, soon!* – but her voice was nothing against the rattle of suspension, the wheels turning. She doubted he heard.

Robert watched him till there was nothing to see, looked sorrowfully at Clara. He knew it, he said as they left Leipzig. He felt it in his bones. They would not see Reuter again.

Reviews had gathered in his absence, a whole handful. Tausch, it seemed, was a marvel as a substitute conductor, a veritable gem. *Connections,* Clara whispered. *Hasenclever told me his cousin works for the press.* Lest there be any confusion, Herr Music Director Schumann made a point at the next board meeting and made it in person: Herr Tausch had done very well, but would return to his former duties. He was quite well, he smiled when asked. He was very well indeed. To show it, he conducted the eighth concert of the series, as indeed he had conducted the sixth and fifth, *with no requirement for assistance,* and it went rather well, if he said so himself. If the newspaper reported otherwise – *the orchestra, tired of waiting for their conductor's signal, began the overture themselves* – the newspaper was wrong, and wrong newspapers bothered him not at all. And despite the rheumatic attack and peculiar fainting spell that brought Dr Pfeffer who brought Dr Müller, despite their medical stricture that He Must Not Work for at Least One Month, Herr Music Director Schumann conducted the ninth concert too. He checked the length of his teeth in the mirror every morning, the skin of his neck, the stray grey hairs in his temples, the extra inch of forehead surfacing like sand beneath the hairline on his brow. This was no time to rest on his laurels or anything else. He had work to do.

Between concerts he composed a requiem, music to save him from the abyss in case, in case. He reworked his *Davidsbund Dances* to trim them of oddity, rubbing out what might seem excessive. He gorged on Shakespeare, Goethe and the Bible in a lust for transcendence. He fended off his wife's damnable fussing – how easily a stream of words could silence her, even one, if well placed! A flame with a fingersnap! – and conducted the tenth. This was challenge such as he had not faced for years! If it had not been for the sleeplessness and sudden bursts of fury that seared his head now and then, he might have called it bracing. And the A. The now and then placeless echo of an A, ringing out on an instrument he did not recognise. It could be distracting.

Clara, however, heard nothing. He wondered if she was entirely well. She looked distant and pasty and down-in-the-mouth, and recently had been given – there was no delicate way to put it – to playing everything too fast. Odder still, she did not seem to know. For her own good, out of love, he spent time telling her the truth, a truth that no one else, not Hasenclever, or Tausch or Hiller, or even her mother, would tell her, viz her playing had been *damnably poor*, and that was the case whatever their friends said. The orchestra rushed and she rushed *more*. And it wasn't the first time. He told her several times over several days, sang the music to her, getting slower to the point of stopping, then started again. Finally, she wept. He took it as contrition, a lesson learned, and was pleased. He almost blessed her as she leaned towards him, bowing her head; he stroked her hair and reassured her. We will fetch doctors if you are poorly, Clara. Do not fear. Never fear.

Not long afterwards, a matter of hours, a chill fear struck him. If his wife was *ill*, what then? What in God's name might it be? He worried himself into a stupor and took to his bed. Insomnia. Rheuma. A raging fit of coughing that would not stop for nearly an hour. Hot sweats and implacable thirst. He lost patience with that too. He was not an invalid! He got up and composed. He composed instead of sleeping, sometimes instead of eating. He wrote himself notes and memos, mottoes, poems, lists. When he suffered a seizure, a convulsion, almost a fit, enough was enough. The aural disturbance and out-of-stepness, frenzy that radiated from him like a halo, was one thing; a *fit*, something with a name, was another. No matter how much he protested he was well, quite well, she called in Müller.

Well then, Dr Müller. What is to be said?

He was not cordial, exactly. Few would have described his manner as *warm*. But he would be thorough, Clara thought, confusing a po-face with a wise one. He spoke hardly at all to Clara when he arrived, exchanged only a little when he emerged from the sickroom, scowling. And since there was something in Clara that responded to scowling and its matching tone of voice, she listened very carefully.

I do not approve, he said, removing his spectacles, of Herr Schumann's *isolationism*. Isolationalism, I am sure is not entirely of *his own choosing.* A touch more socialising, Frau Schumann. A touch more *facing up to life,* hm?

He leered on some words so heavily she barely caught the others, and realised only when he fetched his own hat that he was done.

You have made a diagnosis? she asked, trailing him to the hall. She spoke to the pin-tucks in the back of his coat.

Less composing, less *overwork* to suit the demands of his *family,* in my opinion, are all he needs. He turned, pulling on a glove. Herr Tausch will take over the rest of the season to ensure this is the case. As a senior member of the committee, it is in my power to enforce this.

Clara opened her mouth to speak. Not quickly enough.

Müller turned the doorknob. The deductions from Herr Schumann's salary will be well worth your husband's peace of mind, Frau Schumann. You need not thank me. Your husband will tell you the rest when he is ready. I say, when he is ready.

River bathing. Pills and leeches thereafter, but foremost and certainly first, river bathing. Hydrotherapy: all the rage and all there was. Every day he must walk with her at his side, hire a cabin designed for the purpose, take off his clothes and walk into the Rhine. Something familiar at least. And, just as before, it worked. It worked splendidly. Until, of course, it didn't. Until he would not eat or meet company but only wring his hands and compose in secret, showing her nothing of what he was doing; until he insisted on going to rehearsal, seizing the baton from Tausch and conducting despite his promise to Müller he would do no such thing. Until she told him she was pregnant. Again.

This time Müller chose a reputable spa establishment, a rigorous schedule of cold sea bathing, viz hydrotherapy to the power of ten. Over-stimulation of the cranial nerves, could be simply treated, but only, it seemed — he looked down his nose at Clara — if he sent them away to a place where Herr Schumann was forcibly far from any work *at all.* Not Norderney, then, but Holland; somewhere decently far.

Clara thought all Müller's abruptness was for Robert's sake, the no-nonsense bullying of a man it was not easy to persuade. Why should she think otherwise? She paid for the train tickets in advance, sent Müller some violets. So grateful she sent him flowers! Ah, what supposition does, the desire that all should be for the best, the naïve notion that these lofty professional people dealt their wares impartially! It was years before she saw his report, Müller's queer little observations. Years before she learned he had listed *failure to entertain visiting dignitaries* as *serious* and *attributable to the wife*. Years before she saw that *Herr Schumann's obsessive composing, aphasia, sounds in the head, withdrawal and melancholic morbidity is wholly due to overwork, the which his wife, heedlessly, has done nothing to alleviate.* Years till she understood the doctor she had opened her door to had written: *His present weakness is merely an artistic temperament under strain. A famous wife is a difficulty for any man, and despite her obsequious show, Frau Schumann's overprotectiveness and ambition, personal defects commonly found in women who seek to thrust themselves beyond the scope of normal domestic activity, are much to blame for the depletion of his masculine energies and power of decision-making. Further* — he had formed these words deliberately, dipping his pen in purple ink again, again — *and despite its toll on his sensibilities, she has not the tact to find even the simplest or most obvious means of avoiding her remorseless pregnancies.* Quite, quite. Why, after all, should she have known at the time? Why, after all, should the good Herr Doctor tell her? Or ask for her own observations of her husband's symptoms? His history? Her twelve years' witness as an aid to diagnosis? Because he was the Herr Doctor, that's why. Because he needed no one's say-so. Because he *did*.

So they went to Scheveningen, took Marie for the trip's sake. No question, no demur; the doctor's cold-water bathing, mapped out in rigorous schedule for both of them, folded in a breast pocket like treasure. History, clocks and cycles of the moon. *The simplest means.*

This time they fetched a doctor. Sheet after sheet reddened through, warm, then cooling to a ghastly chill beneath her; her fingers turned marble-grey. She recalls the distant weeping that must have been her daughter; her husband moaning, the papery wringing of his hands. That she had lost the baby should have been mildly gratifying. Perhaps it was, later. When it could be thought through. At the time, there was only a cocoon; these sounds outwith her control or help; the blessed sensation of helplessness. If this was death, she thought, lazy with blood loss, it had its attractions. It was not so terrible after all.

Melodramatic, perhaps. A little self-important. In the event, it was only three days of bleeding, three more of unsteadiness and the worst was done. Most was expelled, the locum assured her, wiping something like a knife into a blotchy rag. He was almost sure she was not poisoned. She could sit up without feeling faint, her fingers had no tremor. There was no question they would not stay. Robert had the shock to recover from, after all, and Müller's schedule could only help. Marie took him bathing instead, sat waiting at the side of the cold-water tank, waving. Her little face was losing puppy fat, almost pinched. Clara bought her some earrings, a gift for no reason but to thank her for being kind to Papa. For the bathing was important, dear me yes. No matter what happened, they would not abandon this place till Herr Doctor Müller's stipulations had been carried out *to the letter*. She would hold her head up when she told him she had done exactly as she had been bid. And slowly, falteringly, the reward for obedience, *please, merciful Heaven*, the Better Times, would begin.

Dear Mother

Warmest wishes for the New Year! I am still not entirely well. Who would have predicted *this particular indisposition* would linger all this time, but I can shift for my household and this is what matters.

I played the first concert of the new season with Tausch officiating (Müller favoured him: we could not argue). The new house in Bilkerstrasse (take careful note of the address) is less noisy and sits neatly in the middle of the terrace here. I have my *own study* and on the second floor! For the first time since we were married, I can compose and practise daily, and not be a disturbance! Robert's cell, on the ground floor, is very quiet and he is transcribing everything he can find. The sounds in his ears that frightened us both so much are almost gone. The health pills from Müller are VERY EXPENSIVE. We have reason enough to be grateful, however: he conducted the first of the winter season in December! (Reasserting authority is an absolute necessity here.) There is still gossip which hurts him very much, but at least now he is being seen to execute his duties. This is his plan, at any rate. All difficulty, I observe, stems from the choir, for whom Tausch has special responsibility when I am unable to attend. They are vile people. We would not stay, but come to you in Berlin if work could be found. Dear Mother, let me know at once if a post arises. It would do everyone good.

The first shoots of something (I hope it is Camomile, but it will be what it will be) are poking through the snow in the window boxes and Robert is planning the new season's programmes. I have a small round of concerts (!) to add my mite to the household wealth. I enclose a money order for a little less than usual, but more will come. Depend upon your obedient

Clara

Köln   Bonn   Barmen   Elberfeld

A new pregnancy alert for once wasn't more than a scare, thank the Lord. And how it sharpened the appreciation of life, the opportunities around them! A little touring, not far, and between times, domestic bliss such as they could cobble together. Sewing plaid trim on the boys' first suits, Ferdinand out of dresses, Robert's pieces specifically for his girls, played for pennies on Sunday afternoons. In the evenings, the copying out of favourite quotations, the creak of the pen and the coals in the grate and something new. Table rapping! The high polish of walnut wood, the scatter of hand-drawn letters of the alphabet, the inverted glass at the centre, waiting for the touch of a human hand; the thrill of the darkened room, the questions aloud to the waiting dead – he liked it all. Dr Hasenclever scoffed but that was what Men of Science did. The Best Families in France held such seances and if they did not, Robert cared very little. Table rapping *enthused* him. It was comfort and entertainment, a bringer of miracles into the common parlour. To commune with the spirits of the Great and the Good, to hear the rhythm to Beethoven symphonies knuckle-thumped *correctly* from the Other Side – what was to ridicule in that? It gave him pleasure and caused no harm. If he drilled the choir only the same sixteen bars for more than half an hour without telling them, if he slowed them to a halt more than once, Herr Music Director Schumann might tell them he was *in direct communion with Beethoven* and therefore had his reasons. Let them whisper, she thought. Stupid people. They failed to see – what was it he had called it? – the *Spoken Metaphor*. Half of them, she thought smugly, would not recognise a metaphor if it slapped them. She entered figures in the household book, checked his inventories. The orderly 'F's, his secret sign for the occasions on which they had sexual congress, fell in spirals among the tobacco and ink bills, their orders for potatoes, muslin, bread; something she no longer questioned. Overhead, in the room above the cellar grating, she could hear the girls beginning their lessons later than usual. There were wood hyacinths in the garden. The darker days were receding.

And wasn't it so? Didn't Joachim come in May? A man now, gathering accolades as fast as critics could pen them, with his face less set, less *flat* against the world. Hearing him play was itself something healing; almost, Clara thought, sacred. He was not Paganini, but a different beast entirely. He was the Music Itself. Nothing virtuosic, tacked on, sleeked over with glitter; he played Beethoven's Violin Concerto as Beethoven himself must have meant it, and nothing more. At the single rehearsal, she could see the effect he had, the look in Robert's eyes. At the concert, the orchestra could see it too. And such audience response! They could applaud like Italians, these Düsseldorfers; they could, after all, bring a house tumbling down about his ears. They applauded in the same way for the Piano Concerto, for Clara herself with no trace of Joachim on stage, but Joachim had brought the means of this re-education, she was sure of it.

And what was it, afterwards, he said? *I have striven* — a flush beginning on his neck — *to emulate only what I have always heard in your magnificent playing, Madame Schumann.* And he recalled their meeting in Madame Hensel's house in Berlin, how Mendelssohn had laughed when he asked if she had really written such beautiful music by herself, allowing the blush to carry to the tips of his wing collar. How could they not love him? He so admired Herr Schumann too, he said, but had never been bold enough to declare it. Now, however, he would. He could say unequivocally that Herr Schumann's work had more of the truth in its slightest pieces than Liszt in his most profound. He could say that if he had a violin concerto penned by one such as Herr Schumann, he would have something upon which to stake immortality. He could ask very humbly if he might consolidate their friendship by sending a composition of his own that none had yet seen, for there was no one he would trust more — and on and on till Robert clapped him on the back, called him a *Young Demon* and could say no more for smiling. *Patience. Obedience.* This boy, she thought, her eyes filling up shamefully, was manna.

And didn't the young demon keep his word? Didn't he send his overture by return, a meditation upon *Hamlet*, moreover, that arrived the day of Robert's birthday? Astounding! The Young Dane and his Ophelia stepping out in the flesh! It could not be more auspicious! And didn't she herself compose more freely than before? Songs and piano pieces, a cache of duets for herself and Joachim to impress upon him that his value was more than he knew? Nothing to provoke the burden of pride, perhaps, but Lord, the luxury of composing! Of losing herself in sound, of seeing Robert cast an eye over her pages, then asking if she would play. *Once more, a weak attempt from your Clara of Old.* F♯ major, F♯ minor, the light to the dark — the Variations that were his birthday gift she made from a five-note falling theme recalling former, glorious, times. C-L-A-R-A. His Clara of almost thirteen years now, he reminded her. She had borrowed the theme he had made of her name only to give it back. And when they went walking to Benrath, out into the clearing of an open field, did a flock of starlings not rise, a speckled sheet, into the clear, wide sky? She recalls the crowding overhead, the sound of them echoing ear to ear, the children tilting back their heads to see. He began to read Jean-Paul again, every book, as if years had fallen away. Now and then he lay awake at night, listing the names on the spines of Schumann Brothers Publishing House, their shapes on the shelf, their colours; the putty softness of his father's hands. He remembered, he said, all sorts of things he thought he had lost, and everything jaggedly clear. He told the story of his missing mother, the story he had told her as a young man on the night of their engagement in Maxen, which she had never forgotten. Sharp as a cut, tearing her heart once more, but he told it as if new. There was a child, once, he said. His eyes were round. He placed his head on her lap. A child on the windowsill, waiting for the dawn.

> The beginnings of a new concerto. Scraps of songs and choruses.
> Partita transcriptions (vl & pf) Exercise transcriptions (vl & pf).
> Transcriptions in general. Pains, paralysis, stiffness of the legs.

Sciatica, the locum said. Exercise.

Overwork, Müller said. Rest.

Robert's own prescription was different. House concerts! *Let none tell Müller how wicked we are. Müller and his flea-trap dog!* He held a finger to his lips, mock warning. Joachim had turned up on the doorstep, passing through, and Divine Providence had *let him know* that his Dear Friends wished to see him. Who were the Schumanns to decide against providence? Robert smiled. His eyes were butterflies. There would be house concerts and no argument! There were two days of playing and singing, and Clara at the helm or at least at the keys — *there is no music without my wife* — both days with as few breaks as possible even to eat, and Joachim didn't raise an eyebrow. He was twenty-two years old. Ravenous only for music, Robert lost weight and looked younger on it, keener. Joachim was a *Blessed Lamb, another Schunke!* Enraptured, the violinist took to calling her *Clara*, confided in her when they were alone.

I had been so afraid of your husband's silences, but now I understand. They are a mark of his depth.

Robert's pupils widened, filling his eye sockets black. They perish who look only at the dark, he said. They find no way out of the clearing. They are lost in the wood and the howl of wolves. An ordinary Russian will not shoot a wolf. This is something I learned in Moscow.

Joachim was delighted. Herr Schumann spoke to him in puzzles and this surely showed him at ease, and playful as well as wise. Herr Schumann was a genius. When the genius found his voice deserting him, his throat overstrained, the serious imbibing of champagne proved everyone a genius and no talk was necessary.

Herr Schumann's mind is on higher things, it flies in the realms of music.

Twenty-two. The night before Joachim left – three days with no need to shave! – Robert sighed so deeply, so horribly, that the boy could not face him on the day itself. He went early instead and left a promise. Another demon would come while Joachim was gone; a friend he had only lately met, but someone so charismatic, so full of the Spirit of Music, he would carry everyone on his coat-tails before he was done! He predicted, given the pace of the younger demon's walking, that he would be there within the month.

Robert clutched the piece of paper as if it might fly away.

We must brace ourselves, Clara! The word of a True Disciple is written here. The spirits hinted the same only the other day, when I spoke to them through the table. Something is coming that will change things in ways we cannot begin to imagine. His face shone. Wonders and portents! We must prepare. What comes toward us is change.

An overture, songs, an introduction and allegro – all for Clara.
Re-orchestration. A fantasy for Joachim, a gift.

The silver shield of the moon is pale in Italy, he read, marking the place in his book. *It hangs among verdant trees.* The crescent was there for all to see in the sliver of sky that marked the end of Bilkerstrasse. He drew a picture of it to keep on his desk, read poems out of his notebooks, checking she had learned what mattered.

> In Moscow, Russia's wondrous town,
> There was the story of a bell,
> So vast and leaden when it fell,
> The cupola that held it once was
> Dragged down to the earth beneath
> And buried there as well,
> Sinking deeper, deeper, deeper. Deeper every year.

When he read, he read most often late at night, sometimes so intent on the words she might undress him into his nightshirt, his head emerging from the broil of cloth still reading. And if she fell asleep, his voice intoning beside her, he would wake her and read her more. Sometimes the words would thrill him to lasciviousness and sometimes to tears, and sometimes to both. Some people couldn't read! Imagine! He read poems to his students and set them to writing songs that he had no time to listen to, no time to amend. What did that matter? He was, he informed them, setting them free. Between times, he placed his hand on hers and stilled her, tilting his head to listen. Could she hear it? Pipes or something under the floorboards, perhaps, but not a voice. The first letter of the alphabet – an A! If this was not a sign of *beginning*, nothing was. The Mind and the Tree. She recalled her father in odd moments, the sound of his voice, lecturing. *The Mind and the Tree, Clara. What do they do?* She recalled it true. They bend.

Well, then! Before the start of the new season he had to make a STATEMENT. His authority had been in some doubt. Let it be the case no more. He would invite some of the choir, so they knew he bore no grudges, some important sorts. A house concert, he announced. Within his own four walls. The day before, she set Bertha and the children to preparing food in the kitchen and discovering what there was in the cellar left to drink and checked their accounts before ordering fresh. They were running out of money. It was quite clear. Not that it stopped anything, but it would eventually. She had, it seemed, been inactive too long.

Did she mention it then? Fastening the clasp of her necklace or spreading the tablecloth last-minute flat, had she made some remark, some trivial thing in passing till the guests arrived, forgotten as soon as said? Lordknew. That she said *something* she has no doubt, for she remembers his reaction: that as she was preoccupied, he turned and stared at her so scornfully, so blamefully, she had drawn back against the wall. *What place has such treachery at a time like this?* Spat more than said. He looked her up and down. *Do you mean to humiliate me?* Whatever she meant, whatever, indeed, she had said, there was no discovering. The bell rang. *No time, no time,* he said, quite level again. And he left the room. No time.

She fixed her face for welcomes and answered the door. Frau Müller in her prettiest dress, Fräulein Leser with marzipan; all the way from Odense, she said, her milky eyes roving corners she could not see; and Hasenclever came and Dr Müller. And Becker with his violin and a pocket full of strings and Reimers, the cellist, and a handful of the loathsome choir and Tausch — she can see his face to this day, the set of his shoulders pressing on to the ribs of their wicker parlour chairs — Tausch.

There was punch and fruit on the side table, Becker's gift of flowers and almost nothing she could think of to say to explain her husband's absence, when he reappeared. He had been to say goodnight to the children, he said, to read them a poem before they went to sleep. The three ladies from the choir cooed appreciatively, made a fuss of an empty seat next to their own. Not long afterwards, with his announcement, the concert began. Beethoven and Gade, Spohr, a great deal of Schumann. And played, so she thought, very well. Not even Reimers lost his place. At the close of the quintet, however, the programme almost done, Robert stood. She saw him from the corner of her eye, walking between chairs. Heedless of the disruption, past her students, past the orchestra committee he so disliked, past Tausch, until he stood behind her. Becker's eyes slid in her direction, looking for a sign as to whether they might stop. Kaase and Sigerland twisted in their chairs. She chose to continue. The end was not far. Perhaps he had come to make a speech, to thank them for their playing of the piece. Perhaps a number of things if she had chosen to think of them, but this was hardly the time and in any case, not her concern. The flow of the music *was*. She took a deep inbreath for the approaching page turn, refocused for the home stretch.

It was then that Robert's hand had come down on her shoulder: heavy, enveloping. He let it sit there a moment, gathering warmth. She kept playing. Then his hand began to rise and fall, rise and fall, an insistent, growing pressure hampering the freedom of her arm. He was, she realised weakly, beating time. She heard some coughing, rustles of distraction from the watchers. This death march pulse upon her shoulder as she played, grinding music almost to a standstill. What else was there to do? She kept playing.

Till Reimers stopped. He held the cello slack against his thigh, put down his bow. Herr Schumann? he said.

Robert didn't hear. He looked around the company, let his eye light on Tausch. Tausch, the startled heron in the front row, dropped his napkin with surprise.

You play, Robert said.

Tausch looked at Clara.

Play, said Robert, waving his finger at the piano. A man understands this kind of thing better. *Play.*

Clara heard blind Fräulein Leser whisper to whoever sat closest, wondering what had happened, and her face burned. Should she have said something herself? Made some light remark, defused this awkwardness? If she had been able to think at all, perhaps. All she did instead was concentrate on her face, refusing to let it register shame, surprise. Refusing to let it register anything at all. She stood from the piano, nodded to her replacement. She met no one's gaze, merely listened. What had remained? A page or two? Less? At the close she applauded, and it was gone through. It was, she hoped, absorbed. What others might have thought she refused to conjecture: it would not help to know. None, however, would fault her professionalism. Not if she could help it.

At the door, Hasenclever was fulsome in his praise for the evening and shook her hand. It was not something he had ever done before. He regretted that she had been indisposed. Fräulein Leser complimented her playing and touched her cheek. Becker looked guilty and almost dropped his fiddle case.

Only Tausch allowed himself to say. To allude. I'm sorry, Frau Schumann, he said, to have been called upon to play. And to have been so unprepared. After your playing, my deficiencies were surely obvious. His eyes searched but she would not look back. I am sorry – and his voice tailed away. He cleared his throat. Sorry. I hope your husband is feeling better soon.

My husband is quite well, she said. Too fast and too loud. I played poorly. My husband, rest assured, is well and looking forward to the new season.

Women's voices sounded past the open door, a straggle of nervous chatter. *An A.* Fräulein Leser's distinctive tones. There was no laughter. *More than once, if I too heard an A.*

And is a birthday not a beautiful thing? Eh, Clara? A sacred thing?

He had written a song from his wedding poem, trained four pupils to sing and play it as she walked over the threshold. He gave her manuscripts and autograph transcriptions, cologne and soap and lengths of satin. He bought her a new piano: walnut wood, sleek and pristine, outrageously expensive. And *hers.* She covered her face with her hands, not caring, and cried. He guided her to the new piano stool, sat her at the keys as the choir drifted away, embarrassed. He drew his fingers along her cheek, let a single tear settle on the tip of his finger.

Water in a diamond, he said. That is Jean-Paul. *The Niagara of thy heaven is scattered in a thousand little rain showers.* Come. There is a great deal of champagne to drink our way through.

Her memory of the rest is cloudy. More poems. Stories. By the end of the night, they sat on the floor together, silent in the half-dark while the lamps, untrimmed, trained soot marks up the pale-blue wall. *You are like a flower, so pure and beautiful.* He sang and poured her another glass. Three bottles, he said. You will tell me I am extravagant! They drank it all, however. She is almost certain they drank it all.

By the end of September, the birthdays and anniversary festivities over, what passed for their routine fell back into its place. Every evening she walked with him to the same coffee house and collected him two hours later. His eyesight, she said, his absent-mindedness. Quite so. Every noontime they took sobering strolls along the banks of the Rhine. Every evening he drew the curtains to one side and checked the street before he rapped his table, asking his questions. Waiting for something. In the end it arrived when they were out. Quite blond, Marie said, and with a staff in his hand. Next morning, as she fished boots out from the kitchen where they had been blacked the night before, her hair struggling loose from its pins, Robert fetched her to the parlour. The young man had come back. *Joachim's friend, Clara – the Demon! The One for whom we have been waiting!*

Her first sight of him was in the parlour, bleached by the sun from the window, the diffuse mesh of white light. Johannes. Little Kreisler. Herr Brahms.

What did she remember, in all honesty, of that first occasion? That the face of an angel appeared from the hazy glare, yellow hair falling to his shoulders? That he said nothing, but merely waited to begin again? *Now, Clara, you will hear something from this young man such as you have never heard before.* That the young man in question looked at her, fleetingly, his hands flexing as he turned back to the keys? Not at all. She remembers that the C major sonata came first, how daring it seemed. She recalls the huge, spidery handfuls of closing chords played thrillingly, if not beautifully; that he almost forgot he was not alone, so vulnerable did he look in his concentration. She remembers the way he sat afterwards, as though he had made an unseemly outburst, waiting for remarks, or encouragement, or *something* that never came. Is there more? Robert asked. There was more. Something else every time he was asked, all of it his own, and difficult, all his things were difficult and they prickled her neck. She recollects fine-boned, pallid hands. You and I, Robert said, we understand each other. He said it several times as he walked the boy to the door. The clock struck noon.

Next day Robert sent her to find him. Taverns, cheap hostels, coffee houses – there were not so many and she knew them, after all. This was already a familiar task. Besides, his hair that colour, his bearing – these things were hard to miss. He seemed unsurprised when she found him and was content to talk. From Hamburg, he said. He had played with a fiddler who abandoned him to hobnob with Liszt, had found Joachim who had sent him on, further on. His shoes had lasted all the way. When Clara took him back to Bilkerstrasse, Robert embraced him and wouldn't take no for an answer. Brahms would stay a month till Joachim came. For the first time in years, he said, he longed for his newspaper. He had something to say and soon everyone would know what it was. Its name? Johannes Brahms! He clapped the young man on the back. *We understand each other, do we not?* From the startled-but-stifling-it, almost defiant look on his face, Johannes had no idea what he meant.

⋗⊶⊷⊶

They spent hours together in the book room, reading. Hoffmann for the Young Kreisler, Robert said. He taught Johannes chess, the patterns of rules hidden in the black and red squares, how best to set up the table to talk to hovering spirits. Clara offered less exotic fare, but he was grateful for her piano lessons and showed her his work that she might criticise, and so she did. Her eye, he observed, was more refined than Robert's, more apt to detect the underlying flaw. Whether he liked this or not he didn't say, but he took the children out walking without asking, made room for her to work if she chose. And he brought her more of his own pieces. In the evenings, raring to play, he offered Hungarian songs made up on the spot. They played the Schubert four-hander she had played with Robert when he had wished to be Moscheles. They played Schumann, Haydn, Handel, Gade. *Brahms.* She too played Brahms and saw his face become soft, unguarded; he all but kissed her hands. Once, she came upon the boy playing wildly in the parlour by himself and he had recoiled from the piano as though to excuse it from blame.

And every night, late into the night, there was talking, a great deal of talking: the function of *programme*, the general foolishness of those who imagined Beethoven listening to birdsong as he wrote his *Pastoral Symphony*, the limitations of Liszt and the New School (*ha!*) who declared the symphony itself dead and gone. The sonata as a form was perfected, he said, his expression fiery: the world needs no more. Clara and Robert and Robert's Johannes. It was how she thought of him: *Robert's* Johannes. The sound of their voices faded behind her as she went to bed. *He fell asleep while Liszt played to him, imagine! A fighter, Clara, a hero to the cause! He turned his back on excess and came directly to us.* Sometimes, when the light struck the young man's profile a certain way, she thought he resembled her husband, her husband when he was not a husband and she was a child.

What Robert saw he stated plain: one sent by God. They composed a surprise for Joachim, a piece requiring three composers if the joke was to work to best effect, but Chiarina was not asked. Robert wrote for two instead, to add to the fun. She might visit Fräulein Leser if she had a mind; he and Johannes had things to discuss! Quite so. This cheerful apple cart her home had become, at least for a time, would surely manage for a short while without her. Besides, almost certain she was pregnant again, she had other things to think about. When Robert, calculating his household book, asked outright, he took the answer in his stride. He was animated, thrilled. *I have been blessed, Clara.* She understood, however, he was not alluding to her present condition. *Heaven preserve for us our dear Johannes's health.* On reflection, over Fräulein Leser's camomile tea, it seemed a reasonable wish. Tactless, perhaps, but no more. Her health was seldom in question; unborn babies were at the mercy of physical whims, things as slight and common as cold water. Things, in short, that wishes had little or no effect upon. Joachim was a precious jewel, but he was not *Johannes*. Robert was quite right in his assessment of priorities. Hannes was particular; the very sound of his name, *Brahms*, an opening chord. He who had finally come was the last part of the cure.

The first rehearsal of the new season was a leaf-blown October day considering frost. He wore his stoutest boots and carried copies of manuscript under his arm, a leather bag with a mass inside. They walked, timed things so no small talk was expected or possible. She removed her cape and sat silent at the piano, her place, while the choir tried to bring itself to order. Hasenclever was nowhere to be seen, but Müller was there, sniffing, Müller's dog. Tausch, in fingerless gloves and new sideburns, counted heads, and Robert ascended the podium, dropping his baton again, again. The fourth time, he placed it inside his palm with deliberate care and turned to face them. They weren't ready. They were never ready. She watched him raise his arms. For want of some indication of what they were to sing, she called out – the *Dies Irae*, from the beginning – her voice clear; Herr Music Director Schumann had indicated they should begin with the *Dies Irae*. When she turned, he stood as before. Just the same. She watched the baton, waiting for it to fall. After page turning, coughing and rearranging of collars and cuffs, so did they. A whole room waiting for the downbeat. Waiting for the downbeat. Waiting.

It didn't come. There was a building rustle of silk and whispering, her own fingers hovering over the keys. They were watching her. She could feel their eyes. She looked at him, instead, willing a sign. It came, thank God it came. The baton fell out of his hand. Before it even hit the floor, she seized the chance. She played: big shapes, driving the music for all she was worth, so they followed after. They followed in several states of shambles, but they began nonetheless. Almost immediately, Herr Music Director Schumann tapped the rostrum with his hands. For the next fifteen minutes, he ran them over the same four bars. When Tausch recovered the stick for him, he chose the *Kyrie* and did exactly the same. The assault on the *Agnus Dei* was barely begun before the disarray was too serious to ignore. Hasenclever was pacing up and down at the back of the hall, two of the singers out of their seats and remonstrating with him. The clatter that followed, however, came from the front. Robert stamped his foot. He threw his baton, apparently deliberately, to the floor. And everything fell quiet. *The flowers only sleep*, he said. He said it very softly. *Shameful people. Shameful!* The silence did not break as he left the hall. She waited some fifteen minutes as the talk grew, as Müller made a great show of blowing his nose and Tausch came forward. When Tausch took the podium, she excused herself and went directly home.

He was there in the music room, playing duets with Marie. She heard them, the sound of quiet laughter as she stood in the hallway loosening the ties of her bonnet, catching her breath. Four hands, then six. Johannes was with them. While the music lasted, she listened in secret, slowing her heartbeat to a more comfortable pace. Why interrupt? It might *excite* things again. Why say? In the evening, there were the children and Hannes to entertain at the dinner table, letters he wanted to write. The opportunity to refer to the morning's irritations did not appear naturally, and she did not force.

Next day, before the full rehearsal began, as the oboe sounded the A and the strings turned their creaky tuning pegs, rosin dust puffing from their bows, she saw Tausch approach the piano to speak, then change his mind. That he had rehearsed the choir himself, that the orchestra were restless, she knew already. It would pass. Hasenclever loomed forward, but she brushed past him, explaining she had no time, no time. The jangle of stands as the timpanist struggled for space made her jump. Then Robert appeared. She smiled as he stood on the podium, a smile she could not feel and was sure he could not see in any case. The glare from the high windows was all but blinding. She saw his arms rise like a swimmer's through the sea of brightness, heard the silence fall as the orchestra took its inbreath. And knew. In that split-second of hovering silence, she knew. It was starting again. As, indeed, it did: the whole charade, the same starts and stops, the same helpless sinking of the heart. Twice, the orchestra fell apart and twice Herr Music Director Schumann failed to notice or much care. Tausch whispered to Hasenclever. Hasenclever paced up and down with his face pink.

It was Reimers who acted. He sat the cello on its side, pushed his chair back with his feet and walked out. Leaderless, his partner set down his bow. The second desks looked at the desks behind, shrugged. Even Clara stopped playing. What else was there to do? Hasenclever, his face red as a flayed rabbit, mounted the platform. He whispered to Schumann, a shaft of dust motes dancing around his head. He whispered again. Clara watched her husband's impassive face as long as she could, then watched the keys. What happened next she heard well enough. Footfalls. Brisk and determined. Leaving. A full second of nothing; the sound of the outer door slamming. When the choir began trading sibilants, Clara stood from the piano and gathered up her music. She asked no one's permission and no one gave it. No one approached her at all. She fetched her husband's score from the podium and walked slowly, unobtrusively, till she left the building. Then she ran.

She pulled aside shutters and curtains the whole afternoon. His pupils came and she took their lessons as if it had been planned that way, but watching the street, listening elsewhere. At six o'clock, when he finally came back, Müller was with him, Müller and Hasenclever and Tausch and a man she had never seen before: Dr Illing. Dr Illing, they told her, they smiled, was an attorney. Might they come in? No, she said. They might not. They might say what they had to say in the hallway or not at all. They looked uneasy and determined both at once, these suits and frock-coats, but Dr Illing came forward. He knew what he had to do. The choir would no longer sing under Dr Schumann. It was the committee's reluctant decision that Dr Schumann should *rest* and relinquish the choir on a permanent basis to Herr Tausch. Herr Schumann might conduct longer works with the orchestra now and then, but Herr Tausch would manage everything else there too. Robert loosened his collar, sweating, his face engorged with rage. Then he turned his eyes to Clara. They all did. A corner, inescapable, unmistakable. A test. She stared hard at Tausch and Hasenclever, hoping to see what to do, perhaps. She ran her eyes over Müller, ignored Illing entirely. Robert watched her. He squared his jaw. He expected something. It came.

This is an intrigue, she said. Her own voice a bloom on the evening air. A vile intrigue and an infamous insult! And more of the same for a short while till she had no more adjectives, no more derogatory nouns. A display, perhaps. Tausch sighed and looked at his shoes.

It was Robert who spoke. Another solution does occur, he said. A solution you lack the perspicacity to find. I propose Herr Tausch replace my wife as *répétiteur* – her work has been poor of late, placing a strain on everyone, as I am well aware. He narrowed his eyes at Clara. Responsibility for a choir is man's work. This is my proposal. I urge you to remember I have a contract. *A contract.* This may not be breached. Replace my wife, gentlemen. Goodnight.

Illing coughed. There was more to discuss, he said, mumbling at Robert's retreating back, Hasenclever butting in, apologising in disconnected phrases, speaking to no one; Herr Schumann perhaps did not understand.

He understood enough. He stopped at the foot of the stairs and raised his hand and pointed at each of them in turn, Clara last. This, he said, is a grave disservice. He was trembling, his collar wings quivering. A disservice to one who has been chosen will find no forgiveness.

And he left her to it, to them. To whatever came next. It was not, it seemed, his affair. Hasenclever intoned about misunderstandings, great pities, no disrespect being meant.

Leave, she said. She managed that much. One word. *Leave.*

They were only too pleased. Tausch opened his mouth on the doorstep, closed it again. She heard Müller's voice, the word *hysteric*, before she closed the door carefully, softly. Johannes was upstairs with the children; Bertha was in the nursery, far enough away, but caution never hurt. It was better that no one else, *no one in the guest room*, become alarmed. She could hear Robert rattling drawers and boxes, biting the words of songs under his breath, being furiously, doggedly cheerful. When the singing and the rearranging stopped, she knew from experience, he would be calmer. Only then was it worth interrupting, taking him something to drink, checking he would arrive at the dinner table later. The chink of metal against the ink bottle rim pealed thinly. He was set to stay in there for some time. No one would miss her. No one would come looking for her if she lay down for an hour, if she kept to herself. If she went upstairs and practised. If she finally wrote to Reuter. She covered her face with her hands as the struggling rose in her chest, a tide of terrible sobbing that she would not let break. A few moments, minutes perhaps – *let nothing show* – and she was ready. As ready as possible. Breathing deep, taking her time, Clara lifted up her head. The waxy wooden banister was firm beneath her hand.

Clarinet, viola, piano. A lot of violin. He was writing, she noticed, a great deal. More, if anything, than before. Orchestration and arrangement. Fairy pieces. The transparent and liquid *Songs of the Dawn.*

Who was to say work was not rest?

She had no answer.

I will write despite them. I will not be silenced by cowards and villains.

No answer at all.

And when Joachim arrived to play, the final version of his overture under his arm, the concert programmes listing Herr Music Director Schumann as conductor already gone to print, what use was sleep? His skin seemed to crackle with energy, with anticipation. Events are ever changing, he said, like rainbow colours; too fast for the human mind to grasp, but angels may decode them with a little patience. He whispered, his words snaking in her ear. A little patience and all will be apparent at last. What use was sleep? What answer could there be? He came to her bed every night nonetheless, wordlessly lustful, implacable in his need. He clamped her hand round his erection, imploring her to feel the intensity of the blood that surged and sparkled in his veins.

By day, every day, he planned house guests, *soirées*, little occasions. Dietrich, Becker, Laurens the painter with his whole family in tow, but best was Joachim. Was it not a wonder and a blessing to see him again? To witness Hannes's face when he played? Was it not an honour that powdery-faced Bettina von Arnim, the Great Woman who had snubbed Clara all those years ago in Dresden, should come to the house and scatter opinions and cake crumbs with equal heedless abandon? This husband *so charmingly eccentric*, von Arnim gushed, glittering her fingers; this Clara (the little Wieck girl!) so changed from her former glories at *every level*. This *funny little house* so near the Rhine and so *fetchingly small!* But there was music, very good music, for which she thanked God indeed. The day of Joachim's rehearsal, he was out of bed early and shaved before dawn. It was possible he had not been to sleep. On his way out of the door, he handed her a piece of paper. It would interest her, he said. She had a letter too; he had received it at the door and tipped the post-boy. Johannes went with them. Alone, she read. Robert's piece first, an article of the kind he had not written for years.

Were I younger I would write a few rhapsodies about a
Young Eagle who swooped down upon Düsseldorf from the

Alps, or like a magnificent torrent that, like Niagara, cascading from the Heights to shores wafted by butterflies and nightingales. Johannes Brahms is another John the Baptist, whose revelations will puzzle the Pharisees for centuries. Only the other apostles will understand the message, including possibly Judas Iscariot. This is he that should come springing like Minerva from the head of Jove, a Young Blood by whose cradle the Graces and Heroes kept watch. This One of the Elect!

She read once, read it again. His style was still a thicket. It was perhaps not as blasphemous as it seemed. Did he mean it for publication? Surely not without Johannes's approval. Later, she would ask him later. The other letter had something else folded inside, something in her own handwriting. Her letter to Reuter, and a note from a stranger. Her invitation, her enquiry, had never reached him. The good Herr Doctor was dead. Her first thought was not pity. It was not sadness. It was, may God forgive her, loneliness.

Honoured Colleague and my dear Hiller

The Düsseldorf you ask after also asks after you. I am in Hannover again with Johannes in my pocket, still reeling with incredulity from his blissful days with the Schumanns. Schumann speaks fondly of you – pay a visit to them soon. He is very restless and Clara, dear Clara whom one cannot picture without also picturing boundless energy, seems in need of her good and trusted friends. My Overture went well, but Schumann's conducting improves not at all. Everything falls from his hands, scores and piles of notes included, and his perception of what happens in the *exterior world of sound* (as opposed to his own interior world, which subsumes him at times, and

375

fills his head with marvels that none but he can hear) has its significant difficulties. During rehearsals, when the crucial horn solo failed to appear because the player was too uncertain of his entry, Schumann merely thought the fellow played too softly. When I pointed out the simpler truth of the matter, he ran the same bars again, but without cues, and, predictably, had the same result. Now the orchestra were grumbling and being disagreeable, and I suggested – as *tactfully* as I could manage, for he will brook no contradiction in such matters – that he rest. It was only fair, I suggested, that I take responsibility for the notes I had written. This he found acceptable, and the rest went perfectly! Out of his earshot, some gentlemen of the Committee begged I take the concert too, and I had the greatest difficulty in smoothing it over. So fine an artist as Schumann might take offence if I did any such thing, I said, and I refused to be implicated. At performance, I sat within eyeshot of the horn player for safety's sake, and everything worked out. Over the rest, however, one should draw a veil. I am concerned for his future there. The atmosphere is most awkward for all concerned. These words, I need hardly say, are between us and NO OTHER. Clara fights his corner like a tigress the better to keep him calm, in which mood he is better connected to the world at large. He is a martinet when roused, a dear and amiable man when otherwise. He tied his baton to his wrist with string and showed me, his face flushed with pleasure. Look, he said, now it will not fall again! Like a child! I would not hurt him for the world. Clara's concerts with me in England have been postponed: she is expecting again and the dates are wholly uncongenial. I am beside myself with regret. She is the best of partners and playing better than ever, if you can imagine that!

Hannes is agog! Dietrich told him a piece has appeared in the *Neue Zeitschrift* about the Genius of a certain Herr Brahms! Everyone is talking about it! I must say it fills him with horror, to be labelled a *genius* already! Heaven defend us all from premature yokes of greatness! Dietrich said the piece was by Schumann, though I am sure he is mistaken. Schumann was too busy to sleep when last I saw him, never mind to write such things without Hannes's knowledge. Meanwhile, we are forming a League called the Band of Silly Arses to fight Philistinism wherever we find it. Wish us luck!

Yr truest Jos. Joachim

✦≡◉≡✦

She opened the door herself. It was Illing and a stranger, clutching matching briefcases. Bookends. No Hasenclever, no Müller. No Tausch. No, she said. Herr Music Director Schumann was not at home. She looked them levelly in the eye, said nothing at all while they foraged for phrases: his genius, the esteemed Madame Schumann, honour and such, before they got to the point. The attorney held out a letter. A legal document. From now on, Herr Music Director Schumann's contract was changed. Herr Music Director Schumann would rest till the end of the season and Herr Tausch would deal with the thankless part. Herr Tausch would conduct. Choir and orchestra. Everything. Did Madame Schumann understand?

I have told them repeatedly, she said.

Illing looked at her.

If he is argued with, he becomes upset.

Illing and the echo repeated themselves as though she hadn't heard properly. Did Madame Schumann understand?

Ask Hasenclever, she said. All they had to do was agree with him.

Illing's glasses were steaming up. Would Madame Schumann, he asked, pass the letter on? It was most important that Madame Schumann pass the letter –

She closed the door, but the hateful thing was in her hand. She had not, she realised, been shocked enough. She had not looked taken by surprise. She had not demanded to know their reasons. She could imagine them well enough. Nonetheless. *Outrage, insult, affront, disgrace, slur.* It would need rehearsal. The picking of the moment. *Slander, misrepresentation, calumny.* The picking of the words. She knew without having to think about it that he would resign. He would sue, perhaps. What else did she know, even then? That the money would stop, certainly. That she could protect him no longer from what seemed wholly determined to come. One pus-filled sore rising to the surface was, however, unavoidable. In Düsseldorf, at least, the tight space they shared together could do nothing but grow tighter.

A copy of Illing's letter arrived by post, a precaution. Robert did not reply. He sent rants and threats to the committee and thank God did not go to rehearsals. He stayed at home, wound-nursing, penning increasingly pompous letters in half-remembered, half-baked legalese that were never sent. *Vult was a black-haired, black-eyed villain. Vult the Whistler,* he said. *He plays only the flute.* He wrote pages of poems and a splay of coded cello pieces that he concealed in a stout wooden box under the piano. Letters to friends, however, he carried to the posting office himself for fear, he said, of interception. A great many letters, his handwriting uneven as his moods.

> Dear Comrade of the War, the Good Apostle Joseph!
> I fired a twenty-pound explosive into the enemy
> camp last week! But only yesterday I heard a former
> comrade had been approached *secretly* by the shame-
> ful enemy to blow me up with an *underground mine*.
> Well! The comrade answered stoutly, *Is it not he who*

should attack you? Clara is quite safe. I will compose a
Wedding Symphony for you with a fine violin solo.

He agreed to go touring with her to Holland – *someone* had to earn – and
did not turn tail. Let it be known, he said, that Robert Schumann
approves of Holland! He ate well and drank well and masturbated every
night. His appetites, he said, were fully aroused. When Verhulst came to
meet them, Clara was pale and Robert exuberant as a volcano. He
noticed everything, anything, stayed up all night arguing with Verhulst
over the legitimacy of Wagner's experiments in artistic fusion. When
Verhulst left, he took to his letters again.

At an assemblage of Royal Personages stupidly asked
my wife what her husband did for his living, was he
a musician too? And she did not laugh, but ran out
into the snow – in only her satin slippers! Thank God
for that!

Thank God. He charmed people, allowed himself to be charmed in turn
and *admired her playing*. Dear God, how happy it made her! The applause
of the many was nothing if he was not pleased with her; his words of
cherishing she grasped like rage. Packed houses! he enthused. One day
they will appreciate *Robert Schumann* in this way. He found his own work
in music shops, bought extravagant dinners, took her *dancing*.

Before long, however, he was melancholy again. He had nothing, he
said worth giving. He was used up, he said, and his head ached horribly.
The fizz had gone from his blood. And these sounds in his ears! He
catalogued everything he had ever written in marching columns,
meticulous as soldiers. The tree reaches towards heaven, he said. I am
done with roots. These things were *secrets*, and only for his *Clärchen*,
his dearest wife, who was sometimes greatly culpable for a nameless
treachery, sometimes worthy of pity, sometimes a blessed guardian of
the citadel. To others, he spoke barely at all. His confidence was eroded,
she thought; his confusions are all the result of this dreadful business
here, this Düsseldorf and its perfidious people – ah, yes, there was always

the place itself to blame. Johannes, he complained, will be sounding trumpets and drums and we are privy to none of it. I am sick of Düsseldorf. Soon, she assured him; they would visit Hannes soon, if that was what he wanted. They were barely back from Holland, but if it would help, she was not inclined to argue. And, she added, more quietly, if she could arrange a concert or two for herself, it might pay for the trip. He hesitated only briefly. The Young Demons, he announced, his face changing as the thought struck him, were exactly what he needed! The Young Demons should hear messages from his own mouth, and since his mouth could hardly go without him – yes! Yes, yes.

A long trip north, then, a deal of playing: variations on the same, the same. He bought presents of champagne for everyone, jovial almost to a fault. Even when the critics hated the violin concerto he had so recently composed for Joachim, he did not care. Joachim, however, felt awkward and Brahms, taken to smoking cigars as though they were essential to his respiratory system, was quieter too. His music was to be published thanks to Robert's efforts. He wished to give gratitude where it was due.

I am grateful, maestro, the boy said. And happy. I confess I am happy. But is happiness a valid state? It is you must guide me, you and Clara both. Is happiness worthy of trust?

Robert took him by the hand. Man must always, he said, be wary in the presence of his happiness. His face was solemn. Soft, gentle dew falls even upon stones, and perfect pearls are found even in stormy seas. He sleeps deeper – his voice dropped here to a whisper – who finds himself on the shore.

A moment of silence followed. Till Robert laughed. He laughed as if it had been a great joke, laughed uproariously, slapping his thigh, his eyes watering. She saw Johannes exchange a glance with Joachim, then look fleetingly at her. No one else smiled. Thereafter, though Robert spoke a good deal, Johannes spoke hardly at all and Joachim remained distant. Slowly, Robert's mysterious pleasure in everything became irritation, then anger. When he was too angry to allow her sleep, too volatile to sleep much on his own behalf, too drunk, at times, to stand, they turned back. Neither of them wanted Düsseldorf, but she at least needed rest, something humdrum. Her own piano, her own room.

> *Flowers only sleep, not the grass.*
> *I slept deeper and found I was standing on a shore.*

He was working too hard, she told him. All these poems. Was there any expectation he would listen?

> My Dear Apostle!
> Clara has set some poems to quite lovely music as you shall hear. But how often you and Johannes are in my thoughts! I have often written to you with *sympathetic ink*, and even now there is a Secret Message written between the lines of this communication which will show itself later. Meanwhile, dear Joseph, I dreamed we were together for three days. In your hands you held heron feathers, from which flowed champagne! How true, yet how prosaic! How true!

Would anyone listen? Whom could she tell? Only Reuter and Reuter could no longer be told. She wept alone in her room sometimes, listening for him seeking her out. Sometimes she heard him waiting outside her door, the creak of the floorboards as he stood there, stood there, did not knock. Sometimes he whispered her name. He knew what she was thinking, he whispered. He could see over mountains, through walls. A suggestion of laughter in his voice that was not warm. Sometimes she thought he was trying to frighten her, sometimes he seemed frightened of and by himself. Sometimes, she hauled the word *metaphor* out of a box in the back of her head and applied it to almost everything he said, whether it fitted or not. She instructed Bertha to take the children out a good deal, to bathe them in fresh air and exercise. Also to close every door found open, and close it tight. In case of what was a question as yet unanswered, unasked. Merely in case.

Why then, you are a publisher! What is easy for you
to enact, then, is one thing; what is just, quite another. While I forge music from indescribable pain and
bliss, what does your ink-factory know? The cost of
paper. Do not bother me again with stupid requests
for less corrections! Music is my master, music alone.

When he answered the door, if he answered the door, he was affable;
when he taught, if he taught, he was a caricature of endearing absent-
mindedness, wondering where his spectacles were while wearing them all
along. When he came to her at night, if he came to her, he was another
self entirely. How was it to be described? To say he was *never one thing* was
to say nothing. He had never been *one thing*. But this change in him, these
several changes that tore at her capacity to think in straight, keen lines,
to think at all, was not how he had been before. Sometimes he was angry,
citing lists of *misdemeanours* and slights and failures of understanding he
thought she had incurred; sometimes he was lustful and kissless, almost
touchless; sometimes he was sad, so crushingly, tenaciously sad she could
feel it through her own skin and she held him, tight and weeping,
till they fell asleep. More than once, he was furious over trifles, over
information she had kept from him because it seemed unimportant. *You
have tried to destroy me with secrecy. Yet I protect you and everything you do.* As if he
meant to break her heart. An impassive face was insolence, he said; a
puzzled face was artifice; if she wept, she was trying to kill him with
guilt. *I will cleanse and absolve you with the justice of my anger.* Sometimes he
placed his hands on her head, as if blessing her, seemed on the verge of
an apology, a realisation that never came. And before long, he would
change again, be bright and brilliant, sure Johannes was writing a
symphony. Or looking uneasily at the ceiling. Or edgy and tender and
in a sweat, hearing distant music. Or clutching his forehead, calling for
her to stop the spinning and take it away, this single tone that would be
the death of him yet. If he hissed at her in the street to *control your face or
you will shame me,* if he saw someone they knew, turned genial as spring
if they drew closer, it was what he did. Who asks a ricocheting bullet
for its reasons?

For the time being, at least, they lived in a kaleidoscope: things rattled and changed and fell into something recognisable, only to melt and slither to pieces again. She waited, fighting her own terrors, the thudding of her pulse, for the moments that hurt less. These moments would come more solidly if she waited, surely; if she stayed perfectly calm and still. *Gentle Papa is not himself,* she explained. *He is overwrought. He is tired. He is excited.* It made her tremble to think it, but it had to be thought. The rippling charge that surrounded him had a suggestion of harm. Without voicing the thought to anyone, she kept her children out of his way. She turned away from her diary, wrote only things that would not disturb him should he read it, which he often did: names and dates; desperate, dull-witted delight.

Hiller, visiting unannounced and briefly, found Schumann an enchanting companion, the household *an oasis of peace.* Immediately after he left, Robert pointed at faeries whirring round their heads, his finger levelled upon nothing. The sounds they made hurt him. Listen! All beauty and fear conjoined! Could she not hear? No, she confessed. Whatever he blamed her for, she could not admit what was not so. Since weeping made nothing better, she did not weep. *Patience, eggshells, pulling through.* What did she do? She called in Hasenclever with his leeches, Müller with his expensive pills. She kept her fingers in fighting fettle. She played.

Signs, everything signs. Soon, the music was beautiful and the music was awful; there was no means by which it could be stopped. His room filled with flakes of paper, his mind with more noises. All night he stared at the ceiling, lighting more and more candles till none remained. *These are not shadows, dear Clara, but angels! One has the face of Johannes — look! If you listen harder, you will hear them speak.* His voice dropped, his face luminous, shored up with infinite content. *We will be with them before the year is done.* When he embraced her, however, she was not calmed. She was, she realised, ashamed of herself while her skin bristled with shock, afraid. Next morning he was up at his desk reworking orchestra parts. He was finishing, he said, what needed to be finished.

Now, however, the angels changed their minds. They were deceivers and devils. They tore at his body and screamed in his ears and he screamed too. They sent tigers to eat him and send the remains to hell where he would suffer for all eternity. Heaven did not exist; he was a sinner, dear Christ, he wept and bellowed like a horse. He had broken the hearts of all he loved. Gentle Papa, she said again, again, watching his door in case it opened, the childrens' eyes fixed on hers, is not himself. This is a sickness, she said. She spoke it to his face. These sights are delusions. Fight them and they will pass.

Thereafter, however, the music turned to voices again and the chance was lost. Voices! He wept. Horrible voices! They told him he was a criminal and must read the Bible, every page, or all hope was lost! If she would not help him in this – his face streaked with misery and water – if she would not understand, then he had no one in this world. Did she think, he said, raising himself to his full height, his face livid, that he would *lie*? Of course not. Of course, of course. That was exactly the pity of it. But what use was it to rationalise, to tell him over and over he was loved? For three days and nights, saying nothing, she sat at his bedside, listening while he suffered, roared, beat the invisible devils away. He told the tale of his drowned sister, the music he had played for her to dance; the tale of his vision in the park, the sky coming to greet him with the face of a woman. He remembered a place where the trees were rustling, where nightingales sang in words he could understand but they told him – he might not repeat the dreadful details – *terrible things*.

When he slept, she slept too or listened to the dark. She spoke to Hasenclever if he called. She did not eat. On the fourth day, however, he got up. He insisted. He had an appointment with Becker that he would not break. What's more, he dressed himself. He ate. He was, he explained, entirely himself. Well, then. What was to be made of this miracle? All this watching and exhaustion, as if he had had a fever, something that might be sweated away or shifted by prayer? Was it possible?

Becker thought so. Herr Schumann is recovered, he said, his young face transfigured with pleasure. I talked with him today and there was no sign of illness; indeed, if Dr Hasenclever had not assured me he had been poorly, I should not have believed it! How fortunate, Frau Schumann, that he has made such a recovery. How fortunate for us all!

Hasenclever thought him more lucid, was impressed by the neatness of the numbers in his ledger. Müller thought Herr Schumann somewhat florid; then again, he observed, flicking a fly from his lapel, Herr Schumann was habitually florid. He had seen nothing of the episodes Frau Schumann described, of course, but wives were prone to exaggeration in matters of masculine health. Also, let us not forget, Frau Schumann was a *performer*. If his years on the music committee had taught him nothing else — he raised an eyebrow at Hasenclever — they had taught him the fondness of performers for melodramatics. As for this talk of angels — where was the harm? It sounded, Dr Müller thought, rather charming. Dr Müller, may he be damned for all eternity for the shame with which he filled her, his carp face grinning. Becker took him out walking, linking his arm. She heard Robert's voice, not clipped or sorrowful, but merely itself when they returned. *I do not think I have been so sick*, he said. *Only travelling in strange lands!* They had discussed politics and the weather, he said; the melody Schubert had sent him through the ether. Charming, a metaphor, his pretty turn of phrase etc. Herr Schumann, if Becker said it once, he said it twenty times, was perfectly fine.

The same night, Robert bathed and put on his nightshirt. He was lucid, distinct and calm. She took away the Bible that agitated him so and read aloud from Jean-Paul — *maids with sickles, the moon in Italy among verdant trees* — to help him sleep. What woke her, cramped in the chair with the book open on her lap, was his whisper. Its closeness.

The songs, he said. This phrase repeated.

He was looking at her. Jean-Paul fell to the rug as she leaned forward, trying to snap to wakefulness, to understand.

This music and terror will never stop.

His fingers were inky, his thumbnail bitten to the bloody quick. He beckoned her towards him, held her face in his hand. His slippers, he confided, a child, were missing. It mattered — each word halting, afraid it was overheard — and *more than she knew* to find them. She tried to stand. She did nothing abrupt. But her shifting at all made him reach and clasp her wrist with his fingers.

His face was lined in the half-dark, a harried face that had seen something it should not. *Don't*, he said. His nightshirt was translucent, sticking to his chest. *Don't. Leave. Me.*

She knew only one thing to do. She knelt at his bedside, took his hands to her mouth. Sour, acrid with ink and sweat, they needed to be cherished. To be kissed. She pressed her lips to his palms, his whitening knuckles, pressed till it hurt. Her tears made a course over his thumb joint, a steady trickle over his wrists. She held his hand tight and kissed his fingers. Lordknew how long they stayed there, she at his feet, he cradling her shoulders. *Do you remember*, he said, *a poem I wrote you oh! long, long ago? I stood on the shore and the water was rising.* Half delighted, half horrified. Whispering. *I have been good to you, Clara. Despite everything? Surely I have been good?*

They must have slept. It stands to reason that they slept. For at five, with no visible sign of fatigue, she opened her eyes to see him standing at the window. On the counterpane beside her, a row of shaving tools, soap and flannel, cigars, matches, pens. While Clara called for Müller or Hasenclever or any that would come, he dressed and made lists of best possessions – *My pocket watch for Ludwig* – and ate very well indeed. He played the piano, a piece she did not know, start to finish. Then he stood. He dusted down his waistcoat. Fear must be faced, he said. He had the children to consider, her dear, dear self. He was – here he faltered, but hardly at all – losing control of his mind and – *feared*, did she understand? – *feared* what he might do. She must call a carriage, quickly. He must go to a madhouse.

It was not serious, she thought. It was unthinkable. It was all a matter of stopping him. Hasenclever got there within the half-hour to find Robert's bags in the hall, labelled clearly. By midnight, he had been persuaded to spend one more night, provided an attendant watched over him in case he became violent. It was his own request. And the next day, while she spoke with Hasenclever – Marie was with him, he was not alone – next day, Bertha rushed distraught into the parlour. Herr Schumann had run out in his dressing gown with no slippers on his feet. Herr Schumann, she said, wringing a rag in her hands, was gone.

She recalls Hasenclever leaving the house, Becker and Müller running, Marie crying at the parlour door, afraid to come in. And herself. The frozen current running under her skin, her muscles, bracing.

◂──◉──▸

The shifts began immediately. Or those things that would become shifts. Not that she knew, entirely; not that she could pin them down with precision. But from the moment of his discovery, their fetching him back through the daylit streets in his sodden nightclothes for anyone to see, the meaning of *Robert Schumann* was changed. More, however. The two hours they looked for him, looked again, the 120 slow minutes of stupefied anguish, were merely a prelude. From the moment of his discovery, the meaning of *Frau Schumann* changed, insidiously and intangibly, into the bargain. Hasenclever shipped her to Fräulein Leser's before she as much as caught a glimpse of her husband come home, with no word of who found him, or how or where. No one knows, he said; no one can say. Through a window on the opposite side of the road, she saw Bertha open the side doors to strangers, attendants, medics, Lordknew who. These gentlemen had come to care for him, Fräulein Leser said, or so Dr Müller had told her. And since Bertha could not cope alone, a letter had been dispatched to Berlin. Frau Bargiel would surely come any day now and attend to the children. Of course, of course. Others, it seemed, were taking her family in hand. The oranges and violets she sent to please him were returned, her notes tucked away in Müller's pocket. Ludwig appeared briefly in the nursery window, a flash of tartan cotton that was surely Elise. Carnival revellers in masks and make-up, a Harlequin and Columbine for Lent, strolled by, singing.

Near eight in the evening, a man with a notebook arrived outside Fräulein Leser's parlour window; from the newspaper, she said. How dreadful! The *newspaper!* Her tone suggesting a veritable fall from grace. And that, she later understood, was when it dawned. Something serious and dreadful had happened; something that would leave a mark; something, finally, public. And these people who surrounded her, who filled her house and made up rules, these people were no longer here at her request. Müller turned up briefly, dosed her with something for shock;

387

Fräulein Leser poured brandy. That night, she pulled her neighbour's spare bed to the window, rested her cheek on the windowsill and did not pull the shutter. She lay that way for a long time, watching the lights in her own house burn till morning.

Well, then! The delegation arrived! Hasenclever and Müller and an army doctor she had never clapped eyes on before stood to attention and invited her to sit. They did not. They stood. A wall of best-quality black woollen suiting, golden pocket-watch chains at her eye level. No small talk, just business. A decision had been reached. They glanced knowingly at each other, nodded. Hasenclever cleared his throat. Herr Schumann wished to be hospitalised. He believed that treatment would help him regain his health and they concurred with his wishes. Did she understand? She looked at them. To ensure his *complete* privacy – this was Müller's turn – they had chosen Endenich. Some distance outside Bonn, not so amenable to visits as the local retreat, but visits would not be recommended in any case. Dr Müller was quite sure Dr Richarz would not permit visits of any kind once he had read Herr Schumann's notes. A fine establishment, Hasenclever said. And Richarz was a fine doctor, a forward-thinking and sympathetic man. Endenich had no leg-irons or handcuffs, its care was humane if expensive, but what was expense? She would certainly approve of Dr Richarz. One wished for *the best* and Endenich had already treated several *moderately distinguished* patients. Endenich was surely for the best.

She looked at them.

By all means take time to consider it, Hasenclever said. Allow yourself a moment to think.

The new man whispered to Müller behind one vulgar, open paw. When is Frau Schumann's baby expected? Has she adequate care? Hasenclever checked his watch and she knew this asking was charade. The carriage was already on its way. They would take him, whether she liked it or not, to Bonn. A place not even they had seen. Might she send a note? Ah. It would not do to *overexcite* him at this delicate stage. Had he received the notes she had sent yesterday? It was best not to *upset* him with anything too personal – Frau Schumann did not wish surely to *upset* him. Sweet Jesus for charity, she cried, would they give in answer one simple word? Might she see him *now*? Might she see him *at all*? Lacking the required restraint, certainly unladylike. A mistake. They did not exchange glances any more. No, Frau Schumann. Dr Hasenclever frowned. One word. *No.*

Robert went without farewells. The children ranged at the nursery window and watched. He wore his green waistcoat, Elise told her, his gloves. Hasenclever had gone with him and held his hand. *Papa will come home soon, quite recovered,* Bertha told them and burst into tears, and someone they did not know gave them sweets. Sugar mice. Ferdinand held his up so she might see. Had he asked for her? No. Had he spoken to his children? No. He accepted the flowers, however. Müller informed her himself. Frau Schumann might wish to know that even if he did not mention her name, though he did not seem to know or care who sent them, he accepted her flowers.

Pens. Fresh nibs. Reams of paper. Notebooks and bottles of ink.

Candles. New wicks for the lamps.

The furious energy of the mind.

How was she to deal with this unrehearsable happenstance? What procedural model, test or maxim was available? *Madhouse. Asylum.* What did she know of such things? Nothing, too much, nothing real. Madmen tore their clothing; they ran half naked if not carefully watched. They were jacketed and chained for their own good. They were sex-crazed and akin to animals, and Liszt had not been able to play for the howls, like wolves he said, like things in traps and Lordknew – she had heard him say it, rolling his eyes – *Lord Alone Knew* what kinds of men had lain sedated or straited in other rooms. *Madmen.* Strangers and attendants, doctors in ranks; this appropriation of the dearest object of her heart. *Asylum.* What was it judicious to say to people who asked how Herr Schumann fared? Where Herr Schumann was? To those who, patently, knew or guessed from the newspaper's hideous blazoning of such a private, domestic calamity? What in God's name did she say, did she explain, trying to hold thought and the facial muscles into a semblance of their normal selves, to her children?

Poor lambs, those pretty children! Fräulein Leser said, sniffing. This dreadful shock! How she felt for the pretty children, as though Clara had not the wit to think of them herself. It would take time, Fraulein Müller said, sobbing, on her visit to empathise; Frau Schumann must understand that these things took time. It could not be argued with. What no one said, however, was that this time it took was only bearable if one trusted that what followed would be something better. Who could even hint it? Dr Müller disappeared, like pissed-on snow, as soon as the carriage left their house with Robert inside it, his work, or so he thought, done. Wasielewski, conducting his orchestra in Bonn, offered to visit Endenich, but what was a fiddle player to ascertain from a doctor he had never met? On what authority might Wasielewski press? Hasenclever's one visit was all she had, his use of the word *price*. Lord, the terrible slowness with which he had scrambled through stupid pleasantries about the weather, finger exercises before the lecture he was about to begin. It came, eventually. It was lucid. She was pleased to understand Dr Hasenclever's lecture from one telling.

Frau Schumann, he said, should know something of Dr Richarz's methods. They were admirably progressive and best suited to the gentler, nobler spirits such as her husband possessed. In accordance with these methods, then, Herr Schumann would not be left alone for a moment. *Further crisis* was possible, and attendants would be vigilant and offer their fullest care. Herr Schumann would see Dr Richarz or Dr Peters daily and Herr Schumann would eat good plain fare. He would not be restrained and never bound. A simple regimen (cupping, perhaps, hot and cold baths, certainly no cuffs or jackets; a spacious white room, a view of the mountains) was likely; he might even walk the asylum gardens when he chose. But this form of care, the freedom this regime allowed, exacted *a price*. And *the price* – here his backside inched near the edge of his chair as he drew closer, the better that she should see his lips move – was that his immediate next of kin must remain *separate*. The maintenance of calm – he looked at her, checking she was attending carefully – was paramount to avoid *requirement for restraint*.

Which means? she asked.

Which means, he said, an edge to his voice, that Frau Schumann and the children must not visit him. They must not write. The entire treatment, she must understand, is predicated on avoidance of excitement for the patient's best protection. He could not stress it enough: the excitement of contact would serve only to remind him of things from which he had been so recently removed. Remain distant, Frau Schumann; allow him to settle and use the freedoms Dr Richarz's methods allow. Or some other treatment would become all too likely.

She looked at him.

The doctors would write when they had something to say. Did she understand? Soon, Herr Schumann would have access to books, writing paper, even quills. A piano. Life's trials and common sense, English model of care, what good fortune to secure Richarz, 50 *thalers* a month, etc Etc. It was difficult to keep her thoughts from wandering, her hands from clenching and unclenching as she sat, but she applied herself. She tried. If what she heard was more woeful than she could express, she would not shame herself by letting it show. Had he not asked for her? Had the doctors not asked for her? Would it not assist their efforts to hear what she knew, what she had seen of him year after year after year? How might he be restored to health when they did not know him, when they did not, in short, know what to restore him *to*? She never asked. The doctors, however, were her best hope. His. *Patience, Obedience, Eggshells.* This was the way of it. Again. Love, it seemed meant self-denial: the Greatest Duty. And if this was the case, which it was, none would say that Clara Schumann failed.

Certainly a great expense, Hasenclever muttered. He was still there, at the close of some rambling paragraph she had not heard at all. He knew from personal experience, from her playing alone, that Frau Schumann possessed tenacious spirit, a formidable strength. *My dear lady, this is a testing time. God has His reasons. You will* — he patted her hand — *come splendidly through.* At the door, he fetched a crushed flower from his pocket, that her husband had given to him on the journey. He would surely wish her to have it.

She waited till he left and climbed the stairs. She placed the violet carefully on the table and closed the door carefully. She bolted the shutters on the window, then fetched a pillow. Hasenclever was moving off down the street in the direction of the square, towards Tausch's house. She waited till he had turned the corner, gone for sure, then sat on her bed. She pressed the pillow to her mouth to deaden the sound. Then she howled and bayed like a cur beneath a coach wheel. She crushed her face against the lace-covered linen and wept. And wept. And wept.

> Dear Wasielewski
> What you are inflicting by not writing! He is there six days now and I know nothing – how he is living, what he is doing, if he hears the voices still. Any word at all would be balm for my wounded soul! Please go for me! You need discover nothing definite, just how he sleeps, what he does during the day, whether he asks after me. Little things will do. If you can't go, pay someone and charge it to me.

Not knowing. It gave her headaches, forgetfulness, cracking in the joints. She did not sleep, but dozed between hollows of fresh realisation, the awareness of the nothing that rested beside her on his pillow. She made her lists and rearranged her shelves, drew up schedules for the children's lessons, exercise, household tasks. Months, she fantasised. He would be home in three months, picking the number from the sky. She said as much when people asked, as they did, their eyes unfathomable. Letters came: regret and condolence; money. They were something to answer, at least. And since she was not a charity case, she returned every offer of money, every offer of concerts or fund-raising to those who had sent them. Thoughtfulness was one thing, money she might earn for herself. And her husband would be back soon. They should understand this without hesitation: his absence was a temporary necessity. She wrote it in those words, in different words, tirelessly inventive with the same assertion: *My husband, for the time being, is unwell. My husband, for the time being, is not at home.* And since weeping stayed away only so long by sheer dint of telling, it was practical to allow for that too. An interval for incapacity was not wasted.

On Mondays at nine the posts from Bonn arrived, if any were to be had, letters reminding her only of what she did not know. Every Monday at 9.30, disregarding whatever the letters contained, she taught just the same. No excuse, no evasion; what would it serve? Only a greater interlude of useless weeping. She was clear from the first that those who called upon Clara Schumann would not find her a burden. They would find her purposeful. They would find her knowing what had to be done. And since her mother was there for the children, and Bertha was loyal and dealt with much else, they would find her involved in the grace of honest toil. A drooping violet was a pitiful thing and visitors who expected to find one would be disappointed. Thank God for work! Work was not only virtue and solace and earnings, but work was Music. There was, she told her children, shooing them to lessons, no other thing on earth that offered so much of healing to the soul.

And to prove it, from the day after her husband left his home, she summoned pupils for lessons as usual. They arrived carrying the notes she had sent, afraid there had been some mistake, and were merely taught. Occasionally they might turn from the keys to see her staring at the wall, unmoving; occasionally they might notice, from the corner of an eye, that her face ran with tears like a winter window, but it passed. Before others, at least, it passed. Frau Schumann had no wish to embarrass. Those who refused bravery and stayed away, who crossed streets to avoid her or missed lessons, she noted. Some she never forgave. Others came but met her gaze for seconds before breaking it, as though her husband's illness might be communicable by eye contact; others again talked only of the weather and the price of veal, refusing to allow that anything untoward had happened at all.

She saw everything, absorbed everything. She watched and took stock. More than anything else, she played. She played the *Carnaval* and the *Arabesque* and the *Davidsbund Dances* and the *Jest* he had sent from Vienna to her girl-self in Paris. She played the children's pieces and songs, the transcriptions she had made herself of *Peri*, the overtures, the symphonies. And if sometimes she could not finish the line of a particular melody, if memory overwhelmed her, then there was tomorrow: a time for better luck, better discipline. How might he be with her, if not in this way? How might the children hear his voice? As if she were a girl again, she played stubbornly, persistently, grandly. She played to her absent father to drown his gloating and his reproaches; to Mendelssohn, the sternest judge, to ensure her best. She played for her husband, persuading herself despite all reason that he would know, somehow; that he would remember the stroke of eleven, their shadows meeting at the Thomas Gate years ago, when they were green enough to believe they understood grief. And she played to a handful who were present in the flesh — the demons, the angels, the tight little group who imagined they kept her sane when, in fact, they kept her company. She would have survived without them, whatever they afterwards thought. Survival was her gift: there was no shaking it. But they were young, Joachim and Grimm and Dietrich, and her gratitude for their loyalty was more than they knew. And with them, Hannes; first and always, Johannes.

No one sent for him, but there he was in the hallway at her return from Fräulein Leser's, primroses in his hand. The carriage left, Hannes came. He had not had to think. He had read something in the paper, had found lodgings round the corner, already moved his things. What else should a disciple do? He should play, he said, when she said nothing herself. She might like it if he played. Into a house changed in no detail and every detail, the resonance of absence tangible in the air, Johannes sat at the piano and simply played. He played that day and every day thereafter, mostly badly. He played with too much rubato, too much timidity or too much crash. He thundered or pulled back, took irritating liberties with the text and pushed her into teaching him all over again. He made awful puns and acid remarks about Fräulein Leser and marked his copy of the Koran, underlining for his own approval those injunctions that advocated the subservience of the female sex.

In the afternoons, he worked with his head bowed over manuscript, a cigar smoking between his fingertips, and at night he read aloud to her, one by one, Robert's essays and notebooks, approving the jokes and laughing out loud. A lodger. Almost. And when Joachim came they played together, all three, to pass the evenings somehow. *Kreisleriana.* Johannes asked repeatedly: would she play the master's *Kreisleriana,* tell the story of how he came to write such a piece? They flicked through his Goethe and his Hoffmann and his letters to her if they chose. The story was there, she said, all of it if they wished to know. Why should she hide them? I should be wrong, she said, her head tilted up to defy the filling of her eyes, to allow myself to be shy of something so fine. And when the men could stay awake no longer, she took herself upstairs and undressed alone for sleep that seldom came.

Was this, she wondered into the hollow noise of the dark, how it had been for him? *Surely I have been good?* These echoes, almost audible in the enveloping, moonless black? Voices, fragments (*Herr Schumann's mind is on higher things*) pieces from letters and life (*in sympathetic ink not shadows*) and sheer imagining (*would I tell you a lie?*) that pitched in her head and denied all peace (*Clärchen are you true?*). And the longer she lay sleepless, the wilder they became. Was this what he heard, even now?

a husband, indeed, an embarrassment. *Disservice will find no forgiveness.*

A great bell dragged down into the earth beneath and buried
if you listen harder, you will hear them speak

Is there anyone in Dresden doesn't know even in stormy seas
or a thousand little rain showers

what place had such treachery at a time like this
sand in his pockets

the music and the terror the music

the terror and the music would never be done.

And Dr Müller, whispering through everything, *hysteric, hysteric;* this casual judgement based on nothing at all. That it should wound her so much, should recur, randomly, when there was so much else she might more usefully have turned her mind to, shocked and shamed her. *Hysteric.* These doctors she had never seen, what intelligence had they discovered? And from whom? What manner of muttering went on behind their private, impregnable, doors? *No, Frau Schumann. No.* She understood the rationale but understanding did not make the longing to see him, to speak to him directly, go away. The echoes of his voice in the mind grew only clearer, sharper as the days slid by; his absence did not make him fade. And though she turned away from whispers in the street, though she pretended not to hear Johannes and Joachim in the parlour, muttering, thinking themselves alone, she knew what they talked about. *What Herr Schumann had done* was a subject. In her room at night, in a place between sleep and wakefulness, the fragments of overhearing began to piece themselves together. Before long, she knew as much as any gossip in Düsseldorf, despite Hasenclever's cover-ups and intrusions; she knew it better. For them, it was a story. She, however, knew the route, its textures and details, the corners of each road. She might picture it all as though she had been there.

What had he done? He had left his house behind and run the length of Bilkerstrasse. He had run in his nightclothes, without his slippers, without a coat to his name. He had turned right into the square, past the statue of Our Lady that faced the church with its chipped stone steps, past the empty window boxes at the corner tavern, its black and gold sign creaking in the updraft from the nearby water's edge. The twist of lanes came next and down the middle of these lanes, the narrowest, he had run with the cobbles bruising his feet to the opening where the carriageway crossed, a broad horizontal band marking the end. He had stood there a moment, perhaps, feeling the cold on his face. He had looked out at the muddy churn of the Rhine that lay beyond, peered into the distance with his eyes watering, to see where it led. He may have looked up, seen the hills and houses, the noontime glitter of the far shore. But the cold had made him shiver in his nightgown, reminded him of what was yet to be done. One naked foot after another, he walked to the toll cabin, clean across the thoroughfare with its carts and cabs and horses and crowds – did no one see and wonder? And, because he had no money, he fumbled in his pocket, found a handkerchief as pay.

Then, before anyone thought to stop him, before anyone could see his face, he moved to the iron railing, stared down at the freezing water and threw himself over the drop into the Rhine. Fishermen saved him. Fishermen. She hoped someone had thanked them. Though none would tell her, would ever tell her or make it plain, she knew the story anyway. She heard his voice – *Clärchen* – quite plain among the host of others that hovered in the dark of her bedroom, caught glimpses of a man by the water's edge, sometimes a man walking on a stage, reciting a prayer – *Remember me, Clärchen. Clärchen are you true?*

This was her present life: a charged and inescapable present tense. By day, a masculine presence in the house, these young men who smoked and read Jean-Paul, who were there when she asked; the nights raddled with reliable anguish, with pain twisting in the muscles of her face, in the pit of the stomach, a proof of remembering. What lifted her heart also broke it: there was no contradiction. She read his courtship letters by candlelight, on her loneliest nights, knowing the man who had written them would never return. Her husband, however, would; she had no doubt. That was the asylum's purpose, for which she must find 50 *thalers* a month. A simple enough demand. Her purpose was to earn. To endure. She had no doubt.

⊷═◎═⊷

No, Frau Schumann. No.

These Monday mornings full of nothings from professional strangers.

> Herr Schumann is agitated and paces his room, but in general seems relieved to be here. He has asked for no one. We are encouraging him to sleep.

No. She sent her mother who said the place was plain and clean. It was admirably clean.

> His calm behaviour has been maintained since the 27th, and he rests a great deal. No anxiety attacks have been noted. He is gentle and friendly. He does not mention his family.

No. She sent Wasielewski and Reimers who said Richarz was brusque. He had not welcomed them, let them see nothing.

He is sleeping a good deal and talking about
Düsseldorf, and is possibly aware he is somewhere
else. He talks of the mountains there and the flowers
he picked. Otherwise mentions little of the external
world.

No. Brahms went of his own accord. This Richarz, he said, is a high court
judge. But there is no screaming. The place seemed calm enough.

For some time, he has not been violent towards his
attendant and indeed has apologised for the trouble
he caused him when first he arrived. He understands
the date. He walks and searches for violets.

No restraints. The exacting of the price. No visitors. No diagnosis.
Hannes fretted with her if she had a mind to fret. He corrected her
playing when he felt like it and encouraged her to swear.

His auditory disturbances have returned and are
uninterrupted. He is almost wholly silent and will
not engage with his attendant.

But still Robert was not home for the birth of his new son, did not
know the birth was almost routine. She named the baby for
Mendelssohn, sure Robert would have wished the same himself. Felix
Schumann: it sounded well. The christening, she insisted, would wait.
Robert would be home soon. How stubborn she was, how insistent! If
Fräulein Leser tutted, well, then, she could tut. She tutted at Johannes
too, calling him a whippersnapper, an upstart. *Intrusive.* She used the
word with no irony. He does not, dear Clara, understand your worth.

On the contrary, Clara retorted, Hannes understands my worth better than most, and Fräulein Leser had taken it ill and gone home.
Emboldened, Clara wrote to Endenich, enclosing a letter for Robert. He
should know, surely, he had a son. If they would not give him the letter,
they might tell him somehow, in the manner they thought best. The

letter came back, unopened, rebound with a fresh seal. No, it said. A clump of hard red wax. *No.*

> His appearance is improved and his appetite reliable.
> He is asking to use the piano and for manuscript,
> which might usefully be sent. Occasionally he wrings
> his hands and prays.

She wrote again, this time enclosing her own stamp for return if that was what they wished. They sent back the lot.

> His sleep disturbance marked. Pleased to converse
> with his attendant and to exchange a joke. He has
> asked questions that suggest he is beginning to recall
> the past.

It was Joachim, then, who told him. Joachim who was not family who was permitted to watch through a window, accompanied lest he break the rules, as Herr Schumann walked in the gardens, peering at the shrubbery through his lorgnette. *He seemed hale, Clara. He looked for all the world contented; for all the world, himself.* One week later Hiller brought a posy: five carnations, three roses. Her husband had picked them, he said; and though he had only hinted at whose they might be, could there be any doubt? And for the first time, the last time, in her own house and alone, Johannes saw Clara whirl on the spot like a child, flowers pressed to her red-eyed, fragile face. She *danced.*

In a matter of weeks she was so agitated she could not sit still. His speech, they told her, was freer; he had no auditory hallucinations and walked regularly to the Beethoven Memorial in Bonn, fully aware of his surroundings. Well, then. Since she might not be at peace, could barely keep from writing, the least she could do was keep herself out of harm's way by earning. She played concerts in Brussels and Ostend, his music. She did not weep. She walked on the seashore and waited for the good news that would surely come.

It was Brahms who delivered it, Brahms who arrived to meet her at the station from the Belgian train. He had been to Endenich. He had seen the Master through an upstairs window, watched him sit at his desk and write, and he looked thoughtful and gentle as the Robert of old. What's more, Dr Richarz said Robert – not Herr Schumann, they used his name, *Robert* – had asked for her. In conversation with his attendant, he had wondered, fearfully, if he had truly had a wife. Had she – he asked with terrible hesitation – passed away? The wife he remembered, he said, would have written to him. Only death would have stopped her.

Clara looked at Johannes, the excitement in his pale-blue eyes. She could not imagine, for a moment, what this story meant.

His memory is undistorted, Clara. Dr Richarz, moreover, wishes Frau Schumann to understand the decision of his last group consultation. Which is to say that Frau Schumann might correspond with her husband with their full approval. They will no longer withhold letters. They are asking you, Clara, finally, in their wisdom, finally – he smiled – to write.

She wrote twice, enclosed both letters for the doctors' scrutiny rather than chance a mistake. Which they let him read, whether they cut holes in each, like the Vienna censors, she never knew. It didn't matter so long as he received *something*. Barely three days later an envelope addressed in a hand she did not know came back. Johannes watched her open it. Not her own letters, rejected and returned, after all. His handwriting: not scrawled but neater, as though he had been schooling his penmanship for seven months. Even so, she could not read. Silent, she handed it to Hannes, who understood well enough. He sat beside her and read it, a flush rising on his neck, out loud.

> Dearest Clara
>
> How wonderful to hear from you, and on our anniversary! I knew you would not forget me. Greet the little ones, kiss them.
>
> How I wish I could see you all, but the distance is so great! Do you still play magnificently? Does Elise sing? Are my pieces selling? Are my autograph copies of Beethoven and Weber and Goethe and

Jean-Paul, of Mozart and my own letters intact? I sometimes think it was a dream that last winter we were in Holland, and that everyone so lauded your magnificent playing and there was the torch-lit procession through the streets and you recollect you played the E♭ major concerto and the sonatas in C and F minor by Beethoven, Chopin *études*, the *Songs without Words* by Mendelssohn and my new piano concert piece in D? Might you send me some poems and some copies of the newspaper I used to publish. And I need badly some manuscript and the Household Book Rules. I want to write some music! Things here are simple but I have a beautiful view of Bonn. I know this letter is full of questions, and I would rather come to you myself and speak for a while. If there is anything you would prefer not to discuss, we can draw a veil over it.

And what joyful news you have given me – a son! His name should be that of the Immortal One. You know who. And Elise and Marie can play my duets! That Brahms is moved to Düsseldorf is news indeed! What has he been composing? Is all the teaching not tiring for you, dearest Clara? Now, will you do something? Ask Dr Peters to give me a little money. When I walk into Bonn, it makes me sad to have nothing to give a beggar. I am now stronger and look much younger than I did in Düsseldorf. Then again, life is less eventful now.

Near the close, Johannes looked up. Her eyelids were tight shut, one hand flat against her breastbone. In the silence as he watched her, she opened her eyes and looked full into his. She was, he thought, a Vision Revealed. She was Fidelio, the wife of Florestan chained in his dungeon, and Faith Incarnate. Read again, she said, all the weather at once in her features. Read again. How could he stop himself? God help him, he almost kissed her. For all the letter was stiff and peculiarly formal, for all it was not the letter he would have written of old, the dear Master was out of danger. There was every sign that, before long, he would be coming home.

Haste and speed. Faith, folly. Johannes might be forgiven, but Clara, after all she had learned, should not have presupposed. Her handwriting, whatever the melodrama of the moment had encouraged, was not medicine and the improvement, if improvement it had been, did not last. The doctors did not stop him writing, not exactly, but for the next few weeks their own missives arrived beside Robert's, spelling out a different story. He feared his food was poisoned, he poured his wine away, he argued with invisible voices, was spiteful, suspicious and confused. Sometimes he wept. Might she see him, talk to him? Might she – whatever the wording the answer remained the same. *Patience, eggshells.* She should have known that too. She did not need to ask Johannes how she might proceed. In this at least, she might act as she chose, and the realisation of her freedom, in this regard at least, was not wholly unpleasant. She planned, then, hired and booked and advertised, scattering letters like lead shot. Fräulein Leser, querying the wisdom of touring *at such a time*, was asked if she had no sewing to do and offered to Hannes that he might show her the door. Clara watched the blind woman cross the street, her arm leaning on the young man's worn sleeve. Fräulein Leser might choose to lean; Clara Schumann had work to do. She had seven children, this house and its help to pay for; two rooms overlooking the hospital gardens just outside Bonn, and she would tour whether Fräulein Leser liked it or not. She opened the window and began her scales, hoping the sound carried. She would play. She would certainly play.

Hannover	Leipzig	Weimar
Leipzig	Frankfurt	Düsseldorf
Frankfurt	Hamburg	Köln

In Köln, it occurred to argue. Bonn was not far. If she climbed the steps to the top of the cathedral, she could see the towers of its churches, the same ones he saw from his window, the same patch of sky. It occurred, for as long as ten minutes together, that she could defy the doctors and *go*. Who were they to keep him from her? To disallow her even to see him through a window, to let him know she was there? Ten minutes before she banished the thought entirely. One piece of folly might exact a dreadful price. She understood the price. She went back to her hotel room instead, and wrote letters, a great many letters. She wrote to Johannes first, for with Hannes there was no danger if she made mistakes. She wrote to her mother and Hiller and Joachim, to Emilie List to whom she had not written for years and Paul Mendelssohn and, almost, to her father. And when she had written enough to trust herself calm, she wrote again; a contained letter to her husband that might satisfy the most stringent of hospital censors, cramped full of codes that he would know. *The Fantasie in C*, she wrote. *You are Like a Flower.* Note for note, the melody of her Variations, a simple five-note, falling call. Next morning, strung as a wire, she climbed the steps anyway and looked out to where he was but the November air had thickened to fog. There was nothing to see beyond the immediate periphery and that was cloudy. Practicalities decided one's course in the end. As they should. She turned back to her schedule, her waiting ticket holders. His music.

Hamburg	Altona	Hamburg
Lübeck	Bremen	Berlin
Breslau	Breslau	Berlin

Johannes met her in Hamburg and Clara almost sent him away. I cannot bear it in Düsseldorf without you, he said, it's full of tedious old women telling me what to do. I am only come to give you courage, to hear you play. How was it to be refused? Even when he told Jenny Lind she sang rubbish to please the public, fought with her husband and denounced the violinist with whom they worked as a pot scraper, Clara felt indulgent as a mother. A guttersnipe, a snob – they could not make up their minds about Johannes. Not that it mattered. Lind was growing foolish as she grew older and Hannes irked her because he was neither. It was time someone argued with her, he said; a beautiful voice was not protection from criticism, whatever *the Swedish Nightingale* seemed to think. It delighted her, this insolence, a boldness she would never dare. *Yet you stand on the platform, Clara, you play to thousands! I have nothing of boldness compared with you.*

She visited Hamburg pubs at his insistence, the dockyards, the cramped-in bustle of the Brahms family home, and found all to her liking. People talked, but that was what people did. Hannes stood at the back of the hall, applauding with his hands raised over his head and she did not give a damn for talk. People always said something. If he was rude to snobs, she could take it. What did it matter if he was not pleasing to everyone? How contemptible, this suggestion that all human qualities, all human endeavour, must be judged by its willingness to please! He was more than any of them, she decided, as Robert had been some twenty years before. The comparison did not shock her. He was Kreisler and Brahms, he said, and it was innocent, surely, a homage to her husband. Even the way he spoke recalled the Robert of old. He was torn in two, he said; he loved her to the point of madness. In the sense that a poet loves, of course. As a poet loves a consummate artist, of course. As a worshipper loves a priestess, the wife of his honoured teacher. *Of course.*

She saw the bloom on his skin well enough, the steadiness of his eyes on hers. It was the breadth of his shoulders, however, that moved her; his care for her children, his devotion to a sick man she was not allowed to see. And his music, music he asked her to share. He brought her manuscript, embarrassed, determined, gazed up at her with wide, creaseless eyes. Is this good enough for the world? Am I worth the Master's opinion? he asked, scowling, and it made her melt. That he was besotted was beside the point. This was kinship; sympathy made of their different isolations. *Someone loves me.* No small thing to be permitted to imagine. *Someone loves me.* But imagining was what it was. What he loved in her was what he saw of himself. It hurt and pleased her both, but was merely the case that what he loved was the striving of music itself. Let him play-act. Let him talk of being under a spell and driven to distraction; let him write her his letters full of veiled love until death. Love until death was something she had already. It attached to the words *my husband*, no one else. And it never would. That was the meaning of love until death. And what Hannes pictured, poeticised or dreamed about in his idle moments was something else. He was living an opera, perhaps. Why not? It was life-giving, an escape. It was not reality. In his closed, tight heart, he knew it too.

After Hamburg, he went back and without a fuss. With Bertha, he took care of the children. He talked to them about their mother and wished himself out of fleshly lust. He wrote a set of variations for her husband, using Clara's own music as his basis: F♯ minor in shocking guises, Robert's themes and hers twined together under his control, an ardent, almost confessional, gift. As if he knew what Robert had always said of him, what his function in their lives was meant to be. *I wish the doctors would employ me as an attendant for him over Christmas*, he wrote, *then I could write to you about him every day, and talk to him, all day long, about you.* Hannes being what he had always been: the final part of the cure.

⋯≡◉≡⋯

Berlin	Leipzig	Düsseldorf
Rotterdam	Leyden	Utrecht
Amsterdam	The Hague	Danzig

Joachim, clucking like a turkey, warned against it – the wrong time of year, the snow – but she would listen to no one. You have become head-strong, Clara, he said. My friend young Kreisler is to blame. He is egoism incarnate, without even knowing. Do not follow his lead, dear lady. Beware. It was nothing Hannes said, however, that made her so restless, so implacable; it was Joachim himself. He had spoken to Robert. Face to face, he said; a visit like any other and what he had seen made her more restless still.

The Master was calm and clear, he said; he played the piano, which was poor and out of tune, but he played. And he read poems aloud. He wished to talk about places more than anything, to list names and weather and things he had seen. But. He was not a doctor and should not voice opinions. But.

She searched his face.

Was there nothing, he said, sighing, nothing more these medical men could do? That they had no name for this illness, no prospectus for his recovery after — *Nine months*, she said. *Nine months and six days*. After all this time. It was surely something to question. But what had they said, these doctors, to make Joachim so uneasy? How did they account for themselves to those who might be permitted to address them — the pang of jealousy did not escape her — *in the flesh*? They were affable enough, he said. Why should they not be? They gave him cold baths and cupping and sedatives. Enemas. And Joachim was not a doctor but, but. He had urged them to try something new. He had been reading. They frowned. Galvanic treatment was the talk of Paris, he told them; they used *shocks*. Others advocated talking and others still used prayer. Surely something new was worth trying. And they had shrugged their shoulders and gently, calmly, shown him out.

I do not believe they are oracles, Clara. He looked her straight in the eye. I do not believe they know all things.

How was she to argue? Might she visit Endenich? Might she see him? Speak to him? Know at least the place he lived? No, Frau Schumann. The method, the hospital's system, the fragility of the situation; restraint, selflessness, the threat of iron bars. No. No. No. What was left but to ask Hannes, who visited within the week and was afforded no objections. And how settled the Master had looked! They had played duets, gazed together at her portrait, barely able to speak. They walked, talking in circles of symphonies and canonic variations and fugues, the pieces the children were playing. They had spoken, man to man, and how they clung to each other at the station in the rain! The Master, Johannes said, was overly emotional, the doctors advising caution. They feared these visits made him *overexcited*, with all that implied. Joachim was not wrong, Hannes said, but he was Joachim. Excitable. Fiery. Not — he looked at her — a creature of aqueous calm, calm to the point of tedium, like himself. He lied, of course. Hannes was not calm, not yet, nor anything like it. But calm was what he strove to achieve. He was here for her, a crag, he said. She had chosen the doctors and should trust her judgement. *Their* judgement. A matter of faith, then. Of not losing one's nerve. *Trust me, Clara.* He smiled, flexed his shoulders, scraped the stubble on his cheek. There is nowhere better he could be.

> Dearest Clara
>
> Last night I had a dreadful thought! What if I should never more see you or the children? How terrible! What a nightmarish idea! Yet everything here is the same, day after day. Is there another place, perhaps, that I could go?

Trust. Wait. Pass time. She had no desire to be still.

Pomerania	Griefswald	Stralsund
Rügen	Bergen	Köln

She sent Johannes. *Ask them. Ask Richarz, speak to Robert. Discover* — she could barely spit the words in order — *discover if he wishes to come home.* Johannes's face did not change but he could not meet her gaze. This was a weight she placed upon him, something almost intolerable. But he went. Past the dark wooden doors of the garden enclosure, to the willow trees at the corner of an open field, where the doctors would not hear, he asked Robert outright what they told him he must not. Did the Master wish to come home? Robert, grown greyer and thinner, peered at him. He seemed not to understand. Hannes asked him again.

My Friend, he said, Noble One who takes care of my Clara!

His eyes were filmy in the clear spring sunlight. Johannes reached for his hand and held it tightly. The older man looked into the distance, mumbling numbers under his breath. He was, Hannes realised, calculating.

Benrath is too near. There are other places, but their names escape me. I would wish, he whispered nervously, to get out of here. Then again, where am I to go? The very thought of Düsseldorf makes me fearful, Johannes! Not there! Those terrible high walls!

He moved from foot to foot, wrung his hands. Perhaps, Johannes thought, this asking him had been a mistake.

Eventually he spoke again. One day in heaven, we will live together, all three.

They sat together at the furthest stretch of the fencing, watching out together into the fields.

Finally, Robert turned. He stood taller and straightened his lapels. I need an atlas, dear boy. He smiled. Paper and pens and a quantity of postage stamps. An atlas! *Do not let them know.*

The moment, for now, had passed. Hannes took him back to his room, gave him the cake that Clara had sent but Robert did not eat. He played something of a sonata that Hannes did not know, missing out whole bars and phrases without noticing or much caring. He was working, he said; *caprices* and a new overture, to show them, these doctors, what he could do. *Paper and pens. Do not forget!* And as Hannes left, he wept. More uneasy than he had ever been in his life, Johannes did not know what to tell her. He did not know what to think. He fudged and reined in and did not mention how harrowed he had felt. But he suspected she knew. Of course she knew.

Robert's next letter arrived on Johannes's birthday, in the midst of the possibility for celebration. Past call-up age, he was twenty-two: half Robert's age exactly. Ciphers, portents! Its timing was no error.

> Dear Clara.
>
> May blossoms! These days have been unquiet, and you will learn more about this from another letter yet to come. A shadow flickers over its pages, but will please where it does not terrify, my darling. My dear.

What it meant there was no end of guessing and nothing of knowing. What was sure was that he sent no more. Her own letters came back and Johannes was forbidden to go.

And in the midst of this fresh crisis, as if it were not crisis enough, Bettina von Arnim arrived at her door. Dressed to humble, her voice oiled smooth, she had, she said, been *passing through*. But Joachim had told her how *dreadful* everything was and she *so wished* – she tilted Clara's chin with one gloved hand – *so fervently wished* to help. Looking back, Clara wondered if she had really been so desperate. Why did she not ask what this sudden request from so slight an acquaintance, so lofty an acquaintance, was *for*? Was it voguish to visit the madhouse, perhaps? Something to which Liszt had added allure? Or had the mention of Joachim's name, the apparent instigator, thrown her? Whatever the reason, Clara did not question. She did not contradict. Worse, Frau von Arnim's express wish (her wishes were always express) to visit dear Herr Schumann and be a Ministering Angel, the One who Understood where Others had Failed, was welcomed. And since ownership of a private carriage permitted it, von Arnim went that afternoon and entirely alone.

She gusted perfume over the doctors and demanded to be taken to Herr Schumann's rooms. Did they know, she demanded, running a finger over the mantel shelf dust, *who she was*? The flurry of their finding out allowed her some half-hour with Robert, after which, blazing with the righteous fury of having been asked to leave, she wrote to Clara as soon as her penmanship allowed. It should not have been read, perhaps. But it was, it was.

Richarz, she opined, was a hypochondriac, Peters a mouse, and both were mere automata in terms of their understanding. To hear them symptomatise and reduce to mere verbal diagrams the Noble Composer's Mind had brought her to tears! Endenich was cheerless and empty, Herr Schumann's rooms were dingy and smelled like a public alleyway and were not fit for a *refined man*. How could his wife leave him in this place, a place for idiots and shufflers, lumpenfolk, *other people*? Musicians were refined by nature and she, Bettina von Arnim, could see how dearly he longed for company of his own stature. Had he not glowed with pleasure to see her? They had let no one near him for a year, he confided, no one! Those who say they saw him in a degraded state had exaggerated or – one shuddered to think it – *lied*. From *her* observation, there was not much wrong with Herr Schumann at all. Had not a terrible error been made? Von Arnim declared it had. A saviour, a seer into souls, she had gained his trust. And what intimacies he shared! Indeed, in his abandonment and loneliness, it was possible Herr

Schumann, *Robert*, had let her hear things she should not know. Would a *loving wife* have surrendered him so? Would not gentle care be his truest salvation, if he had one to offer it to him *unstintingly*? And so on and on, *ad* literal *nauseam*.

Clara, the mother of his children, who had nursed him through the worst nights of his life, who had whiled away eternity with him waiting for the morning to come, who had never been anyone's mistress save her husband's, read and tried to learn. The Great Woman's advice, tacked roughly to the close, was explicit. *Bring him back to the bosom of his friends, Frau Schumann* — her writing grew larger — *he is only in need of coddling and a Good Woman. People talk, Frau Schumann. They judge. Do not have them speak ill of you! Order the doctor to see you at once and announce he is coming home. Do you not pay him? Then for pity, Frau Schumann! Make him do as he is bid! You must save your own reputation and bring him home.*

Well then. Well.

Should she have seen it coming? This package of damnation and sleeplessness, larded with guilt? That on the basis of natural superiority, perhaps, the behemoth von Arnim had made her pronouncement. Had she scribbled this calumny, these horrors that would coil themselves into Clara's ear in the small hours of the night, and posted them, perfumed, without a second thought? God alone knew what possessed her. But she had seen him at least (Clara howled and wept) while she, his wife, had not.

Johannes huffed till he found it would not stop her. He argued instead. He would not for a moment entertain such martyrdom. What did this frightful mare, von Arnim, think to accomplish with her mischief? By whose authority, he thundered, his voice taking on the stature of his words, did she *presume* to condemn such a wife as Clara Schumann for lack of love, when the very thing she most longed to do, to bring her husband home again, was forbidden her? How dared she think this terrible business was open to such sentimental analysis and wishful thinking? Indeed — he inflated — what meaning had such vile presumption in your — he almost said *our*, she noticed that *our* was on his lips — home? And Clara let him rant and damn her for a fool if it offered some relief. If he crushed the letter and threw it in the fire, she did not mind. She had no need of the artefact to be able to recall its words and recall them she certainly would. There was something in these lines yet to learn, whether Hannes would have it or not, and if everything that hurt did one good in the end, this diatribe might save her soul. Even more than the fact of her husband's sickness, this letter and its accusations gnawed at her. She had not expected contempt, much less contempt posing as concern. Contempt earned, it seemed, by Clara's managing the very thing that had been so hard-won.

Could it be that others were watching and weighing in this idle, uninformed way? Now she thought, it seemed likely. They had had time to conjecture and the long summer nights to fill. Why should not Robert's supposed condition, Clara's supposed behaviour, be served up as dinner party conversation for anyone to judge? Were they a story with twists in its tail? A missed opportunity for bet-winning to those who had *seen it coming*, who had *suspected all along*? Was her husband, whose sufferings they could not begin to imagine, an object – she bristled – of pity? And since Clara rejected pity, rejected money, rejected the maudlin lace-hankie-sniffing, child-clutching show that seemed to be demanded of a *Woman in Her Position*, was it not entirely feasible that Frau Schumann, the madman's wife, that nose-in-the-air pianist, was an object of blame? A terrible thing to know, to begin to understand. But that it must be known was manifest. How often had she heard them, casually spiteful at receptions? *Clara Schumann is immodest. Or Clara Schumann is overly modest and therefore false.* Or any one of a number of contradictions that merely added up to the fact that misunderstanding on the basis of scant acquaintance was fine sport. It must simply be endured.

In a rage, Hannes told her she must write to von Arnim, tell the old witch to swallow her letter whole. Clara refused. People would say what they wished, she explained; she would not stoop to a verbal brawl in the gutter. She would not beg for goodwill. What was not given freely was not worth having and the only dignity was silence. One day – she fixed him in her open blue stare – one day he would know. *You are afraid of her!* he said. And he apologised, immediately and unreservedly, but the damage was done. It was partly true and they both knew it.

Frau von Arnim, indeed, had opened a casket of monsters with her letter, more, in all likelihood, than she ever knew. She would dine out upon this vicious nonsense, embroider it for better effect; she would, in all probability, say more regarding Frau Schumann's *young companion*. And those she told, whether they believed it or not, would listen with their ears on stalks to every word and Clara knew it.

When Clara argued with Johannes, she then argued against the hardness of what had to be learned, not with him at all. Truth be told she felt a rush of tenderness for him, her hapless boy. For he must learn it too. The world was as tough as horseshoe nails and Clara Schumann was not invulnerable; she was alone and guilty and terrified. She was also, she realised, appalled by her own stupidity, half in love with Johannes Brahms. From now on she must ensure they were never alone. From now on she must speak to him knowing these new and dreadful things, and must not be so free in his company again. Even as he stood beside her, she was hollow with loneliness. Her only comfort was the hope that Frau von Arnim, in her finest silks, her perfume sparking the flames to pink, would one day burn in hell.

Dr Richarz, when he emerged from the shadows, looked nothing like she had imagined. Not thin, not fat; his features proportionate, bland; his clothes the same. The only thing particular was his fine gold watch and the smooth, almost nail-less fingers that rested their tips on the table in front of him. Muscle-starved fingers, a span that would barely cover an octave. He met her gaze only fleetingly. Many did. Autograph hunters, shy girls or young men with programmes in their hands. He was, she realised with a sinking of the heart, aware. Aware, that is, of her standing, her status, whatever it was they chose to call it; aware, for the sake of calling it something, of her name. She had seen strangers become clumsy for no reason, stammer or talk too much; others become brusque, resentful, as though she had taken something that more properly belonged to themselves. Some, waving flowers at stage doors, flipped from reverence to hostility for no apparent reason at all. She had not expected this variable from Richarz and it threw her from the first.

But then, neither of them was in his or her natural element: a hotel ante-room since he would not countenance Endenich; the choice of venue had been his, even if the demand to meet had been entirely hers. She had pressed, but not, thank God, reminded him who paid. Frau von Arnim had most probably done that for her.

Fifteen minutes. His first words. Time was short and he spoke for most of it. Herr Joachim was full of newfangled ideas but had little idea of their specific application; Herr Brahms was somewhat opposed to hospital rules. He smiled as he spoke. Frau von Arnim, on the other hand, was not given to moderation and had no awareness of the damage she might have occasioned. Frau Schumann might do well to discourage such a visit from recurring. Morphia was an inappropriate sedative in view of Herr Schumann's melancholia, but chloral hydrate seemed free of side effects when he was excitable, except, perhaps some loss of appetite. Herr Schumann sometimes required persuasion to eat, but they had methods to deal with this. These methods were proving successful. Solitude was his best ally. There was no reason why a greater recovery — he looked at his watch — should not take place.

It has been fifteen months, she began, but did not need to continue. He assumed the rest.

And we have made no firm diagnosis. Quite so, quite so. Herr Schumann's case is *many-layered*. Forms of paralysis and overexertion were likely; in general they trusted the notion of inflammation of the cranial nerves, which was always open to improvement. Did he play? Ask for herself and the children? Certainly. Was his memory unimpaired? There was every hope. Were his surroundings — genial? Dr Richarz smiled. Endenich, if he said so himself, was the best asylum in any of the German states. The regime of unrestrained freedom for patients, at least in Herr Schumann's case, had not been breeched. The smile made her feel foolish, as if he had caught her out listening to gossip. Might she see his notes, his records? Ah. For the first time Dr Richarz looked downcast. Alas, he had not brought them. Might she again send letters? Provided she understood that they would be passed on at the discretion of the attendant and other staff.

As she wondered whether to insist, he spoke again. Frau Schumann should have every confidence. With patience, there was no reason why Herr Schumann should not meet his family at Christmas in some wise or another. Occasionally, he wrote the children's names, filling a page with anagrams and ciphers. Christmas was not an impossible hope. Now he must mean as he said: fifteen minutes. His eyes ranged the room as he stood, eyes that lit on her husband every day and had seen God knew what, things she could not begin to imagine, and found the piano. His mouth opened as though it might say something, then closed again. He shook her hand damply, avoiding her eyes, checked his watch afresh. Timing an egg. Meticulous. Her fifteen minutes, to the second, were done.

Düsseldorf   Detmold   Ems

Hannes wrote her letters: sugar loaf and alphabets, her boy children. She moved in and out of court circles, teaching royal children at decorated keyboards; Hannes turned cartwheels down the stairs to cheer her girls. The children ran terrified through the nursery to his room while lightning clashed outside, and he showed them a picture of their mama to make them less afraid. He said nothing of pictures of Papa, nothing, she noticed, of Robert at all. But they were bright, these letters. He seemed content and self-contained.

Until she came home. She looked thin, he said, not entirely herself. She had been overworking and must rest. He waited, however, until they were walking to hand her the envelopes from Bonn. Perhaps he knew what they contained. The first was from Wasielewski, and it melted and folded on the page as she read. *Intolerable, a majestic figure become a broken machine, could barely sit upright at the keys* — a badly written, unabsorbable wallow of words. Whatever it meant, she did not want to know just now. She looked at Hannes and opened the second. Richarz, his own handwriting. She pictured his waxy fingers gripping a quill, dropping it repeatedly. The page was mired with blots. The words rose, flotsam to the surface. Auditory hallucinations, disorders of taste and smell, visual disturbance, aggressive behaviour, weight loss etc. They refused her request he be moved to another institution on the grounds that he was not strong enough to travel. He advised Frau Schumann that her husband had fallen into a sharp decline. Under no circumstances must she visit. Herr Schumann was as comfortable as could be managed at Endenich. He would not be coming home.

◆═══◆═══◆

The world holds more pain than is fair. It holds more beauty.
That is what Music is for. You might play, Clara. Play.

Johannes told her beautiful things and intolerable things; the former to her face, the latter in his letters.

Love ruins people. It breaks their wings. I begin to believe that love is best turned away from, when it brings with it such terror, such harrowing, hollowing loss.

And had she ever played so well? So *nobly*? Everyone came — my dear they *crushed*. In Elberfeldt and Göttingen she played a good deal of Schumann and Schubert, the *Hammerklavier* to full houses and they did not complain. They roared. In Danzig and Leipzig, home to the fold, she played works of her husband's they had not much cared for first time round and watched them clamour.

In Vienna she all but exacted revenge. She played Mendelssohn and forced them to cheer. For Schumann and Beethoven, for the Bach they had always found *dry*, they asked for encores. Vienna's critics raved and wrote eulogies, and could not find enough polysyllables. Liszt, feverish with high emotion, threw his weight behind the rest. *That once-beautiful face, ravaged by sorrows and pain, the floral wreath in her hair barely disguising the Holy Circlet that suffering has impressed upon her weary brow* — great puddles of gush that she was not much inclined to read. How contemptible critics were, she thought; how cleansing and furious her grief! An acid bath, frazzling to the bone. If crowds came to see Liszt's ludicrous vision of suffering, she would play to shame them; if they came to hear Clara Schumann, they would hear more than they paid for. In Budapest, Prague and Loschwitz, they sent flowers in barrowloads.

Back in Leipzig again, free of concerts for a fortnight, she took time to prepare. Marie and Elise must be sent to boarding school; Jülchen to her mother in Berlin. The others — *Ferdinand is lazy, Ludwig is headstrong, Felix is wilful and Eugenie has a temper, but they are good children still* — were settled enough in Düsseldorf, for the time being at least. As long as Hannes and Bertha remained there was no need to fear. Hannes hared off on concert trips now and then, but hating it, hating touring to the roots. It was not a danger to his child-minding. His composing, he said, had dried, and what that meant was anyone's guess and not worth making. What had to come would come in its own good time: she would stop when she had to, not before. If David started a fund for Robert's treatment to allow her to rest from touring, then he was misguided. The need to earn was a blessing, not a burden: it was purpose, a meaning, the exercise of skill. Why was it, she asked him, that men assumed so doggedly that a woman did best to hide at home? In God's name, what better relief might she have but to play? What better service might she offer? And if Hannes wished to keep her near, he was mistaken too. She told him, those words exactly, at the station in Düsseldorf as she left, finally, for London.

A cold place, he said. The people and the weather were the same. She would dislike it and wish to come home. She was headstrong, he said, wilful. Would she not reconsider? She would not. She would send for music from time to time, she said. If helping her was his intention, he could help her best by sending it. He stood, surrounded by children, his collar turned up against the rain. No one had thought to bring an umbrella.

I will fetch you if you write to me, he called. I will come myself.

The children's faces, pallid blurs.

In person. Hannes shook his head and scowled. He did not raise his eyes to look at her. Only Bertha waved goodbye.

Postponement did not lend it charm. London was fog and creeping dampness, drizzle, haar and dirt. The city that did for Chopin, that Mendelssohn took to his heart, it was all they said and worse. Bennett's house in Russell Place was pretty enough when it was visible, and Bennett himself was generous, he was keen. But her bones would not be at ease here. Her hands jittered and her fingers cracked. Hardly anyone spoke German and their English inflected itself out of anything she could comprehend. On the day of her first concert she was tired of the place, longing for something to eat that did not taste of sugar water, when a letter arrived that took all appetite away.

Johannes had been to see Robert. Joachim had said he was a little better, God alone knew why, and he had gone, unsuspecting. *Dear Clara,* he wrote, *it is most unhappy news.* The dear Master had lost much of the power of coherent speech. He recited names instead, mostly names of cities, his children. He copied from an atlas and hardly noticed those who came in and out of his rooms, and he was thin. He was painfully thin. He enclosed a note that she might read the doctor's summary for herself. The word *incurable* slithered on the page as she opened it; *hopeless, the same at best.* And she shut it away. She knew enough. *I will come,* Hannes had scribbled, large letters at the foot. *Say the word and I will fetch you home.* She gave her concert instead, red-eyed, back straight as a whip. Beethoven, Mendelssohn, Schumann, and the gaps between enough to return to the wings and wash her face from the cloy of salt. A stagehand fetched a bowl for her, a towel. He did not complain. The lady was foreign: they behaved differently. And if her eyes watered continually throughout the Beethoven, the Mendelssohn (*play Mendelssohn,* Joachim had said, *they like nothing else*) like melting ice, apparently without her connivance, it was what they did. Clara Schumann played from memory and, however her tear ducts behaved, she had total governance of that.

Bennett was hesitant to let her continue, but Bennett was also English and refused to make a fuss. He conducted without demur and well, she thought, tolerably well. The critics, too, remarked only upon the music and, though their remarks were stupid, it mattered little. Joachim had warned her — the English are stuck in the age of Haydn and rank amateurs to a man — and so it proved. Everything was too modern, too fanciful, too — and this last so absurd she sent it to Brahms that he might be exasperated on home soil — *too ambitious.* They were mealy-mouthed, these islanders, Dresdeners under the skin. Be that as it may, she carried on: an endless trail of London's poky little parlour rooms and draughty, gilded halls, stagehands and backdesk fiddles at every stop learning the great Madame Schumann's eccentricity of pausing to weep. This, she told herself each time she stepped on to a stage, into a crowded, tea-steamed salon, was the life ahead. This was her duty and her calling, and she wished to do it well.

She examined her preparations, the better to refine them, so when little girls asked, as they did, how it was she played, what it was to be on stage, she would have something valuable to say. Wear shoes that do not pinch, she told them; sleeves that do not trail. No jewellery but a wedding ring. Use a handkerchief or drying powder for the hands. Leave time, a closing of the eyes will do it, to clear the head while waiting in the wings. Do not watch at the curtain, but listen; the signal will come soon enough. When the applause begins, hesitate, allow it room to grow and walk into its bloom. Bow. Fix the seat, adjust the cuffs, flex the fingers, hope the piano is willing. Listen to the silence fall. Listen again. Tilt the head back and allow the moment of beginning to arrive with an inbreath. Play. Too much concentration makes for self-consciousness, too little for errors. Find the mean by listening. Moments of blankness, the certainty of not knowing what comes next, will certainly occur. But the fingers produce something. Let them. Find what the composer intended where you can. The rest is merely to play. To get to the end as faithfully as you can. Play.

She played with violinists and singers, in Buckingham Palace and the Hannover Rooms, in Manchester, Liverpool, Dublin. She played Mendelssohn, Beethoven, Heselt, Schumann – concertos and chamber music. On one occasion, for a chorus of her husband's work, she made of herself one voice in a choir. The *Waldszenen*, the *Noveletten*, the *Fantasiestücke*, but not those he had written for her alone, not yet. Not yet. She met people allegedly Great and Good but could not remember names. They, however, knew hers. *Her husband ran mad two years ago and she has seven children to keep.* She was a curio, a porcelain saucer that survived the Dresden war by some quirk of luck. Bennett tried to take her sight-seeing but London was a haunted place, she had read; she had no wish to commune with ghosts. Not knowing, Brahms sent her a present for Robert's birthday, a prelude and fugue in A minor and *quite particularly for my Clara. Particularly.* C-B-A-G♯-A: five notes falling with fearful, over-bearing words. *Be in all thy doings steadfast: what God decrees is for the best.*

Not long after that, the telegram arrived. Her husband was confined to bed, his feet so swollen he could not walk. He had taken nothing for weeks but an infusion of meat jelly and wine, milk and saline. He spoke only to his voices. Enough. She damned the tour and booked the tickets home. Johannes met her from the ship and spent time on persuasion. Things were not as they had been. She must speak to Richarz, there were things only Richarz might say. Self-absorbed and hidebound as they were, the doctors would not deny her now. Go, he urged, it can't be so terrible as imagining. Then Hannes did not know how assiduously she had refused to imagine. How carefully she had guarded her desire to be blissfully, ingenuously, unprepared.

Endenich was not imposing. Attic rooms poked tiny windows from the roof tiles. A fir that had outstretched its roots shed needles at the gates and beyond the whitewashed exterior, the trio of outbuildings, a stretch of low green hills. Carnations and sage: their scents rising to meet her as she stood at the black-bolted door.

Richarz took her walking. He led her to a bench under the lime trees where they might be private, he said. Herr Brahms might wait. They would not be long. There were gardeners, people strolling the grounds; patients or attendants and all men. She wondered, the acrid smell of earth in her nostrils, heartbeat quickening in her ears, if she would see him by chance; if Robert's face might appear at one of these high blank windows and catch a glimpse of a woman following behind his doctor; if he would know who this woman was. But there were no faces. No shouts or calling, no howls of the damned. The building might have been empty for all it gave away. Richarz, as he had promised, was brief. Herr Schumann had no elation. He had persistent melancholia and disorders of taste, had stopped his resistance to being tube-fed. But Frau Schumann must understand they could not promise him another year. If she had questions, she might care to ask them now. Carnations and lavender. Sage. The doctor waited till her breathing slowed. He had a knack for it, a way of suggesting the unbearable might not provoke undue concern.

Should she see him now? She asked it quietly, willing to do what she was told. No. Herr Schumann was sleeping. He slept a great deal under sedation to lessen his restlessness. Herr Schumann, she must understand, was intolerably restless. Besides, her husband was emaciated, not in full control of his limbs and half blind. It would be better if she did not see him, but prepared. He wished Frau Schumann to prepare.

There were roses in the nearest flowerbed, beads of dew clinging. They seared in the sunlight.

It was best, he said, if she came back a second time, prepared.

Four days later he wrote to tell her that second time was now. Herr Schumann has suffered a spasm of the throat. *If you wish to see your husband before he dies, come as quickly as can be arranged. What you will see will not be easy.* But only Hannes saw. The crisis, Richarz protested, had passed. He brought wine to revive her, but sent her packing all the same. He was wrong. In three days' time another summons, another hellish journey south. This time, however, she dispersed the children. Pauline in Schneeberg, friends in Leipzig, her mother in Berlin. The doctor, she was sure, meant for the best, but she would allow it no longer. She would listen, be reasonable, be told no longer. She didn't stand meekly at the gates for this time, she knew the way. Hannes warned her they would not like this stubbornness; they would, he cautioned, *have views.* They would take her to her husband, she said, and damn their views. She would be turned away no more.

They made her wait, certainly. They would not be doctors if they did not make her wait. One look and they spoke to Hannes, to Herr Brahms alone and made their decision. Some time after six o'clock in the evening, then, they led her across the courtyard of the main buildings to a short whitewashed corridor. The third door. No keys, no locks. She might have strolled in by accident, had she tried. Richarz knocked, light and easy, as if he were bringing laundry. No one answered. He is most likely asleep. No matter. He lifted the latch.

The first thing was the quality of light, its whiteness; the shadows of the trees outside that fell across the floor. In the corner of the room, near a scrawny upright piano, was a bed, its top sheet disarranged. It took a moment to realise the disarrangement as a figure. As a man. A tumble of hair on the pillow, the outlines of limbs. She walked closer.

A garden, when Johannes had spoken of it, was where she had pictured him; stout and waistcoated, examining the rose-bushes with a look of surprise. Occasionally, she had dreamed of a man in a darkening room, the candles making mountains on the walls as he fought the voices in his ears. She could not have imagined this. The angles of his shoulders were sharp under his gown, the skin over his cheekbones smooth and translucent as vellum. His eyes were closed, his temples spidered with age-lines. For all that he looked, she thought, like a child; a sleeping boy on a windowsill who might be gathered up and carried without effort. She waited a moment, then pushed the hair back from his brow, ran her finger down his jaw, gently, so he would not wake. The flowers she had brought were not needed, not yet. All that would matter, if anything did, was that she had come at all. A tang of lye and sweat rose from the sheets as she leaned her cheek against the cotton, placed one open palm on his chest to keep him warm. It might be some time. But she had done this before. In Leipzig and Dresden, in Maxen and Moscow and Kreischa and Düsseldorf. She had knelt at his bedside many times and waited. Something familiar in an unfamiliar place: nothing fearful. There was the sound of his breathing, a heartbeat under her hand.

His dying took two days. Once, he struggled on to his side and reached for her, trying to muster an embrace, but his arms would not obey him. She thought he smiled. He spoke to himself under his breath and sometimes swore aloud to God. Sometimes he merely lay there, watching her through clouded eyes. On the second day, with nothing to account for its beginning, he sat up suddenly and looked intently at her face. *I know* — he said, the last word missing. The words, however, were clear. *I know.* What else could it be but *you?*

I am your Clara, she said. She coughed to bring her voice back to itself, then smiled and spoke her name. Your Clara, no one else. A glass of Rhenish on the side table sat close enough. She dipped her fingers in the wine and held them to his lips. He hesitated momentarily, then opened his mouth. He knew. Licking the wine from her fingertips till he could sit no more, he certainly knew. His Clara had come for him at last.

They left him sleeping to fetch Joachim from the train station that same afternoon. When they returned, a trio, an attendant met them at the gates. *Fait accompli.* He had passed over in his sleep, his face showed no expression of pain etc. He had *not suffered.* The doctor said so. It was not, she decided, the time to contradict. Almost beyond this business, dizzy with release, Richarz grew liberal. Of course Frau Schumann might see him. The gentlemen too. Of course, of course.

When Beethoven died, when Mendelssohn died, when Chopin died, crowds came to their doors to snip fragments of clothing or kiss the Great One's hands. Sculptors and painters with bags of waxes and powders arrived to beg death masks, engravings, sketches of the corpse that would certainly sell. Newspaper reporters came to pass judgement, ascertain significance out of little or no knowledge, to describe, if they could, the exact tint of blue about the dearly departed's lips. Seamstresses began mourning cloths and bombazine dresses; coffin makers lavished their silk.

Here, in this room with its white walls, its flaking piles of manuscript, there was no ceremony, no show. Cramolini did not sing, no one played the violin. No music, no poems, no pompous speeches. There was, thank God, nothing but quiet. She wove the flowers she had brought, a scatter of valley lilies, in his hair. She kissed his mouth. She was perfectly calm. It would have been fitting to fetch his children but this was high summer and Richarz planned the autopsy for the morning. There were knives waiting. He had made it plain. This was her farewell. Hannes and Joachim together gathered books and manuscript behind her; his pictures; the stack of letters she had sent bound in pink. His few clothes, the pocket watch for Ludwig, his combs and shoes and God knew what else could wait. When Richarz came, they did not need to be asked. Hannes spent moments on his goodbyes, Joachim less. Frau Schumann, Richarz said, his voice nipped, might have some minutes more.

From the corridor, whispering. She and Robert were not, though she strove to forget it, alone, but it was close enough. It was something. His blanket, in the comings and goings, had fallen part-way to the floor. She smoothed it neat. A ribbon that was surely Eugenie's, a button from

Felix's dress, things found by chance in her pockets, she pressed into his hand. She embraced him. She embraced him. Prayers. It seemed to be what to do. Yet such things had moved or given him comfort hardly at all. She would have played for him, but the piano, out of tune in the corner, was best left silent. His music, braced ready in the stand, would have its day soon enough. All that remained were these. *The unbearable, most of all, is what must be borne. Courageous Confrontation of Great Fear was the Only Path to Salvation. Work alone endures.* Axioms, the comfort of duty. Work alone endures.

It is six o'clock, a summer evening. She unlatches the hospital window and throws it wide. The sound of birdsong rises from the garden and the sky fills blue. It is pretty, she realises, almost with shock, this view beyond the shutters. There are houses, church towers, a path to the mountains, a road wide enough for a two-horse trap. It leads to Köln and Düsseldorf, Essen, Holland. North. Koblenz and Heidelberg lie south, and west is France. East, where the shadows fall, are Zwickau, Leipzig, Dresden. Borders. She imagines a pattern of roads spread onwards, their connections and tributaries ravelling out to the sea. A breeze ruffles his music. The pages turn and fold. She has nothing to do but wait.

ACKNOWLEDGEMENTS

I read a great many books before and during the writing of this book: Berthold Litzmann's classic three-volume biography of Clara (over 100 years old and still the best there is); Nancy B. Reich's *Clara Schumann, the Artist and the Woman*; Peter Ostwald's *Schumann, The Inner Voices of a Musical Genius*: Larry Todd's collected essays, *Schumann and his World* and the Ostwald/Nauhaus edition of the *Marriage Diaries of Robert and Clara Schumann* were those which came under the heading 'invaluable'.

I would also wish to acknowledge the kindness of people who offered advice, encouragement or research materials during the writing of this book. They include Esther Cohen, Archie McLellan, Hamish Whyte, Winifred Whyte, all my respondents at the Davidsbund website and Noreen Marshall at the Bethnal Green Museum of Childhood. Also Mike Crump and the staff of the music department at the British Library, and the TLS who enabled me to act as Research Fellow at the British Library for six months; to Cove Park, Argyllshire, who gifted a week's free residence and to the Scottish Arts Council, who provided a travel grant for the necessary German trips.

For their personal and professional support during the years of writing, I would like to express unalloyed gratitude to Alison Cameron and her family, Richard Milburn and Andrew O'Hagan.

For introducing me to the piano music of Robert Schumann by his extraordinary playing, I am lastingly indebted to Graeme McNaught.

Sincere thanks to Derek Johns, my stalwart agent, and an extraordinarily patient Robin Robertson at Cape go, almost, without saying.